Under a
Summer Sky

Center Point
Large Print

Also by Nan Rossiter and available from
Center Point Large Print:

More Than You Know
Words Get in the Way

**This Large Print Book carries the
Seal of Approval of N.A.V.H.**

Under a Summer Sky

NAN ROSSITER

CENTER POINT LARGE PRINT
THORNDIKE, MAINE

This Center Point Large Print edition is published
in the year 2014 by arrangement with
Kensington Publishing Corp.

The text of this Large Print edition is unabridged.
In other aspects, this book may vary
from the original edition.
Printed in the United States of America
on permanent paper.
Set in 16-point Times New Roman type.

ISBN: 978-1-62899-109-3

Library of Congress Cataloging-in-Publication Data

Rossiter, Nan Parson.
Under a summer sky / Nan Rossiter.
pages cm
ISBN 978-1-62899-109-3 (library binding : alk. paper)
1. Cape Cod (Mass.)—Fiction.
    2. Domestic fiction. 3. Large type books. I. Title.
PS3618.O8535U53 2014
813'.6—dc23

                                                    2014011161

For Cole and Noah

❧ Acknowledgments ❧

With heartfelt thanks . . .

To my editors, Audrey LaFehr and Esi Sogah, and my agent, Deirdre Mullane, who consistently make thoughtful suggestions, give words of encouragement, and guide me toward making each book the best it can be; to all the folks at Kensington—from cover design to sales and sub-rights—who do their very best to make every book a success; to my husband, Bruce, and our boys, Cole and Noah, who inspire me every day and fill my life with joy; to my dad—my number one fan—who continues to tell everyone he meets about my latest publishing endeavors; to all my friends and family who faithfully read and tell others about my books; and to my Lord and Savior—who makes all things possible—I am truly blessed!

Although Joan Benoit Samuelson won the Falmouth Road Race in 1983, her appearance in this book is entirely fiction.

Joan is an inspiration to people around the world, and I hope she won't mind!

Cast of Characters

Asa Coleman—age 73, father of Noah and Micah
Maddie Coleman—age 72, wife of Asa,
  stepmother of Noah, mother of Micah

Laney Coleman—age 52, wife of Noah, mother
  of Elijah, Gabe, Ben, Seth, and Asher
Noah Coleman—age 53, husband of Laney,
  father of Elijah, Gabe, Ben, Seth, and Asher
Elijah Coleman (E)—age 21, son of Laney and
  Noah
Gabe Coleman—age 19, son of Laney and Noah
Ben Coleman—age 16, son of Laney and Noah
Seth Coleman—age 14, son of Laney and Noah
Asher Coleman—age 7, son of Laney and Noah

Micah Coleman—age 45, half-brother of Noah,
  son of Asa and Maddie
Charlotte Coleman—age 6, daughter of Micah
  and his first wife, Beth
Beryl Graham—age 46, Micah's fiancée
Isak—Beryl's oldest sister
Rumer—Beryl's middle sister

Lonnie and Leighton Pacey—Laney's parents
Lyle, Maren, Levi, and Laurie Pacey—Laney's
  brother and his family

Uncle Luke and Aunt Jo—Laney's uncle and
  aunt

Amen (Mennie)—the Colemans' old black Lab
Hallelujah (Halle)—the Colemans' yellow Lab
  pup
Harper—Asa and Maddie's young black Lab

❧ Prologue ❧

Laney Coleman stood at the kitchen window, cradling a steaming cup of black coffee in her hands. She tucked the novel she was reading under her arm and started toward the screen door, but stopped and softly called, "Mennie." The black Lab curled up on the fleecy dog bed in the corner opened one eye, and Laney raised her eyebrows. "Ah-ha! I knew you could still hear. You've just been messing with us." She shook her head. "I'm going out on the porch if you want to come." Mennie closed his eye, and she shrugged. "Up to you, old pie. . . . I'll leave the door open."

Laney loved Saturday mornings. She loved looking in the boys' rooms and seeing them all sound asleep and safe; she loved that the old Cape Cod house—usually spilling over with chaos and mayhem—was quiet and sleepy; she loved being able to go for a long run and not worry about being back; and she loved going out on the porch to read—whether it was the latest novel by one of her favorite authors, her Bible, or a copy of one of the many magazines she subscribed to, but for which she never had time. She also loved the pancakes Noah always made—warm, buttery, and drizzled with sweet maple syrup. Every other day of the week she scrambled to find the snooze button, but on Saturday mornings she was awake before the alarm was even set to go off.

The porch was bathed in early morning sunlight, and she curled up in her favorite wicker chair—the one with the faded cushion that sorely needed mending—breathed in the fresh ocean air, and took her first sip of coffee—coffee so strong Noah called it Fog Buster. She started to open her book but heard a half-snort half-sigh and looked up to see Mennie standing in the doorway, considering her invitation. "C'mon over here, you big lummox," she said softly, and the old Lab stepped gingerly down the one step onto the porch and moseyed over to rest his head on her lap, his whole hind end wagging. "Hi, there, honeypot," she whispered, kissing his noble brow and rubbing his ears just the way he liked it, making him rumble with pleasure. His brown eyes—cloudy with age—gazed at her with deep, unconditional love. "You're *such* a good boy," she said softly, and he leaned against her and slurped his tongue up her cheek. "I love you too, you big mush."

Content that his truest love still loved him, the old dog curled up in the sunny spot at her feet, and Laney tucked her toes under him and rubbed his warm fur. She looked down at his white muzzle and tried not to think about how old he was—he'd already surpassed the average life expectancy for a Lab, and lately she found herself worrying that a very sad day was drawing much too near.

Wistfully, she thought about the first day Noah brought him home. The rambunctious little fellow had scampered through the house with a tennis ball in his mouth that was as big as his head, and the boys—who'd been begging, begging, begging for a puppy—had been over the moon. Elijah must've been nine at the time, which would've made Gabe seven, Ben four, Seth two . . . and Asher not even a twinkle. And, oh, how Elijah and Gabe had argued over his name. Elijah—a staunch Red Sox fan—had insisted on Clemens, and Gabe—who she suspected was only a Yankees fan to annoy his brother—had pressed hard for Mattingly. Personally, she'd thought Clem would be cute, but neither boy would budge. So to resolve the problem, her minister husband had held the puppy up in front of his congregation on Sunday morning and had asked that if anyone had a name suggestion, to please jot it down and put it in the offering plate. To the boys' dismay, eight-year-old Chloe Sanders had printed "AMEN" in big letters on her offering envelope, and Noah had loved it, but the boys had grieved for over a week.

Laney sighed. Now, Amen—which had quickly become Mennie—had reached the venerable age of twelve, but even harder to believe, Elijah had just turned twenty-one—the same age she'd been when she met Noah. And now she was almost fifty-three—*how did that happen?* Time marched on, sparing no one. Loved ones grew old and left us, and young ones came into our world to fill our hearts anew. She looked up and watched a pair of pretty, grayish brown birds with white breasts fluttering from the bushes to a ledge under the backside of the woodshed, and every time they landed, they flicked their tails as if they were trying to keep their balance. As she watched, she remembered a story her grandfather had told her when she was a little girl and an aching sadness filled her heart. She could still hear his deep, southern drawl . . .

"Once upon a time," he'd said, pulling her onto his lap, "there was a beautiful princess who fell into a deep sadness. No matter what she did, she couldn't seem to overcome it. All of the sages and advisors in the court tried to discern the reason for her somber mood, but no one could. Finally, on a crisp autumn morning, the gardener invited her to visit. The princess accepted, but when she arrived, she noticed that all the blossoms had gone by and most of the branches were bare. Seeing her dismay, the gardener quickly pointed out that the garden was still beautiful in its gold and rusty hues. The princess nodded, watching the chickadees, cardinals, titmice, and nuthatches fluttering busily among the vines and berries, and the gardener explained that it wasn't her mind or body that suffered—it was her soul. She went on to say that all mankind endures the ebb and flow of life's joys and sorrows—'the rhythm of the tides' she called it—much like the earthly change of seasons—and she assured her that her heart would once again know joy.

"The princess considered her words and asked how she had come by such wisdom, and the gardener showed her an ancient sundial hidden among the roses. On it were engraved the words, 'This too shall pass.' "

Laney brushed away a tear, and Mennie sat up and rested his head on her lap again. She stroked his soft ears. Noah was right—dogs do have a way of knowing when you're feeling blue. "This'll pass too, old pie," she whispered, holding his sweet head and looking into his solemn brown eyes.

PART I

Now faith is the assurance of things hoped for, the conviction of things not seen.

—Hebrews 11:1

1

August 1983

Laney is an old soul—all her friends say so, but until recently, she wasn't quite sure what they meant. She was a little girl when she first heard her gram say the same thing, and for a long time afterward, she wondered if a person is born an old soul or if having an old soul comes from one's life experiences. She would never forget the first time she'd heard Gram describe her that way.

She'd been lying on top of her sheets in the little room off the kitchen, listening to her brother Lyle snoring softly and wishing she could fall asleep too, but the Georgia night was too hot, and the fiery orange sun was taking its sweet time sinking behind the rolling hills of her grandparents' farm. She studied the familiar, tiny blue flowers on the sun-gilded wallpaper next to her bed, listened to the slow, steady whir of the ceiling fan in the kitchen, and without thinking, started to softly sing the song the local country station had been playing all summer—she'd even heard Gramp humming it earlier that evening, his eyes glistening with tears. Right then and there, she'd decided that the lonely tune about the Wichita lineman was the saddest song she'd ever heard, but that made her love it all the more. She heard the screen door squeak open and the familiar clunk of Gramp's boot as he caught it with his foot so it wouldn't bang. "If we don't get some rain," he said as the latch clicked, "those freestones are going to be as dry as my old bones."

Laney could hear the beans she'd help pick that afternoon plinking into Gram's metal colander. "The Lord'll provide, Lon," Gram replied. "He always does." Laney could tell she was smiling.

"I know," Gramp said with a tired sigh. "But it'd be nice if He'd provide a little sooner."

The plinking stopped, and Laney surmised that Gramp's strong, brown arms were wrapped around Gram's waist.

"That little Laney is such an old soul," Gram said softly, making Laney's ears perk up.

"I know," Gramp agreed with a quiet chuckle.

"She always . . ." But Gram's words were suddenly drowned out by the tap squeaking open, followed by rushing water. Laney knew Gramp was holding his hand under the stream, waiting for it to get cold, so she sat up, trying to hear the rest of Gram's words, but by the time the water was cold enough and Gramp's glass was full, Gram was on to talking about how many jars of jam they'd put up that afternoon. "For six years old, she's a good little helper" were the only words she heard. Laney flopped back down. What did Gram mean? Did she mean she was old—*like Gram, for heaven's sake?* Or did being helpful make you old? Laney waited until Gram turned off the light and Gramp tugged the chain on the ceiling fan; then she slipped over to her brother's bed—Lyle was eight—surely he'd know. "Ly," she whispered. "Wake up." Her brother groaned, and she nudged him. "Lyle, what's an old soul?" she whispered urgently.

"Darned if I know," he mumbled, his words muffled by his pillow.

"You *must* know—haven't you ever heard of it?"

"For Pete's sake, Lane, go back to sleep," he said gruffly, rolling over to face the blue flowered wallpaper and promptly ending the conversation. Reluctantly, Laney shuffled back to her own bed, edged over to the open window, wrapped her arms around her night-gowned knees, and looked out at the last remnants of hot pink flame streaking across the horizon. She thought about Gram's words—and all the other mysteries in her six-year-old world—and then she gazed up at the azure blue heavens, sparkling with diamonds, and quietly whispered the constellations' names—just as Gramp had taught her.

August was by far the best month of the year. Not only did Laney's birthday fall on its last day, but it was also the month she and Lyle spent every summer on their grandparents' farm. Pacey's Peaches and Pecans had been in the family for generations, and it would have been the natural order of things for Lon Jr.—her dad—to take over one day, but young Lonnie, much to his daughter's dismay, had gone off to a small college in Maine and, as her grandfather put it, "fallen head over heels in love with a pretty, smart New England girl dressed in duck boots and a barn coat." Gramp loved to recount the story. "That poor boy was blindsided—just a simple Georgia farm boy—he didn't stand a chance." Gramp always chuckled when he said this—which assured her that he'd forgiven her mom for stealing his son away. But Laney wasn't sure she'd ever forgive her dad. "He should've come back here," she said gloomily, sitting on Gramp's lap in the rocking chair on the porch. She loved the farm more than anyplace else on earth, and she always wished her parents had settled under the endless Georgia sky so she could've grown up under the orchard's gnarled umbrellas of pink blossoms and the shade of its lush green branches, heavy with summer's sweetness. Instead, her parents had become teachers and settled in Maine near her mom's side of the family.

"He should've been true to his family."

"Then he probably wouldn't've had you," Gramp pointed out.

"Oh, yes, he would've," Laney assured him with a long sigh. "And I would've helped him run the farm. After all, I know just about everythin' there is to know—when the peaches are ready 'n ripe and just as sweet as summer . . . how to peel 'em so they don't bruise, and how to . . ."

"*And* how to eat 'em," Gramp teased, wrapping his arms around her and giving her a hug. "Boy, do you know how to eat 'em. In fact, you'd probably put us outta business cuz you'd eat the whole crop."

Laney laughed, her mouth watering for a sweet, juicy Georgia peach. "Oh, Gramp, I would not." Then her eyes lit up. "I know—I could run the farm for you."

"I bet you could too," Gramp agreed, patting her knee.

"I mean it," she insisted.

"I know you do, but until you're a little bit bigger, we'll have to let your uncle Luke help too."

"Okay, but I'm ready whenever you need me," she said matter-of-factly, leaning back against his chest.

"And what happens if you go off to college and fall in love with some cute New England fella?" Gramp teased.

"I would never do that, Gramp," she said matter-of-factly, looking into his summer-sky blue eyes, "because you're my heart's favorite love."

Laney smiled wistfully, remembering her long-ago words as she knelt down to tighten her shoe-laces near the starting line of the 1983 Falmouth

Road Race. It was a cloudy August morning—the first August in her entire life that she hadn't spent in Georgia. But when she'd called her grandparents to tell them about the summer internship she'd been offered, they'd assured her that although they'd miss her, they would manage. Then Gramp had told her how proud he was of his smart, beautiful granddaughter, and he'd insisted she could not miss out on such a wonderful opportunity.

Laney hadn't been so sure. She worried about her grandparents—they were getting older and she couldn't help wondering how many more years they had. *After all, Gramp had just turned eighty that spring, and although the whole family had flown down for the celebration, it had only been for a weekend and that just wasn't long enou—* Laney's thoughts were suddenly interrupted by footsteps sounding much too close, and in the next moment, someone bumped into her, knocking her over.

"Whoa! I'm so sorry," a male voice said. Laney looked up as a tall, slender boy with blond hair and a scruffy, reddish beard tried to regain his balance. "Are you okay?" he asked worriedly.

"I'm fine," she said. He reached out his hand, and she let him pull her up, and then she brushed the sand from her hands and calves.

"I truly am sorry," he said again. "Are you sure you're okay?"

She looked up, and he smiled, revealing perfectly straight white teeth. He was handsome —in a roguish, carefree sort of way—and his eyes, which were the same startling, summer-sky blue as her grandfather's, gazed at her with such sincerity she thought he might cry. She mustered a smile. "I'm fine—honest."

"That's good because it's really my brother's fault," he said, motioning to a slighter, younger version of himself standing off to the side. "Micah was pointing to Joan Benoit, and I turned to look."

His younger version realized he was being talked about and stepped closer. "I hope you're not blaming me for your clumsiness."

"Of course not," the older one said with an impish grin.

Laney looked from one to the other and laughed. She guessed the older one must be in his early twenties and the younger one—whose cheeks were still smooth—might be fifteen. "You ran into me because you were looking at Joan Benoit?"

He nodded. "She *is* famous you know . . . in running circles." He paused and shook his head. "I don't mean she's famous for running *in* circles—I mean in the running world. She won the women's division last year, and she won the Boston Marathon last April, and I'll probably never see her again, except from a distance . . . through the dust. At least she'll leave Micah and me in the dust. I don't know about you—maybe you're a world-class runner too." He paused again, eyeing her. "Are you?"

Laney shook her head, laughing. "No. I'm only running because a bunch of my friends from Woods Hole thought it would be fun. I'll be lucky to finish."

"Do you live in Woods Hole?"

"No, I'm—" But her words were interrupted by the announcer summoning everyone to the starting line.

A chorus of voices called, "C'mon, Laney—it's going to start." Laney looked over and waved to a group of college-age boys and girls.

"Be right there," she called. Then she looked back at the brothers. "Well, have a good race—be careful—watch out for Joan!"

"We will . . . you too," the older one said, captivated by her smile, her friendly eyes, her rosy cheeks, and the sprinkle of freckles across her nose. He wanted to say more, but for the first time in his life, Noah Coleman was at a complete loss for words.

2

From the moment he pulled her up from the sandy pavement and looked into her light sea-green eyes, Noah felt his world shift, and as he watched her run over to join her friends, he murmured the name they'd called her: *Laney*. Suddenly, he felt like love-struck Tony in *West Side Story*—except this time the most beautiful sound was Laney.

His brother gave him a nudge and started to jog away. "You coming?"

"Huh?" Noah looked up, remembered where he was, and trotted after his brother. His heart pounded—as it always did before a race—and he looked around, hoping to see her again, but Laney —not from Woods Hole—had been swallowed up by the sea of people. "Damn!" he muttered, shaking his head.

Micah looked over. "What's the matter?"

"I don't know her last name."

"Well, just run slow and maybe she'll catch up. Then you'll have an excuse for me beating you so bad. Or, if worse comes to worst, she was wearing a Bowdoin T-shirt—you could drive up to Maine and find her." The gun sounded, and Micah took off. "See you at the finish," he called.

"You little sh . . ." Noah said, laughing and chasing after him.

As he ran along the familiar course, Noah fell into an easy stride beside his brother, and his mind drifted back over all the summers he'd spent on Cape Cod—all except one. The summer he'd turned seven his world had been turned upside down, and instead of on the Cape, he'd spent it at a cabin his dad had built on the Contoocook River in New Hampshire. He still remembered looking

27

out the window of the old Chevy pickup as they crossed the Sagamore Bridge and headed north.

The ride had seemed to take forever, and it hadn't helped that the radio kept playing the same songs over and over. One song in particular had puzzled him, and to this day, whenever he heard it, he thought of that long-ago ride.

"Why did someone leave a cake out in the rain?" he'd asked.

His dad had shrugged. "I don't know—it's a silly thing to do."

"Yeah," Noah had replied. "I don't understand why he couldn't get the recipe."

His dad had shaken his head. "I honestly don't know, Noah, but you can change the station if you want."

Noah had leaned over and fiddled with the knob until he found a country station that was playing a haunting song about a lonely lineman, and he leaned back to listen.

"Good choice," Asa Coleman had said with a smile.

Eventually, Noah had grown to love New Hampshire almost as much as Cape Cod—especially hiking its mountains—but the Cape would always be where he went to find solace. The first time he'd seen the ocean in winter he was seventeen, struggling with college decisions and trying to discern what God had planned for his life. The frigid January morning had started out like any other: he'd gone outside to warm up the old pickup—that was now his to use—ran back inside, rubbing his hands together, wolfed down the bowl of lukewarm oatmeal his mom had left for him, grabbed his backpack and jacket, pulled on his hooded cross-country sweatshirt, and headed out the door. But for some reason, when he reached town, he hadn't made the turn toward school; instead he'd just kept driving . . . and he hadn't stopped until the gas gauge was hovering on *E* and he was looking up at Nauset Lighthouse. He'd climbed out of the truck, pulled his hood up, and stood with his hands stuffed in his pockets, looking out at the rugged, weather-weary coastline. Buffeted by the howling wind, he'd watched the waves swell up from the gunmetal gray surf and crash down in angry white foam, relentlessly pounding the frozen bulwark of sand. At that moment, he'd been overwhelmed by the majesty and magnitude of God's power, and he'd felt small and insignificant in comparison, but as he continued to watch and listen to the ocean's fury, he was filled with a sense of peace . . . and he'd suddenly known with absolute certainty what he was meant to do with his life. After that day, whenever something troubled him, Noah went to the ocean—it was like visiting an old friend.

By the time Noah and Micah crested Nobska Light, the sun was peeking through the clouds, and six miles later, when Micah picked up the pace along Falmouth Heights Beach and they raced down Grand Avenue—delighting the crowd with their effort—the sun was high in a cloudless, summer-blue sky.

"Next year," Micah said with a grin, trying to catch his breath.

"Yeah, yeah," Noah teased, reaching out to shake his brother's hand, knowing all too well his victories were numbered. They walked around, cooling off, and Micah stopped to ask an official who'd won.

"Joseph Nzau," the man answered.

"And for the women?" Noah pressed.

"Joanie Benoit."

"I knew it!" Noah said with a grin.

They walked over to the water station, and Noah looked around, hoping to get a glimpse of Laney. "Want to go for a cooldown?" Micah asked, pouring a cup of water over his head.

"In a few minutes," Noah answered, crushing his cup and tossing it in a garbage can.

"Think she came in yet?" Micah asked.

"Who?"

"You know—the girl from Bowdoin."

"I dunno," Noah answered casually, trying to make it sound like it didn't matter. A moment later he said, "All right, let's go," and trotted away from the stream of runners coming in. After all, it was silly to think he'd see her again in this crowd;

besides, she probably had a boyfriend. And on top of that, he was starting seminary school in a couple of weeks, and the last thing he needed was to get caught up in a relationship—especially if it was long-distance.

"Are you sure?" Micah called after him, surprised by his brother's sudden departure and change of heart. He ran to catch up with him. "Maybe she doesn't go to Bowdoin—maybe it's not her shirt. Maybe she goes to Harvard or MIT."

"It doesn't mat—" Noah started to say, but then he caught a glimpse of the young, petite woman with the brunette ponytail walking across the field.

Micah followed his brother's gaze and shook his head. "That's all right. I wanted to get a banana anyway . . ."

Noah barely heard him.

3

"Hey!" he said, catching up.

Laney looked up in surprise. "Oh, hey . . . how'd it go?"

"Good . . . you?"

"Just finished." She reached up to tuck some loose strands of damp hair behind her ear. "I only had to walk once," she added with a grin.

"That's great."

"It's a pretty run. I'd do it again."

"I've been running it since I was sixteen."

"Wow—that's great!" She looked around. "Where's Micah?"

Noah motioned toward the refreshment tent. "He went to get something to eat."

"Did you beat him?"

"I did, but not by much," he admitted with a grin.

She nodded, trying to think of something else to say. "And . . . did you see Joan?"

"No, but I heard she won again."

"She's amazing."

Noah nodded. "Yeah."

"She's an alum of my school. She graduated in '79—right before I started."

"So you *do* go to Bowdoin," he said, nodding at her shirt.

She glanced down to see what she'd pulled over her head that morning. "Yup."

"What brings you to the Cape?"

"I'm finishing an internship at the oceanographic institution."

"That's a prestigious place."

She nodded. "I'm majoring in marine biology, so it's been a perfect fit." She paused. "How 'bout you?"

"Me?" He hesitated, considering his answer and wondering how much she knew about the school from which he'd just graduated . . . or the one he was about to attend. Some folks were turned off by religion, but he didn't have any idea what her feelings were, so he took a deep breath and threw caution to the wind. "I just graduated from Gordon, and I'm starting at Andover Newton in a couple of weeks."

"You're going to be a minister?" she asked in surprise.

He laughed. "Yup . . . crazy, huh?"

She searched his eyes and shook her head. "It's not crazy," she said softly. "I think it's a wonderful profession."

He nodded. "Well, that's good. I mean . . . I'm glad you approve."

Just then, her friends ran by. "Hey, Laney, we've been looking all over for you."

"I'm coming . . . just a minute." She turned back to him. "Well, I guess I better go."

Noah nodded, and then realized he still hadn't introduced himself. "I'm sorry . . . I should've . . . I mean . . ." Flustered, he shook his head at his inability to speak coherently and started over. "I'm Noah."

She smiled and held out her hand. "It's nice to meet you, Noah—future man of the cloth."

"It's nice to meet you too."

"Laney," one of her friends called, "we're heading back to the car. . . ."

Laney looked over and nodded. "Well, I guess I really should get going, or I'll miss my ride."

Noah suddenly realized he was going to miss

his last opportunity. "Would you . . . I mean, you wouldn't happen to . . ." He smiled and shook his head again. "What I'm trying to say is—are you hungry?"

She eyed him skeptically. "Hmmm . . . I usually don't go off with someone I just met."

"Well, it's just that Micah and I are going to The Pancake Man—it's a post-race tradition. Our dad usually goes too, but he's home nursing a knee injury so he didn't come. They have great pancakes, and . . . well, it's not like you'd be going off alone with someone you just met. You'd be going off with someone who's studying to be a minister . . . and his little brother." He paused and then added, "And we can give you a ride back to Woods Hole after."

She laughed. "Well, when you say it like that . . ."

"Have you ever been to Pancake Man?"

She shook her head.

"What?" he teased, feigning disbelief. "It's a Cape Cod institution—you can't say you've been to the Cape if you haven't been to Pancake Man."

"Well . . ." she said with a grin. "I guess I better go then."

"Great!" he said, feeling his heart skipping like a stone across the waves. Then he hesitated uncertainly. "Wait—you meant with us, right?"

Laughing, she nodded, and her smile stole his heart.

• • •

Laney loved The Pancake Man. She and Noah sipped black coffee while they waited for their orders to come, and she told them about the peach hotcakes and peach French toast her gram made, adding that hotcakes—as they were called down south—were definitely the best comfort food on earth, especially when served for supper. Micah contended that scrambled eggs were right up there too, but he eventually conceded that pancakes were probably better—especially on a snowy winter night. Noah listened intently, swept up by Laney's funny, outgoing personality—and decided, right then and there, that he'd love nothing more than having hot, buttery pancakes with her on a snowy winter night. When their orders came, Laney had no problem downing her entire stack of plate-size buttermilk pancakes. "I guess I was hungrier than I thought," she said, swirling her last bite through a puddle of maple syrup, innocently unaware of how impressed they were as they struggled to finish their Pigs in a Blanket—a coronary-clogging dish that included several links of sausage wrapped up in pancakes.

When they got back to Woods Hole, Noah walked her to her door.

"That was fun," she said.

"You made it fun. Thanks for coming."

"Thank *you* for inviting me. I'm glad I got to experience the famous Pancake Man."

"You know," he said, "there are several other Cape Cod institutions you should experience while you're here."

Frowning, she teased, "Well, where've you been all summer? My internship ends Friday and then I'm going to Georgia for a week." She watched a gloomy shadow fall across his face and added, "But I might be able to do something one evening . . . and maybe Saturday if I stay an extra day."

"That works for me," Noah said, his boyish smile returning. "And my family is having a party on Saturday if you'd like to come."

4

On Monday, wearing faded jeans, a blue Gordon College T-shirt, Nike running shoes, sunglasses, and still sporting a scruffy beard, Noah knocked hesitantly on Laney's door.

"Hmm . . ." she teased, eyeing his casual attire. "You don't look much like minister material."

He smiled, taking in what little there was of her short denim cutoffs, smooth, tan legs, and snow-white tank top. "And you make me wonder if I *am* minister material."

They stopped at an ice-cream shop in Woods Hole, and while Noah studied the menu, considering an indulgence called chocolate desire, Laney ordered a small cup of peach ice cream. "Are you sure that's all you want?" he teased. "It can't possibly be enough for a girl who can eat a whole stack of buttermilk pancakes."

"Well, I didn't just run seven miles."

The waitress handed Laney her cup and then handed Noah a monstrous brownie sundae swimming in hot fudge and topped with a mountain of whipped cream. Laney shook her head as he licked his whipped cream. "You want some, don't you?" he asked with a grin.

She laughed. "Well, maybe just a little whipped cream." He plopped a large spoonful—including his cherry—on top of her ice cream, and she laughed. "Wow! Thanks."

They walked along the waterfront, licking their spoons. "So," she said, "how do you know so much about Cape Cod?"

Noah swallowed a bite of warm brownie. "We have a house in Eastham, and I've spent almost every summer out here. The rest of the time we live in New Hampshire. My dad's an English teacher, and my mom works with special ed kids at the elementary school."

"Really?"

"Yup, why?"

"My parents are both teachers too, although my dad was supposed to be a farmer." Noah gave her a puzzled look, and she elaborated on her family's farming history.

"Hence the peach ice cream?" he asked, nodding toward her cup.

"Yup—I love peach ice cream. My gram makes it for my birthday every summer."

"So is that your calling—a peach farmer?"

She sighed. "Well, that's the hard part. When I was little, I promised my grandfather I'd help him run the farm someday, but since then, I've come to love the ocean and aquatic life, so I could definitely see myself working in marine biology. But I also love little kids, so I could also see myself teaching." Her face grew solemn. "Then again, I *do* love the farm . . ."

"Hmm . . . sounds like a tough decision."

"I keep waiting to have an epiphany."

Noah hesitated. "Well, at the risk of sounding religious, have you prayed about it?"

Laney shook her head. "I usually pray for guidance, but I can't say I've prayed specifically about this. I guess I always think God has bigger things to worry about."

Noah shook his head, as if he'd been expecting her answer. "That's just it—people think their problems aren't important enough. I mean God already has a lot on his plate, right? World hunger, war, getting the Red Sox into the World Series . . ." He grinned. "I'm just kidding on that last one. But folks think that just because we humans can only handle one or two crises at a time, that's how God works too; but it's not. He can handle all problems—no matter how big or small—and he can handle them *all* at once. I'm sure you've heard the verse: 'For as the heavens are higher than the earth, so are my ways higher than your ways and my thoughts than your thoughts.' Well, that's just what He's trying to tell us—that he doesn't play on our level—that his playing field is much bigger than ours."

Laney was impressed by his passion and knowledge. "I guess I never really thought about it that way."

Noah smiled. "And, by the way, I think you'd make a great teacher. You have such a warm, easygoing personality—kids would love you."

"You think so?"

"Mm-hmm," he replied, taking another bite of brownie.

"How about you?" she asked.

He looked up in surprise and swallowed. "Me?"

"Yes. How'd you know you wanted to be a minister?"

"Oh," he said, relieved by her clarification. "Well," he began, carefully considering his answer. "I guess it started when I was in high school. I was very involved in our youth group. We were always helping people or raising money to go on trips to help people. Every other summer we went on a mission trip. One year we helped rebuild a cabin in West Virginia. Another time we cleaned up a vacant lot in a poor section of Philadelphia and turned it into a vegetable garden. Other summers we worked as counselors at a Bible camp. We were always doing something—shoveling walks, visiting old folks, having bake sales. Our minister had a knack for coming up with creative ways for us to help others, and I came to realize that those times were the times I felt happiest . . . and most content." He looked over. "I honestly believe we're put on this planet for a reason—and not a self-serving reason. I think we're supposed to find a way to help . . . a way to make a difference."

She studied his profile in the soft light of the late day sun. "You must have a pretty strong faith."

Noah licked his spoon and smiled. "Not always. There've definitely been times when I've wondered if God hears my prayers at all. At one point, I even questioned His existence. Now I just question my ability to hear what He's trying to tell me."

"Have you always found it so easy to talk about?"

He shook his head. "No, I used to keep my faith to myself. I was afraid people would think I was some kind of crazy religious zealot, but then I realized I was—like the Bible says—keeping my light under a bushel. I've come to believe that God is interested in every detail of our lives— even the little things. I have a friend who prays for good hair days and good parking spots." He laughed. "And she usually gets them. I think what God loves most is having an intimate relationship with each of us, and I want to help people understand that."

Laney had never met someone her age that seemed so grounded and comfortable with who he was . . . and she loved that he wasn't afraid to share his faith. Her grandfather was like that too.

On Wednesday, wearing a blue oxford shirt that matched his eyes and stone-colored khakis, Noah tucked a bouquet of freshly cut black-eyed Susans behind his back, smoothed his hair, and knocked on Laney's door; and when she opened it, it was all he could do to keep his clean-shaven chin from hitting the floor—she looked stunning.

"Hi," she said with a shy smile.

"H-hi . . . wow!" he stammered. Her peach-colored sundress accentuated every delicate curve of her body, and her shiny, dark hair fell freely past her shoulders. "You look . . . *amazing*."

She could feel her cheeks flush. "Thanks. So do you. In fact, you might even pass for a minister."

Remembering the flowers, he pulled them from behind his back. "These are for you."

"Wow—thanks! You didn't have to do that."

"I know," he said with the boyish smile she was growing to love.

She held the door open. "Come in while I put them in water."

He followed her inside and saw boxes piled everywhere. "I guess you really are leaving."

"I know—it's a mess," she said, filling a plastic cup with water. "I don't even have a vase."

Noah noticed an old ten-speed leaning against the wall. "Hey, if you come to my family's party this weekend, bring your bike."

"I'm afraid I'll be bringing everything because I'm heading home right after."

"Oh, well, let me know if you need help."

She looked up from arranging the flowers and glanced around the room. "I should be okay. It looks worse than it is."

Ten minutes later, Noah parked the truck on a side street near historic downtown Falmouth, and they walked toward the famous landmark restaurant, The Quarterdeck. He held the door for her, and she teased, "Gee, I could get used to this."

"I hope you do," he said, following her in.

The hostess led them to a table in the corner near an open window, and Laney looked around, admiring the old restaurant. "This is really nice," she whispered.

"I'm glad you like it," he whispered back with a grin, opening his menu.

A waitress appeared to take their drink orders, and Noah looked questioningly at Laney, but she looked uncertain. "Are you having a drink?"

"Yup."

"A drink-drink?"

He grinned. "I'm studying to be a minister . . . not a saint."

She laughed and turned to the waitress. "I'll have a glass of white wine."

"And I'll have a Rolling Rock," Noah added. When the waitress left, he teased, "Are you sure you're old enough to have a drink-drink?"

"I think so, but you never know around here—they keep changing the drinking age. I have a friend in Connecticut who's come of age twice already, and they're talking about raising it again." She paused uncertainly. "What is the drinking age in Massachusetts?"

"Twenty."

She nodded. "I'm good then. I'll be twenty-one on the thirty-first."

"That's my dad's birthday."

"It is?"

"Yup." He paused, thinking. "He'll be forty-one."

Laney looked puzzled. "How old are you?"

"I turned twenty-two on June twenty-first."

"So your dad was . . ." She tried to calculate in her head.

"Young," Noah said, finishing her sentence. "My dad was young—he was nineteen when I was born."

"Oh," she said softly. "Well, back then, people started families at a much younger age."

Noah's eyes grew solemn. "That's not it." He paused. "But it is a long story. . . ."

Laney nodded, not wanting to press him, and when he didn't continue, she looked down at her menu. "So what's good?"

"Everything," Noah said, his smile returning. "The chowder is really good, but if you come out to the house on Saturday, you'll get to have the best chowder on earth."

"Whose chowder is that?"

"My dad's . . . well, it's really my great-grandfather's recipe. My parents are having one of their famous gin and chowder parties—it's a family tradition . . . and a lot of fun."

"Sounds tempting."

"It would be really great if you came."

Laney looked up, her eyes sparkling. "Well, what should I have tonight if I'm going to be having *chowdah* on Saturday?"

Noah laughed. "How about the *lobstah?*"

5

Late Friday afternoon, a loaded-down Honda Civic with a ten-speed mounted on back pulled into the driveway, and Noah came out, wearing white swim trunks and a faded gray T-shirt that said "Go Pre" on it. "Hey," he said with a warm smile.

"Hey!"

"Did you find it okay?"

"Yup. Your directions were perfect. There was a lot of traffic though."

"Yeah, everyone's trying to beat the rush—most of the rentals run Saturday to Saturday—which makes traffic crazy. If I were ever to rent my house, I'd make it Friday to Friday or Sunday to Sunday."

"You have a house?"

"Yup," he said, reaching for her bags. "But that's another long story, and my parents are waiting to meet you."

She looked up at the old, weathered gray house and followed him around back. "Watch this step," he said, tapping his foot. "It's loose."

Laney nodded, stepping over the top step and coming face-to-face with a big yellow Lab, wiggling with happiness.

"Don't mind him—he's friendly."

"What's his name?" Laney asked, rubbing his velvety ears.

"Finnegan," Noah said. "His brother's around here somewhere." As he said this, another Lab nosed open the screen door and moseyed out to say hello too. "That's Mulligan."

"What great names! How do you tell them apart?"

"Finny's a little bigger and a little blonder."

Laney laughed as they sniffed and wiggled all around her. "I don't think I've ever had such an enthusiastic welcome."

"That's how Labs are," Noah said, "always wearing their emotions on their paws."

A petite woman, wearing a white bathing suit with a colorful beach towel tucked around her waist, pushed open the door, carrying a pile of wet towels. She was tan, and her light brown hair was streaked with blond, and she looked much too young to have a twenty-two-year-old son.

"Mom, this is Laney," Noah said. "Laney, this is my mom."

"Hi, Mrs. Coleman," Laney said. "It's nice to meet you."

"It's nice to meet you too," Maddie said, reaching her hand out from under the towels and warming into a smile that reminded Laney of Micah. "Please, call me Maddie though—'Mrs. Coleman' makes me feel old!" She handed the towels to Noah with a look that said, *I asked you to do this before,* and called, "Hon, Laney's here."

"I'm right here, dear," Asa Coleman said. A tall, slender man with blond hair, graying at the temples, limped around the corner of the house carrying a wooden bushel of weeds. "It's a jungle out there," he said, setting the bushel down and brushing off his hands.

"Well, you shouldn't be kneeling if your knee is bothering you," his wife scolded.

"Someone has to do it."

He looked up and smiled at Laney, his summer-sky blue eyes sparkling. There was no doubt in Laney's mind that he was related to Noah, but he looked more like his older brother than his father. "Maybe we can get Laney to do some weeding while she's here," he said hopefully.

"I can weed," Laney said willingly, immediately liking him.

Asa put his arm around her shoulders and eyed his son. "I told you she'd help me weed."

Noah—who was spreading the towels on the railing—rolled his eyes and said, "She's not helping you weed, Dad."

His father feigned disappointment. "What? I thought that's why we invited her."

Maddie laughed and shook her head. "So what *are* you two up to? Will you be here for dinner?"

Laney looked questioningly at Noah, and he shook his head. "Nope, not tonight, but we'll definitely be here tomorrow night." He paused and looked at Laney. "I think we're going to hit Cape Escape, then Arnold's . . . and maybe up to Provincetown."

"I thought you wanted her to come back," Asa teased.

"I do, but she's here to experience the Cape, so we can't skip P-town."

"Well, it sounds like you're gonna hit all the hot spots," Maddie said. "You should try to get to Arnold's early though, or there'll be a line."

"Or we could do what Micah does."

"What does Micah do?" said a voice from behind the screen door.

"Order takeout and bypass the line."

"That's what everyone does," he said defensively.

"Yeah, everyone except the people in line."

"What can I say? Life's short—why should I spend forty minutes standing in line, starving. They'll catch on . . . someday . . . maybe."

An hour and a half later, Noah was standing next to a wooden waterwheel, studying the wrinkled blue scorecard that had been in and out of his back pocket eighteen times and tallying the penciled-in numbers.

"What did I get?" Laney asked, trying to see over his shoulder. "Did I win?"

"I don't think so," he replied.

"How can that be?" she said, reaching for the card. "I had two holes in one, and you were over par at least three times."

Grinning, he held the card out of her reach and shook his head. "Hmm . . . I only see one hole in one," he teased.

"I think I should do the tallying—how do I even know you're good at math?"

"I *am* good at math," Noah said. "I scored a five on my AP calc test."

"If that's true, you should be studying to be an engineer, not a minister."

"That was one of the many conversations God and I had," he said with a smile, finally relinquishing the scorecard. While she studied it, Noah returned their clubs, and then reappeared with a handful of tiny, brown pellets.

"I did win!" she said happily as he walked past, heading toward the steps.

"No need to rub it in."

"Micah warned me you'd be a sore loser," Laney said, following him back up the worn stone steps to the seventeenth hole, wondering where he was going. He stopped next to a dark pool—a pool by which she must've just walked, but because she'd been so focused on the game, she hadn't noticed. She looked down and saw a school of bright orange goldfish and milky white koi splashing about, jockeying for position and puckering their mouths greedily.

"Micah and I call this one Moony," Noah said, kneeling down and pointing to a translucent bluish-white fish that looked as if it might weigh ten pounds. "He's been here for as long as we can remember." Noah held a tiny pellet out to the big fish, and it sucked it up like a vacuum. "Here," he said, pouring some pellets into Laney's palm. She knelt down next to him, accidently dropping several pellets and causing a frenzy of excitement beneath the surface of the water. "Just hold one out. They don't bite. They just suck." Laney held a pellet out, and a small goldfish rushed boldly to the surface and slurped it from her fingers. "See? It doesn't hurt," Noah said. "You're the marine biologist—you should know that."

After feeding the fish and stopping at Arnold's for "THE BEST FRIED CLAMS ON CAPE COD," they continued up Route 6 to Provincetown. It was getting late, but by the time they found a parking spot, the nightlife was just beginning to emerge from the shadows. They walked along Commerce Street, watching the outlandishly clad characters and couples parading on the famous street, and Laney took it all in. They went into some souvenir shops, and she bought a pink Cape Cod T-shirt for herself and two jars of beach plum jam—one for her parents and one for her grandparents. "This is perfect," she said, holding up the jam. "I've been looking for something from Cape Cod to give them . . . and now they'll realize there are other flavors besides peach!" Finally, they stopped in an ice-cream shop, ordered two soft piña colada cones, and walked slowly back to the truck to head home.

A half hour later, when they pulled in the driveway, the house was dark, but as they climbed the back steps, they realized someone had left a light on. Noah pushed open the door, and the two big Labs roused from their slumber and tumbled over each other, blinking sleepily, to greet them. "Hey, guys," Noah whispered, scratching their big heads. Content that everyone was home and safe, they returned to their beds, circled several times, and curled up. Noah carried Laney's bag up to his bedroom, turned on the light, and discovered that his mom had put out a fresh towel and washcloth. "The sheets are clean too," he said with a sheepish grin. "I changed them myself."

"Thank you," Laney said with a smile.

"The bathroom's down the hall on the left. Can you think of anything else?"

She looked around. "No . . . but where are you sleeping?"

"On the couch."

She frowned. "I don't want to put you out. . . . Why don't I sleep on the couch?"

Noah shook his head. "Then what would've been the point of changing my sheets?" he asked. "Besides, we have a lot to do tomorrow, so you need to rest up. *And* I think my dad's making blueberry pancakes."

"I'm ready!" Laney said with a yawn.

He laughed. "You look ready! Okay, well, if you need anything, you know where I am."

"Okay."

"Night," he said, searching her eyes and wishing he could summon the courage to kiss her.

"Night," she said, returning his gaze, wishing he could too.

6

"These pancakes are amazing, Mr. Coleman," Laney said, smoothing butter and drizzling syrup on the two additional pancakes—oozing with plump blueberries—he'd just slid onto her plate.

"I hope you made enough to feed a village, Dad," Micah teased, coming in the kitchen, "because that's how much Laney can eat."

"She's already on her fourth," Noah reported with his mouth full.

"You're keeping track?" Laney asked in surprise.

"Yup," Noah replied with a grin.

"Laney," Maddie said, leaning across the table, "you don't have to put up with their abuse—just kick 'em under the table."

Laney smiled, and at the same moment, two muzzles nudged under her arms, nosing her plate and trying to sneak furtive licks.

"Hey!" Asa admonished. The two Labs pulled their heads out from under Laney's arms and gazed at him innocently. *Do you mean me?*

"Yes—you!" Asa said in an exasperated voice. "You'd think you hadn't eaten in a week!"

"C'mere," Maddie said, motioning to them. "I'm sorry, Laney. Please forgive them. They're both spoiled rotten beggars."

"Nice," Noah said with a hint of sarcasm as he shook his head. "You want her to *forgive* them, but *kick* us."

Maddie just laughed and took a sip of her coffee.

After the breakfast dishes were washed and dried, Noah rolled his mountain bike out into the driveway and lifted Laney's ten-speed off the back of her car, checked their tires, filled two water bottles, strapped beach towels onto the back of his bike, and told his mom they wouldn't be back until late afternoon.

It was another beautiful, blue sky August day, and as they rode down Ocean View Drive—a bumpy, weathered road whose view of the ocean had long been obscured by the gnarled pitch pine and scrub oak that thrived on the sandy, windswept peninsula—Laney took her hands off her handlebars and threw her arms up in the air. "Woo-hoooo!" she sang, sailing past Noah.

Surprised and laughing, he sped up. "Excuse me, miss, but you're not practicing proper bike safety."

"Oh, don't be an old poop. . . ."

"I'm not an old poop," he protested, tentatively letting go of his handlebars.

She looked over at him and grinned. "Now, give those underarms some air."

Noah made sure he had his balance and slowly lifted his arms.

"Now shout, 'Woo-hoooo!' " she commanded, bumping down the weatherworn road.

"Woo-hoooo!" he called, laughing and feeling more alive than he'd felt in a long time.

As they came around the corner, he grabbed his handlebars and shouted, "Watch out for the sand!" Laney grabbed her handlebars too and skidded onto the roadway that led to the Coast Guard Beach.

Noah stood on his pedals as they climbed the hill and then cut across the sidewalk to a path that ran beside the Coast Guard station. He slowed down and stopped, putting his foot on the bottom rail of a weathered split rail fence for balance, and Laney pulled up beside him. "Wow . . . it's beautiful!" she exclaimed breathlessly, gazing at the gorgeous, panoramic view of the Atlantic Ocean.

Noah watched the tide lapping along the long sandbars and nodded. "I love it here." After a moment, he pointed down the dunes. "There used to be a house down there." Laney looked and he continued. "It was built in 1926 by a man named Henry Beston. He lived there for a year or so and wrote about his experience—sort of like Thoreau's *Walden*. A couple of times, Micah and I stopped to look inside. It was a great little house. It had a woodstove, a water pump, a bed, a desk . . ."

"What happened to it?"

"It was swept away in the blizzard of '78."

Laney nodded. "I remember that storm—I was a senior in high school. Maine wasn't hit as hard as southern New England, but I'll never forget seeing the pictures of the deep snow and the devastation."

Noah nodded. "The erosion was so bad this parking lot washed away too, and sometimes, chunks of asphalt still wash up on shore."

Laney shook her head. "That's amazing." She looked around. "Where do people park now?"

"There's a parking lot down the road and a tram that shuttles beachgoers." He pointed to a small white vehicle that was just pulling in, towing a train of open-air cars with bench seats. The tram stopped, and a throng of people climbed out, wearing bathing suits and sunglasses and carrying umbrellas, beach bags, towels, coolers, Boogie Boards—everything needed for a day at the beach.

"Why wouldn't you just go to a beach that has a parking lot?"

"Because the Coast Guard Beach is the best. . . . Besides, the tram is fun, and it drops you off right here."

Laney nodded, suddenly wishing they were spending the day at the beach—the ocean looked so inviting.

As if he was reading her mind, Noah said, "We'll go for a swim on our way back."

"Sounds good," she said with a smile.

They got back on their bikes, crossed the driveway, entered the bike path, and sped down a winding, narrow hill to the long, wooden bridge that crossed Nauset Marsh. The tide was out, and the air was heavy with the thick, briny scent of decay and muck. Noah looked back and pinched his nose, and Laney laughed—she didn't mind the smell. In fact, she loved it! She glanced down at the long marsh grass, swaying in the warm summer sun, and she imagined the plethora of wonderful organisms living in the boggy quagmire—just waiting to be studied.

They followed the hilly terrain out to Route 6 and across the quiet side roads to the rail trail— an old railroad bed that was being converted into a paved path for cyclists, walkers, and runners. Noah cruised along through the shade and sun with his T-shirt billowing around him, and as they passed through Nickerson Park, Laney realized she enjoyed having him in front of her so she could watch his long, muscular legs, his broad shoulders, and the way his short sun-bleached hair cut across his tan neck—she was so busy watching him, in fact, that when he slowed down unexpectedly, she almost rode into him.

"Whoa!" she said in surprise, bumping off the trail and squeaking to a stop. "Excuse me, sir," she said, frowning, "but that was poor use of proper bike signaling!"

"Sorry," he said meekly. "I didn't realize you were that close. Anyway, there's a really good place for lunch just ahead. Are you hungry?"

"That's a silly question," she teased, still frowning. "According to you and Micah, my appetite is insatiable."

He grinned. "You know we were just teasing."

"I know," she said with a forgiving smile.

After a lunch of burgers, fries, and milk shakes at Cobie's, they headed back to the Coast Guard Beach for a swim. As their bicycle tires bumped back across the wooden footbridge, Laney looked down; the tide was coming in, and the marsh grass was now swaying under the gentle current of gray-green water. They climbed the hill, parked their bikes, and while Noah unstrapped the towels, Laney watched the weary line of sunburned people waiting to catch the tram back to their cars. Two little boys were chasing each other and giggling, and although their dad—with the patience of a saint—was trying to reel them in, his arms were full of the toddler his wife had handed to him before hurrying off to the ladies' room. The two little boys, brown and sandy—and sensing their dad's disadvantage—continued to chase each other until the younger one tripped and fell, scraping both knees. He let out a howl that would put wolves to shame, and his mom returned just in time to scoop him up; the tired little fellow wiped away his tears with a sandy fist, realized everyone was watching him, and shyly buried his face in her neck.

"Boys!" Noah said with a grin.

Laney shook her head and laughed. "Yep. Boys are trouble!"

7

Maddie smoothed the white, sun-dappled, linen cloth on the table and set an arrangement of freshly cut black-eyed Susans and blue hydrangeas at its center; then she stepped back and eyed it critically. Asa looked up from lighting votive candles. "That looks nice."

"You're just saying that."

"No, I'm not."

"You don't think the colors clash?"

"Nope."

"Because I could separate them into two . . ."

"I like it just the way it is."

"I don't know. . . ." she said, sighing skeptically.

"Are you ready for a cocktail?" he asked, changing the subject. "Or would you like the whole rooster?"

Maddie smiled. "Where'd that come from again?"

Asa straightened up, his blue eyes sparkling. "My dad used to say it."

Maddie shook her head. "I miss your dad . . . and your mom."

"Me too," Asa said softly, pulling her into his arms.

Just then, they heard laughter on the stairs. "Well, well, look who's home!"

Noah came up the stairs. "I know, I know—we're late," he said. "We stopped for a swim and lost track of time, and then Laney had a close encounter with a seal."

Laney came up next to him, her eyes wide and her hair still damp. "He was right next to me! I don't know who was more surprised, but he just stayed there, gazing at me with his big brown eyes. Then he slipped under the water and swam away, brushing me with his flipper."

"Wow! That is a close encounter," Maddie exclaimed.

"I know."

"Well, if you're going to be a marine biologist," Asa said, "you need to get up close and personal."

Laney laughed, pulling her towel around her. "Noah wasn't kidding when he said I'd get to experience the Cape firsthand if I came here."

"Speaking of which," Noah said. "What time is everyone coming tonight?"

"Soon," Asa said, glancing at his watch.

"Do we have time to shower?"

"If you do it right away," his dad said. "And if you're planning to use the outdoor shower, you better be quick or Uncle Isaac will steal your towel."

Noah nodded. "I'll be quick. Laney, you can use the upstairs shower."

"Okay," she said, brushing the sand off her feet.

After his shower, Noah ducked upstairs with his towel around his waist. Laney was still in the bathroom, so he grabbed his faded jeans and a button-down shirt from his room and retreated to Micah's room to get dressed. Then he headed down to the kitchen to give Laney more privacy, lifted the top off the big pot simmering on the stove, and breathed in the wonderful, steamy aroma of fresh thyme, cream, and clams.

"Is it ready?" a familiar voice asked.

Noah turned around to find that Asa's brother and his wife had just arrived with their girls. "Hey, Uncle Isaac."

"Hey, kiddo, how's it goin'?"

"Really well, thanks," Noah said, shaking his hand. "How 'bout you?"

"Oh, fine, fine—your cousins are all running wild . . . *and* running me ragged, and there's not a damn thing I can do about it." Isaac paused and smiled, eyeing his nephew. "Speaking of girls, I hear there's a pretty brunette here for the weekend."

Noah grinned. "There is."

"Yeah . . . tell me more."

"Her name's Laney, and she's from Maine and . . ."

Just then, Laney appeared in the doorway, wearing white shorts and her new pink Cape Cod T-shirt. "Are you talking about me?" she asked, smiling and tucking her hair behind her ears.

"I am," Noah said, blushing. "Laney, this is my Uncle Isaac. He's my dad's older brother."

"Hey!" Isaac teased. "You don't need to add that when you introduce me."

Noah looked puzzled, and Isaac clarified, "Older . . ."

"Oh, right. Sorry!"

Isaac smiled and turned to Laney. "It's nice to meet you, Laney."

"It's nice to meet you too, Mr. Coleman," she said politely.

"So has my nephew been behaving himself?"

Laney tucked her hands in her back pockets and laughed. "He has."

Isaac smiled. "I hope he's better behaved than his father was when he was . . ."

"Eh, eh, eh," Asa warned, coming in from the porch. "You don't want your daughters to hear about all your escapades, do you?"

Just then, two of Isaac's daughters came in from the living room and leaned against him. "Tell us, Uncle Asa," they pleaded. "What did our dad do?"

Asa grinned, and his brother gave him a warning look. "Who's ready for chowder?" he asked.

❧ 8 ❧

"You have such a great family," Laney said as they walked down the steep wooden steps to the beach. "Your uncle Isaac is so funny, your parents are wonderful, and their friends definitely know how to have a good time."

"Yeah, they're a fun group—they've been getting together for years. My *great*-grandfather was the one who started the whole gin and chowder thing, but it was my grandfather and his best friend, Nate Shepherd, who really got it going. Legend has it that they used to have some pretty wild parties and invite all the neighbors— and all the kids would come along and have a bonfire down on the beach, and now those kids are the friends who are here tonight." He smiled and shook his head. "My grandparents were very old school—cocktails at five, Big Band on the radio, getting dressed to the nines for dinner—but no white dresses or slacks before Memorial Day or after Labor Day. It was very la-di-da," he added wistfully. "But, I guess, after my grandfather died, the gatherings fell apart . . . that is, until my uncle Isaac convinced my dad they should start them up again."

"Well, it's a wonderful tradition."

They continued to walk along Nauset Light

Beach under the moonlight, watching the beam from the lighthouse skim across the clouds. A rogue wave rushed up the beach, and Laney had to scoot around Noah to avoid getting wet. Laughing, she said, "When I was little, I always thought the foam along the edge of a wave looked like the bubbles on the edge of pancake batter when it's poured on the griddle."

Noah laughed. "Why doesn't that surprise me?"

She bumped him playfully, and he smiled, but then grew quiet.

"What's the matter?" she asked.

He stopped walking and searched her face. "Laney, I don't want there to be any secrets between us. I don't want you to ever ask me why I didn't tell you something."

"Okay," she said tentatively.

They continued to walk along in silence, and finally, Noah said, "Remember the other night when we were talking about how young my dad was when I was born?"

She nodded, studying his profile.

"Well . . ." He paused, struggling to find the right words.

"You don't have to tell me."

"I do though . . . because it's part of me, and if we're going to keep seeing each other—which I hope we are . . . I mean I hope you want to."

"I do want to."

"Okay, well then it's something you should

know because I have this thing about being completely honest and forthcoming, no matter what the out-come . . . and this is due, in large part, to my dad taking a very long time to answer questions I'd been asking him since I was little. In fact, he didn't answer everything until I turned sixteen."

Laney nodded, and Noah looked over and smiled. "Well, first I should tell you how incredibly blessed I am to have the family I have. My mom—Maddie—is the best mom on earth, and I know she loves me with all her heart. In fact, I don't think anyone outside the family would even guess she's not my real mom."

Laney looked up in surprise, and Noah's eyes glistened. "My biological mom's name was Noelle—she died in childbirth . . . having me."

"Oh, Noah, I'm so sorry."

He nodded. "More than anything, I wish I'd had the chance to meet her. My dad gave me a photograph of the two of them—it was actually taken at a gin and chowder party," he added. "She was beautiful. Long dark hair—a little longer than yours—dark blue eyes, and young . . . but older than my dad." He paused. "This is one of the biggest questions I had. I knew Maddie wasn't my real mom, but I desperately wanted to know more about the woman who was. And my dad would only say that she died. But, come to find out"—he paused—"she was married." Laney raised her eyebrows, and in the moonlight, she could see the solemn look on Noah's face. "And she wasn't married to just anyone—she was married to my grandfather's best friend."

"No," Laney whispered softly. "How in the world . . . ?"

Noah shook his head, as if he had trouble believing it too. "My real mom was a nurse, and she took care of Nate's first wife, Anna, when she was dying of cancer, so my dad had known her almost all his life. After Anna died, Noelle's job ended, and she went on to take care of someone else, but a year or so later, she and Nate ran into each other, and even though Nate was eighteen years her senior, they fell in love, and married . . . and although my grandparents, Samuel and Sarah, missed Anna, they welcomed Noelle into their lives.

"By the time Nate remarried, my dad was a teenager, and whenever Nate and Noelle came over socially, she was always friendly—always genuinely interested in what was going on in his life and my uncle Isaac's . . . and always teasing them about all the girlfriends they must have . . . even though my dad didn't have any. She was beautiful, thirteen years older than my dad . . . and he thought she hung the moon.

"Then, the summer before my dad went away to college, Nate hired him to paint their house in Orleans, and since Nate worked in Boston, Noelle was often home alone. My dad and Noelle became very close—they talked about everything—even the growing attraction they felt, but Noelle told my dad she could never betray Nate . . . and she didn't . . . until a rainy afternoon toward the end of the summer." Noah shook his head. "My dad said they never meant for anything to happen—it just did—and afterward, they couldn't seem to find their way back to the way things were before. He said he loved Noelle more than life itself, and he would've done anything for her."

"That's so sad," Laney said softly. "Did anyone find out?"

"Well, the summer ended, and my dad went off to college, so he didn't see Noelle for several weeks. But she wrote often, and he started to live for the next time he would see her. An opportunity finally came at the end of September when my dad traveled to Boston to meet Isaac, and my grandfather, and Nate for a Red Sox game. While they were at the game, my dad overheard Nate tell my grandfather that Noelle was out on the Cape alone."

"Noo . . ." Laney whispered with raised eyebrows.

"Yup. After the game, instead of taking the bus back to school, he took the bus to Hyannis and hitchhiked the rest of the way to Orleans. He spent the night with her, and the next day she drove him back to the bus station in Boston. No one ever found out—as far as he knows—and then he didn't see her again until Christmas. And it was on Christmas, in front of everyone, that Nate announced that he and Noelle were expecting. My dad was devastated and jealous . . . it was as if he'd made himself believe she didn't sleep with Nate . . . and this proved she did."

"But how did Noelle know who . . . ?"

Noah shook his head. "I asked my dad the same question, and he said it never occurred to him that he could be the father. And after Nate made the announcement, he just assumed their relationship was over. He was jealous, angry, heartbroken, and confused. Noelle tried to reach out to him, but he wouldn't listen. She wrote to him . . . but he just put her letters in a box and never opened them."

"That's awful."

Noah nodded. "Just before I was born, she tried, once more, to get in touch with him. He didn't want to see her, so he'd stayed in New Hampshire for the summer. She knew he was working part-time at a library in Hanover, and she took a bus all the way up there to find him. My dad wasn't at the library, though, and later, he realized he must've just missed her. Anyway, by the time Noelle got back to Boston, she was in full labor, and when she got off the bus, she collapsed. Passersby called an ambulance and stayed with her until it came. Nate saw her for the last time as she was rushed into surgery."

"That is so tragic," Laney said softly.

Noah nodded. "My dad thinks Nate knew all along, but never said anything . . . and since my dad was still in college when I was born, Nate raised me as if I were his."

"Then what happened?"

"Well, one morning, on his way to work after dropping me off at school, Nate had a heart attack. I was seven."

Laney shook her head in disbelief, tears stinging her eyes. "Oh, my goodness, that's so sad. Then . . . how did your dad find out?"

"Well," Noah continued, "my grandfather was the executor of Nate's estate, and when he was going through his papers, he found a letter Noelle had written to my dad while she was waiting for him that day in the library. It said she would always love him . . . and that he was the father."

"Oh, dear!"

"I know! Talk about grounds for disinheriting someone. But my dad thinks my grandparents already knew by then because I looked exactly like he did when he was little."

Laney shook her head. "You *do* look like him! In fact, if I didn't know better, I'd think you were brothers!" She paused. "So then, your dad, out of the blue, discovers he's the father of a seven-year-old boy—that must've been a pretty big shock."

"Well, if it was, he never let on, but my heart was broken. I loved Nate. He was my dad, and I couldn't understand how I had two dads. But my real dad—who was around twenty-six at the time—did everything he could to help me through it. We went fishing, hiking, played endless games of catch . . . and the following Christmas, my grandparents gave us a puppy . . . and that really helped. He was a little black Lab, and I named him Coal. Nate also left his beach house in Orleans to me . . . and that's how I came to have a house out here too . . . although, right now, it's closed up."

"That's quite a story."

"I know—it would make a great movie."

"It would!"

They were both quiet for a while, and finally Laney looked up. "So when did your dad meet Maddie?"

"He met her the summer I was born—1961. She was doing research at the library where he worked, and they became friends. When my dad returned to New Hampshire after Noelle's funeral, she knew something had happened, and she was there for him. But it wasn't until I came into his life, seven years later, that he realized how much she meant to him." He paused and smiled. "Maddie, on the other hand, says she loved my dad from the moment she saw him."

"What happened to your grandparents?"

"My grandfather died a couple of years later, and my grandmother soon after; my dad thinks my grandmother died of a broken heart."

"That happens sometimes when a spouse can't seem to find a way to go on without their one true love. I bet when one of my grandparents dies, the other one won't last either. They still act like a couple of teenagers!"

"And how do a couple of teenagers act?" Noah asked, reaching for her hand. Laney looked up, and Noah stopped walking. "Or a couple of twentysomethings?" he added.

"Well," she said softly, "sometimes they put their arms around each other . . ."

"Like this?" he asked, slipping his hands around her waist.

"Mm-hmm," she murmured, smelling the clean scent of his aftershave.

"And . . . ?"

"Well, if no one's around, they might . . . kiss," she whispered.

"Like this?" he asked, brushing his lips lightly against hers.

"Mmm," she murmured. He pulled her closer and pressed his lips gently against her forehead, and then slowly made his way back down her smooth cheek . . . to her neck . . . until he found her lips again.

Laney's heart pounded, and her mind raced. *Was this the cute New England fellow her grandfather had talked about?*

PART II

For from his fullness we have all received, grace upon grace.

—John 1:16

❧ 9 ❧

May 2014

Noah leaned against the kitchen counter. "What's one more, Lane?" he asked, avoiding his wife's eyes and looking down at the yellow Lab puppy tugging on her slipper.

"Yeah, Mom, what's one more?" seven-year-old Asher piped as he stroked the puppy's ears.

Laney shook her head in dismay. She'd wondered as she poured maple syrup onto the pancake she'd dropped in Mennie's bowl where her husband and youngest son had disappeared to, and now she knew. "Noah, don't you think we have enough going on?" she asked, drying her hands on a dishtowel. She could still hear her father-in-law's words when they'd told him, eight years earlier, they were expecting . . . *again!* "I don't think God meant for you two to single-handedly repopulate the world," the senior Coleman had teased, and Noah had laughed. "I know, Dad, but Laney's hoping for a little girl this time." His dad had smiled—his sky-blue eyes sparkling mischievously. It was the exact same look Laney often saw in Noah's eyes. And, six months later, when they were blessed with another blue-eyed baby—complete with exterior plumbing—Asa held his tiny, new grandson in his arms, his eyes sparkling with that same playful mischief, and whispered, "Don't you know . . . you're supposed to be a girl?"

"She was the only yellow one, Mom," Asher said matter-of-factly, pushing his round glasses back up on his nose. "The other five were black . . . and all boys. Isn't she cute?"

Laney looked at the tape wrapped around her son's glasses—making him look like Harry Potter—and remembered the tears that had rolled down his rosy cheeks when he'd told her how they broke. She knelt down to pry her soggy slipper out of the puppy's mouth, and it immediately placed its oversized paw on her knee and stretched up to lick her cheek.

"Look, Mom, she likes you! Now there'll be another girl in the house—just like you always wanted, and she'll still have five brothers—six, if you include Mennie."

"Do you see the size of these paws?" Laney said, holding up a paw and eyeing her husband.

Noah shrugged and grinned impishly, but this time, he looked in his wife's eyes and saw her resistance waning. "Don't worry, hon, females don't get very big."

Laney held the puppy's head in her hands and looked into her sweet brown eyes. "And what are we going to call you?"

"We already named her," Asher announced

cheerfully, looking up at Noah. "Dad thought of it—he said we should call her Halle."

"Halle?" Laney looked puzzled.

"Yeah—it's short for Hallelujah. You know, to go with Amen."

Laney smiled at the name, but then a shadow fell across her face. "There's that too—Mennie might not be happy about this." As she said it, she realized the puppy was wolfing down the pancake she'd left in Mennie's bowl.

"Look, Mom. She likes pancakes, just like you."

Laney shook her head.

"Mennie will be fine," Noah assured her.

"He might feel put out."

Just then, twenty-one-year-old Elijah, back from his run, pulled open the screen door and waited for the old dog to limp in. "I don't think Mennie's up to going for runs anymore," he said, wiping his face with his shirt. "He was so excited when I was getting ready, but when we got down to the beach, he just started limping. I brought him back and told him to stay, but he looked so sad, and when I got back, he was still sitting in the same spot." Elijah knelt down to scratch the old dog's snowy muzzle. Suddenly, the fur on Mennie's back bristled, and Elijah looked up.

"Hey," he said softly, realizing there was a newcomer. Asher let the puppy go, and she bounded over and greeted Mennie like a long lost friend, but he took one sniff and turned away.

He wasn't interested in being friends. Then he looked up at Laney, and his forlorn gaze said it all: *How could you?*

"See what I mean," Laney said.

The puppy continued to follow the old dog around, jumping on him and playfully tugging on his ears, but a moment later, a low growl emanated from deep in the old dog's throat, and the puppy backed away uncertainly.

"Uh-oh," Asher said worriedly. "C'mere, Halle." The puppy bounded back over to him, and he wrapped his arms protectively around her neck. "It's okay," he whispered, eyeing the old dog. "You better not be mean to her," he warned, "or we'll . . . we'll change your name to . . . Meannie."

Laney looked at her husband with raised eyebrows, but he just sipped his coffee. "He'll be fine—he just needs to get used to her."

Laney still wasn't convinced. "Ash, why don't you take the puppy out for a walk around the yard?"

"Okay," Asher said, pushing his glasses up on his nose again. He reached for the leash, and Noah tousled his strawberry blond hair as he walked by. "C'mon, Halle, let's go check out your new digs," he said happily.

When the door shut behind him, Elijah let go of the old dog's collar. "I'm goin' to take a shower. Good luck, Dad."

"Thanks, E—nothing like deserting your old man in his time of need."

"You can handle Mom—you're always saying she's a pushover."

"Thanks. Why don't you just put another nail in my coffin?"

"You mean you want me to tell her about the time you said . . ."

Noah gave him a warning look, and Elijah chuckled as he disappeared up the stairs.

Laney turned to her husband. The look on his face was one she knew all too well. "You could've asked," she said.

Noah nodded. "I'm sorry—I should've. I just assumed . . . you know . . . that you'd think it was a good idea. Ash is so much younger than the other boys—it's almost like he's an only child . . . and he's having such a hard time right now. He could use a true blue friend."

Laney nodded, recalling how her youngest son had tearfully struggled to recount—through hyperventilating breaths—the latest "incident" on the bus. "Move, Asser!" nine-year-old Jared Laughlin had commanded, shoving him into a seat. Asher's head had hit the seat, and his glasses had flown into the center aisle, and then Jared had held his foot over them and sarcastically said, "Whoops!" as he stomped down. "Oh, no, I'm sooo sorry, Ashhole," he'd sung sarcastically before kicking the broken glasses under the seat and pushing his way to the back of the bus.

"You have to talk to Jared's mother," Laney said.

"I'm going to," Noah said, putting his mug on the counter. "But in the meantime, I really think this puppy will be good for Ash. Dogs have a way of knowing when you're feeling blue. And he'll grow up with her, just like E and Gabe and Seth and Ben grew up with Mennie." He paused. "Mennie *is* getting older, you know—and having another dog will make it easier when . . ."

"Don't even go there. . . ." Laney said, tears springing to her eyes. "You don't know how long he has, and if he doesn't adjust to having another dog around, his last years will be miserable."

"Hey," Noah said softly, seeing the sorrow in his wife's eyes and pulling her into his arms. "I'm sure he'll be fine." He held her close and whispered, "He has *you* . . . and we all know you're his favorite. I'm sure he has no plans of leaving his true love any time soon." Laney nodded, and the old Lab nudged his way in between them. "See what I mean—I'm not even allowed to hug you." Laney laughed, knowing it was true. She reached down to scratch the big head between them, and Noah cleared his throat. "There is one other thing that I forgot to mention. . . ."

Laney pulled back and eyed him suspiciously, and Noah pressed his lips together, trying to calculate how much trouble he was in. "It's just that . . . well, Micah called yesterday, and . . . you know how he and Beryl hadn't set a date yet?"

Laney nodded slowly.

"Well, they have now . . . August something . . . and he asked me if I'd be willing to officiate, and I said, 'Of course.' And then, he asked if . . . well . . . if they could have the wedding on the . . ." Noah swallowed, suddenly realizing the magnitude of the commitment he'd made without consulting her first.

"Yes?" Laney said, suddenly feeling worried but not knowing why.

Noah nodded. "He asked if they could have the wedding on the beach . . ." He paused and then softly added, "Here." He cleared his throat. "*Here* . . . on the beach," he repeated. "It would just be our family and Beryl's . . . and maybe a couple of their friends."

Laney stared at him in disbelief and shook her head. "And . . . you . . . said . . . ?"

Noah rubbed his brow, wondering how he'd managed to paint himself into that same troublesome corner again. "Well, actually, I said yes . . . but obviously, now that I've had time to think about it, I realize I should've talked to you first. In fact, Micah even suggested I talk to you, but I told him that you love weddings and it wouldn't be any problem. However, if you feel differently, I can call him. . . ."

Laney held up her hand, signaling that it was

time for him to stop talking, and Noah immediately clamped his mouth shut like a clam that didn't want to be disturbed. She knew she should be used to this by now. After all, in the three years they'd dated and in the twenty-nine subsequent years that they'd been married, Noah had neglected to check with her on countless occasions before committing them to all kinds of obligations: impromptu dinner invitations *to their house,* last-minute cookies for the youth group's bake sales, unsolicited appointments to temporarily vacated committee seats, and filling in for Bible study leaders or youth group leaders who were under the weather. And she'd been willing to go wherever and do whatever was needed. After all, she was a minister's wife—it came with the territory. *Didn't it?* And, not only had she always made herself available, she'd done it while juggling the busy lives of their five sons and working full-time as a first-grade teacher at a nearby elementary school.

She knew her husband had a lot on his mind— he had an active flock to tend, people to counsel, sermons to write, shut-ins to visit, endless meetings to attend. But a wedding . . . *at their house?* Had he lost his mind? Had he looked around at the house he'd inherited but barely maintained? Had he considered how a stranger might see it or the critical appraisal a Realtor might give it? The kitchen alone looked like it was a throwback from the fifties, with its yellow Formica counters, retro wooden cabinets—the knobs of which were chewed on, or worse, missing because they'd been eaten—and then there was the olive-green refrigerator and the brown enamel stove that desperately needed new burner liners . . . not to mention new burners. For years, they'd talked about updating the kitchen, but with five boys and a dog—make that *two* dogs and a fluffy orange cat that had recently decided they were a good family to adopt—they'd never had the time . . . or the money. And now, with Elijah and Gabe in college, the dream of a new kitchen wasn't even on the back burner—that didn't work anymore.

And the rest of the house wasn't much better: the walls were cracked and scuffed, and the finish on the hardwood floors—from soccer cleats and Labrador paws clicking across them—was worn through in all the main travel paths. And the exterior looked as if it hadn't been painted since the fateful summer when her father-in-law had painted it.

Laney turned to her husband, and with quiet conviction, announced, "If we're going to have a wedding here, we will need a new oven and the outside of the house has to be painted."

And when Noah didn't blink, she wished she'd asked for a new fridge too.

❧ 10 ❧

A wedding! Laney thought as her husband disappeared into his study to work on his sermon. She looked out the kitchen window. Her mind spun with the news—as overwhelming as it had seemed, it was also exciting. She pictured their yard, sparkling with strings of white Christmas lights. She pictured Tiki torches around the yard and down on the beach. *What would everyone wear to a wedding on the beach? It would have to be semiformal . . . but casual . . . pretty, flowing sundresses and sports coats, rolled-up khakis and bare feet.* She could picture her handsome boys with haircuts and new jackets. At least E and Gabe would need new jackets; Seth and Ben could wear their hand-me-downs . . . Asher too. Heaven knows they had enough boys' jackets to open a thrift store.

Oh, and what about the food? She'd have to send Micah the link to her friend's catering company. Everyone raved about A Moveable Feast. Ruth was an amazing chef, and her staff was always professional.

Laney's reverie was suddenly interrupted by Asher coming through the porch with Halle still on her leash. "Mom!" he shouted. "Halle loves the yard!" He was beaming, but as he reached the kitchen, he realized Mennie was blocking their entrance, and a shadow of worry fell across his face. Immediately, Mennie's fur bristled and his ears went back. Without lifting his head, the old dog looked sideways, searching Laney's face for a clue.

"Oh, Mennie," Laney consoled, kneeling down next to him. "Stop being an old poop." Mennie lifted his head and continued to search her eyes. "Halle *is* staying," she said softly. He sighed heavily—as if he'd just received the worst news on earth. "But she's going to need an older, wiser dog to look after her and show her the ropes." His tail thumped slowly, and he rolled onto his side to have his belly rubbed. Laney gently scratched up and down. "You don't have to worry, old pie," she said softly. "She'll have her own bed *and* her own bowl."

"Do you think he understands, Mom?" Asher asked. "I was just praying that he'd stop being mean."

Laney looked up and saw the concern in her little boy's eyes. *He's too young to have so many worries.* "I think he understands, Ash—we'll just have to make sure Halle respects his space until he gets used to having her around."

"Well, she can sleep in my bed until she gets her own."

Laney laughed. "We'll see—we have to make sure she's housebroken first."

They heard jostling and laughing out on the porch and then the room filled with commotion as sixteen-year-old Ben and fourteen-year-old Seth came in, followed by nineteen-year-old Gabe, who'd just picked them up from track practice. "I so beat you in that last split," Seth said.

"You did not," Ben argued. "I easily beat you!"

Gabe looked at his mother and rolled his eyes. "They've been like this all the way home!"

Laney laughed. "Don't tell *me*. It's the story of my life—you and E were no better! Thank you for picking them up though."

All at once, the boys saw the puppy in Asher's arms. "Hey! Who's that?" Seth asked, kneeling down and petting the puppy's soft head.

"This is Halle," Asher said protectively, "and she's *my* responsibility." Halle licked Seth's cheek, and he laughed, and Ben knelt down too. Pretty soon all the boys were on the floor playing with the puppy while Mennie watched with his head between his paws.

"Don't forget your other pal," Laney gently reminded.

They all looked over and saw Mennie's sad eyes, and quickly scrambled over to pet him too. "Don't worry, Mennie," they gushed. "We still love you." The old dog thumped his tail, and Laney shook her head. *How quickly they forgive.*

After lunch, Laney plopped the puppy on the

floor of Noah's study and told him she was taking Asher to get new glasses.

Noah looked up from his laptop.

"She was just out, but I can't promise anything." The puppy was already nosing along the edge of the couch, curiously nudging a pillow. "Maybe she'll take a nap," Laney added with a conspiratorial grin, "or maybe you can get one of the boys to puppy-sit."

Noah knew from his wife's tone that this was payback—the first of many, he was sure, but he wasn't going to give her the satisfaction. He could handle a puppy *and* write a sermon. "Not a problem," he said with a smile as the puppy pulled the pillow off the couch and started chewing on the corner. He looked down. "Not a problem," he repeated. Laney smiled, and as she closed the door, he murmured, "I didn't like that pillow anyway."

"Why is Jared mean?" Asher asked, settling into his booster seat in the back of Laney's old Honda Pilot.

"I don't know, hon," she said, looking at him in her rearview mirror.

He was gazing out the window, and she could tell his wheels were spinning. At seven, Asher was already showing signs of being extraordinarily bright—especially in math and science. He loved to take on challenging problems that were well above his grade level, and he refused to give up until the problem was solved. Unfortunately, real-life problems—like the one with Jared—couldn't be solved using mathematical logic.

"His brother's mean to him," Asher said thoughtfully, "so maybe that makes him mean to other people."

"Maybe," Laney agreed, surprised by his insight. That was another thing about Asher—he was very sensitive to other people's feelings, and he was a bit of an old soul—just like his mom. Laney smiled at the thought. She'd finally figured out that being an old soul meant people perceived you to be wise beyond your years. And this surprised her because, most of the time, she didn't feel very wise at all. As for Asher, being sensitive and perceptive just made him a bigger target for bullying.

She stopped at the end of their driveway and sent a quick text message to her husband, reminding him to call Jared's mom. And as they drove along, she thought about Jillian.

Jillian Laughlin had grown up in their church—she'd even been confirmed there. Her parents had been good people, but they were an older couple when they had their two daughters, and now they'd both passed away. Laney knew Jillian was having a hard time. In fact, if anyone needed prayers, Jillian and her boys did. Unfortunately, at the moment, Laney couldn't muster any prayers . . . she just wanted to wring Jared's neck!

Jillian's situation, like the situations of so many other single moms, was the unfortunate result of poor choices. The first time she'd gotten pregnant, she was nineteen. She'd been working at a bar in Chatham, and after she got off work, she went out drinking with a bunch of rich college boys who were out on the Cape for the weekend . . . and she'd ended up sleeping with one of them. The next morning, Jillian had woken up alone. A month later, she realized she was pregnant, but she didn't even know the boy's last name or where he lived.

After her first son was born, Jillian went to live with her sister Liz in Wellfleet; she started dating a friend of Liz's boyfriend. John was a bad decision from day one. He was six years older than Jillian, and his favorite pastime was drinking. He didn't work; he just lounged around all day at Liz's. Liz finally got tired of hosting endless parties for her boyfriend and all of his buddies, and she kicked them all out. At the time, she begged her little sister to stay, but Jillian moved in with John and, before she knew it, she was pregnant again. John never warmed up to fatherhood. He barely looked at Jeff, except to swat him against the wall . . . and after Jared was born, he disappeared.

Now Jeff was in sixth grade, and he was always in trouble. In fact, he'd just been suspended for the second time. Laney knew if he got in trouble again, he'd be expelled. And Jared was no better—following right in his half-brother's footsteps. He was a bully! And for some reason, he'd zeroed in on Asher . . . and he got the other kids to pick on him too. It was almost as if picking on Asher Coleman was cool. Laney's heart ached for the loss of her son's innocence. Jared called him every name he could think of: *Ashhole, Ashwipe, Ashtray.* And Laney had come to rue the day they'd picked the name Asher over Samuel—his great-grandfather's name. Sam would've been a much better choice.

She pulled into Nauset Optical and helped Asher climb down. As they walked across the parking lot, he reached for her hand. "I want to get the same glasses," he said, pushing the taped pair back up on his nose. "You know, Mom," he continued. "Harry was bullied by all kinds of people, so when anyone's mean to me, I just think of him."

"Harry who?" Laney asked, forgetting all about Asher's favorite character.

"Harry Potter, Mom," Asher said matter-of-factly, skipping along. "They were way meaner to him."

Tears filled Laney's eyes. It was a good thing Jared Laughlin was not standing in this parking lot right now!

"Mom, can we get a bed for Halle after this?"

Laney knelt down and pulled her little boy into a hug.

"Why are you crying?" he asked in a worried voice.

"I'm not," Laney whispered.

"Yes, you are," he said, pulling back and touching the tear on her cheek. "Don't cry. If Harry can handle Uncle Vernon and Aunt Petunia and Dudley . . . *and* Voldemort, I can handle Jared."

"I know you can, Ash," Laney said, mustering a smile. "I just wish you didn't have to."

"Can we get a bowl too?" he asked, pulling away.

"We can," she said, brushing away her tears.

"And a new collar and leash? I think we should get blue."

Laney nodded.

"And we should probably get her one of those tags with her name and phone number on it too, in case she gets lost."

"You're right. We should," Laney agreed. "Maybe we can get her a new tennis ball too."

"Yeah, she'd love that," Asher said with a grin.

Laney looked down at her son's smile. Noah was right. Halle was a good idea.

❦ 11 ❦

Sunday mornings were always hectic in the Coleman house. Even when Elijah and Gabe were away at college, there were still three other boys to round up, feed, make sure their shirts were ironed—or at least, not too wrinkled—and load in the car. But now that E and Gabe were home for the summer, life was back to its normal state—total chaos. Or as Noah like to call it: blessed pandemonium!

"Has anyone fed Lucky lately?" Laney asked, noticing the fluffy orange tiger cat sunning on the screened-in porch.

"Not me," replied a chorus of voices.

Laney shook her head. "That poor cat—he didn't pick a very good family to adopt."

"We're a good family," Ben protested with his mouth full of Froot Loops. "It's the woman who takes care of us that needs help."

"The woman who takes care of you needs help all right. It's called a maid." Laney bopped him with a cereal box as she opened the cabinet to look for the cat food.

"Hey!" Ben said, rubbing his head.

"Oh, I'm sorry. Did I hit you?"

"There's no hot water left," an angry voice called from the top of the stairs.

"Sorry! Maybe you should get up earlier," Gabe called back with his mouth full of Corn Pops and his hair still damp.

"Maybe you shouldn't take such long showers," the annoyed voice replied, then added, "Guess I'm not going to church . . ."

Laney shook her head, and in an exasperated voice, called, "E, could you just skip the shower? You took one yesterday."

"No, Mom, I can't."

"Take a cold one," Gabe shouted. "It'd be good for you." He looked up at his mom. "Chloe Sanders is gonna be in church," he said with a conspiratorial grin.

"Chloe Sanders?" Laney said in surprise, remembering the little girl who'd grown up in the church with her boys, and who, years earlier, had been the one to name Mennie. "I didn't know she and E kept in touch."

"Oh, yeah, they keep in touch all right . . ."

Laney looked puzzled. "Where does she go to school?"

"Smith . . . right near E at Amherst."

"I know where your brother goes to school, Gabe. The question is: how do *you* know so much?"

"Facebook."

Ben and Seth, who'd been pretending to study the back of their cereal boxes, snickered. "E's got a girlfriend!" they sang merrily.

"Shut up, Gabe!" Elijah warned, coming into the kitchen and tying his tie.

"You're wearing a tie?" Gabe teased. "You're such a dweeb."

Elijah glared at him and reached for the coffeepot, but it was almost empty, and he slammed it back on its burner.

"I'm sorry, hon," Laney said apologetically, looking up from the cat kibble. "I forgot you drank coffee. Do you want the rest of mine? You can nuke it."

"No, Mom, I don't want yours," he said, reaching for the orange juice.

"I'm leaving," Noah said, coming into the kitchen and putting his empty cup in the sink. He kissed Laney's cheek. "I'll see you guys there."

"Okay . . . oh! What time did you say your parents are coming tonight?"

"I don't think I said a time," he replied uncertainly. "They'll be in church, though, so you can ask them." He looked at the boys. "Grandpa said he'd like to hear some poems tonight, so be prepared."

Asher was just coming in with Halle. "I have my poem!" he announced.

"You do?"

Asher nodded, beaming. "I picked it out after our last poetry night."

"Good for you," Noah said, ruffling his hair and eyeing his other sons. "You guys should learn from your little brother." And as he stood to leave, he looked down. "Hmm, looks like there's a puddle here."

Asher looked down too. "That wasn't there before. Maybe Mennie did it."

"Mennie didn't do it, Ash. But don't worry. Halle's not in trouble."

Laney reached for the paper towels. "I guess we should leave her in the crate then." She motioned to the ancient dog crate Noah had pulled out of the basement the day before when he wasn't getting anywhere with his sermon.

"Do we have to?" Asher groaned. "She just spent the night in there. It's not very cozy."

"It's the best place, Ash. She can't get in trouble, and she'll be safe. It's just at night and when we're not here—until she's housebroken."

"Can we at least put her bed in there?"

Laney looked perplexed as she wiped up the puddle. "Oh, hon, we can't put her bed in there. What if she has an accident?"

"Lane, I'm leaving," Noah said. "You got this?"

"Yes, dear," she said, giving him a wilting look. "I've got it."

"You guys help Mom," he called to the boys as the door swung shut behind him.

Laney finished cleaning up the puddle and put the cat food out on the porch. "Ash, did you have breakfast?"

He shook his head, and she suddenly remembered the treat they'd picked up after they'd ordered his new glasses. "Do you want a doughnut?"

Four other heads looked up in surprise. "We have *doughnuts?*"

Laney pulled a bag of cider doughnuts from behind the coffeepot and handed it to Asher.

He grinned. "I forgot we got these, Mom," he said, beaming. He reached in, pulled one out, and took a big sugary bite. Immediately, his brothers all clambered for the bag.

"Hey!" Laney shouted, and they stopped. "There's enough for everyone," she said calmly. Then she eyed her fourteen-year-old. "*You* are not wearing jeans and a T-shirt to church. Go find nice pants and a button-down shirt."

"I don't have any nice pants. They're all too short. Besides, everyone wears jeans."

Laney looked at him as if she was seeing him for the first time—when had he gotten so tall? He was standing next to Ben, and it dawned on her that they were practically the same height. She shook her head. "Not everyone, dear. *We* don't. Maybe Ben has a pair that will fit you."

Seth grumbled, knowing there was no point in arguing, and Laney sighed. When she was a girl, she'd always worn a dress to church—her Sunday best—and her brother Lyle had always worn pressed slacks and a button-down. *Those days are long gone,* she thought sadly. *Pretty soon, people will be wearing shorts and T-shirts!*

She glanced at the clock. "Leaving in five—plan accordingly," she called as she ran up the stairs.

Noah looked out at his congregation. It was Memorial Day weekend and the sanctuary was almost full, so he decided people were taking advantage of the nice weather and opening up their summer homes early. He scanned the sea of faces, looking for his parents, and his dad caught his eye and smiled. Noah smiled back. Then he glanced at his watch and frowned. It wasn't the first time his family was late. In fact, it was unusual if they weren't late, but he'd hoped Laney would be there for the first hymn. He nodded to the organist, and she ended the interlude with a playful flourish.

"Welcome!" he began. "This is the day the Lord has made. Let us rejoice and be glad in it." He glanced at his bulletin. "Would everyone please stand and join in singing our opening hymn, number twenty-six?" He leafed through his hymnal, hoping Laney would get there soon, and as he turned the pages, he heard a loud commotion in the vestibule, and then his oldest son pushed open the door and Laney—who'd been wearing baggy sweatpants and a Nike JUST DO IT T-shirt when he'd left—swept in, wearing a light sea-green linen sundress. She looked stunning. But then again, she looked stunning no matter what she was wearing—his favorite being nothing at all! He watched as she masterfully ushered their five boys down the aisle and into the pew in front of his parents, and then slipped in before E so he could sit on the end. His dad leaned forward and handed Laney his open hymnal, and Laney, hearing the beginning notes of the familiar hymn, looked up at Noah and smiled. Beethoven's "Ode to Joy"—also known as "Joyful, Joyful, We Adore Thee"—was one of the hymns they'd played at their wedding.

❧ 12 ❧

Sunday evening, Asa Coleman sat on his son's porch with a gin and tonic in his hand and Mennie's head in his lap. He listened to Maddie and Laney chatting in the kitchen as they put the final touches on supper and stroked the Lab's noble head. "You're getting as old as me," he said, looking into Mennie's soulful brown eyes. He gazed at the doorway into the kitchen and a long-ago memory slipped into his mind . . .

He'd just run back from his pickup truck through the summer rain to get his shoulder bag. As he had, he'd noticed Noelle struggling to collapse the umbrella by the pool. He'd stopped to help her . . . and then they had both run back to the porch, soaking wet and laughing . . . and she'd stood in front of him . . . so close . . . too close. . . .

He could still smell the sweet scent of her sandal-wood soap. . . .

"What do you want?" she'd whispered.

He'd searched her eyes. "You," he'd murmured —his voice barely audible.

She'd stepped closer . . . reaching for him. . . .

"Dad?"

Asa looked up, startled.

"Sorry," Noah said, and nodded toward his glass. "I just wondered if you needed a refill."

"Hmm?" Asa glanced down. "Nope. I'm all set."

"Okay, I'm just going to grab a beer and I'll be right out."

A moment later, he sat down across from his dad and noticed Mennie's head resting on his lap. "Is he being a pest?"

Asa stroked the old dog's silky black ears. "Nope . . . we were just reminiscing. . . ."

"And . . . what were you reminiscing about?"

"Our salad days," Asa said with a slow smile. He paused thoughtfully. "You know, I thought of something the other day . . . about your mom . . . Noelle."

Noah waited, listening. Through the years, he'd often felt as if half of his family history was missing—and all the information that went with it. It hit him especially hard when he was filling out medical forms at the doctor's office. He'd stare at the list of questions about health history and try to picture his maternal grandparents: What health problems had they faced? How had they died? Did they have cancer or heart problems? Did they have high blood pressure or a history of strokes? Diabetes or dementia? What possible ailments did he have to look forward to?

"Her father was a minister."

"Really?" Noah sputtered, choking on the sip he'd just taken.

Asa nodded. "I don't know why I never thought of it before—especially when you were in seminary." He smiled and shook his head. "I've become very forgetful lately, but occasionally something comes to me, and it's as clear as if it happened yesterday."

Noah nodded, and Asa took a sip from his glass. "Your mom could recite all the books of the Bible—Old and New Testaments . . . *and* she could do it backward."

Noah laughed. "I love these old tidbits you come up with."

His dad nodded, smiling wistfully. "She was quite a lady. She gave me this book." He patted the ancient tome beside him. "It's my poem for tonight," he added with a conspiratorial grin.

"Must be a good one," Noah said.

"It is." He paused thoughtfully. "I told you she had a brother. . . ." It was more of a statement than a question.

"No, I think you left that part out too," Noah replied.

"Pete. He was killed in the war. Her family was devastated—even her father's faith was shaken. They were never the same."

Noah nodded, his heart aching for the tragedies that had struck his family—the family he'd never known. He took a sip and slowly realized that since the day he was born, he'd had his very own cloud of witnesses—people who would have loved him, had they lived—watching over him.

Asa closed his eyes, and Noah leaned back in his chair and recalled the countless times he and his dad had stopped by to check on this house. Back then, it had been empty except for an old piano, which they still had and which Gabe sometimes played, but he'd never given any thought to the house's owner. He just remembered it vaguely from his childhood and assumed it belonged to someone in his dad's family; but then, on his sixteenth birthday, when they'd stopped by to check on it, his dad had revealed that it belonged to him, and then he'd searched his young son's eyes and finally answered all the questions he'd been asking.

"Noah?" Laney appeared in the doorway, wiping her hands on the dish towel. "Oh . . . I didn't know you were . . ."

Asa opened his eyes, and Noah smiled. "We were just reminiscing, weren't we, Dad?" he said, winking at him.

Laney nodded. "Well, is the grill almost ready?"

"Yup."

"Did you happen to find out how many hamburgers and hot dogs we need . . . and if anyone wants a cheeseburger?"

"No, but I will." He looked at his dad. "Cheeseburger, Dad?"

"Sounds good," Asa replied.

"The boys are down on the beach with Halle," Laney said, as she turned toward the kitchen. "If the grill's ready, they need to come up."

Noah looked at his dad. "Want to take a walk down with me?"

"No, I think I'll stay here," Asa said, scratching Mennie's ears.

"Everything okay?" Noah asked, realizing his dad didn't have his usual spark.

"Yup—just tired. I haven't been sleeping well." He sighed. "Don't get old, son."

"There's not much of an alternative, Dad," Noah said, pushing open the screen door. "I'll be right back."

He headed down the path to the beach to round up the boys, and Asa leaned back in his chair and closed his eyes. Something *was* going on, but he couldn't put his finger on it. He hadn't said anything to Maddie. He didn't want her to worry, but he didn't feel quite right. It wasn't just forgetfulness and having trouble sleeping; his vision was sometimes blurry too, and he was having headaches that the usual remedies didn't touch. Maybe he needed new glasses—he couldn't remember the last time he'd had his eyes checked. He started to doze off . . . and then, somewhere in his subconscious, he heard the screen door swing open, and he woke with a start.

"Grandpa, did you meet our new puppy?"

Asa tried to focus on his grandson's face. He sat up and rubbed his eyes. Finally, they came around. "No, hon, where is he?"

"He's a she, and she's right here."

Asa realized Asher was holding the puppy right in front of him.

"Oh, she's a cutie," he said as Asher gently placed her in his lap.

"Her name's Halle. It's short for Hallelujah."

"Well, that's a perfect name." He looked around for Mennie, but he was gone. "What does Mennie think of her?"

"Oh, he's still gettin' used to her. Mom says he's an old poop."

Asa chuckled. "Well, she's probably right. Your grandpa's an old poop too."

"No, you're not," Asher said, giving him a hug.

"What happened to your glasses?"

"They broke. C'mon, Halle," he said, lifting up the puppy.

"There you two are!" Maddie said, peering around the corner. "Supper's ready."

"All right! I'm starving," Asher said, hurrying off with Halle in his arms.

Asa stood unsteadily and Maddie eyed him. "Are you okay?"

"Yup . . . fine, fine."

"How's that old head of yours?" she asked, gently touching his white hair. She'd recently noticed they'd been going through a lot of Tylenol.

"It's old," he said with a smile.

The picnic table in the side yard was festively set to celebrate Memorial Day *and* the official kickoff of another Cape Cod summer. Laney had spread her old, favorite, extra-long, red-and-white-checked tablecloth down the extra-long picnic table her father-in-law had built when they'd told him they were expecting another baby. Small red lanterns lit with votive candles dotted the length of the table, their flames dancing in the breeze, and a lush bouquet of white tulips in a blue glass pitcher sat at the table's center. "The table looks lovely," Maddie said. "So festive!"

A second table with a blue-and-white-checked tablecloth was covered with the traditional spread of a summer cookout: red and blue plates and napkins; a platter of hamburgers and hot dogs, baked macaroni, baked beans, potato salad, tossed salad, Jell-O salad, deviled eggs, and at the end of the table was a box of graham crackers, a bag of marshmallows, and a package of Hershey bars.

"All right . . . s'mores!" Asher announced happily.

"I don't think you have enough food, dear," Noah said as the boys jostled to be first in line. He counted heads and realized one was missing. "Where's E?"

"He's still down at the beach with Chloe," Seth announced, rolling his eyes as he said her name in a singsong voice.

"Watch it!" E said, sneaking up behind him and yanking down his swim trunks.

"Hey!" Seth said, turning around awkwardly, his face turning beet red. "You're lucky I have boxers on!" he said, pulling his trunks up while his other brothers howled with laughter.

"You mean *you're* lucky!" E teased with a grin.

Seth turned to Ben—who was laughing the hardest—and tried to pull down his suit too, but Ben pushed him and he fell backward, his face turning even redder. When he got up, he stormed toward the house.

"Oh, stop being a baby!" Ben called after him, which only added to his humiliation.

"That was mean." Asher said softly.

"He deserved it," Ben protested. "He tried to short me."

E stood by and watched—he hadn't meant for his little brother to get so upset.

"Maybe you should apologize to him," Laney said, eyeing her oldest son. "He's been looking forward to this all day."

E nodded, but he wanted to introduce Chloe to

his grandparents first, and after a few pleasantries, they got in line behind Gabe. Asa watched his oldest grandson talking to the pretty redhead and eyed Noah with raised eyebrows, but he just shrugged and shook his head—as usual, he was out of the loop. A moment later, E disappeared into the house. "I'll be right back," he said, leaving Chloe and Gabe to fill their plates.

"After you," Noah said, offering plates to Laney and his parents.

"As usual, Laney," Maddie said with a smile. "Everything looks wonderful. You've been busy."

Laney laughed. "Busy is a relative term around here, Mom!"

"I hear you guys are hosting the wedding," Asa said.

"We are?" a chorus of surprised voices called from the far end of the table.

Laney nodded.

"Are you sure you're up to it?" Maddie asked.

Laney looked at Noah and smiled. "It'll be fun. I'm really happy Micah found someone—not just for him, but for Charlotte."

They filled their plates and sat down, and as Noah poured iced tea, E reappeared, carrying his giggling brother over his shoulder.

Noah looked down the table. "Now that we're all here. . . ." he said, and they reluctantly put down their forks and bowed their heads.

13

After the kitchen was cleaned up and everyone had had their fill of s'mores—including Mennie and Halle, who'd each happily chomped down two marshmallows, one fresh from the bag, snow-white and pillow-soft, and one charred and flaky from catching on fire—they perused the poetry books Noah had set out on the porch. Laney turned on the sparkling white Christmas lights that hung on the porch year round—making it festive and cheery, and to add to the ambience, Noah lit several old Boy Scout lanterns.

"Would anyone like some coffee?" Laney asked.

Asa, Maddie, Noah, and E all looked up and nodded.

"How about tea?"

"That sounds good," Chloe said. "I'll help. I already have my poem."

"Tea?" Elijah said in surprise. "I thought you liked coffee."

"I love tea," she said, smiling at him.

As she disappeared into the kitchen, Asa peered over his glasses at his grandson. "When it comes to women, E, don't ever assume *anything*."

Noah laughed. "Truer words were never spoken."

A few moments later, Chloe reappeared, carrying a tray of steaming mugs and offered them around. Then she settled next to Elijah with her cup cradled in her hands.

"So who's goin' first?" Asa asked, peering over his glasses again.

Asher's hand shot up. "Me!"

Asa nodded. "The floor is yours, sir."

Asher could hardly contain his smile as he lifted Halle off his lap and stood in the middle of the porch. With the lantern light reflecting on his glasses, he looked solemnly at his grandfather and started off softly—his voice barely a whisper. But as the dramatic tale unfolded, his voice rose with excitement. His grandfather immediately recognized the famous poem by William Rose Benét and listened with rapt attention as his youngest grandson perfectly recited all fourteen verses of the legendary poem "Jesse James."

Asher finished with a dramatic flourish and promptly received a standing ovation from his audience and a hug from his grandfather. "That was super!" he whispered. "How long have you been working on it?"

Asher grinned. "Since last summer."

When Asa sat back down, he was still smiling. "Well, does anyone think they can top that?" he asked, eyeing the crowd.

"Nope, definitely not," Elijah conceded. "Guess we better call it a night."

Chloe elbowed him, and he laughed. "I have one," she said. "But I don't know if I can top

Asher. That was great!" She smiled at him, and he beamed.

Chloe stood up, cleared her throat, and glanced back at E for support. He nodded, and she started off in a soft, mysterious voice, her brown eyes sparking in the candlelight.

" ' 'Twas brillig, and the slithy toves
Did gyre and gimble in the wade;
All mimsy were the borogoves,
And the mome raths outgrabe.

'Beware the Jabberwock, my son!
The jaws that bite, the claws that catch!
Beware the Jubjub bird, and shun
The frumious Bandersnatch!'

He took his vorpal sword in hand:
Long time the manxome foe he sought—
So rested he by the Tumtum tree.
And stood awhile in thought.

And as in uffish thought he stood,
The Jabberwock, with eyes of flame,
Came wiffling through the tulgey wood,
And burbled as it came!

One, two! One, two! And through and through
The vorpal blade went snicker-snack!
He left it dead, and with its head
He went galumphing back.

'And hast thou slain the Jabberwock?
Come to my arms, my beamish boy!
O frabjous day! Callooh! Callay!'
He chortled in his joy.

'Twas brillig, and the slithy toves
Did gyre and gimble in the wabe;
All mimsy were the borogoves,
And the mome raths outgrabe.' "

Everyone cheered enthusiastically, and Asa winked at his oldest grandson and gave him a thumbs-up. Any girl who could recite "Jabberwocky" had his approval! Chloe smiled and bowed, and when she sat back down, E leaned over and whispered, "You *do* know that Lewis Carroll was . . ."

"Shhhh," she said, putting her finger to her lips.

"Next?" Asa asked, looking at his oldest grandson with raised eyebrows.

E opened the slender book on his lap. "I have one," he said, "but I don't have it memorized."

"That's all right," his grandfather said.

He cleared his throat. "Lord Byron . . .

'She walks in beauty, like the night
Of cloudless climes and starry skies;
And all that's best of dark and bright
Meet in her aspect and her eyes:
Thus mellowed to that tender light
Which heaven to gaudy day denies.

One shade the more, one ray the less,
Had half impaired the nameless grace
Which waves in every raven tress,
Or softly lightens o'er her face;
Where thoughts serenely sweet express
How pure, how dear their dwelling place.

And on that cheek, and o'er that brow,
So soft, so calm, yet eloquent,
The smiles that win, the tints that glow,
But tell of days in goodness spent,
A mind at peace with all below,
A heart whose love is innocent!' "

"Ahh . . . romance is *not* dead," Asa said with a smile.

Laney laughed. "Not when there's a Coleman in the house." And Maddie, who was sitting beside her with Lucky purring contentedly on her lap, laughed and nodded in agreement.

Chloe smiled and slipped her hand into Elijah's, which made Ben and Seth snicker.

"Ladies? Do you have anything to offer?" Asa asked. "And I wasn't talking to you two," he added, eyeing his middle grandsons.

As the evening slipped by, they each shared a poem or part of a poem: Maddie recited Robert Frost's "The Mending Wall"; and Laney, with her toes under Mennie's warm fur, read the anonymously written "A Dog's Soul"; Noah recited Tennyson's "The Higher Pantheism"; Seth read Thayer's "Casey at the Bat"; Ben recited the last verse of Edgar Allen Poe's "The Raven"; and Gabe recited Walt Whitman's "O Captain! My Captain!" And when he finished, Asa smiled. "My poem's by Walt Whitman too."

He opened the fragile book on his lap, carefully turned to the last page, and scanned the words. Suddenly, his heart began to race. He couldn't read the words. They were an incoherent gray blur. He took off his glasses, rubbed his eyes, and looked again. Finally, he cleared his throat. "Ahh, here we go. . . ." Haltingly, he pretended to read the words he'd memorized a long time ago.

" 'Great is life, real and mystical, wherever
    and whoever;
Great is death—sure as life holds all parts
    together, death holds all parts together.

Sure as the stars return again after they merge
    in the light, death is great as life.' "

He closed the book, and although his head was pounding, smiled.

"Is that from *Leaves of Grass*?" Chloe asked.

"It is," Asa said. "It's also signed."

"Really?" Chloe said.

Asa stood to pass the book to her and lost his balance, but Gabe, who was sitting next to him, reached up to steady him. "Whoa, Grandpa, are you okay?"

"Thanks, Gabe," he said. "I'm fine." Gabe passed the heavy book to Chloe, and she opened it and reverently touched the famous signature. "Wow," she murmured softly. "This is such a treasure. Where did you get it?"

Asa smiled. "An old friend gave it to me."

She handed it back to him, and everyone began to stand, ready to call it a night, except for Asher, who was curled up, sound asleep in his chair— he'd already called it a night.

"Well, you each picked out perfect poems," Asa said. "Thank you for humoring an old man. It warms my heart and makes me believe there's still hope for this old world." He glanced at his watch . . . and then at his wife. "Shall we?"

Maddie nodded, her face shadowed with concern.

Noah and Laney walked them to their car. "Are you sure you're okay, Dad?"

"Yes, yes . . . just tired. Don't fret." And at that moment, as he strode briskly to the car, Asa truly did seem fine.

"That was really nice, my dears," Maddie said, giving them both hugs. "Everything was delicious—as always."

Noah shook his dad's hand and then pulled him into a hug. "Make sure you go to the eye doctor— if that's what you think it is."

"I will," Asa replied with a smile. "You two have done such a great job with those boys—they're all keepers! I can't believe Asher memorized that whole poem. . . . And Chloe—she's a keeper too . . . reciting 'Jabberwocky'!"

Laney laughed and gave her father-in-law a long hug. "Thanks, Dad," she said softly. She pulled back and searched his eyes. "You take care of yourself."

"I will . . . and I'll let you know what the doctor says."

"Okay. We're gonna hold you to that," Noah said, eyeing him. He turned to his mom. "Make sure he does."

Maddie smiled. "I will."

Noah and Laney waved as they pulled away, and as they walked up the driveway, Noah put his arm around his wife's shoulder. "Do you believe him?"

"I don't know," she said, shaking her head. "Sometimes people have a hard time facing what's really going on."

Noah nodded, praying it wasn't anything serious.

❧ 14 ❧

Laney was so caught up in the end-of-the-school-year activities she barely had time to sit down—never mind worry. Her in-laws had headed back to New Hampshire on Monday, and her father-in-law had promised to go to the eye doctor. E had driven Chloe home on Sunday night and been late getting back. She was trying very hard to give him space—after all, he was in college. But it didn't make her worry less. Noah had tried calling Jillian Laughlin, but her phone didn't seem to be working. And Mennie seemed to be ignoring them—was he going deaf or was he still put out by the new puppy? The week had flown by, and before she knew it, it was Friday again, and her six-year-old charges were lining up with their backpacks over their shoulders, ready to head home for the weekend.

She stood by the door. "Don't forget to do your reading. Reading logs are due Monday!"

"Have a good weekend, Mrs. Coleman!" they sang as they filed out of the room. "Don't forget to do *your* reading," Charlie Lathrop teased with a grin that revealed his newly missing tooth.

"I will, Mr. Lathrop," she said, ruffling his hair. "You too. And make sure you leave that tooth under your pillow tonight."

"I will. And I'm going to read about dinosaurs."

Laney loved teaching first grade. It made her feel as if she was actually making a difference. Six-year-olds were still sweet and innocent, and first grade was such a critical year—especially for reading. She watched them weave down the busy hallway and remembered how young they'd seemed in September—a lifetime ago! She smiled and whispered a prayer that their lives would always be full of blessings.

She went back in her classroom, picked up the pencils and crayons that had fallen on the floor, erased the blackboard, looked up at the clock, shuffled through the papers on her desk, and slid a manila envelope of report cards into her canvas bag—she hoped to get started on them over the weekend. She turned off the lights, remembered she needed to send a text, pulled her phone out of her bag, and typed a quick note to Noah, reminding him she had a doctor's appointment.

As she reached her car, her phone vibrated, and she stopped to read his response.

THANKS FOR THE REMINDER. WANT ME TO PICK UP PIZZA?

She smiled in wonder—after nearly thirty years of marriage, he was finally getting the hang of reading her mind.

SOUNDS GOOD! ☺

WHAT SHOULD I GET?

1 BACON, 1 HAWAIIAN, AND 1 PLAIN—ALL LARGE! AND MAYBE A SALAD?!

YOU GOT IT. C U LTR. <3

She slipped her phone back in her bag, thankful to have one less thing to think about.

Ten minutes later, she was signing the clipboard at the window in her doctor's office. "Hi, Etty," she said, waving through the glass. Etty was an old friend—she'd been working for Dr. Jamison forever—and Laney, the prolific reproducer of five, was one of their best customers.

Etty rolled her chair over and slid the window open. "Hi, Laney! How're the boys?"

Laney smiled. "They're fine."

"Are E and Gabe home for the summer?"

"Yup—both lifeguarding again."

"Well, make sure they use sunblock, or they'll end up with wrinkles like me."

"I'll try," Laney said with a weary smile.

"And how are you? You look tired."

"I am a little tired, but I didn't think it showed." She'd always wondered when someone voiced this observation. Usually, it happened on a day when she'd really tried to pull herself together, but then some thoughtless cur always came along and said, "Is something the matter? You look *really* tired." She knew, deep down, it was a message of sympathy: *You deserve a break. You shouldn't be working so hard.* But on days when she actually felt good or had really tried to be conscientious when she applied her makeup, it felt like a backhanded compliment. And on those days, the only response she could come up with was a somewhat sarcastic, "Thanks a lot!"

But that afternoon, when Etty said it, she *was* tired. She'd actually felt out of sorts for weeks, but she'd attributed it to the growing need for summer vacation. At fifty-two, she wasn't a spring chicken anymore. In fact, at the moment, she felt like an old hen!

She settled into one of the chairs in the empty waiting room and sifted through the magazines on the table. A headline on the cover of one of the parenting magazines caught her eye: "What To Do When Your Child Is Bullied." She picked it up and leafed through the pages, looking for the article, and when she found it, the accompanying photo startled her. It was a close-up of a boy, and his face was filled with despair. The single tear trickling down his cheek had left a glistening trail on his smooth skin. In the background, there was a computer screen, and on it was a mock Facebook page, symbolizing the prevalence of cyberbullying among today's youth. Laney shuddered at the thought. Asher wasn't even on the Internet yet, but he would be. *Was this what his future held?*

Laney had just started reading the article when Dr. Jamison's PA, Martha, opened the door. "Hi, Laney."

"Hi, Martha," Laney said with a smile before

stopping at the window with the magazine. "Etty, can you copy this for me?"

"Sure thing, hon. It'll be ready when you come out."

Laney followed Martha down the hall. "How've you been?" Martha asked over her shoulder.

"Pretty good. You?"

"Busy . . ."

"Too busy, I'll bet," Laney commiserated.

"Always too busy!" Martha said with a grin. "Will we ever learn?"

"I doubt it," Laney said with a laugh. "We haven't learned yet."

Martha stopped in front of a scale, and Laney eyed it skeptically. "Do I have to?"

Martha laughed and nodded. "It can't be that bad. Look at you. There's nothing to you!"

Laney shook her head and stepped on the scale. "Is that why I have to walk around with the top of my slacks unbuttoned all the time . . . and why I can't wait to get home to my baggy sweatpants?"

Martha slowly moved the leveling weight on the scale to 120, but the bar didn't budge. She slid it to 130, and it rose a tad; 140 sank it, so she slid it back to 130, and Laney exhaled and held it. The bar leveled at 134, and Laney breathed in. "Maybe you could take a couple pounds off for shoes and clothes," she suggested hopefully.

"That sounds fair," Martha said marking her chart and then measuring her height.

"Didn't I weigh one twenty-nine last year?"

Martha flipped back a page and shook her head. "One thirty-one."

Laney shook her head in dismay. "I watch what I eat. I exercise. But it just doesn't seem to matter . . . so why bother?"

Martha smiled. "It's perfectly normal. Once you hit fifty *or* go through menopause, it gets harder and harder to keep the weight off." She marked Laney's height. "Still five feet two inches though," she said with a grin. "Did you have a bone density test last year?"

"I think so."

Martha flipped through her chart. "If you did, we'll have it. We're converting all of our records over to the computer this summer. Next year when you come, I'll have a laptop and hopefully I'll know how to use it."

"I know what you mean." Laney nodded in agreement. "The school's doing the same thing with report cards. It's supposed to be simple and user-friendly, but I'm pretty clueless when it comes to technology. I can barely figure out my iPhone, but Asher uses it like a pro."

Martha chuckled. "My grandson is the same way! I think babies are born knowing how to use iPhones. When they come out of the womb, their little fingers just naturally know how to sweep across the screen."

Laney laughed, knowing it was true.

They went into an exam room, and Martha took her blood pressure, pulse, and temperature, reviewed her meds and daily supplements, and handed her a soft, cotton robe and a paper skirt. "You know the drill—open in front, everything but your socks."

"No more paper robes?" Laney asked, feigning dismay.

"Nope." Martha smiled. "Everyone hated 'em!"

"Are you kidding? I *loved* those crinkly, stark-white, gaping-open fashion statements!"

As Martha closed the door she said, "Dr. Jamison will be right in. You're her last patient."

Laney undressed, slipped on the robe, and scooted awkwardly onto the paper-covered exam table while trying to keep the robe closed. She wondered why they even bothered with a robe? Everything ended up exposed anyway. She sat on the end of the table, feeling chilled, and eyed the metal stirrups. This was definitely her least favorite appointment of the year. She dreaded it—it was worse than getting a tooth pulled. At least then, you were dressed! You'd think she'd be used to it after five pregnancies. But no, she wasn't. The sooner it was over, the better!

There was a soft knock, and Dr. Jamison peered around the door. "Hey, Laney."

"Hi, Dr. Jamison." Laney said. She couldn't help but smile. Johanna Jamison was one of her favorite people . . . and a wonderful doctor. Her bedside manner was kind and caring, and she had completely mastered the art of chatting during an exam, keeping her patients' minds off what was really happening.

She swept into the room. "How are my handsome young men?"

"They're all fine," Laney said with a smile. "I'm still trying to wrap my mind around the fact that E's twenty-one."

"Nooo! Has it been that long? He was one of my very first deliveries. In fact, he was so easy he made me think I'd wasted a lot of money on medical school!"

Laney laughed as Dr. Jamison motioned for her to lie back. Laney closed her eyes and focused on the funny story Dr. Jamison was telling about the new rooster they had who thought dawn was at three in the morning, and before she knew it, the worst was over.

"Are you doing regular exams?"

Laney nodded, moving her arm over her head and watching Dr. Jamison's expression as she methodically checked her breasts. Without saying anything, she stepped away to look at Laney's recent mammogram, and then gently touched a spot on the outer curve of her right breast again. "You've always had dense breast tissue, Laney," she said, "and that makes exams a bit more challenging. I think I'd like you to have an ultrasound this year."

"Is something wrong?"

Dr. Jamison covered her up and smiled reassuringly. "It's just a precaution. Lots of women have dense breast tissue. You can sit up." She consulted her chart. "Martha said you've been feeling tired . . ."

Laney nodded. "I don't seem to have the same energy I once had, but I've been so busy at school . . . and with the boys. I just attributed it to getting older."

Dr. Jamison nodded. "You are getting older, my dear. But you're far from old, so I'd like to get some blood work too." She scribbled out some prescriptions and handed them to her. "Etty can set everything up for you." She searched Laney's anxious eyes. "Now, don't start worrying! I want you to go home, relax, enjoy the weekend, and I'll be in touch next week after I get the results."

"Okay," Laney said with a nod, knowing full well she was going to worry.

Twenty minutes later, as she walked up toward the house, Laney stopped to look at the brightly lit windows welcoming her home. Noah's car was in the driveway, so she knew he was already home with the pizzas, and she could hear laughter and giggling drifting through the open windows. She stood still, listening, savoring the lovely sound. Then she remembered the concern she'd seen on her doctor's face, and a wave of anxiety swept over her. *What if something is wrong? What if there's a day when I'm no longer here to hear these wonderful sounds? What if my boys have to carry on without me?* She pictured her six handsome men lined up tearfully at her graveside, and the image broke her heart. "Oh, God," she whispered, "please don't let anything happen to me—not until I'm really old and they're ready to let me go. . . ." She shook her head, trying to push the heartbreaking image from her mind. "I can't think like this," she admonished. "Even if something is wrong, I have to stay positive."

She shifted her bag to her other shoulder and resigned to be strong. Noah didn't need to know yet. There was nothing to tell. It was just a routine follow-up. Lots of women had them. She forced a smile and pulled opened the door.

"Mom's home!" announced a chorus of happy voices.

"Hi, Mom!" Asher gushed, rushing over to wrap his arms around her.

"Pizza's still hot," Noah said with a smile. "Want a slice of Hawaiian?"

❧ 15 ❧

Asa tried to focus on the illuminated chart at the far end of the room. "E, A, Z. Hmm . . . that last one might actually be a two. . . ." He shook his head, as if shaking it would rattle his eyes into alignment.

The young optometrist switched on the light. "Mr. Coleman," he began slowly, "I think you already know. It's not your eyes." He jotted something on a piece of paper. "This is the name of a neurologist in Boston. I'd like you to make an appointment as soon as possible."

Asa nodded.

"I don't mean to alarm you. It could be any number of things, but you shouldn't wait."

Asa nodded again, wondering why his unsettling symptoms couldn't be caused by a simple astigmatism or cataract, even glaucoma— something a new pair of glasses or a quick in-office surgery would resolve.

He returned to the waiting room, and Maddie looked up from her book and smiled. "I was look-ing at some frames I thought you might like. . . ."

Asa pressed his lips together, shook his head, and headed for the door. Maddie got up to follow. "Thank you," she said, smiling at the receptionist as she walked past.

Once they were outside and he could breathe again, Asa handed the slip of paper to her. "There's something putting pressure on my optic nerves. Possibly a tumor."

Maddie felt her heart race as she looked at the paper.

"That's the name of a neurologist in Boston. He said I shouldn't wait."

She nodded. "We'll make an appointment as soon as we get home."

The following week was a blur of appointments and tests. Asa endured each and every one—from blood draw to CT scan to MRI—all while feeling increasingly like a lamb being led to slaughter. And although Maddie was beside him every step of the way, he also became increasingly withdrawn and reticent. Maddie expected it. Throughout their married life—and even before—when something weighed heavily on her husband's mind, this was his way of dealing with it, so she gave him his space and tried to be strong. Even though, deep down, she was terrified.

On Monday morning, they were both up early for yet another appointment. Maddie gazed out at the dull, gray sky. It looked like it might rain any minute, and she realized she hadn't seen a forecast in days. She turned on the kitchen TV, and the weatherman's cheerful voice sounded oddly comforting . . . and normal. *Oh, if we could just have our normal lives back,* she thought as she reached for the coffee, *I would never ask for anything again.* She heard the shower come on in the upstairs bathroom and wondered if Asa would want any breakfast; he hadn't had much of an appetite lately. She'd just started to open a new can of coffee when she heard a loud thud. She literally dropped what she was doing, spilling coffee grounds everywhere, and rushed up the stairs.

"Asa?" she cried, pushing on the bathroom door. "Asa!" She put all her weight against it and was finally able to pry it open just far enough to see her husband's naked, shuddering body slumped against it. "Oh, God! Asa!"

16

"Ash, are you up?"

Asher opened his eyes and felt a warm body curled up next to him. He stroked Halle's soft fur, and remembering what day it was, leaned over and whispered, "Rabbit, rabbit." Halle opened her eyes and yawned, her thumping tail caught under the sheet, making it flop up and down.

"How'd she do?" Laney asked, peering in his room.

Asher put on his glasses, inspected the floor, and felt his sheets. "Good . . . I told you she could do it."

Laney looked skeptical. "Well, take her outside before she has the chance to prove you wrong."

"C'mon, Halle," Asher said, scooping the puppy into his arms—he wasn't taking *any* chances. He went downstairs, saw Mennie dozing in a sunny spot, and gave him plenty of room. Then he put Halle down by the door, clicked on her leash, and followed her outside in his pajamas. The warm, damp grass tickled his bare feet as he wandered around the yard. He breathed in the fresh morning air. It looked and smelled like summer, and he couldn't wait until it *really* was summer.

When he came back in, Laney was putting his lunch in his backpack. Ben and Seth had already left for school. And Gabe and E were still in bed since they didn't have to be at work until ten, so it was just the two of them. Laney glanced at the clock. "You need to get a wiggle on, hon. The bus will be here in twenty minutes."

"Did you say 'rabbit'?" he asked.

Laney looked puzzled. "Rabbit?"

"You know—for good luck."

"Oh!" She suddenly realized he was talking about the age-old superstition to say "rabbit, rabbit" as soon as you woke up on the first day of the month and then you were assured to have good luck all month long. "Oh, hon, June first was yesterday."

Asher looked utterly distressed. "It was?"

Laney saw his dismay and frowned. "Ash, it's just a silly superstition. I don't know why your brothers fill your head with such nonsense. I'm sure June will be a fine month. Now, hurry up and get dressed."

As he disappeared up the stairs, she murmured, "If anyone should've said 'rabbit, rabbit' yesterday, it was me."

Ten minutes later, they were sitting at the bottom of the driveway, waiting. "*Where* is your bus?"

"Maybe we missed it," Asher suggested hopefully, his mouth full of strawberry Pop-Tart. "Maybe you should drive me," he added with crumbs spewing everywhere.

"If you missed it, that won't be very lucky, because I'll be late for school."

"It'll be lucky for me," Asher said with a grin, "cuz then I won't see you-know-who."

"Who? Voldemort?" she teased.

"Very funny, Mom."

"Maybe I can get E or Gabe to drive you."

"Waking them would take even longer."

Laney sighed, knowing he was right. Waking her two older sons was like waking a pair of bears from winter hibernation. "Okay," she conceded, still hoping the bus would magically appear. "Hop in back."

"Yes!" Asher cheered, climbing over the seat. "Maybe it'll be a lucky month after all."

❧ 17 ❧

Elijah sat on the edge of his bed, scrolling through the pictures on his phone. Chloe had been leaning against his car the night before, posing seductively, and he'd taken several pictures. "I don't know if your mom's going to like seeing these photos of her daughter on Facebook."

"You better not," she'd warned.

He'd laughed, his blue eyes sparkling mischievously. "Hmm . . . what's in it for me?"

"What would you like to be in it?" she'd murmured, brushing against him and feeling how aroused he was. He'd slid his hands down her back and pulled her against him. "You," he'd whispered with a smile.

His reverie was suddenly interrupted by his phone vibrating, and he lightly tapped the screen.

R U UP?

He glanced at his boxers and chuckled.

YUP!

I MEAN AWAKE

THAT 2

LAST NIGHT WAS NICE . . .

MMM . . .

MISSED U AS SOON AS U LEFT

MISSED U 2

GOIN RUNNIN?

YUP
WILL I C U LTR?
DEFINITELY
CAN'T WAIT . . .
MIGHT NOT . . .
WELL MAK SUR UR THINKIN OF ME . . .
ALWAYS!
GOOD. LUV U!
LUV U 2

Elijah leaned back against his pillow and smiled. Then he glanced at the time on his phone and realized how late it was. If they were going running, they needed to get moving. He threw a pillow at his brother. "Gettin' up?"

Gabe muffled a sleepy reply.

"Is that a yes?"

"Mm-hmm."

"How far are we going?" E asked, stripping off his boxers and pulling on his running shorts.

"Ten?"

"Well, get moving or we won't have time."

Fifteen minutes later, they were trotting down the shady driveway and Gabe was still yawning. "You got in late."

"Don't tell Mom."

"Do I ever?"

"Yes."

"I only told her you were seeing Chloe. She was going to find out anyway. So . . . where were you?"

"Down at the beach."

"Doin' what?" Gabe teased, knowing full well he wasn't going to get an answer.

"None of your business."

"Hmm. That just makes my imagination run wild."

"How 'bout *you* run wild, instead of your imagination?" E said, picking up the pace.

🎕 18 🎕

"So that's that?" Asa said with a resigned nod. "There's nothing that can be done?" He felt like he'd been kicked in the stomach. Tears filled Maddie's eyes, and when she tried to breathe, her breath came out in a muffled cry. Asa wrapped his hand around hers, and Maddie felt how cold he was.

"Inoperable doesn't mean there's no treatment," Dr. Raines said gently. "It means the tumor can't be removed surgically, but it can still be treated with radiation, and the seizures you've been experiencing can be treated with medication."

Asa squeezed Maddie's hand, and his voice wavered as he spoke. "Our son is getting married this summer. Will I still . . . be here?"

The doctor nodded. "You will be here." He smiled. "It's not the end of the world, Mr. Coleman—at least not yet! And your attitude will play a big part. Our goal is to shrink the tumor. External beam radiation therapy is noninvasive and it's done on an outpatient basis. You will come in for your treatments, and you will walk out and carry on with your life."

"What are the side effects?" Maddie asked, starting to feel hopeful.

"Oh, the usual suspects—hair loss, fatigue, short-term memory loss, possibly muffled hearing, weight loss."

"And when would I start?" Asa asked.

"As soon as possible. And once we start, it's important that you get plenty of rest—which shouldn't be a problem because you're going to be tired, and you'll need to keep up your strength. So you must eat . . . even if you aren't hungry."

Asa nodded, trying to absorb everything the doctor was saying.

Twenty minutes later, after scheduling the treatments and taking care of all the other details, they stepped out into the beautiful June morning, and Asa pulled Maddie into his arms. "I'm sorry," he murmured.

"It's not your fault," she said softly.

"I'm sorry I've been so . . . unreachable. I just didn't want to believe it was real."

"It *is* real."

"I know," he said, pulling back and searching her eyes. "I wish it wasn't. I wish we didn't have to go through it. I wish *you* didn't have to go through it."

"We'll get through it together."

He nodded solemnly and looked up at the cloudless, blue sky. "I don't want to say anything to the kids . . . with the wedding coming."

Maddie frowned. "Asa, how can we not tell them?" she asked, gently laying her hand on the side of his head. "They're going to figure it out—especially if you lose your hair."

He rested his hand on hers. "Maybe I won't lose my hair. Let's just take one day at a time. If we have to tell them, we will, but for now, I don't want to be a dark cloud hanging over their happiness."

Maddie nodded uncertainly. She understood how he felt, but deep down, it seemed like an unforgivable betrayal of trust. "You're going to have to take their calls then, because I can't lie. Noah and Laney already know something's going on, and they're going to ask."

Asa nodded. "Fine, I'll take their calls."

They were both quiet as Maddie drove home. They stopped at the pharmacy to pick up the new seizure medicine, and then they stopped at the market to pick up a couple of steaks for dinner. "I guess I don't need to worry about my cholesterol anymore," Asa said with a wry smile.

"Yes, you do," Maddie admonished as they turned onto their street. "You're going to beat this, and you're going to continue to have all the same health problems you've always had."

As they drew near the house, they saw Micah's car parked in the driveway, and Asa turned to her. "Please remember what I said."

Maddie nodded, but she could already feel tears stinging her eyes. Micah was in the yard, throwing a tennis ball for Harper, their black Lab. He looked up and waved, and almost immediately, a little girl of about five peered around the corner of the house. She smiled shyly and then started to run toward them, her blond curls bouncing around her rosy cheeks. Asa opened his door, and she threw her arms around his neck. "Hi, Grampa," she whispered.

Asa held her tight, his heart in his throat. "Hi, honey." He stood up with her still in his arms.

"We came to see you," she said matter-of-factly.

"You did?"

"Mm-hmm." She nodded, then squirmed from his arms and ran to give Maddie a hug too.

Her grandmother scooped her up. "Hi, sweetie," she said cheerfully, pushing away her new reality.

Harper bounded over and dropped a soggy tennis ball at Asa's feet, her tail wagging. Asa gave it a kick, but Harper pounced, stopping the ball in its tracks, and then dropped it at his feet again. Asa leaned down to pick it up, and a sudden, sharp pain exploded through his head. He stood up unsteadily with the ball in his hand as

Harper bounced expectantly in front of him. He tossed it weakly over her head, and a wave of nausea swept over him and he had to hold onto the car for support.

"Dad, are you okay?" Micah asked, coming up to steady him.

"Yup, fine," Asa insisted, rubbing his temple. "I just stood up too quickly."

Maddie ran her fingers through her salt and pepper hair and blinked back tears. Just then, an attractive, petite woman with short dark hair came up behind Micah.

"Hi, Beryl," Maddie said, giving her future daughter-in-law a warm hug.

"Hi," Beryl replied, hugging her back. She loved Micah's mom, and she wanted to call her "Mom," but the word just wouldn't come out yet. It was still too soon.

"We've been trying to reach you all day," Micah said. "So we finally decided to come over and make sure there wasn't something wrong with your phone."

"How come you didn't try our cell?" Asa asked, giving Beryl a hug too.

"I did. No answer."

Maddie suddenly remembered she'd left their cell phone plugged in on the counter. "That's because we forgot it, dear." She shook her head and smiled. "What can I tell you? Your parents are getting old and forgetful." She gave her son a long hug and purposely avoided his eyes.

Micah reached into the backseat for the grocery bags, handed the smallest one to Charlotte, gathered up the rest, and followed his parents inside. "So where've you been all day?"

"We had some errands to run."

"All day?"

"We haven't been gone all day. We've been in and out. You must've just missed us."

"Well, if you ever need us to let Harper out, all you have to do is call." He set the bags on the counter, and Charlotte pulled the prescription out of the bag she'd carried in. Micah took it from her and glanced at the label. "What's Depakote?" he asked.

"Oh, that's just my cholesterol medicine," Asa said casually, leaning against the stove. Micah nodded and put it on the counter with everything else.

"Can you stay for supper?" Maddie asked.

"I wish we could," Beryl said, rubbing Harper's ears. "But we're going out for pizza with Rumer, Will, and Rand." She paused. "We wondered if you guys might like to come. We're going to be talking about the wedding menu." She looked over at Micah and grinned. "Micah thinks we should have an old-fashioned clambake."

"A clambake sounds perfect!" Maddie said, glancing at her husband to see if he felt like going out for pizza, but his face was pale and she could tell he was trying to hide the fact that he didn't feel well. "I think we'll take a rain check on pizza though. We've had a busy day."

Micah looked at his watch. "Okay, well, I guess we better go then." He kissed his mom's cheek. "Love you, Mom," he murmured.

"Love you too, hon."

Then he turned to shake his dad's hand. "Make sure you let me know if you need help with anything. Now that school's out, I'm free anytime."

"I will," Asa said with a nod.

Beryl and Charlotte gave them both hugs and followed Micah to the car. Maddie watched from the window as Beryl helped Charlotte into her car seat and smiled. "Beryl is such a treasure," she said, but when Asa didn't reply, she turned around and realized he was already making his way out to the deck with Harper at his side. She reached for his new prescription, studied the directions, and filled a glass with water. She followed him out back, kissed the top of his head, and handed him the glass and one of the pills.

"Thanks for covering for me," he said.

"You're welcome. But I can't promise I'll be able to keep it together every time." She squeezed his shoulder. "I'm going to start the grill. Would you like a baked potato?"

"I'll split one."

Maddie nodded, and while she busied herself in the kitchen, Asa watched the pair of Canada geese that called their pond home every summer. Mr. and Mrs.—as they affectionately called them—had been late arriving this year. In fact, it had been almost June before Maddie had spotted them as she washed the supper dishes. "They're here," she'd called.

"Who?"

"Mr. and Mrs."

Asa had pulled himself off the couch and stood beside her. "Yup," he'd said with a smile. "There they are. I was beginning to worry."

"I was beginning to worry too," Maddie had agreed.

As he watched now, they gracefully swam along, side by side, in the late day sunlight, and he marveled at their lasting devotion. He stroked Harper's soft ears and wondered how much time he had left. At seventy-three, his life had been full and lovely—he had no regrets, and if God wanted to call him home, he was ready. But his heart ached for Maddie. He didn't want her to be alone.

❧ 19 ❧

"Move, Ashhole," Jared commanded as he climbed the steps onto the bus, pushing Asher roughly. Asher tried to catch himself, but his arm slipped behind the handrail and got caught.

"What's the matter, Ashwipe?" Jared taunted. "Did the little baby hurt his arm?" His voice was sarcastic and snide, and his laugh was cruel. "Hey, everybody, little Ashwipe hurt his arm," he announced as other kids on the bus joined him in jeering Asher.

"I did not!" Asher said defiantly, brushing away hot tears and ignoring the pain in his arm.

"Hey, dipshit!" a voice called. "How 'bout you leave him alone?"

At the sound of the familiar voice, Jared's heart stopped and he turned to see his older brother coming down the aisle behind him. Asher, sensing a brewing storm, ducked into an empty seat, his heart pounding. "Yeah, loser, I was talking to *you*." Jeff sneered derisively, coming face-to-face with his brother and shoving him so hard that he landed on the floor in the aisle. Asher sank lower in his seat, wishing he could disappear. "In fact, turd-face, if I see you bothering him again, I'm gonna beat the pulp out of you."

"Shut up, Jeff," Jared said, getting to his feet and trying to save face.

"What?" Jeff said, glaring at him.

"I said, 'Shut up,' " Jared repeated softly, his face pale with rage and humiliation.

By this time, Asher was practically under his seat and his heart felt like it was going to beat right out of his chest.

"You little shit," Jeff seethed. He glared at Jared

and whispered, "I'm gonna effin' kill you." Asher looked up, saw the rage in Jeff's eyes . . . and believed him.

At the very same moment, Mr. Anderson, the bus driver, climbed up the steps, looked down the aisle, and saw Jeff's clenched fist connect squarely with his brother's face. Jared fell back, howling in pain and holding his nose as blood squirted everywhere.

"That's it!" Mr. Anderson roared. "Off my bus!"

Jeff turned around, and with profanity spewing from his mouth, stormed off the bus, while Jared, fighting back tears and holding his nose, shuffled after him. Asher glanced up as Jared passed and saw blood spattered all over his shirt. Everyone on the bus watched as Mr. Anderson escorted the two wayward boys back into the building. Moments later, he reappeared, shaking his head, climbed back on the bus, and closed the door.

"Hey, Mr. Anderson," someone in back yelled. "Are they off for good?"

"Damn straight," Mr. Anderson answered, glancing in his rearview mirror, putting the bus in gear, and turning the big steering wheel.

Asher gazed out his open window as the trees zipped by, felt the cool, early summer breeze, and wondered why he didn't feel lucky.

When Laney finally got home after her ultrasound and blood work, Asher was sitting on the porch with Halle in his lap. "Whatcha doin'?" she asked, peering around the doorway.

"Thinking," he said without looking up.

"I heard what happened," she said softly.

"Yeah," he said sorrowfully.

"Jeff is suspended for the rest of the year, and Jared isn't allowed back on the bus."

"I know."

Laney studied her youngest son. "How come you're so gloomy? I thought you'd be happy."

Asher sighed. "Mom, aren't you the lady who always says not to rejoice in the misfortunes of others?"

Laney leaned against the doorframe and smiled. "I *am* that lady! But I didn't think anyone was listening."

Asher looked up. "I listen," he said, sounding wounded, and then added quietly, "I thought I'd be happy, but I just feel sorry for Jared. It must stink to have a brother like Jeff. I only have to put up with Jared on the bus, but he has to put up with Jeff all the time. Jeff told him he—" Asher stopped. He couldn't even say it. "Jeff says such awful things," he blurted.

Laney sat down, slipped her arm around him, and said softly, "How come God made you so good?"

"How come he made Jeff so bad?" he asked, playing with Halle's ears.

"I don't know, hon. I don't know why some

people do mean things. I guess the only thing we can do is pray for Jeff . . . and Jared."

"That's just it," Asher said, looking perplexed. "I've been praying for Jared to stop bothering me, but I didn't mean for this to happen. I didn't mean for him to get hurt."

Laney pulled him close. "I'm sure God didn't answer your prayers by hurting Jared. He doesn't work that way."

"Are you sure, Mom? In Sunday school, we talk about God revenging people all the time. Look at what he did to the Egyptians."

Laney nodded. "You're right," she said as Halle climbed over onto her lap and licked her cheek. "That's why these questions would be good for your father. Why don't you ask him?"

"I don't feel like it," he said. "I don't even want to think about it."

"Well, do you feel like helping me make brownies?"

His face lit up. "Sure!" He plopped Halle on the floor and stood right up.

As they came into the kitchen, Noah looked up from his laptop. "Uh-oh. What are you two up to?"

"We're making brownies," Asher said with a grin. "So after supper we can have your favorite dessert."

"Brownie sundaes?" Noah said with a grin, gathering him into a hug as he walked by.

"Mm-hmm." Asher nodded.

"Well, I'm glad Mom found a way to cheer you up."

"Moms have a way," Asher replied matter-of-factly.

"Is that so?" Noah said, tickling him.

Asher giggled. "Stop! Stop!" he pleaded as Halle jumped up on them. "Dads have a way too!" he squealed, trying to escape. Finally, Noah let him go, but by this time, Mennie had gimped into the kitchen to find out what was going on. "Now look what you did," Asher said, trying to keep the two dogs apart.

Just then, Ben and Seth came in, laughing, and dropped their backpacks and duffel bags in the middle of the floor.

"I thought practice was over at five," Noah said, glancing up at the clock.

"We got done early," Ben said, pulling open the refrigerator door.

"How'd you get home?"

"Tommy Baker's brother."

"I don't even know Tommy Baker, never mind his brother," Noah said.

"It's okay, Dad. He's a good driver," Seth piped.

"I don't care if he's a good driver. I don't want you two riding with other kids. That's the rule, and you know it."

"You worry too much," Ben protested, gulping orange juice from the container.

Noah stood and took the container from him.

"Use a glass! And you are to call if you need a ride. Or you won't be on the team." He eyed his middle sons. "Got it?"

"Yes," they grudgingly agreed.

"Holy cow!" Noah grumbled. "I don't understand what the heck is so hard about following the rules. Your mother and I make sure one of us is always available."

"We just don't want anything to happen," Laney added.

"We got it," Ben said impatiently, hoisting his backpack on his shoulder.

Seth followed him, and when he thought they were out of earshot, he whispered, "I told you we should've said *Mrs.* Baker . . ."

"I heard that," Laney called after them. "And you'd be in bigger trouble if you'd lied."

She turned to get her mixer out of the cabinet and realized Asher was sitting on the floor with one dog on either side of him, each with a head in his lap. He looked up and grinned. "I think Mennie's getting used to Halle," he said happily.

❧ 20 ❧

Laney rolled onto her side, listening to Noah snoring peacefully beside her, and looked at her alarm clock. The numbers glowed brightly: 1:23 a.m. She reached for her phone, wishing it would beep, but it didn't. She slid it on and touched the icons to make sure a new message hadn't magically skipped directly to her inbox, but the last message was still the one she'd gotten from E that afternoon, telling her he wouldn't be home for dinner. She'd written right back, asking when he would be home, but he'd never replied, and she'd been fretting ever since. In fact, at that very moment, worried, angry thoughts were charging around her head like out of control children: Didn't he know she wouldn't be able to fall asleep? Didn't he know she had to work the next day? Where was he? Was he with Chloe? Had they been in an accident? Was he lying in a ditch, bleeding and unconscious . . . or worse? Had he gone for a swim and been swept away by a riptide? Damn it! Did he have any idea how inconsiderate he was? She would certainly tell him. *If he would just come home!*

She rolled onto her back and blinked at the darkness, her mind drifting to the ultrasound she'd had that afternoon. She recalled telling the technician it was nice that the gel was warm, but the technician had gruffly replied, "It doesn't stay warm," and on that pessimistic note, she'd continued her task, staring silently at the screen, moving the handheld device methodically around Laney's breasts and clicking her mouse. Laney had turned her attention to a water stain on the ceiling and tried to think of something else, but when the technician started to spend a lot of time gliding back and forth over the same area, Laney good-naturedly teased, "You're going to wear that spot out." The technician had only responded with a solemn "Mmm," and Laney had felt like saying, "That's not very reassuring." But instead, she'd endured the rest of the test in silence, and when it was finally over, she'd wiped the gel off with a towel, pulled on her blouse, and stuffed her bra in her bag, giving her breasts a well-deserved break. They'd been through enough prodding that week . . . and she was only going home anyway.

Now, as she lay in bed, she gently touched the outer curve near her right nipple—the area that had seemed to be the center of attention. Both of her breasts were tender, achy. She'd once heard someone say that cancer doesn't hurt, and she wondered if it was true. Was the pain she felt right now a good sign? Or was it just a result of the mammogram and ultrasound? If it was the latter, it was neither a good or bad sign. *It was nothing*. She had nothing to grasp on to for hope. It didn't matter that she dutifully followed every recommendation touted in the health magazines: she exercised regularly, drank black coffee and green tea—even though the tea sometimes made her nauseous—ate copious amounts of broccoli, spinach, kale, tomatoes, wild-caught sockeye salmon—even though it was more expensive—as well as berries and other cancer warriors. And she stayed away from red meat and artificial sweeteners. And on the rare occasion when she indulged, she only drank red wine—which studies showed was chock-full of antioxidants. But all that didn't seem to matter, she decided. If cancer wanted you, it found you.

"That's positive thinking," she chided, tears stinging her eyes. "I'm not a very good fighter, God," she whispered softly. "Please don't make me go through this. If you do, who will take care of the five wonderful boys you gave us? They need their mom to guide them. Especially that oldest one who doesn't seem to know when to come home."

Without realizing it, her whispering had gotten louder, and Noah snorted and slipped his hand into hers. "Everything okay?" he murmured.

She nodded, brushing away her tears. "Mm-hmm . . . except that E's not home."

Noah looked at the clock and immediately became more alert. "Where the heck is he?" he growled. "He needs to learn that college rules don't apply at home! I know he has unlimited freedom at school, but when he's home, he needs to be more considerate. He could, at the very least, call."

"My sentiments exact—" Laney started to say, but before she could finish, they heard the screen door, and she looked at the clock again—it was just after two.

Noah threw back the covers and headed for the stairs.

"Noah, don't lose your temper," Laney said in a hushed voice as she pulled on her robe and followed him.

The only light in the kitchen was coming from the open refrigerator—in front of which stood their tall, slender son . . . with the orange juice container in his hand. When Noah turned on the light, Elijah quickly put on the top and tried to make it look like he was getting a glass.

"Where the heck have you been?"

"I—"

"Do you realize what time it is?"

E looked up at the clock and started to answer.

"You aren't away at college. And although we realize you're very close to being an adult—in fact, in some societies you would already be considered an adult—a little common courtesy, like calling your mother, would be very much appreciated."

"I—"

"If you want us to treat you like an ad—"

Laney put her hand on her husband's arm. "Let him answer."

"I'm sorry," E began, his eyes glistening. "I should've called . . . it's just . . . Chloe's grandfather died, and she was really upset . . . and she didn't want me to leave . . . and then I lost track of time, and when I realized how late it was, I thought it was too late to call."

Laney was stunned. "Oh, E, I'm sorry," she said, suddenly feeling foolish for being so angry and suspicious. "Oh, poor Chloe."

Noah shook his head remorsefully. "I'm sorry too, E. For jumping on you . . . and for Chloe."

Elijah nodded. "It was so unexpected. Chloe's grandmother had gone to the store to pick up a few things for lunch, and her grandfather was working in the yard. When she got back, she found him lying in the grass—he'd had a heart attack."

"Oh, no . . . that's awful."

"Chloe was really close to him. She's . . ." His voice broke as tears spilled down his cheeks. "She's a mess."

"Oh, hon," Laney said, wrapping her arms around him. She felt him lean against her just as he had when he was a little boy turning to her for comfort. She reached up to brush away the tears on his tan cheeks. "It's not easy," she said softly.

"He's not even my grandfather, and I feel terrible," E whispered. "I don't even know what to say to her."

"Sometimes there aren't any words, E," Noah said, putting his hand on his shoulder. "The best thing you can do is just be there."

Elijah nodded wearily and opened the refrigerator to put the juice back. "All I want to do is go to bed."

Laney nodded, and at the top of the stairs, she gave him another hug. She noticed Mennie lying on the rug beside his bed. "Your pal's waiting," she said, nodding to the old dog, and E nodded too, smiling sadly.

Laney went back to bed and listened to her son wash up; she heard him turn off the bathroom light and talk softly to Mennie as he got into bed. She was thankful he was home and safe, but her heart ached for Chloe and her family . . . and her son.

She lay still, trying to fall asleep, but her mind slipped back to the beautiful spring day near the end of her senior year at Bowdoin. She'd just come out of the library with friends, heading to lunch, and she remembered thinking she'd never seen such a pretty day. Then one of her friends had pointed across the quad.

"Laney, isn't that your dad?" Laney had followed her friend's gaze and watched as a figure had walked toward them. What was her dad doing here?

"Dad?" she'd called, leaving her friends. He'd looked up, and immediately, she'd seen the despair on his face; her heart had pounded as she'd searched his eyes. "What is it, Dad?" she'd pleaded. "What happened?"

"Oh, Lane," he'd said, tears spilling down his cheeks, his voice choked with emotion. "It's Gramp . . ."

"Is he okay?" she'd cried.

He'd shaken his head and pulled her into his arms.

Through the years, the memory of that day had never been far from Laney's mind. She still remembered the anguish in her dad's eyes as he'd explained what had happened. Just like Chloe's grandfather, Gramp had been working outside on his old John Deere orchard tractor while her dad's brother—Uncle Luke—had run into town to get a part, and when he'd gotten back, he'd found Gramp lying, faceup, under the peach trees.

After her dad had left that afternoon, Laney had called Noah, and he'd dropped everything and driven up to be with her. She'd still had two exams left but, to this day, she had no recollection of taking them. The only thing she remembered was that Noah was there. And that when she didn't want to go to graduation, her dad had insisted, saying Gramp would've wanted her to go—he would've been so proud. And Noah had nodded in agreement.

A week later, Noah had flown with her to Georgia for her grandfather's service. And although the entire service had been amazing and beautiful, the part that always stayed with her was when her cousin John had played his guitar, and sounding hauntingly like Glen Campbell, had sung Gramp's favorite old song about the lonely Wichita lineman, and Noah, with tears in his eyes, had slipped his hand into hers and gazed out the window, smiling sadly.

❧ 21 ❧

Noah lifted the calendar off the kitchen wall and looked at the many handwritten appointments and commitments that had been kept over the last thirty-one days—almost every square had something written on it. "Well, May flew by like nobody's business," he said, trying to decipher his wife's scribble.

"It sure did," Laney agreed, drying her hands on the dish towel, "and it's about time someone changed the calendar. June started a week ago."

"By the way, how was your physical?" Noah asked as he turned the page and rehung the calendar.

"Fine," Laney replied vaguely.

"Was it fun?" he teased, knowing how much she loved her annual.

"It was. Sorry you missed it."

He grinned and pulled her into his arms. "I'm sorry I missed it too."

Just then, Seth wandered into the kitchen. "Geez! Get a room, wouldja?" he said, shielding his eyes in mock embarrassment as he opened the fridge and stood in front of it, gazing at its contents. "What's for supper?"

"Believe it or not, that appliance is not an air

conditioner," Noah admonished, ignoring his question.

"Well, maybe if we had a *real* air conditioner, I'd know what one looked like," Seth answered sarcastically. "This family really needs to join the twenty-first century. It's primitive to live the way we do."

"Primitive?" Noah retorted. "You don't know what primitive is. Not to mention, we have a year-round ocean breeze, so we don't need an air conditioner."

"Yes, we do! Our room is so hot!"

Noah eyed his wife. "I think someone needs an attitude adjustment. I think there's a bridge falling down somewhere."

"Is it in London?" Laney asked with raised eyebrows.

"Oh no, it isn—" Seth started to protest, but before he could escape, his parents' arms had dropped down on both sides of him.

Noah and Laney immediately broke into the old song about the fate of London Bridge, swaying their son back and forth. "I'm too old for this!" he shouted, trying not to laugh.

"You're never too old," Noah said, laughing.

Finally, as they sang "My Fair Lady" at the top of their lungs, they squeezed him and he started laughing so hard he had tears rolling down his cheeks.

Hearing the commotion, Asher came running

with Halle at his heels. "I'm not too old," he shouted. "Do me! Do me!"

Laney and Noah left their next to youngest son in a heap on the floor, still trying to catch his breath, and circled their arms around their youngest son, who was already giggling. They started to sing, and Halle jumped up on them, wanting to join in on the fun. As they reached the famous finale, Laney looked up and realized E was standing solemnly in the doorway, wearing his black dress pants and a white shirt and with his jacket draped over his arm. He smiled wistfully, remembering the simpler times when he was the one being swung in the safety of his parents' arms.

"Hi, hon," Laney said. "How did it go?"

Noah looked up too, and they gently laid Asher, still giggling, on the floor with Halle on top of him.

"It was nice," he said with a sad smile. "Chloe's a little better. I had no idea she had such a big family. Her grandfather was the second oldest of nine, and they all still live up near St. Johnsbury. Two of his brothers and one of his sisters spoke. I guess her grandfather was pretty mischievous when he was a kid. The stories were funny. They made everyone laugh, and it seemed . . . less sad. Even Chloe smiled when her great aunt told a story about him being chased by a Tom turkey when he was little."

Laney smiled. "When people recall the good

times and the light someone has brought to their lives, it definitely helps ease the sadness."

E nodded. "It's funny. I never met him, but after today, I feel like I did."

Laney smiled. "Did Chloe come back with you?"

"No, she's staying up there for a few days. She wanted me to stay too, but I told her I couldn't miss work. I think she was glad I was there today though."

"I'm sure she was," Laney said.

Elijah pulled his tie free. "Well, I'm going for a run. Is Gabe around?"

"No, he's not home yet," Noah said, glancing at his watch. "In fact, I have to go pick him up, but I think he went running this morning anyway."

"Supper will be ready soon," Laney added.

"I'm not hungry," E said, unbuttoning his shirt.

"I am," piped Asher.

"Me too," added Seth. "What are we having?"

"Spaghetti," Laney said with a smile, knowing the menu would be well received.

"Yay!" they both cheered.

"How soon?" E asked, his interest peaking a little at the mention of his favorite dish.

"How soon can you be back?"

"An hour?"

"We can wait . . . *if* I can hold off the hungry masses," she said, eyeing her two youngest sons.

"An hour?" Seth groaned. "I can't wait that

long. I'm hungry now. Can I have a Pop-Tart?"

"How about an apple?" Laney offered.

"I'll have an apple," Asher piped. "Can you cut it up, Mom?"

"I just want a Pop-Tart," Seth mumbled, reaching for the knob of the cereal cabinet, hoping she wouldn't say no, but his mom was busy talking to his brother again, so he took advantage of the opportunity to slip a silver foil package from the box with one strawberry Pop-Tart left in it.

Ten minutes later—after Noah had left to pick up Gabe, E had headed out for his run, Seth had stolen furtively up the stairs with his Pop-Tart, and Asher was contentedly sharing apple slices with the dogs and watching Harry Potter—Laney filled her big pasta pot with water. As she did, she looked out the kitchen window and noticed the same grayish brown birds she'd seen earlier flying from the scrub pine up to the back of the wood-shed. She set down the half-filled pot, typed "small gray bird with flickering tail" into the search box of the family computer, and clicked enter. The first site that came up was the Cornell Lab of Ornithology's allaboutbirds.org. She clicked on it, and several pictures of flickers came up. She frowned and tried again, this time deleting the word flicker and typing in "white breast." New images popped up, and she slowly scrolled down through them: white-breasted nuthatch, tufted titmouse, white-crowned sparrow, mockingbird. Finally, at the bottom of the page, she saw a picture that resembled the birds in the backyard, and she clicked on it—that was it! Eastern phoebe. She scanned the page, reading more about the little bird, including its unique tail movement and the interesting fact that it likes to build its nest on a ledge under an overhang.

Curiously, she pushed open the screen door, and immediately, the two birds flew up to the roof and cocked their heads. She peered under the back of the shed overhang, and to her delight, discovered an intricately woven nest with five creamy speckled eggs in it. The nest was made of small twigs, strips of bark, and a single strand of white ribbon, and it was lined with soft, green moss. "Oh, my," Laney said softly. She backed away slowly and looked up at the anxious parents. "Good job," she said softly.

As she walked back through the porch, she noticed Lucky stretched out lazily on the swing and warned, "Don't you dare bother them!" Lucky blinked innocently, and she knew she'd have to keep an eye on him. She went into the living room, excited to tell Asher, but he was sound asleep with a dog curled up on each side of him.

Laney watched through the kitchen window as the pair of phoebes flew back under the shed roof. Then she turned on the water to finish filling her pasta pot, and as she did, she remembered the phone call she'd gotten that afternoon and forgot all about the phoebe nest.

Dr. Jamison had called to tell her that her blood work revealed she was vitamin D deficient and slightly anemic—both of which could be easily remedied with supplements and diet. But then she'd gone on to say the ultrasound had been inconclusive and she wanted to get a biopsy.

"A biopsy . . ." Laney had repeated in quiet alarm, and Dr. Jamison had quickly reassured her it was just a precautionary measure. But the word had sounded surreal and now Laney wondered if maybe she'd dreamed it. At the time, there'd been so much commotion in the house, she hadn't had time to absorb everything, but now—alone with her thoughts—she could feel the icy fingers of fear wrapping around her heart. *Biopsy* was one of those worrisome words—like *malignant, inoperable, metastasize,* and *mass*—that people always associate with cancer. She put the pot on one of the working burners, and as she chopped an onion, she pictured herself pulling a soft pink hat on her bare head. Is that what her future held? Was she going to be bald and have ominously dark circles under her eyes? Would she be bone thin—almost skeletal—and not have the strength to protect her bullied son?

Through the blur of tears, she scraped the onion into a puddle of hot olive oil. It sizzled, and she gave it a quick stir. Then she wiped her cheeks with the back of her hand and minced a clove of garlic into the oil too. Suddenly, she remembered something Noah had said when they'd first started dating: "Lane, I don't want there to be any secrets between us. . . . I don't want you to ever ask me why I didn't tell you something." Her heart ached from not telling him, but she couldn't bring herself to say the words. It was almost as if saying them would give life to the specter of cancer.

Lane, I don't want there to be any secrets between us. . . . His words continued to echo through her mind. They'd never kept secrets. It was true. Noah sometimes forgot to tell her things —important things—but he never purposely withheld information. And how many times had they had this same conversation with the boys? Withholding information was just as bad as lying!

"All right all ready," she mumbled, plopping a pound of ground sirloin into the hot pan. "I'll tell him. . . ."

"Tell him what?"

Laney looked up, startled. "I didn't hear you come in."

Noah smiled. He was holding a bottle of red wine.

"What's that for?"

"Us," he answered simply. He riffled around in the drawer, looking for the corkscrew.

"I think it's over there," Laney said, nodding to a drawer at the far end of the counter.

Noah found what he was looking for, took down two wineglasses from an upper cabinet, eyed them critically, blew on them, frowned, and ended up rinsing and drying them. While he poured the wine, Laney drained the fat from the pan and added crushed San Marzano tomatoes and fresh basil. She started to reach for the garlic bread, but Noah put his arm around her shoulder and handed her a glass. "There's truth in wine," he said softly.

"What?" she asked uncertainly, her heart skipping a beat. *Not now,* she pleaded silently. *Not now—I'm not ready!* She suddenly wondered if he already knew—if he'd heard her talking on the phone or if the doctor's office had left a message on their machine.

He searched her eyes, and she tried to look away, but he gently turned her chin back to face him. "Lane, what's wrong?"

"Nothing."

He eyed her skeptically, and she shook her head. He knew her too well, and she was going to lose it if he kept looking at her that way.

"It's nothing," she insisted.

"Then why does it seem like you're carrying the weight of the world on your shoulders?"

She leaned against the counter. "I just have a lot on my mind—the end of the school year, Asher being bullied, your dad not feeling well, Chloe and E. And now Chloe's grandfather, which reminds me so much of what happened to

Gramp. . . ." Her voice trailed off, her eyes glistening.

Noah didn't say anything. He took a sip from his glass, set it down, and started to get out plates and silverware. Laney swallowed, realizing she'd sunk to an all-time low. She'd gone over the edge—from withholding information to outright lying—and she realized, by the nausea churning in her stomach, that speaking an untruth *was* worse than saying nothing.

"I didn't want to—" She stopped, struggling to find the right words, and Noah looked up. "What I mean is I just need summer to be here."

Noah pulled her into his arms, and Laney could feel hot tears stinging her eyes, but she laid her head against his shoulder and blinked them back.

Just then, Ben came in from mowing the lawn. "Good grief! Get a room, wouldja?" he said, pretending to cover his eyes. "When's supper? I'm starving." He pulled open the fridge door and stood there, enjoying the cool air that drifted out.

Noah looked over. "Believe it or not, that's not an air conditioner."

"It's not?" Ben said with a hint of sarcasm. "It feels like one."

❧ 22 ❧

Micah pulled Beryl into his arms and kissed her softly.

"Mmm, what's that for?" she murmured.

"Do I need a reason to kiss my fiancée?"

She smiled, her cornflower blue eyes sparkling. "Now there's a word I never thought would be associated with me."

"You just hadn't met the right guy yet," Micah said, pulling her closer.

"Well, actually, I had met the right guy. I just didn't know it at the time, and then I let him slip away." Beryl smiled, picturing a much younger Micah stocking shelves and ringing up customers in her mom's tea shop, Tranquility in a Tea Cup. She'd only recently found out that he'd had a crush on her back then and that he'd even been planning to ask her to their prom, but by the time he'd mustered up the courage, she'd already accepted an invitation from someone else. Her sisters, Isak and Rumer, had known more about Micah's plan than she had, and in hindsight, she wished she hadn't been so clueless. Fortunately, life's paths have a way of twisting and turning until they intersect again, and theirs had serendipitously crossed again twenty-five years later.

Beryl would never forget that blue sky September day. She'd been taking her mom to see a neurologist in Boston, but the appointment hadn't been until late afternoon, so they'd had time to have a leisurely lunch in Quincy Market before doing a little shopping. Their last stop had been a bookstore at the far end of Faneuil Hall called The Bookend. Beryl's mother, Mia, had been stepping away from the counter after making a purchase when she accidently knocked over a display of books, and a slender man in his early forties, wearing stylish, round glasses and a neatly pressed blue oxford, had quickly come to her rescue, assuring her it was his fault because he'd put the display too close to the register. Beryl had knelt down to help too, and the man had looked up and quizzically said her name. She'd looked up too and immediately recognized him—it was Micah!

They'd all stood, and he'd hugged them both— which had startled Mia because she didn't remember him—and then they'd chatted for a few minutes. Micah had told them that working at Tranquility had inspired him to start his own business, and because he loved literature, he'd decided to open a bookstore. Beryl had complimented him on his efficient use of the small space, and then she'd suddenly realized how late it was and explained about the appointment. Micah had nodded, and as they'd said good-bye, she'd promised to stop by again. Later that afternoon, however, her mom had received the devastating diagnosis of dementia—most likely Alzheimer's —and their lives had been turned upside down. And with Isak and Rumer both living across the country—Isak in California and Rumer in Montana—Beryl had willingly assumed the role of primary caregiver for their mom. At the same time, she'd continued to run the tea shop, and the combination of responsibilities had consumed so much of her time, energy, and emotions that she'd never been able to keep her promise.

The months had slipped by, and although Beryl didn't know it, Micah's life was turning upside down too. When they'd gone into his store that day, his wife Beth had just reached the third month of a fragile pregnancy—she'd already suffered several miscarriages—and Micah had been bursting with the news, but he'd never had the chance to tell Beryl, and later on, he wondered if she even knew he was married. Two months later, his wife had felt an odd lump in the curve of her breast, but she'd refused to acknowledge it. *It's nothing,* she'd told herself. *It's probably just my body getting ready to nurse . . . and besides, I'm not having any treatments that could jeopardize our baby.*

The following March, Beth had given birth to a little girl, and they'd named her Charlotte—after Beth's grandmother—but their joy had been bittersweet because the worrisome lump was still there, and she'd finally had to tell Micah. She'd assured him it was nothing, but at the same time, she'd prodded and touched the spot so many times—willing it to go away—her skin had become red and irritated.

Beth's diagnosis had been alarming, and she'd suddenly realized what treasure was at stake. There was no way cancer was going to take her life. She was going to live! She was going to be there for her daughter—for her first steps, her first day of school, her birthday parties, her proms, her graduations, her wedding . . . and when she was expecting her own baby. She was going to see her baby *and* her grandbaby grow up.

Beth fought fiercely, accepting every possible treatment—no matter how savagely it ravaged her body. She fought with every fiber of her being, and Micah stayed by her side every step of the way, keeping his anguish and terror buried deep inside.

But on a rainy morning in late June, Beth held her daughter for the last time. She had lived long enough to see her baby's first smile and hear her first, sweet laugh. She knew, deep down, that their little girl would be the light of Micah's life, and she made him promise to be happy . . . and to try to love again. Micah had been inconsolable.

Soon after Beth died, Micah closed his little bookstore. The introduction of e-books and Internet sales was making it very hard for small, independent booksellers to survive. And as if that wasn't enough, he also had a mountain of medical bills to pay. In the end, with his world crashing down around him, Micah moved back to New Hampshire with Charlotte, and his parents welcomed them with open arms.

Beryl had no idea what was going on in Micah's life—she'd been so busy caring for her mom that she sometimes didn't even know what day it was. Alzheimer's had slowly cast its long, dark shadows across her mom's bright, wonderful mind, leaving her confused, disoriented, and silent. And, eventually, her care became so overwhelming that Beryl was forced to move her into a nursing home.

She'd visited as often as she could, bringing Flannery O'Connor, her mom's old bulldog, with her and learning the names of all of the other residents too. But every time she had to say good-bye, it broke her heart. She'd look back to see her mom sitting in her wheelchair at the end of the hall, waving to her and tears would fill her eyes.

About a year later, the nursing home was plagued with a recurring respiratory infection, and although Mia's hadn't seemed too bad, it blossomed overnight into pneumonia, and the next morning, as she was being rushed to the hospital, Beryl tearfully called her sisters.

"Isak and Ru are coming, Mom," Beryl had whispered, touching her mom's soft, white hair.

"They're coming to see you." Tears had streamed down her cheeks. "Please don't go. . . ." With her heart breaking, Beryl had gently kissed the hand that was so like her own and held it against her wet cheek. She'd gazed at her mom's lovely face and whispered, "Oh, Mom, I love you so much."

Within an hour, Mia slipped away.

Everyone who knew the Graham family—and that was just about everyone in town—was saddened to hear about the loss of the cheerful, little lady who ran the tea shop, but Micah was the first to share his condolences. Beryl had been sitting in the airport, waiting for Rumer's flight to get in, and she finally had a minute to check her phone. She'd been surprised to see she had two messages and a text, but she'd been even more surprised to hear his voice. "It's Micah," he'd said, "Micah Coleman." She'd smiled at his clarification because—just as he'd gone on to say in his message—how many Micahs could she possibly know. "I'm so sorry to hear about your mom," he'd said solemnly. "She was a wonderful lady. If there's anything you need . . ."

In the week that followed, Micah had become a fixture in Beryl's life, supplying just about everything she needed. He'd stopped by with an apple crisp that his mom had made and ended up staying for dinner; he'd hauled boxes of clothes to the thrift store in his old Honda wagon; he'd borrowed his dad's lawn mower and mowed the dandelion farm, as Charlotte called it; and he'd stayed to listen with Rumer and Isak as Beryl read a memoir their mom had left behind. And then he'd been able to provide some unexpected insight into the secret relationship about which their mom had written. But the most important thing Micah did that week was simply be there when Beryl needed someone.

After the funeral was over and everyone had gone home, Micah stayed and helped out in the tea shop until Henry—a local boy from the high school—finished his track season. Beryl decided Micah was the perfect temp—not only was he smart, helpful, and cute, but he didn't need to be trained. He already knew *where* everything went and *how* everything worked. And the best thing he knew how to do—at the end of a long day—was turn over the sign in the window, lock the door, close the blinds, and pull the weary shop owner into his arms and hold her tight. And Beryl, at forty-five, couldn't believe how her life had changed.

As they stood together, Beryl's stomach suddenly rumbled.

"Are you hungry?" Micah teased.

Beryl laughed. "I must be. What's your mom making for dinner?"

"I think we're having baked ziti, Caesar salad and garlic bread."

"Mmm, that sounds good."

"Well, my mom's a little worried about cooking pasta for an Italian girl."

Beryl pulled back. "She shouldn't be. I love your mom's cooking!"

He chuckled. "It's probably my fault, because after you made your mom's sauce that time, I talked about it for weeks."

Beryl laughed, recalling the snowy day she'd finally made her mom's gravy for Micah. Even though she practically knew the recipe by heart, she'd carefully studied the faded recipe card that had been passed down through generations of the Gentile family. Making the gravy was always an all-day event because the directions—written in her grandmother's handwriting—explicitly said, "Simmer forever!"

That snowy Sunday morning, she'd skipped church and chopped, browned, diced, and carefully measured all the ingredients, and then she'd set the stovetop to simmer. Late in the afternoon, Micah had appeared with a bottle of wine, and when he opened the door, the wonderful aroma of tomatoes—which she'd canned the previous summer from a bumper crop of Romas—onions, green peppers, garlic, fresh basil, parsley, brown sugar, sausage, and beef wafted through the kitchen. "Oh, my," he'd murmured, taking off his jacket.

Beryl had lifted the top off the pot and spicy steam had drifted through the kitchen. She'd smiled seductively. "My mom always called it 'mantrap gravy.' "

Micah had laughed and leaned over her shoulder, breathing in slowly. "Mmm . . . consider me happily snared."

It had been snowing lightly all day, but after Micah's arrival, the snow had really started to come down. He'd gone out on the porch to get more firewood, and when he stepped back in—not a minute later—he'd looked like a snowman. "Is this supposed to keep up?" he'd asked.

"I don't know. I haven't seen the weather."

He added several logs to the cheerful fire crackling in the fireplace and then opened the wine. As she stirred in the spaghetti, he'd handed her a glass. "Well, if it does, you might have to put up with an overnight guest."

"Well, I hope he brought his sleeping bag," she'd teased.

In the warm, flickering candlelight, Micah had tasted the famous sauce for the very first time. "Mmm," he murmured, slurping his spaghetti. "What kind of meat is in it?"

Beryl opened her napkin. "Ground sirloin and sausage."

"Wow," he said softly.

Beryl sprinkled freshly grated Romano across her plate and then deftly twirled her fork into her spoon, neatly swirling a ladylike portion of angel hair around its prongs.

"You're good," Micah said, watching her and obviously impressed. "I never learned how to do that."

"I can tell," she'd said with a laugh.

He'd grinned, as Beryl took a sip of her wine.

After the kitchen was cleaned up, Micah had turned on the outside light to check on the snow and realized it was still very much a blizzard outside. He'd called his mom to tell her—as long as she didn't mind looking after Charlotte—that he was probably going to stay over, and Maddie assured him she didn't mind one bit. In fact, her granddaughter was already sound asleep.

Beryl and Micah had settled in front of the fire with the last of the wine. They'd watched the fire crackle cheerfully and listened to the fierce wind blowing snow against the windows outside, and they'd luxuriated in the warm comfort of being cozily inside together. Micah had pulled Beryl into his arms, gently laid her back on the rug in front of the fire, and they'd made love for the very first time. The next morning, he'd asked her to marry him.

"That was a fun night," Beryl said with a smile.

"It was," Micah agreed, laughing. "I will never forget that gravy. It was amazing."

"Hey!" Beryl said, sounding wounded.

"Well, it was a mantrap," he said, laughing and pulling her against him. "And as much fun as it would be to let you have your way with me now, we probably shouldn't keep my parents waiting. But maybe I'll let you later," he added, kissing her softly.

"Mmm, that would be nice," she murmured, feeling how aroused he was. "Let's not forget the pie . . ."

23

As Laney buttoned her blouse, she glanced down at the area from which the biopsy had just been taken. "Maybe I should just have a double mastectomy like Angelina," she mumbled, "then I won't have to worry anymore." She knew one thing: she was getting tired of buttoning her blouse after being prodded and examined. And she couldn't wait until summer—when her attire would consist exclusively of T-shirts, tank tops, shorts, bathing suits, and an occasional sundress.

There was only one more week of school, but everyone considered it the longest week of the year—the time for learning had passed and the kids were ready for vacation. In fact, most were already mentally checked out, and Laney was ready to join them. She thought about the coming week's schedule: Monday was Field Day, weather permitting; Tuesday was their class party; Wednesday was the all-school assembly with the ever-funny Bill Harley—an event her kids couldn't wait for because they'd already memorized Bill's silly song about the pea on his plate; and finally, Thursday would bring the always emotional and much anticipated Moving Up Day when all the kids brought in thank-you gifts and the sweet cards they'd made, hugged their old teachers good-bye, and then trooped down the hall, looking excitedly, and anxiously, for their new ones.

As Laney stepped out into the bright sunshine, she caught herself singing Asher's favorite Bill Harley song, "You're in Trouble," and in spite of herself, she smiled—maybe she *was* taking life a little too seriously. She'd even woken up in the middle of the night, clenching her teeth, and now her jaw ached.

She climbed into her hot car, cranked the AC all the way up, and texted Noah to make sure all the boys were where they were supposed to be. She was on her way to the teachers' party, and she'd only be able to relax if Noah had the home front under control. She was relieved when he wrote back almost immediately: ALL'S WELL—HAVE FUN! ☺

Laney pulled open the door of The Lobster Claw Restaurant, humming the ringtone on Gabe's phone. Somehow her creative son had figured out how to record the restaurant's radio ad, and now, whenever his phone rang, the cheerful jingle filled the air. "The Cape in the summer is magic. The sun and the sea and the wind on the shore. These days were made for families. That's what we're here for." She smiled. Gabe said he liked hearing the song when he was away at school because it reminded him of home, and besides, his class-mates all thought it was a hoot.

"Are you with Eastham Elementary?" the hostess asked, looking up.

Laney nodded and then saw her best friend Mara—one of the other first-grade teachers—coming down the stairs. "Hey, Laney! I wasn't sure if you were coming, but I saved you a seat. Dottie already has everyone rolling on the floor, and she's only had one drink!"

Laney smiled as she followed Mara up the stairs to the Surfboat Room. "I'm going to miss Dottie so much."

"Me too, but she deserves it."

"I don't know how she did it. I don't think I'd last fifty years."

All the teachers stood to give Laney a hug, and Dottie held her at arm's length and searched her eyes. "How'd it go, dearie?" she asked gently.

Laney looked puzzled. "Fine?" she said uncertainly, looking over Dottie's shoulder at Mara, who shrugged and tried to look equally puzzled.

As soon as Laney could break free from Dottie,

she confronted Mara. "You're the only one I told," she said in a hushed voice.

"I'm sorry, Lane, but she asked me where you were," Mara whispered remorsefully. "I didn't realize it was a secret."

"Mar, I haven't even told Noah . . ."

"Don't worry, Lane, I'm sure Dottie won't say anything."

Just then, another first-grade teacher, Pam Travis, sat down across from them and smiled sympathetically at Laney. "Lane, I just want you to know, I'm keeping you in my prayers."

Laney practically choked on her water. "Thanks, Pam," she sputtered, "but there's really nothing to pray about. Everything's fine." She gave Mara a wilting look.

"Well, that's good," Pam continued, "because one of my mom's friends had to go for a biopsy, and she ended up with stage four. It was awful. She didn't last six months."

Laney blinked and wished she could go home.

Just then, a waitress came around, taking drink orders, and Mara ordered a Cape Codder. "Want one, Lane?"

But Laney shook her head. "No, thanks. I'm just going to have water."

"Laney, I'm really sorry," Mara said softly, her eyes glistening, which only made Laney feel worse.

"It's okay, Mar, don't worry about it." Laney

knew her friend meant well, and if she excused herself, Mara's evening would be ruined too, so she stayed, but when her baked scallops came, she barely touched them.

Finally, it was time for Dottie to open her gifts—many of which had a retirement theme, including a whole stack of beach novels. "I love to read, but I've never had the time, so I'm looking forward to these. Especially this one!" She held up a paperback with a very muscular, very tan lifeguard on the cover, and all the ladies hooted.

"Oh, Dottie, you're too much!" Shirley said, making everyone laugh all over again.

"They're both too much," Mara whispered, knowing Shirley, the other kindergarten teacher, would be retiring soon too.

Laney nodded and then sighed. "I think I'm going to head out. . . ."

"But we haven't had dessert."

"I'm not very hungry," Laney said, giving her friend a hug and wishing everyone else a good night. As she left the room, their hushed voices followed her.

Laney looked up at the slate sky as she walked across the parking lot. Her heart felt just as heavy as those dark clouds looked, and she wished she hadn't confided in her friend. Now she *had* to tell Noah—if he heard the news from someone else, he'd be crushed.

The air was ominously still as she got in her car,

but by the time she pulled out onto Route 6, it had begun to stir, and as she turned onto Ocean View Drive, gusts of wind were thrashing the trees, sending leaves spiraling and spinning in front of her headlights. Finally, she pulled into their driveway, thankful that a tree limb hadn't fallen on her car; almost immediately, she realized E's car was gone, and she wondered where he was on this stormy night. She hurried toward the house, and lightning split the clouds; a second later, a huge clap of thunder exploded above her head. Almost tripping on the walkway, she saw a shadow of gray fly up under the shed roof, and she stopped to look. A glint of resolute and dutiful black eyes blinked at her; she looked in the nest and saw five tiny dark bundles of feathers. She backed away slowly, smiling, as the first fat drops of rain splashed her shoulders.

"I'm home," she called, setting her things down. The house was oddly quiet, except for Mennie who struggled to his feet and padded over to greet her, his whole hind end wagging. "Hi there, old pie," she whispered, kissing his snowy brow. "Where is everybody?" She looked down the hall and saw the light on in Noah's study.

With Mennie at her heels, she walked quietly toward the light and leaned against the doorframe. "Hey," she said softly.

Noah looked up in surprise. "Hey," he said, taking off his glasses. "I didn't hear you come in."

"Probably 'cuz there's a storm brewing."

"I know. They said on the news we were going to get walloped, but hopefully it will cool things off a little."

"I hope so."

"How was the party?"

"Good."

"What'd you have?"

"My usual," she said with a smile.

"Scallops and Cape Codders?"

"Just scallops."

Noah frowned. "No celebratory indulgences?"

"No." She paused. "Where is everybody?"

"Asher and Halle are in bed."

"Already?"

"Yup. He said he wasn't hungry and then he went upstairs, and when I looked in on him, he was sound asleep."

Laney frowned. "I hope he's not coming down with something."

"I hope not. And as for everyone else, Seth and Ben are on PlayStation, and Gabe is reading."

"Where's E?"

"Chloe came home, so he went to see her."

"Did you ask him to try to be home at a decent time?"

"I did."

Laney sat on the couch and picked up one of the pillows. "What happened here?" she asked, eyeing the stuffing coming out of the corner.

"I got hungry," he said with a grin.

Laney rolled her eyes. "So do you think they're getting too serious?"

"I don't think they're *getting* too serious. I think they *are* too serious."

"They're too young. . . ."

"And how old were we?"

Laney smiled. "We were too young too."

"Well, he's pretty smitten, just like I was. . . ."

"Was?" Laney asked.

Noah's eyes sparkled mischievously. "And they've known each other forever. Besides, any girl who names a puppy Amen and is able to recite 'Jabberwocky' has something special going on."

"I know. I'm just not ready for this. And I hope they're being careful."

"That's all we can do," he said, "hope and pray." He sat down next to her. "So did Dottie like your gift?"

"She did," Laney said, remembering Dottie's happy surprise when she'd opened the gift cards from the first-grade teachers—it was for a spa weekend in Lenox. "I could use a gift like that," she added wistfully.

Noah put his arm around her. "Well, maybe after you teach for fifty years, you'll get one."

"*If* I live that long . . ."

Noah frowned. "I'm just teasing."

"I know," she said, closing her eyes.

"Are you still stuck in worry mode?"

Laney nodded, and then shook her head, tears stinging her eyes. "I didn't want to say anything until I knew for sure. . . ."

A shadow fell across Noah's face as he watched her, and she took a deep breath. "Okay, so I had my mammogram last week, and then I had to go back for an ultrasound because the results were inconclusive because I have dense tissue," she explained, purposely leaving out the word *breast*. "But that was inconclusive too . . . so today I had to go for a noninvasive proced—"

"A biopsy?" Noah asked in alarm.

Laney nodded, and Noah shook his head in disbelief. "Why didn't you tell me?"

"I didn't want you to worry. I wanted to be sure."

"Lane, we're in this together. . . ."

Tears spilled down her cheeks, and she tried to brush them away but they just kept coming. "I'm sorry, Noah. . . . I just want it to go away."

Noah didn't say anything. He just put his fist against his chin and stared at the light on his desk. Finally, he wiped his eyes with his thumb and fingers.

"I'm sorry," Laney said again softly. "I should've told you."

Noah turned to look at her, and she could see the pain in his eyes. "I asked you outright the other night . . . and you told me nothing was wrong." He shook his head. "Lane, I want so badly to take you in my arms and tell you everything's going to be okay. But now . . . I feel like you purposely kept this from me." He looked away, wiping his eyes again. "I'm probably overreacting, but you know how I feel about this kind of thing. How many times have we drilled it into the boys' heads?"

"I know. You hate it. But this isn't like that. I wanted to tell you. . . . I even tried to tell you . . . but the words just wouldn't come out."

Noah stood up and walked over to his desk. "So when do you get the results?" he asked, sounding like she was the only one who *would* be getting the results.

"Next week, I guess," Laney said, her heart aching.

Noah saved the sermon he'd been working on and closed his laptop. Then he turned off his desk light and leaned on the back of his chair, looking out into the darkness. Finally, he turned to her, his eyes still glistening. "Lane, if anything were to happen to you, I don't know how I'd go on. Don't you see? Everything that happens to you . . . happens to me."

Laney bit her lip. "Honestly, Noah, I just didn't want you to worry."

"Well, thanks for looking out for me."

"You know, if you think about it, you forget to tell me stuff all the time."

"This is different, Lane. *You* didn't forget. You

purposely didn't say anything." He paused. "I'm heading up."

"Okay," Laney said sadly, feeling the sting of his words. "Good night."

"Good night."

Laney listened to the thunder rumbling through the heavens and realized how much Noah was like her grandfather. A long-ago memory from her childhood slipped into her mind. . . .

She must've been six or seven at the time, and she'd been standing on a chair, admiring her grandparents' twenty-fifth anniversary plate. And then, because she couldn't really see it that well, she decided to take it out of the china closet for a closer look . . . and just as she'd gotten it over her grandmother's Hummel figurine of a little girl feeding chickens and ever so carefully through the door, it had somehow slipped from her hands, and Lyle, who was in the next room, ran in to see what happened. He found her sitting on the chair with her hands over her face, and the plate in a million pieces on the floor. In a worried, hushed voice, he told her to go hide in the barn and he would clean it up. An hour later, Gramp started looking for her; he called everyone—including Uncle Luke and all the neighbors—but Lyle never spoke up. Finally, Uncle Luke found her hiding in the loft of the barn, and somehow, later on, Gramp found out Lyle had known all along, and he ended up in more trouble than she was. She got a big hug from Gramp—even though the plate was broken—but Lyle had to sit on the porch the whole next day and think about what he'd done. She tried to tell Gramp it was all her fault—that Lyle had been protecting her—but Gramp wouldn't hear it.

"That boy needs to learn to come out with it," he said sternly, "no matter what the consequences." Lyle did learn, and Laney would never forget the tears of relief that had streamed down his brown face when Gramp finally took him aside and talked to him . . . and hugged him too. There was no greater relief than being forgiven, and she knew in her heart that Noah would forgive her too . . . eventually.

Laney listened to the torrential rain spilling over the gutters, and then she heard an odd sound coming from the kitchen. She went to investigate and realized that one of the phoebes was frantically fluttering against the window. It was ten o'clock at night—how come she wasn't tucked into her nest with her babies? Laney turned on the outside light, pushed open the screen door, and peered outside, wondering if she'd become disoriented. The bedraggled bird was perched on top of the railing, and it blinked at her and then flew to the back of the shed. Laney stepped out into the rain to make sure everything was okay, and although it was dark, she could see the nest. And now the phoebe was on the edge of it. "I wish

I knew what was wrong," she said, backing away. She hurried inside, and as she slipped off her wet shoes, she noticed Lucky curled up on the couch. He opened one eye and blinked at her.

Noah was snoring peacefully when she climbed into bed, and she listened to his steady breathing and wished she could fall asleep that easily. She'd often wondered, as she lay in bed at night, if her husband's ability to fall asleep before his head hit the pillow was because he was so well versed at giving his problems over to God. She tried to give Him her problems too, but then she always pulled them back—lest they get away! On this night, she stared into the darkness, fretting about the odd behavior of the little bird and hoping E would get home safely. She also prayed she'd wake up to the smell of coffee and pancakes—a sure sign that Noah had forgiven her.

24

"So, Dad," Micah said, reaching for the garlic bread. "I've been telling Beryl about the famous Coleman family chowder, and I was wondering if you might be willing to make a big pot of it for the clambake."

Asa smiled. "I can't see why not. In fact, I'd be honored." Then he eyed his granddaughter. "But only if Charlotte will help shuck the clams."

"I will!" Charlotte said, beaming.

Her grandfather nodded. "And maybe we can get Asher to help too."

"Thanks, Dad," Micah said. And then he added conspiratorially, "Then Beryl will realize she's not the only one with delicious old family recipes." He winked at her as he said this and she laughed.

"This baked ziti is delicious," Beryl said, turning to Maddie.

"That's very kind of you, hon, although I'm sure it's nothing like your mom's. Micah raved about her sauce for weeks after you made it last winter. In fact, I was wondering if you might share the recipe with me sometime."

"I'd be happy to."

Maddie took a sip of her wine. "So how are the wedding plans coming?"

Beryl nodded and held up one finger. "Good," she said after swallowing.

"I think a clambake is a wonderful idea, and by the middle of August, the local corn will be in season too. Have you decided if you're going to use a caterer?"

"We are," Micah confirmed. "Laney gave us the name of a friend of hers—Lucy Paxton, who has a catering company called A Moveable Feast."

Asa chuckled. "What a great name."

"I know. Anyway, she comes highly recommended, and we want to make it as easy as possible for Laney, especially since Noah said yes to the wedding without asking her first."

Beryl looked up in surprise. "He did?"

Micah nodded. "He constantly forgets to tell her stuff. Or he assumes she'll love whatever idea he has, and she's always so forgiving and easygoing about it. She truly is a saint. He even brought home that puppy without asking her."

"I didn't know that," Maddie said. "Although that puppy is cute—I can't imagine she'd be able to say no."

Asa leaned back in his chair. "Have you seen her?"

"No, not yet," Micah said, taking a bite of his bread.

Asa nodded toward Charlotte and smiled. "Well, you-know-who will fall in love immediately. In fact, you should ask Noah if there are any left in the litter."

Micah looked at his dad over Charlotte's head, hoping she hadn't realized what he was suggesting. "I think we have enough going on, Dad. Besides we already have Flan and Thoreau," he added, referring to the two senior citizens Beryl had inherited from her mom. Flannery was her mom's beloved, homely old bulldog and Thoreau was her sweet, orange tiger cat.

"Oh, yeah, I forgot about those two old coots," Asa said with a chuckle. "Well, a puppy would definitely put a hop in their step," he added, his blue eyes sparkling mischievously. "After all, look how much Flan loves Harper!"

"Can we, Dad?" Charlotte piped brightly.

Micah eyed his father and then patiently explained to his soon-to-be seven-year-old daughter why a puppy wasn't a good idea at the moment. Beryl smiled at the way he handled it— he was such a good dad and she could only hope to be as good a mom.

"Anyway," Micah said, turning back to his parents. "We haven't had a chance to get to the Cape, but we have to soon because we need to meet with the caterer and finalize the menu. We also need to talk to Laney and Noah about the rest of the arrangements. I'm thinking we should get a tent in case the weather doesn't cooperate, and if we're going to get a tent, it would be fun to get a dance floor too." He paused. "We're also going to ask Asher if he'd be the ring boy."

Maddie smiled. "He'd love that! He's such a gentle soul—just like his mom. Did Dad tell you he recited all of 'Jesse James' the other night?"

"No," Micah said, recalling the familiar poem his dad used to recite to them when they were younger.

"Yep," Asa said with a nod. "Not a single mistake."

"That's amazing," Micah said, obviously impressed.

"Laney says he's been having a hard time at school though," Maddie continued. "An older boy on the bus has been pushing him around and calling him names. He even broke his glasses."

"Oh, no," Beryl said. "That's awful."

"Did they call the school?" Micah asked.

"Well, they know the boy's mother, and Noah tried to call her but he was never able to get through, and then the boy had some kind of altercation with his older brother and they've both been kicked off the bus. In fact, I think the older one has actually been expelled."

Beryl took a sip of her wine. "I don't know why some kids are so mean."

"It begins at home," Asa said matter-of-factly. "In all our years of teaching," he said, nodding to Maddie, "it's the kids that come from broken homes or have parents that don't discipline them that get in the most trouble."

"That's not entirely true," Maddie said, eyeing him. "We've both had kids from the same family who have parents that are involved"—she looked at Micah and Beryl—"but then one child can be as good as gold and the other can be Mr. Mischief. It depends on their personalities."

Beryl laughed. "That's like my sisters and me. We came from the same home, but we're as different as can be . . . and Isak was definitely Miss Mischief!"

Asa laughed. "That's true, your sister did have a mischievous streak," he said, remembering Beryl's older sister from his tenth-grade English class and the cross-country team he coached.

"But I still think home life plays a big part . . . in most cases," he added, eyeing his wife, waiting for her to agree.

"Most," she conceded, "but not all."

Beryl turned to Maddie. "Micah said you used to work with special needs kids."

"I did. My older brother Tim had Down Syndrome and he inspired me."

Beryl nodded. "Micah told me about Tim," she said softly. "Did he tell you that Henry Finch works in the tea shop now?"

"He did. How's he doing?"

"Really well. He's very conscientious."

"I've known Henry since he was a little boy. He was in my Excel preschool class—and this was before autism was as widely understood. His mom, Callie, is the nicest person."

"She is. She picks him up every day, and Honey, his golden retriever, is always waiting for him. Callie told me Honey has made a huge difference in Henry's life."

Maddie nodded. "Well, when Henry was little, he didn't talk at all, but then a yellow Lab named Springer came into his life, and they developed a very special bond. It helped him open up. Animals have an amazing effect on kids with autism. There's even a place in New York—Guiding Eyes for the Blind—that specializes in guide dogs, but some of the dogs that aren't cut out to be guide dogs are now trained to work with kids who have autism. The program is called Heeling Autism. They've had some remarkable results."

Beryl nodded.

"Back to the wedding," Maddie said with a smile. "Any idea how many people?"

"Well, I wish we could invite everyone," Micah replied, "but even if we only invite family, the number would hit sixty-five, and I don't think Noah's septic tank could handle that."

"They make fancy porta-potties now," Asa offered with a grin. "You could get a couple of those."

"That's a thought," Micah said with a laugh. "But I also don't want to put a strain on their marriage. We'll have to get a sense of things when we see them."

"What else are you going to have at the clambake?" Maddie asked.

Micah sopped up the last of his sauce with a piece of bread. "The traditional fare—steamers, mussels, lobster tails, red potatoes, corn on the cob . . . and filet mignon for anyone who's not fond of seafood."

"And a cake?"

"Nope." Micah grinned. "Laney's going to make her grandmother's peach cobbler."

"Mmm . . . that sounds good," Maddie said with a smile.

Micah nodded. "Noah is trying to convince Laney to go to Georgia to get the peaches so he can put in a new kitchen while she's gone."

"Does she know that?"

Micah laughed. "What do you think?"

Maddie shook her head. "Well, you guys let us know if you need help with anything. Dad's happy to make the chowder, but we can also help take care of some of the expenses. Maybe the bar and the dance floor? By the way, if you're going to have a dance floor, you must be planning on music. Are you getting a band?"

"Nope. We're going to see if Gabe would DJ. He seems to know a lot about music."

"Well, it sounds like it's all coming together," Maddie said as she stood to clear. "Oh!" She looked at Beryl. "Did you get a dress?"

"Not yet," Beryl said. "As soon as Laney's done with school, my sisters and I are going to meet her in Boston. And I was going to see if you'd like to come too."

"That would be fun," Maddie said. "Just let me know when." She looked over at Asa and realized his face was very pale.

Micah followed her gaze. "What's the matter, Dad?"

Asa squeezed his eyes shut. "I don't know. I seem to be getting a headache."

"Do you want to lie down?"

"No, no, I'll be fine," he said, rubbing his temple.

A shadow of worry fell across Maddie's face, but she didn't say anything. "Who'd like coffee?"

"I would," Micah said, standing to help clear. He looked at Beryl. "Tea?"

"Whatever's easier," Beryl said.

"It's not hard to put on a kettle," Micah said.

"Okay," she said with a smile. "Tea."

"Dad?"

"I'll have some coffee. Maybe it'll help my head."

Micah reached for his dad's plate, but then realized he'd hardly touched his food. "Are you finished?"

Asa nodded, and Micah took his plate and followed Maddie into the kitchen. At his heels was Harper, who'd been patiently waiting for a tidbit. Micah scraped a little ziti from his dad's plate into her bowl, and then set the plates on the counter and reached for his mom's tea kettle. "What's up with Dad?"

Maddie busied herself making coffee and avoided her son's eyes. "He's been getting some headaches," she said. "What kind of tea would Ber like?"

"What do you have?"

"The usual—Earl Grey, Darjeeling, Lady Earl . . ."

"Let me ask." A moment later, he reappeared and reached for the Darjeeling. "So has he been to the doctor?"

"He has. This blueberry pie looks like a picture," she said admiringly. "Did Beryl make it?" she asked, rummaging through the utensil drawer for the pie spatula and the ice-cream scoop.

"She did. *And* what did the doctor say?" Micah pressed.

"Tylenol helps. Can you bring the whipped cream and the plates?" she called as she disappeared into the dining room with the pie.

Micah got out the whipped cream, picked up the plates, and followed her, and because he wasn't getting any answers from his mother, he turned to his dad. "How long have you been getting head-aches?"

Asa looked up, and Maddie realized that the color had returned to his tan cheeks. "All my life," he said with a grin. Then he added, "Wow! That pie looks like a picture!"

❧ 25 ❧

"I can't, E," Chloe said sadly.

"That's okay, Chlo. We don't have to."

"I'm sorry."

"Don't be," he said, wrapping his arms around her.

"I couldn't wait to get home . . . to be with you again . . ."

"Shh. . . ." He pulled her blouse closed and gently kissed her forehead. "It's totally okay."

Chloe leaned against him, tears welling up in

her eyes. "I keep having these waves of sadness wash over me, and I feel like I'm drowning. It's crazy—I'm fine one minute, and then I'll remember he's gone . . . and I lose it all over again. I thought it would be easier by now."

"It'll get easier," E said softly. "A day will come and you'll think of him, and the memory will make you smile."

Chloe shook her head. "I don't know if I'll ever get to that point."

They were both quiet, lost in thought—Chloe thinking of her grandfather, and E recalling the blur of that morning. . . .

It had been hot, and the beach had been packed. He'd been on the chair alone for the first hour, before the crowds had really started to arrive, and then, Jim, another lifeguard, had climbed up with two water bottles and joined him. The tide had been coming in, and just as he'd opened his water bottle, a rogue wave had crashed onto shore, surprising everyone and washing away several sand castles, including one that two brothers had been working on all morning. He'd immediately scanned the water, counting swimmers, and then, as was protocol, he'd checked the water's edge, making sure everyone was accounted for, but something was wrong. *Where was the little boy who'd been collecting stones in a yellow pail all morning?*

At the very same moment, a woman had stood with her hand shielding her eyes. "Tyler!" she'd called.

He'd scanned the water's edge again, trying to get a visual. *Where is he?* He'd felt his heart start to race. He'd blasted his whistle, signaling an emergency, and shouted to Jim as he jumped from the chair. "Look for a little boy in a red suit!"

He'd raced across the beach, and as he reached the woman, he saw a yellow pail bobbing up and down in the waves, taunting him; the woman had followed his gaze and cried out in alarm. By this time, the two older boys were by their mother's side, calling their brother's name, and people all along the beach had stopped what they were doing and looked up. "He was just here!" the mother cried. "I only looked away for a second."

E had scanned the water again . . . and then, in the white foam of a receding wave, he saw a blur of red and tan. He'd jumped through the waves, lifted the small, lifeless body from the surf, carried him back to shore, and laid him on the sand. The little boy's face had been blue, and his limbs had hung limply. The crowd had continued to grow, surrounding them—suffocating E—and as he'd checked to see if the little boy was breathing or had a pulse, in the back of his mind, he'd heard the mother screaming.

"Focus!" he'd told himself . . . and then whispered a prayer. "God, please help."

He'd checked the boy's mouth and pressed on his chest. "Breathe," he'd commanded as he leaned over to breathe for him. And then, suddenly, a spout of water had dribbled from the little boy's mouth, and he'd turned him on his side and more gray water had drained out. The boy had sputtered and started crying, and the woman had rushed forward to hold him. As more emergency personnel arrived, E had stepped back, his heart still pounding, his eyes glistening.

E looked down at Chloe's strawberry-blond hair, pulled loose from her ponytail, and realized she was sound asleep. He hadn't had the chance to tell her about the rescue, and now it seemed like ages ago. The boy's mother had tearfully hugged him and repeatedly thanked him, and when he'd dropped his favorite Red Sox hat on the little boy's head, the boy had looked up at him with his eyes full of life, and whispered, "Thanks, Elijah."

Rescues were not uncommon on the busy Coast Guard Beach, but they always set him back on his heels and left him feeling emotionally spent. In the four years he'd been lifeguarding, he'd witnessed more than one drowning—although it had never happened on his watch—and he prayed it never would.

You never know, he thought, closing his eyes wearily.

❧ 26 ❧

"Ready?" Maddie asked, looking up as Asa came out from radiation.

He nodded, rolling down his sleeves. "Are you cold?" he asked, shivering.

"No," she said, closing her book, "but you must be. How else do you feel?"

"Okay," he said, rubbing his head, "just cold."

"Well, the air conditioning is on in here. You won't be cold when you get outside."

Asa nodded, walking beside her. "I actually don't feel that bad."

"Well, give it time. It might not've hit you yet."

"Only five more to go. Do you realize I'll be done right before the wedding?"

"Then we'll have two reasons to celebrate," Maddie said. She looked over at him. "Do you feel like getting a bite of lunch?"

"Sure. Why don't we go to that little outdoor café in Hay Market—the one that has the Waldorf salad you like so much."

"Sounds good to me," Maddie said with a smile, starting to believe that maybe the doctor was right —maybe they would be able to go on living their lives.

By the time they got home, it was late afternoon. "Harper probably has her legs crossed," Asa said, looking at the time.

"Mmm," Maddie agreed. "You know, Micah said he'd be happy to come over and let her out. It's really not fair to keep her waiting so long."

Asa looked over. "I don't want to ask Micah, and I'm sure Harper will survive. You don't need to come every time. I can go by myself."

Maddie sighed as she got out of the car. "I don't think it's a good idea for you to go by yourself, and I also still think it's wrong to not tell them."

Asa shook his head. "Micah has been through enough heartache. I don't want to spoil his happiness."

"That's how Beth felt too. She didn't want to spoil his happiness either."

"Well, she didn't tell *anyone* . . . at least I told *you*," he said, putting his arm around her. "And *we're* doing something about it."

Maddie smiled. It was true. They were doing something about it, and hopefully that *something* would work.

Asa opened the door, and Harper greeted them happily, wiggling all around. "Hey, there, missy," Asa said. "Why don't you go get busy. Your mother thinks you can't hold your water, but you and I both know she's the one with *that* problem."

Laughing at the truth of his statement, Maddie hurried down the hall.

❧ 27 ❧

The sun was streaming through the bedroom windows when Laney opened her eyes. She looked over at Noah's side of the bed and saw the sheets strewn about. Then she looked at the clock—how had she slept so late? She remembered the pouring rain from the night before and felt the cool ocean breeze drifting in, rustling the curtains. What a difference a day makes.

She pulled on her robe and shuffled down the hall, looking in the boys' rooms as she passed. Ben and Seth were still sound asleep in their bunk beds and Asher was in the small twin bed against the opposite wall with Halle curled up beside him, but when she saw Laney in the doorway, her tail started to thump. "Do you need to go out?" she whispered, and the puppy yawned, hopped off the bed, and padded over. "C'mon, then." She glanced into the older boys' room as they walked past, but then she backed up and frowned. Gabe's bed was a mess, but E's was still neatly made . . . which meant he was either super-organized or he hadn't slept in it.

She heard voices and followed Halle down the stairs. Gabe was standing in front of the refrigerator with the open orange juice container in his hand and E was leaning against the counter with a large glass of water. They were both wearing running shorts and dripping with sweat. "Hi, Mom," Gabe said with a grin as Halle started pulling on his shoelaces.

"You know," she said, eying him, "if one of you comes down with the plague, you're all going to get it."

"People don't get the plague from drinking out of the same container," Gabe said matter-of-factly. "They get it from being bitten by insects."

E took a long drink of his water and swallowed. "Actually, that's not true," he corrected. "You can also get it from being near infected people who are coughing and sneezing, so I'm sure you can get it from drinking from the same container."

"Well, Asher won't get it," Gabe assured her. "He'd never drink from the container. So you'll always have one son."

Laney rolled her eyes and turned to E. "Well . . . ?"

"I know . . . I know. I'm sorry I didn't call, but I fell asleep. I already talked to Dad."

"And he's okay with that?"

"Yup."

"Boy, Mom," Gabe said. "I hope you remember this moment when I use a lame excuse like that."

Laney eyed him. "I probably won't remember, so don't even try." She looked out the kitchen window. "Is Dad here?"

"Nope. He went to the church. He said he had to

finish his sermon, and it would be easier there."

Laney looked around the kitchen. The coffeepot was clean . . . and empty, and it didn't look like there was much hope of pancakes either. It didn't even look like he'd had a bowl of cereal. *I guess he's not over it,* she thought glumly. "C'mon, Halle," she said. Then she looked at the boys again. "Do you know if Mennie's been out or had breakfast?"

"I imagine Dad took care of him," E offered, "but I'm not positive."

"He usually leaves a note," she said, glancing around. Then she eyed their older dog. "Have you had your breakfast yet, mister?"

Mennie thumped his tail, and Gabe chuckled. "He wouldn't tell you if he had."

Laney briefly considered calling Noah, but decided against it—if her husband couldn't bother to leave a note, Mennie could have two breakfasts. "Let's go," she said, leading the way with the two dogs happily following her.

"So, Mom, are you making pancakes?" Gabe asked.

"Nope, that's Dad's job," she said as she pushed open the screen door, "but I will make your lunch."

"We have to be at work by nine."

"Okay, I'll be right back in."

"Shotty first shower," Gabe said.

"No," E replied, moving toward the stairs.

"You take too long and you use all the hot water."

Gabe started to move toward the stairs too. "No, I don't." He reached for his brother's arm, trying to gain an advantage, and laughing, they tumbled over each other up the stairs.

"Someone's going to get hurt," Laney called, but all she heard was bumping and laughter. She shook her head as the screen door closed behind her.

The world was wet and glistening with fat, heavy raindrops hanging from every surface, but the oppressive humidity had finally pushed out to sea. Laney looked up at the blue sky and thought about Noah. And, for the millionth time, she wished she'd told him at the outset.

She watched the dogs nosing around the yard, investigating all the new scents that had been created overnight, and then Mennie stopped to stuff his nose deep into the daylilies behind the shed. She frowned. "Mennie, come away from there." The old dog pulled his head out and gazed at her. She walked across the wet grass in her bare feet, and as she drew closer, she saw one of the phoebes snatch a moth in midair and fly up to the ledge with it. But then the little bird just perched on the edge of the nest, cocking its head. "What's the matter?" she asked softly. She stepped closer, and it flew up to the roof. Laney looked in the nest and then covered her mouth in dismay. "Oh, no," she cried. She gently parted the lilies and then looked all around the shed. She even looked in the shed, but there was no sign of the babies . . . *anywhere*—where could they be?

Laney looked up at their mother. "I'm so sorry," she said softly. "What happened?" The little bird cocked its head and blinked at her, and Laney's heart ached. The bird had been so frantic the night before. It was almost as if it had been pleading for help, but Laney hadn't understood . . . *and* she hadn't helped. She'd just gone to bed. Now the babies weren't anywhere—what in the world could have happened to them?

With a heavy heart, Laney fed the dogs. Then she pulled out the boys' coolers and filled them with ham and cheese sandwiches, pickles, cookies, chips, water bottles, a Coke for E, and a Sprite for Gabe. As she closed the tops, they came down the stairs wearing their red lifeguard suits and white T-shirts. "Don't forget to wear sunscreen," she said.

Gabe put in two Pop-Tarts. "We won't," he said. "Forget, that is."

"And drink plenty of water."

"We will," E said, picking up the coolers. He smiled at his mom. "We didn't just start this job yesterday, you know."

"I know. I'm just reminding you."

"Are you going for a run today, Mom?" Gabe asked, handing a Pop-Tart to his brother.

"Maybe," she said with a smile.

"You don't have any excuses today. It's not too hot, *and* you don't have to work," E pointed out.

Laney knew her runner sons were giving her a hard time because she hadn't run in over a week, and every time they asked her, she had some kind of excuse.

"Maybe I will," she said with a smile. "You never know."

" 'K . . . we're gonna ask you later," they warned.

" 'K," she answered in the same singsong tone. And as soon as they left, she went upstairs to change into her running clothes.

❧ 28 ❧

As the congregation closed their hymnals, Laney felt jostling in the pew beside her. She looked over to see her two middle sons trying to gain possession of the only stubby pencil in the rack. She gave them a wilting look, and Ben let go, but Seth, looking vindicated and pleased, proceeded to draw on his program. She sighed. E and Gabe were both working, leaving her with only three to shepherd, but even so, two of the three couldn't seem to behave. In fact, they were acting like two-year-olds!

Noah finished reading a passage from the New Testament about the last supper, and then invited the congregation to join him in prayer. Everyone bowed their heads, except Laney, who was lost in her own thoughts.

Noah had been quiet all day, and she looked up to watch him, standing behind the pulpit with his head bowed. His blond hair had started to come in darker underneath, and it was showing signs of silver in his sideburns. She listened to the sincerity in his solemn voice as he prayed, on behalf of the congregation, for forgiveness.

"Amen," he said finally, looking up. He shuffled some papers and took a sip of water.

"Recently," he began, "I came across a story about a young mother who was tucking her six-year-old son into bed, and as she did, she asked him, 'Do you know what it means to be a Christian?' The boy looked up at her, and with all the innocence of a child, answered, 'Of course. You look at the cross, you think about what Jesus did, and then you become one of God's guys.' In that little fellow's mind, it couldn't have been simpler.

"Oftentimes, though, being one of 'God's guys' means stepping out of one's comfort zone, crossing that boundary, and sharing a bit of oneself. Today is one of those times . . ."

Laney's heart pounded. Was her husband's sermon going to be reflective of the personal struggles they'd experienced over the last few days? Was he going to talk about trust and honesty? Surely, these subjects had been foremost on his mind as he wrote his sermon this week. She looked in her bulletin for the title of the sermon. It said "The Last Time."

Noah looked up and smiled. "Of late, I've found myself wondering about the passage of time. In fact, for weeks now, I've been wondering where spring went. Woefully, we humans overschedule our lives . . . and the lives of our families. Our days become filled with activities, and the weeks and months become a blur, until finally, we pause, shake our heads, and wonder, 'Where did the time go?' "

As he spoke, Laney became captivated by his words, and her racing heart slowed.

"It is a blessing that we humans are, for the most part, blissfully unaware when some task or daily ritual occurs for the very last time. When our boys were younger, we read countless books together at bedtime. Fortunately, we still have one little one who enjoys listening to stories, although he's growing up much too fast." Noah looked at Asher as he said this, and Asher grinned and blushed. Hearing their father's reference to their little brother, Ben sat up from his slouch and stopped scowling, and Seth looked up from his drawing. "But all our boys have had their favorites: *Mike Mulligan and His Steam Shovel*, *The Biggest Bear*, *Tractor Mac*, *Rugby and Rosie*, and the perennial classic, *Goodnight*

Moon. We know some of these books by heart, and I can still smell that sweet little boy scent and see their little index fingers pointing to the mouse on each page." He paused. "But . . . when was it? When was the moment when we closed *Goodnight Moon* for the last time? If I had known it was the last time, I probably would've cried.

"Reading books before bed was only part of the nighttime ritual in our house, because reading was always followed by 'running hugs.' Laney and I would sit on the floor at the far end of our bedroom, safely clear of furniture, and brace ourselves while pajama-clad bundles of energy stood at the other end . . . waiting. Then, laughing and giggling all the way, the boys would run full tilt *at* us . . . into our arms and push us right over onto the floor in a hug." He smiled wistfully. "Now, even Asher is too big to give us a running hug—because one of us might get hurt!" Everyone laughed when he said this.

"Every night . . . night after night . . . reading . . . running hugs . . . and flying like airplanes into bed—I remember it all as if it were yesterday." His voice was choked with emotion, and Laney felt tears welling up in her eyes. "But then, a night must've come . . . when I wasn't paying attention . . . when we didn't do it. What night was it? It's a good thing I didn't realize, at the time, that it was the *last* time . . . because it would have broken my heart." He paused.

"But God's grace is with us every step of the way. As each chapter of our lives ends, as every door closes, He is standing right there. Whether we are innocently unaware of the preciousness of a moment or if we are all too well aware that it is the last time, God is with us.

"Anyone who has ever sold a home knows the keen sadness of walking through empty rooms one last time, gazing at the familiar way the sunlight falls through a window and realizing that it will still shine through even after we are no longer there to see it; or we picture the Christmas tree that always glittered festively in the corner and remember all the happy memories that were made beneath it; and then we turn to look in a different corner—where our favorite chair was and the side table where we kept our Bible—and we think of the many whispered prayers we prayed while sitting there. We move from room to room, and we can almost hear the laughter and the lovely voices, and we wonder how we can bear to leave such a sacred place.

"But with tears in our eyes, we eventually close the door for the last time; and God is there, waiting for us, waiting to ease our pain and guide us.

"There are also times when we have no way of knowing that the moment at hand is the last time. We see images of military families that are facing separation. Through tearful eyes they hug and whisper good-bye, and we imagine their silent prayer, 'Dear God, don't let this be the last time. . . .' Or sometimes, it is our turn to face the mortality of a loved one. We linger at their bedside after being beside them all day. We hold tightly to their hand; we are so weary. And we know we must go home, but we continue to hold on, wanting to never let go. And we silently pray, 'Please don't let this be the last time.'

"God is here most of all.

"Today's New Testament passage tells us about one of the last moments that Jesus shares with his disciples. He is well aware that it's the last time he will have supper with them, and even though they don't seem to fully understand what is about to happen, Jesus reassures them that he will always be with them. He tells them, 'I will not leave you desolate; I will come to you. Yet a little while, and the world will see me no more, but you will see me; because I live, you will live also.' His words are enough to sustain them but he continues, 'Peace I leave with you; my peace I give to you; not as the world gives do I give to you. Let not your hearts be troubled, neither let them be afraid.' These timeless words of reassurance that Jesus gave his twelve disciples so long ago are still the cherished words that we, as God's guys, have the honor of carrying in our hearts today.

"So this morning we've paused to reflect on the treasured moments that make up our days. And now, as we leave this sacred place and rush back to our hectic lives, perhaps we will remember to notice each moment . . . each of the ordinary, simple, mundane moments that make up our lives. We can never have them back, so we must try to squeeze in as many running hugs as we can. And as each chapter of our lives comes to a close, we must also remember that God is there at every turn . . . waiting to ease our way.

"In closing, there's a country song that is known—in our house—to make my eyes mist over. But don't worry, I'm not going to sing it." He smiled as he said this, and everyone laughed.

"It's called, 'Remember When,' and throughout the song, the singer reminisces about the different stages of life until he finally gets to the part about getting older and turning gray and the kids moving away; but he goes on to sing that they won't be sad. They'll just be thankful for all the good times."

Noah looked up. "So no matter how busy I am today, or how tired I am tonight, my boys and I are going to sit together . . . because we have a book to read . . . and maybe it won't even be the last time."

Laney looked up at her husband with tears in her eyes, and he looked back at her . . . and smiled.

❧ 29 ❧

"Hurry up, Ash," Laney called up the stairs, "or you're going to miss the bus."

"Mom, can't you drive me? It's the last day, and everyone's gonna have water guns. I'm gonna get soaked."

"No, hon. I need to be at school early," she called back as she rinsed the breakfast dishes and put them in the dishwasher. "Besides, you need to give Mr. Anderson his gift." The phone started ringing, and Laney dried her hands and hurried to answer it. "Hello?" she said, wondering who could be calling so early.

Asher appeared at the bottom of the stairs dragging his backpack. He saw his mom on the phone and frowned. Then he went over to the counter, peered inside his lunch pack, zipped it up, and pushed it into his backpack. "Mom, we gotta go," he whispered, but Laney didn't hear him.

"Yes. Hi, Dr. Jamison," she said.

Overhearing his mom's greeting, Asher groaned and plopped down on the floor next to Halle. "Maybe I'll get a ride after all," he whispered softly, and Halle thumped her tail and climbed on his lap. He stroked her soft ears, watched the second hand on the kitchen clock ticking steadily, and listened to his mom's side of the conversation. "Yes . . . yes . . . it was?" Long pause. "Okay . . . yes . . . mm-hmm." Long pause. "I understand . . . I will . . . okay." Long pause. "Thank you so much, Dr. Jamison. Yes, you too . . . enjoy the summer."

She hung the phone back up and leaned against the doorway.

"That phone call took four minutes and thirty-two seconds," Asher announced cheerfully.

Laney quickly brushed away her tears and turned around.

"Mom, what's wrong?" he asked in alarm, scrambling to his feet. "Why are you crying?"

Laney pulled him into her arms. "Nothing's wrong, honey. Nothing's wrong," she whispered. "Everything's okay."

Asher pulled back and searched her face. "Then why are you crying?"

"Because I'm happy."

He looked puzzled. "I don't think I've ever cried because I was happy."

"Someday, you might, sweetie, someday you might."

Asher wasn't so sure, and then he frowned. "I think I missed the bus."

"That's okay, I'll drive you," Laney said with a smile. Suddenly, there was no problem on earth that was insurmountable. She was going to live. She was going to see her boys grow up, and that was all that mattered.

Asher looked at his mom curiously. Something was different. Something had changed. He couldn't tell what it was, but it was almost as if she looked prettier. He smiled. "Good," he said, reaching for his backpack. "Now I won't get wet."

As they got in the car he asked, "How come I can't bring a water gun?"

"Because kids aren't supposed to bring toy guns to school."

"They do anyway."

"Well, *we* try to stick to the rules," she said, looking at him in her rearview mirror.

"Seth says, 'Rules are meant to be broken.' "

"Well, Seth is testing the waters."

Asher didn't reply right away, and Laney looked in her mirror. He was looking out the window with his brow furrowed into a frown, and she could see his wheels spinning. "Does that mean he's stick-ing his big toe in the water to see how cold it is?"

Laney laughed. "Sort of. But he's also seeing how much he can get away with. It's not easy, at his age, to have three big brothers and still be cool."

"I have four big brothers, and I don't think it's hard."

"That's cuz you're just naturally a cool dude."

Asher grinned and Laney went on. "So who do you think you're gonna get next year?"

"I hope I get Mrs. Delpha," he said. "She's

nice. She always waves to me when I walk by."

"Well, I hope you're happy . . . no matter who you get. They're all good teachers."

"I know."

Laney pulled into the driveway in front of his school, and Asher unstrapped his seat belt. He climbed out, and she came around to give him a hug. "Last time this year!"

"I know," he said, giving her a hug. Then they gave each other double fives and kissed each other's palms—a trick they'd learned from the little raccoon in the children's book, *The Kissing Hand*. That way, later, if one was missing the other, they could press their palm against their cheek and feel the kiss.

"Keep the faith," Laney said, hugging him again.

"Fight the good fight," Ash replied with a grin.

"I can do all things through Christ, which strengthens me."

"Inch by inch, it's a cinch."

"Love you."

"Love you too!"

Asher turned to go, but then stopped. "Mom, do you still do that with E?"

Laney nodded. "Sometimes."

"Good . . . because I want to do it forever."

He waved and hurried inside. She watched him go. "I want to do it forever too," she said softly.

❧ 30 ❧

Beryl peeked around the dressing room door and smiled. "Ready?"

Six heads nodded, and as she pushed open the door and slowly walked out into the center of the room, she heard a chorus of "ohhhs!" The round-mirrored room in Ros-Lyn's dress shop was circled with velvet-cushioned benches—and on them sat her sisters, her niece, and her future sister- and mother-in-law.

She looked down at the delicately embroidered, hand-beaded bodice and the smooth silken skirt with the perfect-length chapel train. "Do you think so?" she asked uncertainly, although, deep down, she knew it was the one.

"It's perfect," Isak said, motioning for her youngest sister to turn, and when Beryl obliged, she saw infinite nodding heads in the circle of mirrors.

Maddie smiled. "You look beautiful, Beryl."

"I love it, Aunt Ber," Meghan said.

Laney nodded in agreement. "Gorgeous."

Rumer stood up to straighten the train. "It's so *you,* Blueberry," she said, using their mother's nickname for her.

Beryl nodded and felt her eyes fill with tears. "I wish Mom was here," she said softly.

Rumer wrapped her arms around her and whispered, "She is here. Can't you tell?"

Beryl brushed back her tears and nodded, but deep down, she still wished her mom really was there—in person—to see her wearing a wedding gown!

"You're going to have to work on those tan lines," Isak teased.

Beryl reached up to touch her bare shoulders. "You mean my farmer's tan?" she said, laughing. "I know. I have to get outside more."

"Actually," Isak said, reaching into her bag, "Rumer, Meghan and I got you a Northern Tropics gift card."

"You did?" Beryl asked, trying to hide the dismay in her voice.

"Don't worry," Isak said, hearing her uncertainty. "A few visits to a tanning salon before your wedding day won't kill you—as long as you don't make a habit of it. Besides, you don't want to go to Bermuda without a little color."

"Yeah," Rumer agreed. "And this way you won't have *any* tan lines."

Beryl looked puzzled, and Rumer laughed. "You're the only one in there, silly, so you can wear as little as you want."

Maddie smiled. "Since we're giving gifts," she said, "Laney and I got you something too . . . because we heard, through the grapevine, that you've never had a manicure."

215

"Or a pedicure," Laney added.

"You didn't have to do that," Beryl said, blushing.

Isak eyed her sister. "You're not going to have the same old neatly trimmed nails with clear nail polish on your wedding day."

Beryl rolled her eyes. "I might," she said, unwilling to give in to her sister. Then she looked at Laney and Maddie. "Thank you very much. I'm sure it'll be fun."

"It will be lots of fun," Laney said, still smiling, "because we're all going. It's for Salon 16 in Orleans, and we've made reservations for first thing Saturday morning. We're getting our hair done too."

"You guys are too much," Beryl said, shaking her head. "I still can't believe it's happening, but all these plans make me realize it really is."

"It really is," Maddie said, giving her a hug. "And we couldn't be any happier."

Tears filled Beryl's eyes again, and she brushed them away. "Okay, so if you guys think this is the one, than I guess we're all set." She looked at Isak, Rumor, and Laney. "And you're all happy with your dresses?" They nodded. They'd loved the ocean blue color Beryl had picked out and the mid-calf length. It was perfect for the beach.

"Since ours are strapless too, it's going to look like we planned it," Rumer said.

Beryl nodded. "Oh, and wait 'til you see the

dress Maddie and I found for Charlotte. It's the cutest white, cotton sundress."

Maddie nodded in agreement. "Yes, I'm afraid she might steal the show."

Beryl laughed. "That would be completely okay with me!" Then she looked at Maddie. "Did you want to look at dresses while we're here?"

"Actually, I found a lovely sea-green dress at Mulberry Corners in Osterville last Saturday."

Beryl turned to Ros, one of the owners of Ros-Lyn's, and smiled. "I guess this is the one."

Ros nodded. "It's beautiful."

31

"It's going to be really nice to have two more girls in the family," Laney said as she and Maddie crossed the Sagamore Bridge back onto the Cape.

Maddie nodded. "It will be, especially since we already have more than our share of testosterone."

Laney laughed. "I know. We definitely don't have to worry about carrying on the family name."

"For generations to come!" Maddie added with a smile. She looked out the window at the boats drifting along the canal. "Beryl is such a sweetheart, and it'll be nice for Charlotte to have a mom too. I wouldn't be surprised if Beth has been pulling some strings up in heaven."

"It's funny you should say that," Laney said.

"Because I heard Rumer telling Beryl that their mom has been pulling some strings too—to bring Micah back into her life."

"Well, that's proof right there. Women do run heaven!"

Laney laughed. "You know, I bet you're right." They were both quiet for a while. Then Laney looked over. "What happened to Beryl's mom?"

"She had Alzheimer's—which is the most devastating disease. When she was first diagnosed, Beryl moved back home to look after her. But eventually it became too much. Mia wandered off on a couple of occasions, and Beryl couldn't find her. So it reached a point where it just wasn't safe, and finally, even though it broke her heart, she had to move her into a nursing home."

"Where were Rumer and Isak?"

"When this was all happening, Rumer was living in Montana and Isak was in California. Ironically, they both ended up moving back east after their mom passed away. Rumer's husband Will—who's in construction—had been out of work when they lived here, so they'd moved to Montana, but the only job he could find was working for a company that makes prefab houses, and he didn't like it. But then, at the funeral reception, he was offered a job as construction foreman, and they moved back. They're living in the family's old farmhouse and fixing it up at the same time. And Isak's husband, Matt, is a heart surgeon. They moved back east because his mom lives in Rhode Island. She's getting older too, and he didn't want the same kind of burden to fall on his sister."

"Do they have kids?"

Maddie nodded. "Rumer and Will have a son, Rand. He's around twelve . . . or thirteen by now, and Isak and Matt have a son and a daughter. Tommy—who's named after his grandfather—just graduated from Stanford, and Meghan is a junior at Columbia. That was another reason they moved back East—because Meghan is out here. I think they're all coming to the wedding, so you'll get to meet them. By the way, have they come up with a final head count yet?"

Laney laughed. "Nooo . . . nowhere close, but I'm not gonna worry about it. What will be, will be." She paused. "You mentioned Tommy's grandfather. Do you mean Beryl's dad?"

"Yes, Tom Graham was killed when he was just twenty-six years old. He and Mia had gone out to dinner to celebrate their fifth wedding anniversary, and on their way home they were hit by a drunk driver. Their pickup truck was pushed down an embankment, and Tom was thrown from it, and Mia, who was almost full term, went into labor. Beryl was born the same night her father died."

"That's awful," Laney said softly.

Maddie nodded. "And Mia was left to raise those three little girls all by herself."

"Well, she did a wonderful job. They're all amazing women."

"Mia was amazing too, and Beryl is just like her in every way. You've often commented that Noah looks like Asa, but Beryl and Mia were even more alike. I know Beryl wishes her mom had lived to see her get married." She paused thoughtfully. "There is someone else she might invite—although I doubt he'd come. After Tom died, Mia fell in love with a famous artist. He lives in North Conway. Beryl and her sisters only recently found out about him. They were going through their mom's house, and they found a memoir she'd written and some portraits he'd painted of her. They were very provocative!"

"Noo!"

Maddie nodded. "Yup, and then, to their surprise, he came to Mia's funeral. He's in his seventies, but he seems much older—maybe it's because he uses a cane—and I honestly don't know if he'd make the trip."

Laney nodded. "Micah and Beryl asked me if I'd be willing to make my peach cobbler."

"Are you going to?"

"I said I would," Laney said with a nod, "although I don't know where I'm going to get the peaches."

"You could always drive down to Pacey's Peaches and Pecans," Maddie suggested.

"You don't know how much I'd love to do that.

Asher has never been to the farm, and I'd love to take him, but how can I possibly leave for a week when there's going to be a wedding at my house? There's still so much to do."

"You could let Noah worry about that," Maddie said. "After all, he's the one who said yes."

Laney smiled. "That's true, but I'm still afraid it won't get done, and then I'll come home to an even bigger mess."

Maddie looked over. "Aren't you the one who said, 'What will be, will be'?"

Laney laughed. "I guess I am."

❧ 32 ❧

Harper heard the car door, rounded up her soggy tennis ball, and bounded down to the yard with her tail wagging.

"How'd it go?" Asa asked as Maddie came up the stairs with Harper at her heels.

"It was fun, and Beryl found a gorgeous dress. Then, afterward, we had a nice lunch at the same place you and I had lunch last week—the one with the yummy Waldorf salads. Beryl said she and her mom ate there the day her mom was diagnosed. She said it's funny how something like that sticks in your mind. She also mentioned the neurologist who made the diagnosis, and it's the same one who diagnosed you."

"I'm not surprised. He's supposed to be the best in New England."

"I had to bite my tongue not to say anything."

"You didn't though?"

"No, dear," she said with a sigh. "But, you know, Noah is going to be very upset when he—"

"Hon, if we tell Noah, we have to tell Micah, and now just isn't a good time."

"Asa, there is no good time to tell someone you have cancer."

"The treatments aren't so bad. I'm hoping we can get through this without ever having to say anything."

Maddie shook her head. "You can't do that. The boys should know—if only so they have a complete record of their medical history. There is a section on medical forms for family history, and even now, Noah knows only half his history."

"It's not a big deal, Maddie. Orphans don't know their family history and, somehow, they survive."

"Noah is not an orphan, and you're being selfish," she said, her voice edged with frustration. "You just don't want anyone to make a fuss."

Asa looked away. It was true—it wasn't only that he didn't want to put a damper on the wedding; he didn't want anyone's sympathy. He didn't want people coming up to him and saying how sorry they were. He just didn't want to talk about it. Period.

Maddie looked at her husband's back and shook her head. She knew the conversation was over. She turned to go inside, and moments later, she reappeared wearing shorts and a T-shirt. "I'm taking Harp for a walk." When she heard her name and the word *walk* in the same sentence, the black Lab bounded over, barely able to contain herself. In fact, she was wiggling so much, Maddie had trouble hooking her leash to her collar. As they headed toward the stairs, Harper rounded up her tennis ball and Maddie paused to look at her husband. "Do you want to come?"

Asa shook his head.

"You know, it's wrong for you to expect me to be a part of this deception."

But he didn't answer. He just stood at the railing and watched the waves roll in.

Maddie sighed. "C'mon, Harp."

Asa looked up at the azure blue sky—the stars were just beginning to appear and he could almost hear his father's voice. "The waves are as constant as the stars," he'd said as he'd pointed out the constellations to his two young sons.

And it was true. The endless rhythm of the waves was as constant as the night sky. The waves were just the same as they'd been years earlier when he was a boy and a riptide had caught him off guard and pulled him out to sea. The Lab they'd had back then—Martha—had seen him, barked frantically, and charged out into the surf, circling him until he wrapped his arms around her neck and held on to her thick, black fur. Somehow, she'd instinctively known to let the current carry them parallel to the shore until they were free of the rogue current.

The waves had also been the same when he'd stood next to Noelle on his nineteenth birthday and asked her to meet him on the beach that night. He still remembered the sadness in her eyes as she said, "If I don't come, it's not because I don't love you. . . . It's because I do."

And as he stood there, watching the waves, he realized the scene would still be the same long after he was gone. The earth would turn. The tide would follow the moon. The seasons would follow the sun. And the waves would follow each other into shore . . . for all eternity.

33

It was dark by the time Laney turned onto their road. It had been a fun day, and she was glad she'd gone, but now she was looking forward to a cup of tea and relaxing. She was thinking about how happy Asher had been when he'd come home and reported that he'd gotten Mrs. Delpha for second grade, and she'd just pushed the release button of her seat belt and slid it over her shoulder when two boys careened out of the woods on bikes and cut right in front of her. She slammed on her brakes, lurching forward in her seat, and barely missed them.

"Watch where yer goin'!" one of the boys hollered as he sped alongside the car, banging it with a stick.

"You watch where *you're* going," she shouted back in frightened anger, but they'd already disappeared into the shadows. Her heart pounded as she gathered herself. What were they doing on their quiet cul-de-sac at this hour? All of their neighbors were older, so there was no reason for them to be here. She wondered who they were— one of them looked vaguely familiar.

She pulled into their driveway, and as she crunched along on the gravel, she noticed an animal limping slowly through the grass. Frowning, she stopped and saw that it's long light-colored fur was matted with blood. "Oh, no!" she cried. "Oh, no, Lucky, what happened?"

She climbed out of the car, and the sweet cat looked up at her, meowing pitifully. He could barely stand, and one of his eyes was bloody beyond recognition. She gently scooped him up and hurried to the house. "Noah!" she shouted. "Hon, come quick—I need you!" Within seconds, the entire family was in the kitchen.

"Holy cow," Noah said, running his hand through his hair. "What the heck happened?"

"I don't know. He was in the driveway."

"Maybe he was hit by a car," Gabe said.

"Looks like he was hit by a truck," Seth observed gloomily.

Tears streamed down Asher's cheeks. "Is he going to be okay?"

"Yup," E said, picking Asher up and stepping back. "Head injuries always bleed a lot. They look a lot worse than they really are."

Lucky cried mournfully, and Laney eyed her oldest son, as if to say, *Don't make promises you can't keep*.

Noah hurriedly searched through the Post-it notes taped around the phone. "Where's Aiden's number?"

"It's on the fridge," Laney answered, her voice sounding frantic. "I'm just going to go. I'm just going to take him. Tell him we're on our way. If you don't reach him, call my cell and I'll take him to the emergency clinic in South Dennis."

"I'll drive," Gabe said.

"Grab a towel," Laney directed.

As they went out the door, she heard Noah talking on the phone. It was a reassuring sound, and she whispered softly, "It's okay, Lucky. Everything's going to be okay."

Laney had left her vehicle running, and Gabe opened the passenger door, helped her in, and laid the towel on her lap before climbing into the driver's side. As they passed the wooded area at the end of the road, she remembered the two boys. "Just as I was coming home," she said, motioning to the side of the road, "two boys came flying out of the woods on bikes. I almost hit them, and one of them had a stick and banged the whole side of the car with it. I wonder if they had anything to do with this."

"Why would they hurt a cat?" Gabe asked skeptically. "I think he was hit by a car. Animals run out in traffic all the time and, at this time of day, it's hard to see."

"You're right. It is hard to see, so I shouldn't say anything, but I really think one of them looked like Jared Laughlin."

"What would he be doing up here?"

"Who knows? I'm not sure where they live, but he was on Asher's bus so it must be nearby. Maybe they were on their way home from the beach. Come to think of it, they did have towels around their necks."

"Well, I doubt they had anything to do with this."

Laney sighed. He was probably right, but she couldn't seem to shake the feeling.

Gabe passed the barely legible sign that had once clearly read, "Cape Cod Animal Hospital," and turned into an overgrown driveway. Dr. Aiden Hatch's circa 1800s run-down office was behind his circa 1700s run-down house, but the condition of the buildings didn't matter one bit to his four-legged clientele or their human counterparts. The only thing that mattered was his gentle touch, his soft voice, and his unmatched wisdom when it came to caring for furry friends; he was an old-time treasure in the modern world of veterinary care.

As Gabe pulled up next to the office, a small troop of dogs came around from behind the house and announced their arrival, and then, an older gentleman with a lanky frame and a mane of white hair came out of the house, wiping his mouth on a napkin. Dr. Hatch had always cared for the Coleman pets—he'd even cared for Martha, the old black Lab who'd saved Asa from a riptide when he was a boy.

"Did we interrupt your dinner?" Laney asked worriedly.

"Nope. What have we got?" he asked, motioning to the bundle in Laney's arms.

"Oh, Dr. Hatch, it's Lucky, that stray cat you checked out for me a couple of months ago."

He nodded, pushing open the rickety screen door of his office and turning on the light. "And what brings Lucky here tonight?"

"Well, we think he might've been hit by a car," Laney said, laying him on the table.

Dr. Hatch gently stroked Lucky's side and let him sniff his hand. "Well, Lucky, you've gotten yourself into a heap a trouble, haven't you?" he murmured, looking at the bloody eye. Lucky cried plaintively as if he was telling the old vet the whole, sad story. Dr. Hatch nodded. "I know, I know. I'm sorry to hear that," he said sympathetically. He carefully examined him, and then looked up. "Well, he's definitely experienced some kind of trauma, but I don't know if he was hit by a car. I think his jaw is broken, and he may lose that eye."

Tears stung Laney's eyes. "Is he going to be okay?"

Dr. Hatch pressed his lips together and looked down at Lucky again. "It's hard to say. If he makes it through the night, his chances will greatly improve, but until I get an X-ray, I don't know what's going on inside."

Laney nodded.

The old doc looked up. "Jot down your number," he said, pulling a tattered assignment pad from his shirt pocket.

Laney opened the small notebook full of scribbled notes and tried to find an empty page.

As if reading her mind, he assured, "Don't worry. I'll find it."

Laney jotted down her name and number and handed it back to him, and he tucked it in his pocket. "I'll call you first thing in the morning."

Laney leaned over and gently kissed the one spot on Lucky's head that wasn't covered in blood. "Love you," she murmured, fighting back tears. "Don't you leave us."

Gabe gently stroked Lucky's side, his solemn

eyes glistening. "Live up to your name, bud," he said softly.

Dr. Hatch looked up. "Can you stop at the house and tell Marnie to come?"

Laney nodded and, feeling helpless, they turned to go.

Marnie was the youngest daughter of the ten redheaded Hatch kids, and even though she was twenty-eight, she still looked like a teenager. She had long, reddish blond hair pulled into a ponytail, a smattering of freckles across her nose, and she had her dad's kind blue eyes. She'd never married. Instead, after her mother's death, Marnie, who'd always been close to her dad, had taken it upon herself to look after him and help him take care of his large flock of four-legged patients.

"Marnie," Laney called, peering through the screen door. A young woman standing at the sink, washing the supper dishes, turned around.

"Hi, Laney," she said. "Noah said you'd be over."

Laney nodded. "I'm sorry to interrupt, but your dad says he needs you."

Marnie nodded, dried her hands, and abandoning the dishes without a second thought, pushed open the squeaky farmhouse door.

"Thanks," Laney said as she hurried past. But Marnie, intent on what her dad needed, only waved over her shoulder.

Later that night, Laney lay awake, listening to Noah snoring peacefully. Her heart felt like it weighed a hundred pounds. *How can he sleep?* she wondered, staring into the darkness. *How can he sleep when Lucky's life is hanging by a thread . . . if he's even alive?* She rolled onto her side and looked out at the stars. A breeze whispered through the window, and she remembered the old, orange barn cat her grandparents had had when she was a little girl. Her grandmother had called him Peaches, but her grandfather had called him Ned.

"How come you call him Ned, Gramp?" she'd asked one day when they were sitting on the porch.

" 'Cause he looks like a Ned," Gramp said matter-of-factly.

"He does?" she'd asked, watching the old cat sunning in a nearby chair and puzzling over this answer.

"Yep."

"I think he looks like a Peaches," she said.

"Now, how can you call a big ole tomcat *Peaches?* He'll have a complex."

"Gram calls you honeypot, and you don't have a complex."

Gramp laughed. "Oh, yes, I do."

"Oh, stop your nonsense, Lon," Gram said, pushing open the screen door. "C'mon, Peaches," she called softly, and the cat hopped down and trotted into the kitchen after her.

"He doesn't look like he minds," Laney observed.

Gramp just shook his head, but when the old cat died the next winter, and Laney visited the following summer, she spied a little wooden cross in the garden with Gramp's handwriting on it. It said, "PEACHES." But when she'd knelt in the grass for a closer inspection, she'd realized that down the cross—using the first *E* in *PEACHES*—was written the name "NED."

"Oh, Gramp," she whispered now. "I wish you were still here. . . ."

She tossed and turned all night, dreaming about a pack of boys careening crazily out of the shadows on bikes. "Watch where yer goin'!" they yelled over and over and then, *"Bang, bang, bang!"* She woke with a start to the sound of the phone ringing. "Noah?" she said, disoriented and fumbling for the phone, and when she finally managed to pick it up, she heard Noah's voice talking. "Yes, thank you, Dr. Hatch. I'll tell her," and then the phone clicked.

She sat bolt upright. *Lucky!* He was calling about Lucky. Grabbing her robe, she pulled it on as she hurried down the stairs. Noah was watching *The Rifleman* while he mixed pancake batter. "How is he?" she blurted.

Noah looked up. "He made it through the night, but he's still in pretty rough shape . . . and he did lose that eye."

"Can we pick him up?"

"I don't think so. I got the impression he's going

to be there for a few days. He's still sedated, and they don't know how much trouble he's going to have eating with a broken jaw."

"Oh, dear," Laney said. "How can he survive if he can't eat?"

Noah shook his head. "I don't know, but the good news is he didn't have any internal injuries."

Laney nodded, sat wearily at the table, and absent-mindedly started watching the old western TV series *The Rifleman* and heard Chuck Connors's character Lucas addressing the marshal.

"I forgot the marshal's name was Micah," she mused. "I don't think I've ever heard of anyone else named Micah except your brother."

Noah smiled. "There's a Micah in the Bible."

"I know," she said. "Is that where your parents got his name?"

"Actually, I think they got it from this show. It was one of my dad's favorites."

"It was one of my grandfather's favorites too. That's where my uncle Luke got his name. Good thing it started with an *L*." Noah looked up with a puzzled expression, and Laney said, "Lon, Lonnie, Lucas, Laney. And my niece's name is Laurie and my nephew's name is Levi."

Noah laughed. "I never thought of that. And just think, we didn't consider any names that begin with *L*."

"That's okay. I like the names we picked . . . although I sometimes wish we'd named Asher

Samuel." She paused. "Did Dr. Hatch say anything more about what he thinks happened to Lucky?"

"No," Noah said, dropping broken eggshells into the garbage. "I thought we decided he was hit by a car."

"Well, Dr. Hatch didn't sound convinced by that theory." Then she went on to tell him about the encounter she'd had with the two boys. "Which reminds me," she added. "I need to see if he did any damage to the side of the car."

"You think they purposely hurt Lucky?"

"I don't know. The timing is kind of odd . . . and what were they doing on our road?"

"Well, we have no way to prove it. We don't even know who they were."

"I know, but one of them really looked like Jared, and it's a little scary to think he might have targeted a pet."

Noah took a deep breath and shook his head. "It is scary, but you can't blame someone without proof."

"I know, but I think we should keep an eye on the dogs and make sure they stay in the yard—especially Halle. I don't think Mennie would wander off."

Noah nodded, and Laney stood up to make coffee, but then realized the pot was already full. "You made coffee?"

"Yup," he said with a nod. "Fog Buster—just for you."

"Thanks," she said, pouring a cup. "By the way, there're blueberries in the fridge."

"No, there aren't."

"Yes, there are," Laney said, pulling open the fridge. She spent five minutes looking on every shelf and behind every condiment and juice container. "Well, they were in here," she said in a puzzled voice.

She noticed Noah's eyes sparkling mischievously, and she looked in the bowl and realized the batter was already full of dark blue lumps. "You," she said, laughing.

"Me," he said, pulling her into a hug.

"How long before breakfast?" she murmured.

"Not long. Gabe and E have to be at work by nine."

"Can I help?"

"Nope," he said, letting her go. "You just take your coffee out on the porch and relax."

"Are you sure?"

"Yup. Lucas McCain and I have it all under control."

"You just don't want me talking while you're trying to watch," she said as she headed for the porch with both dogs trailing behind her.

Noah laughed and shook the orange juice container. "We need OJ," he called.

"I know," she called back as she sank into her favorite chair. "We always need OJ."

The dogs wagged their tails, and Mennie rested

his head on her lap while Halle put her paws on the edge of the chair. "You two are silly," she said softly. "And, you, missy, are getting big." Halle leaned forward and licked her right on the lips. "Nice," she said, laughing and wiping her mouth.

The dogs lay down at her feet, and Laney took a sip of her coffee. She looked out at the yard and noticed one of the phoebes fly from the clothesline to the ledge under the shed roof. She frowned. "I hope you're not still looking for your babies," she murmured sadly.

When it continued to fly back and forth, Laney put her coffee down, stepped over the dogs, pushed open the screen, and walked over to investigate. The little bird immediately flew to the clothesline and cocked its head, watching her. Laney peered into the nest. There were three new eggs.

❧ 34 ❧

The bell on the shop door rang cheerfully, and Beryl looked up.

A tall, slender boy with short blond hair carefully closed the door behind him, and Beryl smiled. "Hi, Henry."

"Hi," Henry answered solemnly.

"Are you here for your check?"

He nodded, and Beryl sifted through some

papers and handed an envelope to him. "Here you go."

"Thanks," he said, taking it but not moving.

Beryl looked up and searched his face. "Are you going to the fireworks tomorrow?"

Henry shook his head. "I don't like fireworks," he said, "but I am running in the Firecracker 5K."

Beryl smiled. Anytime Henry volunteered information without being asked was a good thing. When he'd first started working in the shop, Callie, his mom, had explained that he hadn't spoken at all when he was little, and even though he'd come a long way, he was still quiet.

"That's great, Henry. Micah's running in it too, so now I'll have two people to cheer for."

Henry smiled—another rare occurrence. "I'll take it easy on him," he said softly, and Beryl laughed.

"I hope so. Otherwise you'll make him feel old."

"My mom said you're getting married."

"We are—next month. In fact, we're going on vacation the same week you're going on vacation."

"Where are you going?"

"Bermuda."

Henry frowned. "I don't know where that is."

"It's an island off the Carolinas."

Henry nodded. "We're going to Maine."

"I know," Beryl said. "That'll be fun."

"My dad and I are running in a 10K."

"You're going to be busy."

Henry nodded. "It's called Beach to Beacon because it starts at a beach and ends at a lighthouse. We ran it last year."

The bell jingled, and they both looked up. Callie, Henry's mom, peered around the doorway and waved to Beryl. "Comin', hon?"

Henry nodded. "See you tomorrow."

Beryl smiled. "I'll be there. Good luck!"

"Thanks," he said, smiling shyly. "Tell Micah good luck too."

"I will."

"Thanks, Beryl," Callie called, holding the door for her son.

As they left, Callie continued to hold the door as Rumer and Rand came in. "Was that Henry?" Rumer asked in surprise.

Beryl nodded, giving her nephew a hug.

"No wonder he's such a good runner—look how tall he is!"

Beryl laughed. "Look how tall *this* kid is," she said, holding Rand at arms' length. She grinned. "Okay, back-to-back," she said.

Rumer rolled her eyes. "We don't need to stand back-to-back. You can see for yourself he's got four inches on me."

"C'mon, Mom," Rand said, turning around. Rumer gave in and stood back-to-back with her son.

Beryl eyed them critically. "Hmm . . . I think it's more like five inches."

Rumer laughed. "What can I say? Look at Will's side of the family. His dad is six foot four."

Rand grinned, pushing his dark hair out of his eyes.

Beryl smiled. "He's all Swanson," she teased, ruffling his hair. "Look at this mop too!"

"Don't worry," Rumer assured her. "He's getting it cut before the wedding."

"Don't do it for me," Beryl said, touching his curly locks. "I think his hair's beautiful."

"See, Mom," Rand said, looking at Rumer. "You're the only one who thinks I need a haircut."

Rumer gave her younger sister a wilting look, and Beryl laughed. "Sorry! I shouldn't have said anything." She turned to Rand. "You look very handsome with short hair too," she said with a grin. "Would you like a chocolate croissant?"

"Mmm, I'd love one, Aunt Ber."

Beryl busied herself warming up two croissants, and Rumer came around the counter and poured a cup of coffee. "Have you been busy?"

"Very," Beryl said. "I think half of New York City has come up for the holiday."

Rumer laughed. "Guess you didn't realize we live in a tourist destination."

"I guess not."

"So how're the wedding plans?"

"Good. We ordered the flowers, the menu is all set, and Laney and Noah said it was fine to get a tent. There's plenty of room in the side yard . . .

but if the weather cooperates, we're still going to have the ceremony on the beach."

"It all sounds wonderful," Rumer said wistfully. "And then you're flying out of Logan first thing in the morning?"

"Yup, Micah made reservations at a hotel near the airport because our flight is at seven. We're really looking forward to it. Micah said he and Beth never got to go on a honeymoon, and he always regretted it. I just hope there aren't any hurricanes."

"That's right," Rumer mused, sipping her coffee. "You're going right in the heart of hurricane season."

"I know. I've already started watching the long-range forecast, and they keep saying it's going to be a busy year. There've already been five named storms."

"Well, fingers crossed that the third week of August will be smooth sailing . . . pardon the pun!"

Beryl put the croissants, oozing with melted chocolate, on two plates. "I hope so," she said. She handed a plate to her nephew. "Milk?" she asked.

"Yes, please," Rand answered, sitting down at one of the nearby tables.

❧ 35 ❧

E poured a second helping of Corn Pops into his cereal bowl while Mennie watched his every move. He tossed a puffy, yellow kernel to him, but the old dog missed, and Halle deftly scoffed it up. "Here, Mennie," Gabe said, giving him the last morsel of his third slice of cinnamon toast.

They listened to their mom talking on the phone. "Thanks, Dr. Hatch," she said, and their ears perked up. "When can we pick him up?" Laney continued, cradling the phone against her shoulder while she made sandwiches. She nodded, almost dropping the phone. "Okay, thank you again." She hung up, and the boys looked at her expectantly.

"This morning," she said. "But he said he has to be an indoor cat."

"That stinks," E mumbled. "He loves going outside."

"Yeah," Gabe agreed. "He's not gonna like that."

"Well, he can still go out on the porch, and if you think about it, he's lucky to be alive."

"He may not think he's lucky after he figures out he's confined to the house," Gabe said glumly.

"Is one sandwich enough?" Laney asked, dropping ice packs into their coolers.

241

"No," they replied in unison.

"Well, you both brought one home yesterday."

"That's cuz Chloe brought pizza," E said. "She's working today, so she won't be stopping by with food."

"That reminds me. Uncle Micah wondered if you'd like to invite her to the wedding."

"I thought it was just family."

"Well, I guess Grandpa told him about her, and Uncle Micah specifically told Dad that you're welcome to invite her."

"Okay, I'll mention it," E said, picking up his bowl and draining the last of his milk. He eyed his brother. "Ready?"

"Ready as I'll ever be," Gabe mumbled, putting his sunglasses on top of his head.

"Don't forget your sunscreen," Laney reminded as she handed them their coolers.

"Of course, Mom," Gabe said.

"See you later," E added.

"Will I see *you* later?" she asked, eyeing him.

"Yup, I'll be home to run and shower, but then Chloe and I are going to P-town for the fireworks, so I won't be home for supper."

"There're fireworks in Barnstable."

"I know, but we'd rather go to Provincetown."

"I'll be in the car," Gabe said, kissing her on the cheek.

"Okay, go," Laney said.

E kissed her too. "Thanks for lunch."

"You're welcome."

"Mom, are you goin' for a run?" he called over his shoulder.

"I might," she called back. "Falmouth's only a month away."

E turned, his face lighting up. "That's right. Wait . . . isn't that the day after the wedding?"

Laney nodded, following him down the walk.

"And we're still running?"

"We are."

"Well, you better get training," he said with a grin.

"I know," Laney replied, watching him get in the car. With the radio thumping, they pulled away, waving.

She waved back, shaking her head, and then knelt to pull a couple of weeds from between the slate stepping-stones. It had rained overnight, and as she pulled the weeds, she recalled one of her grandfather's old axioms: "It's always easier to pull weeds after it rains."

"That may be true," she murmured, surveying all the weeds coming up between the stones, "but I don't have time right now."

"Mom," a small voice called. "Are you out there?"

"Right here, hon." She heard the screen door squeak open and then the sound of scampering paws, and from around the corner of the house, Halle charged toward her, jumping up with wet, muddy feet. "Ash, you're not supposed to let Halle out without a leash."

"I didn't," Asher said, standing barefoot in his pajamas, his strawberry blond hair sticking up in all directions. "She pushed the door open."

"Okay, well, we'll have to have Dad look at it," she said, holding on to the puppy's collar.

"Can we pick Lucky up today?" he said, yawning.

"Yup. Dr. Hatch said we could pick him up this morning, but he also said he has to stay indoors from now on."

"He does?" he asked in a voice edged with sadness. "Why?"

"Because he only has one eye and that makes him vulnerable."

Asher frowned, scratching his head. "He won't like that."

"Well, that's the way it is," she said, smoothing his hair and putting her arm around him. "How 'bout we go have some breakfast and then we'll go get him."

Asher nodded and reached for Halle's collar. Pulling the puppy toward the door, he coaxed, "C'mon, Halle."

An hour later, Asher had attempted to tame his hair with water and a comb, and then he stood by the door, wearing his favorite John Deere T-shirt and shorts. "C'mon, Mom," he called.

"Coming," she called back.

Laney peered into Seth and Ben's room. "Time to rise and shine," she said cheerfully.

Both boys groaned and pulled their pillows over their heads.

"Ash and I are going to get Lucky. You two need to be up and moving when we get back. That means dressed, breakfast, dishes in the dishwasher . . . and beds made. Seth, it's your turn to mow, and Ben, I'd really appreciate it if you'd do some weeding."

They both mumbled something unintelligible. "Get moving—the day's a wasting!" She looked around at the clothes strewn about the floor. "And put your clothes in the laundry . . . or you're not going to have anything to wear."

She hurried down the stairs, grabbed her bag, and spied her youngest son sitting on the floor with Halle on his lap. He pretended to snore and then discreetly opened one eye to see if she was watching. "Very funny," she said, nudging him with her foot. "Let's go."

Asher lifted Halle off his lap and scrambled to his feet. "Starting to feel like Rip Van Winkle," he said solemnly, suppressing a grin.

Laney laughed at the reference her husband always made when he had to wait for her. "What's your name? Noah Coleman?" she teased, ruffling his damp hair.

"Hey!" he protested. "I just combed that."

"I know. I can tell."

Ten minutes later, they pulled into the Hatch's driveway, and Laney parked between the two cars already near the office door. They climbed out, and as Asher pulled open the screen door leading into the waiting room, a young woman stepped out. Her face was tearstained and her eyes were rimmed with red. "Thank you," she said softly, wiping her eyes. Laney and Asher went inside, but Asher stayed by the door, watching the woman as she opened the back of her station wagon and smoothed an old blanket that was there.

"Ash, come here," Laney said quietly, but Asher didn't seem to hear. Instead, he continued to watch as Doc Hatch came around from the back entrance. He was carrying an old dog with long, wispy, golden hair; its eyes were closed and its muzzle was silvery, white. It was oddly still, and when Doc Hatch laid him gently on the blanket, Asher realized what had happened. He breathed in suddenly, and the rush of dusty air through his throat choked him. "Oh, no," he cried out. "Mom," he said, turning, his eyes filled with tears, "that lady's dog died."

Laney bit her lip and nodded. "Come over with me," she said, motioning to the seat beside her, but Asher didn't move. Instead, he turned back to watch as Doc Hatch closed the back of the woman's car and stood talking to her. She nodded, wiping her eyes again, and then the old doc gave her a hug.

Finally, Asher walked over and sat next to Laney. She put her arm around him, and he slowly shook his head. "I've seen dead animals on the road before," he said softly, "and dead fish and crabs on the beach, but I don't think I've seen anything important dead."

Laney sighed. "I don't think you have either, hon, but I'll bet that dog had a good life. I'll bet that lady loved him a lot."

Asher nodded, and Laney could tell—by the faraway gaze in his solemn eyes—that he was trying to understand.

Just then, another lady came out of one of the exam rooms, leading a bowlegged, happy-go-lucky bulldog. The funny bulldog waddled right over to Asher and looked up at him, and Asher couldn't help but laugh at the dog's soulful expression. He reached out to pet him, and the woman smiled, and when Marnie came out, she paid her bill. "C'mon, Winston," she called, and the funny dog waddled out the door after her.

Marnie looked up and smiled. "Here for Lucky?"

Laney nodded.

"He's doing great," Marnie said. "He still has some trouble eating. You'll have to keep him on canned food at least for a while, but he's a real trouper . . . and a sweetheart." She disappeared, and moments later, Dr. Hatch appeared with Lucky in his arms. Asher frowned at the cone around the injured cat's neck and stared at the spot on Lucky's face where his eye had been. It was stitched closed.

"Oh, my goodness," Laney said softly. "You poor guy."

"He's doing really well, all things considered," the old vet assured her.

Laney nodded as he explained Lucky's care.

"Soft food and this antibiotic twice a day," he said, producing a small bottle from his shirt pocket. "It's liquid, so you don't have to pry open his mouth. It might be a little challenging, but as long as you get some of it into him, it'll help. Keep the collar on for a week or so—just until everything's healed. We don't need him licking or scratching, and opening up any wounds. I'd give you a sedative, but I don't think you could get it down his throat. I think he'll be fine without it . . . and just call if you have any problems or questions."

Laney nodded, and he handed him gently to her. "Oh, Dr. Hatch, I can't thank you enough," she said.

The old doctor looked down at Asher and saw the concern on his face. "Now, you've got yourself a pirate cat."

Asher smiled. The idea of a pirate cat somehow made it seem a little better.

❧ 36 ❧

"Asa," Maddie said, holding the phone against her chest. "Micah wants to know if we'd like to go to the fireworks."

Asa opened his eyes and blinked, trying to focus. "Do you?"

"It's up to you—only you know how you feel."

They'd left the Cape early on Monday, stopped in Boston for Asa's treatment, and headed straight home to New Hampshire to escape the Cape Cod crowds, so going to a fireworks display—which would also be crowded—wasn't Asa's idea of a peaceful evening.

"Micah says Charlotte asked if we were coming," Maddie added.

Asa rubbed his chin thoughtfully. How could he disappoint his only granddaughter? "All right," he said finally.

Maddie put the phone to her ear. "We'd love to," she said, and Asa shook his head at her exaggeration. "What time?" She paused, listening, and then said, "Hang on." She held the phone against her chest again. "They're all meeting at Beryl's for pizza at eight and going from there."

"Okay," Asa agreed, even though he'd actually been hoping for a quiet supper, watching the Boston Pops on PBS, and turning in early.

"We'll be there," Maddie said. "Oh, anything . . . yup, you know your father . . . any form of meat . . . pepperoni, sausage—the healthy stuff. Okay, thanks, hon. See you later."

Maddie retreated to the kitchen to hang up the phone, leaving Asa to resume his nap. They'd had a quiet week, and the burden of their disagreement still hung heavily between them. Except for the fatigue that continuously dogged his steps, Asa's treatment had been uneventful.

Maddie had been cool and distant, only speaking when necessary—just enough to be cordial, and every evening she turned in early with her book . . . or stayed up late, if Asa headed to bed first. Even Harper sensed the discord between her two favorite people, and with her head between her paws and her ears in their worried position, she followed the movements of her dear ones with sad eyes. Dogs don't take sides, but after countless walks, she started to be less than enthusiastic when Maddie reached for her leash; they'd already put in more than thirty miles that week and her pads were tender, but Maddie, remember-ing a tip Aiden Hatch had told her years earlier, pressed wet tea bags against them because he'd said the tannic acid in the tea would help toughen them up. And afterward, she encouraged Harper to walk on the grass. Maddie would not sit in the house. She wanted to make sure her husband knew she was unhappy.

And Asa, for his part, knew his wife wasn't happy. He tried to be helpful, and he made every effort to catch up on his honey-do list, but nothing seemed to help. He knew what she wanted, but he refused to do it, so it finally came down to who would be more stubborn.

When seven thirty rolled around, Asa pulled himself off the couch. The house was quiet, and Maddie was nowhere to be found; Harper was gone too. Deciding they must've gone for a walk, he went out on the deck to watch the geese. The female, with her pointed tail feathers, sat dutifully on the nest while the gander, with his rounded tail feathers, swam back and forth protectively like a soldier on watch. Asa smiled at their devotion. He heard the front door, and moments later, Harper limped out onto the porch, her tail wagging.

"Are you trying to wear her out?" Asa asked with a wry smile.

"No," Maddie replied coolly. "Are you ready to go?"

"Just need to change my shirt. Are we bringing chairs?"

"They're already in the car."

Asa retreated into the house, and Maddie filled Harper's bowl with fresh water. "We'll be back," she told her as she lapped up the water. She filled a glass for herself, and taking a long drink, looked out the window to watch the geese. *What do they say to each other as they wing their way north?* she wondered. *Does he encourage her with tender words, "Just a little farther, dear"? And when they arrive, does he say, "Here we are, my love . . . our summer home"? And what happens when the day comes when she is too weak to make the trip? Does he stay by her side, his heart aching . . . realizing the end is near?*

"Ready," Asa said, interrupting her thoughts. Maddie turned and looked at her husband as if she was seeing him for the first time. "You look nice," she said quietly.

Surprised, Asa smiled. "Thanks, I always try to look nice for my girl."

"I know you do," she said with a sad half smile. Then she walked over and gave him a hug, and he wondered what had changed while he was upstairs.

"We'll be back, puppy," he said, releasing Maddie and leaning down to scratch Harper's ears. "You rest up," he teased. "Who knows how many miles your mother has planned for tomorrow." Harper thumped her tail, happily sensing a change in the demeanor of her beloved people.

Twenty minutes later, Flannery greeted them at the front door with a bark announcing their arrival. Beryl's apartment in a beautifully restored Victorian had high ceilings and dark mahogany trim, as well as a fireplace that took up the better part of one wall and beautiful wide oak flooring.

Micah had moved in with Beryl soon after they'd gotten engaged, and Charlotte—who loved Beryl with all her heart—adjusted to their new home like a Lab to water.

"How'd the race go?" Asa asked as Micah led them into the kitchen.

"Pretty well," Micah answered. "I thought I might see you out there."

Asa sighed. "I'm afraid my running days are behind me—ever since I had that knee injury."

Micah nodded. "Well, I saw Linden. He asked how you were, and I told him as ornery as ever. He also asked if you ever fixed up your old Chevy pickup . . ."

Micah eyed his dad, but Asa just smiled. "I'm going to. It's on my bucket list."

"Yeah," Micah said skeptically, "you keep saying that."

"Well, if I don't get to it, you can. . . ."

"I'd like to do work on it together."

"We'll see . . . maybe when you get back from your honeymoon." He paused. "Did Henry run?"

Micah laughed. "He did. In fact, he won. He was two minutes ahead of the next runner."

"Good for him," Asa said with a smile. "Between running and his computer skills, he's going to get a scholarship somewhere."

After pizza and beer, they parked on a dirt road outside of town and walked down a worn path that led to an outcropping that looked out over the valley. Although the spot was usually a popular hangout for local teenagers, the teens must've found somewhere else to watch the fireworks that night. The family's voices cheerfully filled the air, making it seem less desolate, and as the youngsters clambered up on the rocks, Asa set up the chairs they'd brought. He settled into one, feeling as if he could fall asleep right there, but when the first rocket screamed into the air, piercing the night sky, Charlotte scrambled off the rocks and leaped into his lap.

"It's okay, hon," he whispered in her ear, but she wasn't convinced, and he smiled. For the first time, he was glad they'd come.

❧ 37 ❧

E opened two bottles of Samuel Adams and handed one to Chloe. "So how'd you like to be my date for the wedding?"

"I'd love to be your date," she said with a smile. "When is it?"

"The sixteenth of August."

"Hmm . . . should I get the day off?"

E frowned. "I think it's later in the day."

She nodded and took a sip of her beer. "Mmm, this tastes good after a long day."

"How was work today?" E asked, remembering

she'd worked too. He smoothed the blanket behind him and leaned back.

"Busy," Chloe answered. This was her fourth summer working at Hot Chocolate Sparrow—a favorite coffee shop for the locals and the summer folks. "I think every tourist in Orleans came in today . . . and I have to be there at six thirty again tomorrow."

"You should've said something," E said, rolling onto his side to lean on his elbow. "We didn't have to drive all the way up here. My mom said there were fireworks in Barnstable too."

"I know, but I wanted to come here," she said, lying back on the blanket next to him. "This is my favorite spot."

"Why's that?" E asked, leaning over to kiss her.

"You know why," she murmured, tasting his sweet lips.

"I don't remember," he said softly, "maybe you could remind me."

She laughed and reached for his hips. "You should remember . . . but I'd be happy to remind you."

E slipped his hand inside her tank top and rested his hand on her flat stomach. Then he lightly ran his fingers along the curve of her hip bone, and she laughed and pulled away.

"What's the matter?"

"It tickles."

"It does?" he teased.

255

"Yes—let me show you," she said, slipping her hand inside the top of his jeans and running her fingers lightly along the same area.

E shrugged and shook his head.

She frowned and unbuttoned his jeans so she could get a better angle. "How about now?"

He shook his head again. "Nope . . . nothing."

She pushed him onto his back so his hip bone was more prominent, and then she ran her fingers lightly over it. He kept a straight face for as long as he could and then, laughing, he grabbed her hand.

"Aha! I knew the sweet spot was there somewhere!"

Smiling, he slid his hand between her thighs and murmured, "And where's your sweet spot?"

She didn't answer as he slid down her shorts, but she pushed down his jeans and boxers and pulled him on top of her. "I can't wait," she whispered, and he kissed her softly. Slowly, she arched her back and took all of him in.

"I love you so much," he whispered.

"I love you too," she murmured, rocking her hips slowly back and forth.

Finally, he eased off and lay beside her, lightly tracing circles on her smooth skin. "I don't want this summer to ever end," he said wistfully.

She smiled. "Only one more year 'til you graduate."

"Two for you."

"It'll go quick."

"Not quick enough. I want to be with you all the time. I want to get married and be together every minute."

"That day will come," she said gently.

"I don't know . . . I don't even know what I want to do. Sometimes, I feel like college is a waste of time. Any job I get will take me away from here . . . and this is the only place I want to be."

"I don't know what the future holds, E, except that we'll be together . . . and that's all that matters. I just know we should enjoy every moment . . . and tomorrow will take care of itself."

E smiled sadly and kissed her. "You sound like my dad."

She looked back up at the stars. "My grand-father used to say that all the time. *Tomorrow will take care of itself.* And he's right. That's how I want to live my life."

The dark waves lapped rhythmically against the sand, and they watched the bobbing lights of party boats floating in the bay. Suddenly, the first fireworks soared into the starry sky, exploding in thundering booms of brilliant, cascading lights above Pilgrim Tower. Elijah looked over at Chloe's sweet smile, and his heart ached for the future.

❧ 38 ❧

"I think it's a great idea," Noah said as he splashed milk into the bowl of pancake batter and stirred. "You've been talking about taking Asher for years. Besides, it would be good for you. You haven't been back since before he was born."

Laney stroked Lucky's long fur and sighed. "I'd like to go," she mused softly, "but with the wedding just around the corner, it would be crazy. We haven't even started painting the house or picked out a new oven." She looked up at her husband. "And if I go to Georgia, none of that will get done."

"Yes, it will," Noah countered. "The boys and I will take care of everything. You won't even recognize this place when you get home," he added.

Laney eyed him skeptically and laughed. "You don't really expect me to believe that," she said, knowing her husband's lack of success at finishing projects.

"I know I don't have a good track record," Noah began slowly. Laney raised her eyebrows, waiting to hear how he would finish this admission. "But with the wedding coming, I know we'll get it done. Besides, if you go, you can bring home a whole crate of fresh peaches for the cobbler."

Laney sighed, considering his words and feeling her heartstrings tugging south. "Okay," she said finally, "I'll go."

Noah beamed. "Great!" Then he paused. "We better go look at ovens today."

Just then Asher appeared at the bottom of the stairs with Halle behind him. "We're getting a new oven?" he said sleepily, rubbing his eyes.

"We are," Laney said, pulling him onto her lap as he walked by.

He snuggled against her and gently patted Lucky's back too. "Is breakfast ready?" he asked, looking up.

"It is," Noah answered, "*and* your mom has some news for you."

Asher pushed his glasses up on his nose, his eyes wide. "She does?"

"Yup."

Laney frowned. Although she'd said she'd go, it would've been nice to have a little wiggle room in case she changed her mind—and once Asher knew, there'd be no backing out.

Her young son peered at her expectantly, and Noah looked up from pouring pancake batter on the griddle and eyed her questioningly. "Well?"

"What?" Asher asked in an excited voice.

"You could've waited," Laney admonished.

"Why?" he asked, crinkling his brow. "You just said yes . . . and it will give him something to look forward to."

Laney sighed and shook her head.

"Tell me, Mom," Asher begged.

"Well, your dad thinks we should take a trip . . . to the farm."

"Are we going to?" Asher asked, hopping off her lap.

"Do you want to?"

"Yes!"

"It's a really long ride," she warned.

"I don't care."

"It's just going to be me and you."

"Woo-hoo!" he shouted, jumping up and down. "Wait," he said, stopping in mid-jump. "Can Halle come?"

"Oh, I don't know, hon, it's so far."

"She loves car rides," Asher said hopefully.

"She might be better off at home, Ash," Noah said, turning the pancakes.

"Please . . . it would be fun," Asher pressed.

"We'll see," Laney conceded. "But if she stays home, does that mean you want to stay home too?"

"No," he said softly, kneeling down next to Halle. "I'd just miss her."

Laney sighed.

"Okay, who's ready for pancakes?" Noah asked, slipping his spatula under the golden orbs and flipping them onto a plate.

"Me," Asher said, raising his hand and sliding into a chair.

"I'll get the boys," Laney said, pouring a cup of coffee and heading for the stairs.

"Gabe and E are out running," Noah called and she nodded.

After the breakfast dishes were stacked into the dishwasher and the dogs had been fed and treated to small pancakes drizzled with syrup, Laney packed lunches for Gabe and E and headed up to take a quick shower. Meanwhile, Asher settled onto the couch to watch cartoons with Halle curled up next to him while Seth and Ben vied for use of the family computer.

"Dad," Seth whined. "Can Ben use your laptop?"

"Not right now, pal. I need to start my sermon."

"I need my own computer," Seth complained bitterly.

"Get a job and you can buy your own computer," Ben said matter-of-factly.

"How 'bout you get a job," Seth retorted angrily. "You're sixteen."

"I *have* a job—mowing lawns. Remember?"

"Then *you* should buy *your* own computer."

"I can't. I'm saving for an iPhone."

"Well, I need the computer too."

"For what? So you can play that stupid game?"

"It's not stupid!" Seth shouted, trying to push his brother out of his chair.

"Hey," Noah said, looking up. "That's enough.

Do we need to set the timer like we did when you were little?"

"No," Seth growled, stomping from the room. "But I get the computer in fifteen minutes!"

Laney came down the stairs, towel drying her hair. "What *is* the problem down here?"

"Seth's a baby. That's the problem," Ben said.

"I'm not a baby!" shouted an angry voice from the next room.

Laney raised her eyebrows and looked at her husband. "Can one of them use your laptop?"

Noah stared at her. "I have to start my sermon, dear . . . unless you want me to ad-lib."

"You're good at that. Besides, I thought we were going to look at ovens."

"Now?"

"Yes, now."

"It's Saturday. Traffic will be a nightmare."

"I know what day it is," she replied with a hint of sarcasm, "but if you want me to go on this trip, we need to find an oven."

"What trip?" Ben said, looking up from his Facebook page.

"Mom's going to Georgia," Noah said, "and, no, you're not going."

"Can I go?" a pained voice called from the next room.

"If I can't go, you can't go," Ben called back before his parents could answer. "No one wants to travel with a baby."

"I'M NOT A BABY!"

Just then, Gabe and E came down the stairs. "Holy cow! You two are the biggest whiners," E said, reaching for his cooler.

Gabe laughed. "We were never this bad," he said, kissing his mom's cheek. "Bye."

"Thanks for lunch," E added, kissing her other cheek and heading for the door.

Laney rolled her eyes. "No, you were worse."

As the door swung closed behind them, Noah shook his head. "I don't think we can leave these two alone. They might end up killing each other."

"Not if you let one of them use your laptop."

"Seth," he called to the next room. "Do you want to use my laptop?"

"No," a sulky voice mumbled.

Noah frowned. "Why not?"

And when he didn't answer, Ben answered for him. "Because his game's not on it."

"Well, then . . . *you* use it," Noah said.

"Fine," Ben said, purposely shutting down the computer and shoving the chair back so that it toppled over.

"Why did you shut the computer down?" Noah asked, his voice rising.

"Because," Ben answered insolently.

"Well, then, on second thought," Noah said, trying to control his voice. "You can forget about using my laptop. In fact, you're off the computer for the rest of the weekend."

Ben shrugged defiantly. "Fine," he said, pretending not to care and turning to the stairs.

"Honestly, Ben," Laney said. "What is the matter with you?"

"Nothing," he mumbled, looking crestfallen.

"Is it the trip?"

"No," he answered, looking away.

"Asher's never been to the farm," she explained.

"Asher's going?" he asked in surprise.

"How come he gets to go?" a sullen voice called from the next room.

"Because he's never been," Noah said in an exasperated voice. "And there's no way your mother is going to put up with you two on a long car ride." He turned to Laney. "If you want to look at ovens, we need to go. I have work to do."

"Does anyone want to go with us?"

"Nooo," answered a chorus of voices.

❦ 39 ❦

"Are you sure you're up to this?" Maddie asked as Asa gently backed her against the wall, and reached for the buttons of her blouse.

"Mmm," he murmured, kissing her neck and pressing his body against hers.

"I guess you are," she teased, gazing into his blue eyes. "Didn't your doctor tell you to take it easy?"

"I am taking it easy," he whispered, pulling

her toward their old sleigh bed while slowly undressing her.

She lay back on the soft comforter and watched his eyes take in her body as if they were seeing it for the first time. A soft summer breeze rustled the curtains, and he lay on the bed next to her, pulling her body against his. The gentle touch of his hand was as familiar to her as the warmth of the sun on her skin. Even before he touched her she knew where his fingers would trace long slow circles . . . where they would linger . . . and where they would explore. He knew her body as well as he knew his own . . . and he knew how to bring her to the edge, and with a mischievous smile, stop . . . until she could barely hold on. Then he would cover his body with hers, and with the easy rhythm that was ancient and familiar as time itself, they would once again find each other's heat and pleasure.

On rare occasions, Asa closed his eyes, and it always made Maddie wonder if he was thinking of a time long ago. She never asked. She didn't want to know. She knew he'd always been faithful . . . and that was enough, but sometimes she couldn't help but wonder—when his eyes were closed—if he was remembering Noelle. Maddie knew Asa's first love had been painful and real and deep. But did he still slip back into the memory of her?

"I love you," he murmured, kissing her softly and easing to her side.

"I love you too," she whispered, pushing the thought from her mind. *It didn't matter,* she thought, reaching for his hand and drifting off.

Asa looked out the window at the stars and listened to the cicadas in the trees. The droning summer sounds at this time of year always reminded him of the bittersweet day he'd left for college . . . and all of the lonely autumn days that followed. Sometimes the memory still made his heart ache. Suddenly, the peaceful night was shattered by terrified squawking. Maddie woke up in alarm as Asa flew down the stairs with Harper barking at his heels. He turned on the back light just in time to see a fox disappearing into the woods. "No!" he shouted, pushing open the door and running toward the pond, but it was too late. The fox was gone. Asa stood in the yard, naked, his chest tightening in anguished pain as the distraught gander called out frantically for his mate.

❧ 40 ❧

Noah looked up from his pulpit. "Today's sermon," he began, "touches on one of my wife's favorite topics." He paused, surveying his flock, and everyone, including Laney, waited, wondering what her favorite topic was . . . especially since the title in the bulletin, "My Yoke

Is Easy," wasn't very revealing. In fact, Stewart Nicolson, sitting in the back row, wondered if his minister liked his eggs over-easy. But Noah, famous for his long, dramatic pauses—which he believed kept his audience on the edge of their seats—looked down at his notes again, and when he finally looked up, he said, "Worry."

The congregation chuckled and turned to look for their minister's lovely wife. She was in her usual pew surrounded by her five handsome boys, and they knew she had good reason to worry. Noah nodded. "For a woman of abiding faith, my wife loves to keep her worries close to her heart.

"In our kitchen, there are several hand-painted signs that the boys have given her over the years to gently remind her to rise above her one . . . *and only* . . . fault." He grinned impishly, and everyone laughed. "The sign over the oven boldly states: 'STRESS LESS . . . PRAY MORE.' And the one on the mantel is from Proverbs. It commands: 'TRUST IN THE LORD WITH ALL YOUR HEART. AND DO NOT LEAN ON YOUR OWN UNDERSTANDING. IN ALL YOUR WAYS ACKNOWLEDGE HIM, AND HE WILL MAKE STRAIGHT YOUR PATH.' The one in the downstairs bathroom reminds, 'CAST ALL YOUR ANXIETY ON GOD, BECAUSE HE CARES FOR YOU.' And the one on the windowsill over the kitchen sink—where she spends most of her time—is from Philippians: 'DO NOT BE ANXIOUS ABOUT ANYTHING, BUT

IN EVERYTHING BY PRAYER AND SUPPLICATION WITH THANKSGIVING LET YOUR REQUESTS BE MADE KNOWN TO GOD.' "

The boys all turned to watch their mother's reaction, but she just smiled and Noah continued. "But it's not just Laney that worries . . . it's me . . . it's Tom . . . it's Barbara . . . it's Sue . . . it's Lynn . . . it's every one of us.

"So why is it then that, despite all of God's loving reminders, we humans insist on carrying burdens of the world on our shoulders? Even our reading this morning cautions us against this sin . . . and it *is* a sin because it means we don't trust God to take care of us. And for all you worry warts out there, Matthew 6:25–27 bears repeating: 'Therefore I tell you, do not be anxious about your life, what you shall eat or what you shall drink, nor about your body, what you should put on. Is not life more than food and the body more than clothing? Look at the birds of the air: they neither sow nor reap nor gather into barns, and yet the heavenly Father feeds them . . .' Through my wife I might add." He smiled and everyone chuckled. Then he continued to read. " 'Are you not of more value than they? And which of you by being anxious can add one cubit to his span of life?' " Noah looked up and repeated, " *'Which of you by being anxious can add one cubit to his span of life?'* " And then, in classic Reverend Coleman style, he paused. "The answer is: none of us can add a cubit . . . or any other length of time . . . to our life by worrying. In fact, there have been numerous studies that prove anxiety can have a negative effect on one's health. . . . So, in reality, the act of worrying can actually diminish the number of cubits we have left."

He looked down at his notes. "There was a time, early in our marriage, when my wife was a carefree spirit. She took life as it came . . . and saw it as a cycle of changing seasons . . . a rising tide followed by an ebbing tide . . . a world where joy is often paired with sorrow . . . but, even so, she always had a cheerful, positive outlook.

"And then, she gave birth to our first son . . . and she's never been the same."

The congregation chuckled.

"When a woman becomes a mother, her old perception of the world is set back on its heels. The love she feels for her child is as fierce as a grizzly bear's . . . and there is nothing that will stop her from protecting it. In fact, without a second thought, she will lay her life on the line for that new little human being; and the world—which she once viewed as a welcoming, wonderful place—becomes a giant danger zone, complete with yellow tape, and filled with endless reasons to worry.

"From the moment we brought Elijah home from the hospital, my wife was a changed woman. Was the car seat strapped in properly? Were we using the right diapers? Was every cabinet baby-proofed? Should he be allowed to use a pacifier or suck his thumb? Should he be sleeping on his side . . . his stomach . . . his back? Was he breathing? Was he getting enough fresh air? Was he warm? Was he too warm? Was he eating enough? Sleeping enough? Pooping enough? And why was his poop that awful green color?"

He looked up. "Sorry, E, I didn't know you were going to be in church today."

His oldest son smiled. It wasn't the first time he'd been included in his father's sermon.

"I will never forget the first time we took E and Gabe to the Barnstable County Fair. E was probably around two, and Gabe was still pretty new. In fact, I was carrying him in one of those baby carriers. Well, we went into a crowded tent that was serving a sit-down chicken dinner, and as we juggled our plates and looked for a place to sit, Laney realized E wasn't with us. She turned to me, and with utter panic in her eyes, squeaked, 'Where's Elijah?'

"I looked around. 'He was just here,' I said, but in the sea of people, we couldn't spot him right away. As we looked for him and called his name, time seemed to slow to a crawl. Pretty soon, everyone in the tent had stopped what they were doing and were looking too . . . but when Laney started to frantically make her way toward the exit, shouting his name at the top of her lungs, the

270

crowd parted like the Red Sea . . . because a grizzly bear mother had lost her cub.

"Well, needless to say—as you all can see—he was located. In fact, it was just a moment later that my dear wife found him, standing outside, looking around innocently, completely unaware of the heart attack he'd just given his mother . . . and with tears streaming down her cheeks, Laney scooped him up, wrapped him in a bear hug, and held him so tightly I thought she'd never let him go."

Noah smiled. "For years afterward, our boys had to hold hands at all times at the Barnstable County Fair. In fact, they're lucky they don't have tracking chips surgically implanted in their necks."

At this, the congregation chuckled, and Noah smiled.

"Well, fast-forward twelve years and imagine E in middle school, announcing that he would *not* be holding anyone's hand at the fair. He even ventured to say that he planned on hanging out with his friends . . . and not us. Needless to say, it was a rough night for his poor mother, whose memory of the traumatic night twelve years earlier was still ingrained in her memory. And to this day, although E is now twenty-one, Laney still has a hard time letting him go. Thank goodness someone invented the cell phone!"

Noah paused and looked down. "We all know how hard it is to let go. Every mother and father, since the beginning of time, has struggled with letting go of their offspring, but we must remember that our children are gifts from God, and they are put in our charge to love and raise and nurture . . . and through them, God teaches us to trust him. Even when illness or loss or tragedy strikes, He promises to be with us . . . and with them.

"Life isn't easy for anyone. When we are facing difficult times, and it feels like our world is crashing down, and we look at other folks walking down the street or on the beach—and they are smiling or chatting with friends—we ask, 'Why can't that be me? Why can't my life be easy like theirs?' It's then that we need to remember that we are not alone in our suffering—although it may seem like it at the time—there's not a soul on earth that doesn't face struggle at some point . . . but God is always there to give us the strength to soldier on.

"In chapter eleven, Matthew shares Jesus' invitation: 'Come to me, all who are heavy laden, and I will give you rest. Take my yoke upon you, and learn from me; for I am gentle and lowly in heart, and you will find rest for your souls. For my yoke is easy, and my burden is light.' " Noah looked up, his eyes sparkling. "And these, my friends, are some of the most comforting words in the Bible." He smiled. "We would all do well to inscribe them on our hearts. Amen."

Asa stood on the porch, listening to the mournful cries of the gander as he swam slowly back and forth in the last golden rays of sunlight. For as long as he could remember, he and Maddie had looked forward to the pair's arrival every spring —they'd even had an unspoken rivalry as to who would see or hear them first. And they never tired of listening to the gander's deep *a-honk,* or her loving reply—a higher *ca-honk* that assured, "I'm here, dear." But now the male's calls were heart wrenching—it had been two days since the fox had killed his beloved mate, and he was still grieving.

"What will become of him?" Maddie asked.

"I don't know," Asa replied.

"I wish we could help."

"I don't think there's anything you can do for a broken heart."

"We have that old incubator. Maybe we could incubate their eggs. They must've been pretty close to hatching."

Asa shook his head. "They've been neglected for two days now . . . and even if they do hatch, he may not take care of them. What will we do then?"

Maddie looked thoughtful. "Raise them ourselves."

Asa shook his head. "Hon, I know you want to help, but we have a lot going on. We certainly don't have time to be playing Father and Mother Goose."

"I have time."

"What about the weekend of the wedding?"

"I'll get Bella to take care of them," Maddie said, thinking of the young daughter of their next-door neighbor.

Asa sighed, suddenly realizing his wife had latched onto an idea and had no plans of letting go. He put his arm around her. "What if taking the eggs from the nest causes him more trauma?"

Maddie looked skeptical. "I don't think he even remembers they're there."

"Can it at least wait 'til morning? I don't have the energy to dig out the incubator tonight."

Maddie nodded. "First thing . . ."

Asa agreed. "First thing."

42

Beryl sat on the porch of her childhood home and watched as her mom's old bulldog waddled along behind her sister's big black Lab, Norman, trying to sniff his hind end. "Flan-o," she called. "Could you try to be a little more ladylike?" But Flannery ignored her and continued to stop and pee wherever Norman peed.

Rumer looked up from husking corn and laughed. "She's just reclaiming her territory."

Isak took a sip of her wine and added, "It was her territory first, and she can't understand why it smells like Norman everywhere."

"She's too much," Beryl said with a resigned sigh, reaching for another ear of corn. "Is this corn from Kimberly's?"

"Yup. Just picked this morning," Rumer said.

"I wonder if we should get our corn for the clambake from them."

"You should. They have the sweetest corn around."

Beryl nodded. "Maybe we'll stop and talk to John on our way home."

Isak reached for an ear. "How come Micah's parents aren't coming tonight?"

"His dad hasn't been feeling well," Beryl confided. "He's a little evasive about what's going on," she added quietly, "but Micah says he's always been that way."

"Will's parents are like that too," Rumer said with a sympathetic nod. "I hate it when people aren't forthcoming. Whatever it is, just come out with it."

Beryl stacked several ears of corn on the arm of her chair. "They also had a Canada goose killed in their yard."

"Oh, no!" Rumer said. "That's awful."

"It *is* awful. The same pair has been nesting on

their pond for years, and the other night, the female was killed by a fox . . . and now her mate keeps calling for her."

"That's so sad," Isak said, reaching for another ear. "Don't geese mate for life?"

"They do," Beryl said. "And now Micah's parents are worried about what will happen to him. He's so heartbroken."

"Okay," Micah interrupted, coming out on the porch with a plate in his hands. "Who's having a burger and who's having a hot dog?"

Isak frowned. "I thought we were having steak. . . ."

Micah laughed. "I knew that would get you going," he teased, and as he went down the steps to the grill, Isak threw a cushion at him.

"You're not funny, Coleman," she called.

Beryl laughed. "Micah is really looking forward to Bermuda," she confided softly. "He's like a little kid. He even bought a new bathing suit."

Rumer laughed. "I'm so jealous. Will and I never got to go on a honeymoon."

"Micah and Beth never did either."

"Well, you guys are going to have such a good time."

Beryl nodded. "I hope so. I hope there aren't any hurricanes."

"You don't need to worry," Isak reassured. "Hurricane season doesn't really get going until September."

As she said this, Matt and Will came around the corner of the house, and Matt stopped to admire the porch Will had just restored. "It needed new flooring and posts."

"Well, it looks great," Matt said with a nod. "Everything you've done to this old place looks great."

"Thanks," Will said. "We still have a long way to go. Ru wants to re-do the kitchen, but I'm so busy right now I think it's going to have to wait until winter."

"I heard that," Rumer called over the railing, and Matt and Will both laughed as they walked over to join Micah at the grill.

"You're not supposed to be doing that," Will said apologetically.

"Not a problem," Micah said with a grin.

"Well, can I at least get you a beer?"

"Sure," Micah said.

"How about you, Matt?"

"Sounds good."

"Are the steaks almost ready?" Rumer called.

"Just turning 'em now," Micah called back.

Will came back out on the porch with three frosty bottles as Rumer gathered up the corn. "Hon, can you round up Charlotte and Rand. I think he's showing her the tree house," she said.

Will nodded and held the door for her.

Beryl and Isak picked up the ears they'd husked

and followed Rumer inside, and as Isak refilled their wine glasses and Beryl pulled salads out of the fridge, Rumer plunged the corn into the steaming pot on the stove.

Moments later, giggling Charlotte chased her new cousin into the kitchen with Norman at their heels and Flan waddling as fast as she could to keep up. "Go wash up, Char," Micah commanded as he held the platter of sizzling steaks up so it wouldn't get knocked from his hand.

"You too, Rand," Will called.

When they were all finally seated around the kitchen table, Rand reached eagerly for an ear of corn, but Charlotte nudged him and whispered, "Grace!"

Rand frowned, and Rumer raised her eyebrows. "You know what grace is."

Sheepishly, Rand bowed his head, and everyone else turned to look at Micah.

"Me?" he said with a groan.

"Might as well be you," Matt said matter-of-factly. "You're closer to the cloth than any of us."

Micah shook his head, but then looked down and paused reflectively. Before he spoke, he glanced around the table at the bowed heads—including Rand's and Charlotte's, whose eyes were squeezed shut—waiting, and he bowed his head again. "Thank you, Father," he began softly, "for the blessing of a beautiful summer day . . . a bountiful table . . ." And then, in traditional

Coleman style, he paused before adding, "And a big, crazy, wonderful family."

They all chuckled, and Beryl squeezed his hand.

"Amen!" Matt said, holding up his drink.

A chorus of voices responded, "Amen!" and then cheerful chatter and laughter filled the kitchen as bowls of potato salad, Caesar salad, and Beryl's famous three bean salad circled the table, followed by steak, corn on the cob, and deviled eggs.

43

Maddie woke to the cheerful sound of chirping —the cardinal was first, then the chickadee, and then a titmouse joined in. She rolled onto her side, smiled sleepily, and was about to doze off again when she realized something was amiss— the traumatized honking that had haunted them for three days was silent.

"Asa, wake up," she said, pulling on her robe and hurrying down the stairs with Harper at her heels. The pond was gray and misty in the early dawn light so she pulled on her gum boots and went out into the yard. As she walked along the edge of the pond, her heart pounded. She noticed Harper nosing near the nest. "Harp, leave it," she commanded, and Harper backed away. She stepped closer, and then her eyes filled with tears—the gander's lifeless body was lying among the cattails.

After a quiet breakfast, for which neither of them had much appetite, Asa rooted around in the garage for plywood to make a box while Maddie looked for the incubator. After twenty minutes, she groaned, "I don't see it."

"It has to be here," Asa said. "Did you look under that drop cloth?"

Maddie lifted a folded drop cloth up off the shelf behind their bicycles, and there it was. "You could've suggested looking there ten minutes ago."

"I didn't know," he said innocently.

"Mmm," she said, eyeing him skeptically. She brushed away the cobwebs and lifted the incubator off the shelf. Years earlier, after checking the prices of incubators at Agway and Tractor Supply, Asa decided he could make one that worked just as well. He found plans online, constructed a simple box out of plywood, and cut a hole in one end of it for a lightbulb and socket. It worked perfectly.

Maddie set the incubator on the workbench and plugged it in. The lightbulb flickered to life. "It still works," she said in a surprised voice.

"Why shouldn't it?" Asa asked. "We used it last year for the Bantams," he said, referring to the laying hens they'd had the previous summer—before the fox discovered their yard was a perfect hunting ground.

"That's probably why he took the goose," Maddie surmised. "He was mad because we didn't have any chickens this year."

"Well, now there isn't anything for him to snack on so he'll have to move on. That is unless you're successful at hatching those eggs. Then he'll be back."

Maddie frowned. "I didn't think of that. . . ."

Asa stopped what he was doing and looked up. "It certainly would be sad if the goslings met an unfortunate end too."

Maddie shook her head. She knew what her husband was doing, but she wasn't falling for it. "I guess that's a chance we'll have to take," she said as she disappeared to gather the eggs.

By lunchtime, their appetites had returned. The box had been built, a hole had been dug, and an old, soft towel had been folded into it. Together, they gently laid the gander in the box, and while Asa nailed on the top, Maddie folded another soft towel into the incubator and put the eggs under the warm light. They buried the goose under the pine trees on the far side of the pond, and while Asa put his tools away, Maddie checked on her eggs.

"A watched egg never hatches," Asa teased.

"Very funny."

"What's for lunch?"

Maddie paused thoughtfully. "How about grilled cheese and tomato soup?"

Asa smiled. "That sounds good."

❦ 44 ❦

The next two weeks flew by in a flurry of activity. The new oven, and to Laney's delight, a matching stainless steel refrigerator with an ice and water dispenser were both ordered from Cape Appliance, and then several gallons of dark red paint with wooden paint stirrers appeared in the garage, along with new drop cloths, scrapers, and brushes.

Ben and Seth were immediately set to task, scraping loose paint off the front of the house, and although they were getting paid by the hour, it was tedious work and they were thankful it was only the front of the house that needed attention as the sides and back—in traditional Cape Cod style—were shingled.

On the morning the appliances were to be delivered, Laney cleaned out the contents of the old fridge and realized they had two bottles of ketchup, three jars of mayonnaise—two of which were nearly empty—and three flavors of mustard: spicy Dijon, classic yellow, and honey. They also had enough bottles of salad dressing to open a restaurant, and several of them looked like they'd been in there for years. There was every flavor jam and jelly—also of vintage origin—as well as eggs, carrots, celery, cold cuts, one container of orange juice, and an almost empty gallon of milk.

When she finished with the fridge, she dragged in two old beach coolers, filled the bottoms with ice, and packed them full with several half gallons of ice cream, Popsicles, waffles, frozen vegetables, chicken nuggets, French fries, Ziplock bags of mystery meat, and numerous cans of frozen lemonade. Next, she carefully plucked off the outer layer of magnets that were holding up years of photographs, notes, and phone numbers and put them all in a box for safekeeping.

Hours later, after the delivery men had carted off the old appliances and she'd almost filled the new fridge, Ben came in from scraping paint and stood in front of the open door with beads of perspiration dripping down the sides of his face. "I like our new air conditioner," he said with an approving nod.

Laney closed the door. "It's not an air conditioner," she said, reaching for the box of magnets and photos. She picked out the magnet from the Double Dragon Inn and put it against the door, but it fell to the floor. "Oh, no!" she cried.

"I don't think magnets stick to silver refrigerators," Ben observed.

"I didn't even think of that when we ordered stainless," Laney said in dismay.

"That's okay," Ben consoled. "I think it looks better without all that stuff."

"You do?"

He nodded.

"Well, what am I going to do with it?"

Ben shrugged. "Throw it away?"

Laney looked as if he'd suggested she cut off her hand. "You want me to throw away this picture of you running in your first race?" she asked, holding up a faded newspaper clipping.

Ben looked at it. "Well, no . . . but you can throw everything else away."

Laney was still shaking her head when Noah came in ten minutes later. "The magnets don't stick," she announced mournfully.

"Oh, well," he said with a grin. "That's the price you pay."

"Thanks a lot," she said, stuffing ice cream into the drawer of the new freezer. "Want a melting Popsicle?"

"No thanks," he said, sitting in a kitchen chair and admiring the new appliances. "Do you like 'em?"

"I do . . . except for the magnet issue."

"Hey, did you know there's a bird nest under the back of the shed?"

Laney looked up. "I did, but I kind of forgot about it. There were babies in it earlier this summer, but after we had that really bad rainstorm, they all disappeared. And then I saw there were new eggs."

"Well, now there are four new babies, and they are keeping their parents very busy."

"That's wonderful. I felt so bad for them after

that storm. They kept bringing food to an empty nest."

Noah nodded. "You should go see them."

"I will," she said, putting the last of the canned lemonade in the door and closing it. She collapsed wearily into a chair across from him, and Mennie moseyed over to rest his head in her lap, thankful that the kitchen was finally getting back to normal. She rubbed his ears and saw the Double Dragon Inn magnet lying on the table. "Feel like Chinese?"

"What?" Noah teased. "We have a brand-new oven and refrigerator. I expect a five-course meal."

Laney laughed. "Maybe tomorrow."

"Well, I wish you'd thought of that before I left the church. I could've picked it up on my way home."

"I could have the boys pick it up."

Noah shrugged. "If that's what you want. Make sure you order enough egg rolls this time or we'll have World War Three on our hands."

Laney nodded, remembering that the last time they'd ordered Chinese they'd been two egg rolls short. She looked down at Mennie. "Are you ready for your supper too?" she asked, and Mennie's whole hind end wagged as he slurped his tongue around his jowls. The words *supper* and *breakfast* always caused him to lick his lips.

As she stood up, they heard the screen door, and

Gabe appeared, looking tan, tired, and sandy. "You were supposed to pick up Chinese."

"Did you text us?" Gabe asked.

"Not yet."

"Oh, well," E said, following him in. "We have to run anyway," he said, setting his cooler on the floor.

"I hope that's not sandy on the bottom. I just cleaned."

"It's not," he said, picking it up to show her and leaving a light-colored rectangle on the floor. "Well, maybe it is. . . . Sorry."

Laney sighed and reached for the dustpan.

"Nice fridge," Gabe said, leaning against the counter.

"Yeah," E agreed, pulling the door open and admiring the interior.

"It's not an air conditioner," Noah reminded.

"I know," E said. "I'm just getting some OJ."

"Use a glass," Laney added.

"Of course, Mom. I don't want to get the plague."

Gabe reached into the cabinet for two glasses.

"So when will you be back?" Laney asked, sweeping up the sand.

E shrugged. "I dunno . . . seven?"

Laney looked at the clock. "Well, I guess I can go get it," she said, thinking out loud. "We need milk anyway."

"Get orange juice too," E said, shaking the empty container.

"What kind of Chinese do you want?"

"Sesame chicken," Gabe said.

E nodded. "And make sure you get enough egg rolls this time."

Laney rolled her eyes, and twenty minutes later, after taking everyone's order—including several more reminders to get enough egg rolls—she headed out so she could get milk and OJ too. As she turned onto Ocean Drive, she saw two boys on bikes riding on the opposite side of the road. She slowed down as she passed, and although she couldn't place the second boy, she was certain the first one was Jared Laughlin, and as she watched him, she saw him laugh as he swerved to hit a squirrel that had scampered into the road.

❧ 45 ❧

The last week of July was a blur. "I don't think we should go," Laney said the night before they were to leave. In her arms was the last load of laundry.

Noah looked up from his laptop. "You can't back out now. Asher's all packed. He even packed Halle's things."

"I know, but this house is a disaster, and I can't come home two days before the wedding and have it all cleaned . . . *and* have time to make enough peach cobbler for sixty plus people. Do you have any idea how long it takes to peel that many peaches?"

"I'll help you. We'll all help. In fact, while you're gone, I'll get more peelers, and when you're ready to make the cobblers, we'll have a peach peeling party."

Laney frowned and shook her head. She had no reply for such an absurd solution. She just felt like crying. She turned to head up the stairs with the laundry.

"Don't worry about the house," he called.

She dumped the laundry on the bed and spread it out so it wouldn't wrinkle—most of the clothes were hers—things she planned on taking: T-shirts, shorts, underwear, a pair of jeans, a sweatshirt, her running shorts, and a sports bra—in case she had the chance to go running, which she was beginning to doubt. Glumly, she opened her suitcase, folded each item and laid it in. Her heart just wasn't in it.

"Rabbit, rabbit!" Asher said softly, blinking at the darkness. There was just the slightest hint of gray outside his bedroom window, and his heart pounded with excitement as he pushed back his sheet. "C'mon, Halle," he whispered. "We've got to get ready." The puppy, who'd grown considerably since they'd brought her home, yawned, and settled her head back on her paws while Asher shuffled to the next room.

"Mom," he said in a hushed voice, shaking her. "It's time to get up. You said we have to leave early."

Laney mumbled, "It's too early for school, hon. Go back to bed."

"Mom," Asher persisted. "We're going to Georgia . . . remember?"

Laney sat bolt upright, opened her eyes, and looked at the bedside clock. "Crap," she grumbled. She looked at Asher. "You didn't hear that."

He grinned. "Nope."

Laney nudged her husband. "Hon, I overslept . . . and I'm going to take my shower."

Noah rolled over, looked at the clock, and immediately pulled himself out of bed. Sleepily, he carried Laney's suitcase down the stairs, turned on the coffeepot, and started to pack a cooler with snacks and drinks.

Asher pulled on his John Deere T-shirt and shorts, made his bed, brushed his teeth, packed his toothbrush, and thumped his suitcase down the stairs, with Halle at his heels. "I'm ready," he announced.

"Mmm . . . you look ready," Noah said with a smile. "Why don't you go get the comb and we'll try to tame that wildfire on the top of your head."

Asher reached up to touch his hair. "Oops!" He dropped his suitcase and turned to run up the stairs, almost knocking Laney over.

"Be right back," he called.

Laney dropped her backpack by the door, and Noah handed her a cup of coffee. She took a sip and smiled. "As much as I'd love to drink this right now, I think I'm going to put it in a travel mug and drink it when we're a little farther down the road. I'd like to at least be off the Cape before we have to make our first stop."

Noah chuckled. He knew all about Laney's pit stops when they traveled.

"It's not funny," Laney admonished. "*And* it's your fault."

"My fault?" Noah asked, feigning innocence.

"Yes, your fault for impregnating me so many times."

"Yeah, well it would be nice to have the opportunity to try to impregnate you again," he said, putting his arm around her shoulder.

"Well, you have a long wait," Laney said wryly, "with this full house. Besides, in case you forgot, you're fixed and I've paused . . . so they'll be no more impregnating."

"We could still go through the motions once in a while . . ."

"We could . . . if there weren't so many little ears around."

"Well, maybe we'll have to get away for a weekend."

Laney poured her coffee into her travel mug. "I don't think ministers are allowed to go away for the weekend," she teased.

"I'm sure something can be arranged . . . maybe Nantucket?"

"Nantucket sounds nice," she agreed, sounding doubtful. "When you figure out when and how we can afford Nantucket for a weekend, let me know." She missed their lovemaking too, but she was usually too tired to dwell on it. She was perfectly happy to have him cuddle next to her at night. "I'm going to miss you," she said.

"I'm going to miss you too," he said softly, pulling her into a hug.

Just then, Asher bounced down the stairs with the comb and a spray bottle full of water. He pretended to shield his eyes and teased, "Get a room, wouldja?"

Noah pulled him into their hug, which made him giggle. "I'm gonna wet my pants," he said breathlessly.

"Well, you better go to the bathroom then," Noah said, laughing and releasing him.

Twenty minutes later, after quick bowls of cereal, a reminder to keep an eye on Lucky, and a walk around the yard for Halle, they loaded everything in the car. The eastern sky was just beginning to brighten, and Laney looked out at the ocean. "I can't believe we've only been down to the beach a couple of times this summer," she said sadly. "And by the time we get back, summer will be almost over. The kids have hardly been in the pool."

"That's not true," Noah consoled. "They've been in the pool—even Halle's been in the pool," he said, scooping up the puppy, kissing her head, and putting her on the backseat. "And when things settle down, we'll make a point of getting down to the beach. Things've just been a little hectic this summer."

"Halle loves the pool," Asher piped, climbing into his seat.

"Hey, where's my hug?" Noah said, eyeing him in dismay.

"Right here," Asher replied, jumping into his arms.

"Have you got Halle's leash?"

"Yup."

"And you're gonna be good?"

"Yup."

"And help Mom?"

"Yup."

"And not eat all the peaches on the way home?"

"Yup."

"And not let Mom eat all the peaches on the way home?"

He giggled. "Yup!"

"Okay, then you can go." He kissed his forehead. "Love you," he said, plopping him into his seat.

"Love you too."

Noah turned to Laney.

"Don't eat all the peaches," he said with a grin.

I will. I mean *won't*," she said with a laugh.

"Do you remember how to go?"

"Like the back of my hand," she assured him. Then she looked up at the house. "Do you think I should wake them?"

"No. You said good-bye last night. They're fine."

"But, what if—"

"What if nothing," he interrupted. "We'll be fine . . . you'll be fine . . . and like it or not, you'll be back before you know it."

Laney half smiled and nodded, and he pulled her into one last hug. She lay her head on his chest and felt the rhythmic beat of his heart. It was as steady as he was. "I love you," she whispered with tears in her eyes.

"I love you too," he said softly, holding her tight.

Asher cleared his throat, and Laney smiled although her eyes were glistening, and Noah looked over and realized Halle had her head out the window. "You make sure her window stays up a bit so she doesn't fall out," he reminded.

"I will."

Laney opened her door.

"Got your phone?"

She nodded.

"Charger?"

She nodded again.

"Call me when you get there?"

"I will."

Noah smiled, and as Laney turned the key, he stepped back and waved. She smiled wistfully and waved back. And as she pulled away, watching him continue to wave, hot tears spilled down her cheeks.

"Don't cry, Mom," Asher said cheerfully. "We'll be back."

As the sun came up over the Sagamore Bridge, Laney glanced in back and realized that Asher had fallen asleep with Halle's head in his lap. Smiling, she slid the top of her travel cup open and took a sip—the coffee was still hot. She was glad she'd waited. Now Asher could sleep, and she could probably make it all the way into Connecticut . . . maybe even New York . . . before she had to stop.

Cape Cod to Georgia was an eighteen-hour trip without stops, but she didn't plan to drive straight through. They'd go as far as Virginia today, and then hopefully make it to the farm by early Sunday afternoon. She felt less anxious about going now that they were finally underway. She knew all along that leaving would be the hardest part. As she reached for her sunglasses and turned on the radio, her thoughts drifted to the rolling hills of the farm and the bear hugs they'd get from Lyle. It had been much too long.

❧ 46 ❧

The receptionist ushered Asa and Maddie into the doctor's office. "Dr. Raines will be right in," she said. Asa nodded and walked over to the window. The office had a commanding view of Boston Harbor, and he murmured wryly, "I guess oncology is the right business to be in." He turned to Maddie, who was already sitting across from the desk with her hands folded. She mustered a smile in response, and Asa studied her. "Bracing yourself?"

She shook her head.

Asa looked around the room. It was not like most doctors' offices, which were usually paneled with dark, somber wood and decorated with important-looking degrees. In fact, Dr. Raines's office was painted a soothing tan, and the back wall was covered with strikingly beautiful photographs of snowy mountains, crashing surf, and rustic townscapes.

"I don't remember his office being so bright," Asa observed.

"I think it was raining that day . . . or maybe it was just cloudy. . . ." Maddie said, trying to remember. "Or maybe it was just our world that seemed dark."

"Maybe," Asa agreed. He stood in front of one

of the photographs. "These little towns must be out west somewhere," he mused thoughtfully. "That's something I always wanted to do—travel out west to see the Grand Canyon . . . the Redwoods . . . El Capitan. I guess that'll never—"

Just then, the door opened, and the tall, young doctor came in and immediately walked over to shake Asa's hand. "Good to see you again, Mr. Coleman."

Asa shook his hand, looking puzzled. "Good to see you too, Dr. Raines. It's funny, but I don't remember you being quite so tall . . . or so young."

Dr. Raines laughed. "I'm not surprised. You had a lot on your mind that day." He turned to Maddie and shook her hand too. "How are you, Mrs. Coleman?"

"I'm fine," she said with a polite smile.

"I was just admiring your photographs," Asa said, motioning to the walls.

"Thanks," the young doctor said with a smile. "Photography is an old hobby of mine."

"You took them?" Asa asked in surprise.

The doctor nodded. "When I was in college, I wanted to be a photographic journalist—travel the world and document everything I saw. It seemed so . . . romantic. But my parents—you know . . ." He grinned. "They wanted to make sure I was going to be able to support myself, and since I was interested in science too, they

296

pressed hard for medical school." He sighed. "In the end, it worked out. Now I can afford to travel, and I still get to photograph everything I see."

"Where'd you grow up?"

"Under the wide, blue skies of Montana."

Asa nodded. "I always wanted to travel out west," he said wistfully.

"Well, it's never too late," the young doctor said, opening the file on his desk. "In fact, you're going to have time to travel the whole world if you want to." He looked up and smiled. "Mr. Coleman, your response to the treatment has been remarkable . . . even textbook noteworthy. In fact, your case will be included in all of our future published reports. It's not unusual, with this particular type of laser radiation, to have significant shrinkage, but in your case, after only six weeks, the tumor you had is undetectable."

Tears filled Maddie's eyes as Asa squeezed her hand. His hand felt warm and strong—so different from the last time they'd sat in this office.

"Now, of course, you'll need to follow up so we can make sure there's no recurrence." He looked at the calendar on his desk. "The first time I'd like to see you is in four weeks—so around the beginning of September. After that, every six weeks for a year or so."

Asa's eyes glistened as he shook his head in disbelief. When he finally spoke, his voice was choked with emotion. "I can't thank you enough,

Dr. Raines," he said, standing to shake his hand.

The doctor stood too. "In my experience, it's the patients who have a strong faith—who believe in some kind of higher power—that have the most profound results. And from the moment I met you, I had a feeling you would have a positive outcome."

Asa smiled at Maddie. "Maddie's the one with the strong faith," he said, squeezing her hand. "I think she has a direct line to heaven."

The doctor put his hand on Asa's shoulder. "Well, she's a keeper . . . and so are you."

The doctor reached out to shake Maddie's hand, but Maddie bypassed his outstretched hand and hugged him instead. "Thank you," she whispered.

"You're welcome," he said softly.

Asa held the door for Maddie, and as she stepped out into the late-day August sunshine, she felt as if the weight of the world had been lifted from her shoulders: Asa was going to live . . . their lives would be normal again . . . they would grow old together. Her heart sang with joy.

"I think we should celebrate," Asa said, putting his arm jauntily over her shoulder.

"What about Harper?"

"She'll be fine, but if you're really worried, call Micah."

"He's not home. He's out on the Cape, helping Noah."

Asa frowned. "How about Bella?"

"Okay," Maddie said with a nod, reaching for her phone.

Twenty minutes later, they were sitting at a table near a window at the Union Oyster House, sipping cocktails and perusing the menu when their cell phone rang. Maddie looked at the screen. "It's Bella," she said, flipping it open.

"Hi, Bella," she said. "What's up?" As she listened, a smile spread across her face. "Oh, that's wonderful," she said, laughing. "Thank you so much for letting us know." She paused. "Yup, we'll be home in a couple of hours."

Maddie closed her phone and beamed. "Two of the eggs hatched!"

"Great," Asa said, laughing. "I can't wait to be followed around by fuzzy little goslings."

47

Micah and E stood on either side of Noah, holding up the new granite countertop while Noah spread silicone along the plywood base; then he quickly squeezed a bead of caulk around the rim of the new sink, and they gently set the heavy granite down and slid it into place.

"When is Laney due home?" Micah asked.

Noah frowned and gave the granite a gentle nudge to center it better around the sink. "I think she'll be home on the twelfth. She didn't want to have to freeze the peaches because she worried it would make the cobbler watery, so she planned on getting back as close to the sixteenth as possible while still allowing enough time to get everything done. And she wanted to be home for Asher's birthday, which is the thirteenth."

"We shouldn't have asked her to make the cobbler," Micah said regretfully.

"If you hadn't asked her to make the cobbler, she wouldn't have gone to Georgia."

"Well, it's too much. It's bad enough that we're having the wedding here. She must be absolutely frazzled."

"She's okay," Noah assured him.

E looked up and caught his uncle's eye, and Micah nodded in understanding. Everyone in the family knew that Noah—ever the optimist—was notoriously bad at gauging his wife's stress level. "I still think we should make it up to her somehow. Any idea what she might like?"

Noah surveyed the counter and took a sip of his beer. "You really don't have to do anything," he said. "She's getting a new kitchen."

"I know, but that's from you—because she's put up with you all these years," he added with a grin. "We should do something too."

"Well, we were just talking about how nice it would be to get away . . . and since E and Gabe are heading back to school soon, maybe you guys could stay with the boys for a weekend."

"Where are you thinking of going?"

"We talked about Nantucket, but she thinks it's too expensive."

Micah nodded. "Well, how about if we give her a gift card for the Century House *and* stay with the boys."

"She'd love that," E said, before his dad could answer.

"She would," Noah agreed, "but don't you think the Century House is a little extravagant?"

Micah took a sip of his beer. "Nope, Laney's worth it. She's always been there for me, and this is long overdue."

Noah shrugged and turned his attention back to the countertop. "When are they coming with the tent and the dance floor?"

"Probably the same day Laney gets home."

"Perfect," Noah said with a chuckle. "She'll come home to the usual—blessed pandemonium."

"Well, at least the kitchen'll be done," Micah said.

"Maybe," Noah said with a smile. "E, can you hand me that cloth?"

"Where did you learn how to do all this any-way?" Micah asked.

"We ministers have all kinds of hidden talents," he said with a grin. "Actually, I learned a lot when I helped Dad update their kitchen."

"When did you order the cabinets and counter-tops?"

"Oh, back when Laney started talking about getting a new oven—that was the easy part. Convincing her to go to Georgia was the hard part."

Micah looked around. "She's going to be so surprised."

Noah nodded. "I tried to get an idea of what color scheme she liked when we were picking out the oven, and she seemed to be drawn to the darker colors."

"Well, it's gorgeous. She's going to love it."

"I wanted to refinish the floor too, but we have to be off of it for three days afterward, so I don't think we'll be able to fit that in."

Micah took a sip of his beer. "Maybe you can do it right before you go away. And we'll have the boys come stay with us in New Hampshire."

Noah looked skeptical. "That would involve bringing the dogs too . . . and trying to work around Ben and Seth's cross-country schedule. It's a nice thought, but nothing is ever that simple around here."

Micah laughed. "Well, I guess you'll just have to camp out in the yard one weekend."

"Dad," E interrupted, looking at the clock. "Do you need me anymore?"

"Why? Where are you headed?"

"Out."

Noah raised his eyebrows, waiting for him to continue.

"I need to go running, shower, and then Chloe and I are going to a movie."

Micah looked up. "That reminds me—I'm supposed to find out if Chloe's coming to the wedding."

"She is," E said with a smile. "Thanks for inviting her."

"Good! Beryl and I are looking forward to meeting her. We've heard so many good things . . . especially her poetry reciting skills."

E laughed. "Yup, she definitely impressed Grandpa."

"And he's not easily impressed," Micah noted.

Noah eyed his oldest son. "Well, just because your mother's not home, doesn't mean you can stay out all night."

Micah eyed his brother. "You're kidding, right? He's a twenty-one-year-old college senior, and he still has a curfew?"

"Hey, I don't make the rules," Noah said defensively. "I just follow 'em."

"Don't worry, Dad," E interjected. "Chloe and I both have to be at work tomorrow, so I'm sure I'll be home at a decent time."

Just then, Gabe came in, drying his hands on a paper towel. "Well, the front is all done—two coats. But I'm not responsible for how much paint Ben and Seth spattered on each other . . . and the hydrangeas."

"I thought you covered the bushes."

"I did, but they still managed to get it everywhere." He looked at E. "Are we running?"

"Yup."

"Hey, are you guys running Falmouth?" Micah asked.

"We are," Gabe answered.

Noah eyed his brother. "Poor planning on your part."

Micah frowned. "When is it?"

"The day after the wedding."

"It's late this year. Oh, well, maybe next year." He looked at Gabe. "Are you still going to be our DJ?" he asked hopefully.

"Yup. In fact, I'd like to go over the music with you sometime."

"I'm staying over tonight . . . so maybe later?"

"Sounds good."

The screen door squeaked open, and Ben and Seth tumbled in, covered in red paint, and Noah groaned and shook his head.

"It's his fault," Seth said, pushing his brother.

"You started it," Ben protested, pushing back.

Micah just laughed. "I'm so glad I have a girl."

"You are *now,*" Noah said. "Wait 'til she's a teenager."

"Yeah, Uncle Micah," Seth added. "You'll wish you had five boys!"

❧ 48 ❧

"There it is," Laney exclaimed, pointing to an old wooden sign by the side of the road. "Want to stop and take a picture?"

"Sure," Asher said. "Can Halle be in it?"

"Yup," Laney said, stirring up a cloud of dust as she pulled over. She helped Asher climb out and then clicked Halle's leash onto her collar and lifted her out. "Hold on to her," she warned, handing the leash to him.

Asher nodded and led Halle—sniffing happily—through the tall sprays of goldenrod and milkweed. "Get busy," he said, and he didn't have to ask twice—Halle promptly squatted. "Can I go too?" he asked.

Laney looked up from her phone. "Go ahead."

Asher turned away and pushed down his shorts. "Look how far I can make it go," he said proudly, glancing back over his shoulder.

Laney shook her head—after five boys, male peeing prowess was old news. "You're definitely a Coleman," she said as Asher pulled up his shorts and studied the hand-painted sign.

PACEY'S PEACHES AND PECANS
PICK YOUR OWN
OR VISIT OUR GIFT SHOP AND TAKE HOME

A DELICIOUS HOMEMADE PIE,
COBBLER, OR JAM
2 MILES AHEAD . . . BUSES WELCOME!

"Someone needs to repaint it," Asher called, critically eyeing the peeling paint.

"You're right," Laney called back.

Asher turned around, pushed Halle's hind end down, looked up at Laney, and grinned. "Perfect," Laney said, taking the picture. She studied the image and gave him a thumbs-up. "If I had a Facebook page, this would be a perfect post."

Asher walked back toward the car, looking puzzled. "How come you don't have a Facebook page, Mom?"

"Oh, I don't know," she said, showing him the picture. "I guess I'm kind of old school. I keep in touch with my friends the old-fashioned way—with letters and phone calls." She lifted Halle back into the car.

"Does Dad have a Facebook page?" Asher asked, climbing.

"He does. He says it helps him keep in touch with his congregation."

Asher nodded thoughtfully. "I don't think I want a Facebook page."

"How come?"

"Cuz kids post mean stuff."

"How do you know that?"

"Ben and Seth were talking about it. They

thought I was asleep, but I heard Ben tell Seth about some older kids that posted some really mean things about a girl . . . and she ended up in the hospital."

"She did?" Laney asked in surprise, wondering how she'd missed this. "Was she okay?"

Asher shrugged. "I dunno because they started whispering."

Laney frowned. "Well, sometimes kids do say mean things . . . and it's usually because they're having a hard time or they aren't happy."

Asher nodded, stroking Halle's head. He looked back at the sign. "Two miles, Mom! Let's go!"

Leaving a trail of red dust behind them, Laney pulled back onto the road, and as they crested the next hill, she pointed. "There it is!"

Asher looked out at the rows of gnarled, ancient trees, their limbs heavy with rosy, golden fruit. "Wow!" he said.

"And those are the pecan trees," she said, motioning across the road.

Asher gazed at the majestic trees on the opposite side of the road—they were twice as big as the peach trees. "Mom, how come *we* don't live here?"

Laney laughed. "I don't know, Ash. When I was your age, I was certain I'd live here someday . . . but sometimes life doesn't work out the way we plan." She turned into a long, winding driveway shaded by peach trees and drove slowly up to an old rambling white farmhouse sitting on a hill. "This is where Gramp and Gram lived," Laney said softly, tears filling her eyes.

As she pulled up next to an old Chevy pickup, a lanky reddish-brown hound loped out of the barn, bellowing a deep-throated greeting. "C'mere, Red," a broad-shouldered man with a tattered John Deere hat called out gruffly, following him.

Laney climbed out of her old Honda Pilot and stood with her hands on her hips, watching the man as he tried to suppress the grin that was spreading across his face. Laney slowly shook her head as she walked toward him, and when they reached each other, he swept her off the ground in a powerful bear hug. "Oh, man, yer a sight for sore eyes," he said, laughing and swinging her around.

"So are you," she said, resting her hand on the side of his tan face and searching his bright blue eyes. She lifted his hat off his head and laughed. "Oh, my goodness! Look how gray you are!"

"You'd be gray too if you were running this place," he said, laughing.

"Mom!" Asher called, eyeing the big hound warily.

Lyle looked up. "Oh, man, look at this kid—does he ever look like his father! Are you sure you had anything to do with him?"

Laney laughed. "I'm sure. I felt every contraction."

Lyle walked over and smoothed Halle's soft ears. "You don't need to worry about Red. He's a big mush—big wind, no rain."

Asher nodded and opened the door for Halle to jump out; immediately, she ran fearlessly over to the old hound and jumped on him, but he just wagged his wiry tail and sniffed her. Satisfied that his uncle was right, Asher started to climb down too.

"Hey, man, you got a hug for me?"

Asher grinned and jumped into his uncle's strong, brown arms.

Lyle chuckled. "Man, you're heavy! What'd you have for breakfast?"

"Pancakes, sausage, and orange juice."

"All that? Well, heck, I hope you saved room for dinner."

"You're having dinner now?" Asher asked in surprise.

"Yup."

Asher gave his mom a puzzled look, and she laughed. "You're in the south now, Ash. Life's a little slower down here."

Lyle set Asher down and grinned. "I like that shirt," he said. "Do you think it would fit me?"

Asher looked down. "Nooo," he said, laughing.

"What if I let you drive my John Deere?"

Asher's eyes grew wide. "You have a John Deere?"

"Yup, didn't yer ma tell ya?"

Asher shook his head and then frowned. "I still don't think it'll fit you."

Lyle ruffled his hair. "That's okay, Ash. I'll let you drive my tractor anyway," he said. "A little later though, cuz everybody's waitin' and dinner's gettin' cold."

"What are we having?" Asher asked as Laney reached into the back of the SUV for the gifts she'd brought.

"Let's see," he said, scratching his chin. "We're havin' fried chicken, mashed potatoes, gravy, coleslaw, biscuits . . . and peach pie with home-made ice cream."

"Peach ice cream?" Laney asked, her eyes growing wide.

"Is there any other kind?" Lyle teased.

They turned toward the house, and as they came up the walk, Lyle's wife, Maren, came out on the porch, drying her hands on her apron. "They're here," she called, and a tall, dark-haired boy and a younger girl came running toward the door. Maren gave Laney a hug and knelt down in front of Asher. "You must be Asher," she said with a kind smile. "I'm Aunt Maren and these are your cousins," she said, motioning to the boy and girl standing beside her, "Levi and Laurie." Asher smiled shyly and nodded.

The screen door squeaked open again, and a tall, slender man with a shock of white hair politely held it open for a sprite, petite woman in her early seventies. Laney looked up in surprise. "Hi, Uncle Luke and Aunt Jo."

"Hi, Laney, dear, it's so good to see you," Aunt Jo said, reaching up to hug her.

The older gentleman leaned on his cane and smiled at Asher. "Hello there, young man," he said, his ice-blue eyes sparkling.

"Hello," Asher said politely.

"Uncle Luke is Grandpa Pacey's brother," Laney explained.

Asher nodded, suddenly feeling overwhelmed by the introduction of so many new family members.

Laney smiled—struck by how much her uncle looked like her father . . . and her grandfather. She gave him a warm hug. "It's so good to see you," she said softly, her eyes filling with tears. She looked around at her family. "It's so good to see all of you."

❧ 49 ❧

As Noah poured fresh paint into the roller tray, he heard Lucky meowing sadly and went out on the porch to investigate. Lucky was sitting by the screen door, watching the birds. "Sorry, pal, no more roaming . . . or hunting. Even if you could go out, those birds are off-limits." Lucky looked up at him and cried pitifully. "C'mere," he said, sitting down on the step. Immediately, he padded over, swishing his tail, and swept back and forth between his legs, making figure eights. As he came through the last time, Noah stopped him and gently cupped his head in his hands to get a better look at the wound where his right eye had been. "Looking good," he said softly, scratching his ears. Lucky purred loudly, continuing to swish his long tail. Then he padded back to the door. "You don't know how much I wish I could let you out," Noah said sadly, "but the doc and Mom said no."

As he said this, he thought about the conversation he'd had with Laney earlier that morning. She'd chatted endlessly about the wonderful time they were having—especially Asher who loved his new cousins and was especially fond of ten-year-old Laurie, who'd immediately taken him under her wing and was teaching him everything there was to know about farming—from canning peaches to making jam —and Lyle had even let him drive the John Deere up and down the driveway.

"He's in seventh heaven," she'd reported happily. "He's already eaten a whole bushel of peaches. I have a great picture of him eating one with sticky juice running down his chin. His face is lit by the setting sun and it just glows. Wait 'til you see it."

"It sounds like *you're* in seventh heaven too," he'd said. "I think you two would probably stay there forever if you could."

"Probably," Laney had said, laughing.

Noah had smiled. He couldn't remember the last time Laney had sounded so relaxed and happy.

"I'm glad we came."

"Good," he'd answered quietly.

"Lyle said my parents are coming down after the wedding."

"That's a good idea. They're coming all the way from Maine. They may as well keep going."

"How are you guys doing?" she'd asked, changing the subject.

"We're fine," he'd said, running his hand over the new countertop. "Same old, same old."

"Are you getting any projects done?" she asked, and he could hear the worry creeping into her voice.

"We're working on it," he'd answered honestly, opening the new cabinet and reaching for a coffee mug.

"How are the boys? Is everyone behaving?"

"Yup," he'd said, pouring the freshly perked coffee. "No problems."

"Okay, good. Well, I guess I should go. Laurie's teaching Ash how to make peach hotcakes."

"Well, tell him I expect him to make them for us when he gets home."

"I will," Laney said, lingering. "I miss you."

"I miss you too."

They were both quiet, picturing one another far away.

Finally, Laney had broken the lonely silence. "Okay, well, I'll call again soon."

"Okay."

"I love you."

"Love you too."

Noah had hung the phone up and looked out the window. He'd taken a sip of his coffee and wondered if Laney ever regretted the decisions she'd made. He still remembered how much she'd loved the farm when they first met—and how torn she'd been at the time. In the end, she'd been firm in her decisions—once she'd made them—and, as far as he knew, she'd never looked back. . . . Or had she?

Just then, the phone started to ring again, and Noah pulled himself up, wondering who was calling so early in the day. It persisted until he finally lifted it off the hook. "Hello?"

He paused. "Yes, this is he." He slowly shook his head, absorbing the news the caller was sharing. "Yes, of course," he answered. "I'll come right away."

❧ 50 ☙

"I think I might go for a run," Asa mused, lying in bed.

"Do you think that's a good idea?" Maddie asked in surprise. "You were just saying how good your knee's been feeling."

"That's why I'm going."

"Hmm," she said skeptically. "Don't hurt yourself or I won't have anyone to dance with at the wedding."

"You have two sons and five grandsons, I'm sure you'll have plenty of dance partners. In fact, I'll probably end up being a wallflower—there won't be any room for me on your dance card."

"There's always room for you," she said, kissing him.

Hearing their pillow talk, Harper got up, rested her chin on the bed, and gazed at them lovingly, her whole hind end wiggling.

"Are you taking your pal with you?" Maddie asked, reaching out to rub her ears.

"That depends. Are her pads better?"

"I think so."

Asa looked over at the happy-go-lucky Lab. "Do you want to go too?" he asked, and she immediately wiggled over to his side of the bed, thumping her tail. "Okay," he said, getting up. "You and me. Just a short one though—a couple of miles to see how it feels."

He turned to Maddie. "Are you checking on your new charges?"

"I am," Maddie said, getting up and pulling her robe around her. "Right after I start the coffee."

Ten minutes later, Asa clicked Harper's leash to her collar and walked to the end of the driveway. "Which way should we go, ole girl?" he asked.

Harper wagged her tail, and Asa nodded. "I agree, let's go this way. There're less hills." And Harper just continued to wag her tail. She looked like she was smiling as she trotted along beside him.

As Maddie measured coffee, she couldn't help but recall the loud crash, followed by the image of Asa's naked, trembling body against the bathroom door. She wondered if the simple act of making coffee would always trigger that memory or if, now that he was better, the image would fade. Without realizing it, she sighed—it was definitely one she wanted to block out.

She turned on the news and heard the tail end of a story that was unfolding in Massachusetts. "We'll come back as soon as we have more information. This is Mike Johnson, reporting to you from Cape Cod." Maddie frowned, changed the channel to see if another station was covering it, and then she turned on her laptop.

She lingered, waiting for it to warm up, but even online, the only news from the Cape was a recent shark sighting off the Coast Guard Beach, and she wondered if E and Gabe had seen it. After a few more searches, she gave up and went out to the garage to check on the goslings. The last two eggs had hatched the day before, and now all four babies were nestled together in one big, downy

316

ball. She gently stroked the back of one of them and smiled. She went back inside and poured a cup of coffee, and by the time Asa came in, she'd forgotten all about the news. "How was your run?"

"Good," he said, dripping with sweat. He released Harper's leash, and she splayed out on the floor with her water bowl between her paws, panting and drinking sloppily, splashing water everywhere.

"And your knee?"

"Pretty good," he said, filling a glass with water.

"Is pretty good less good than plain good?" she asked.

"A little less," he said with a smile. "I had a pain in my other leg, which took my mind off my knee. Not sure what that's all about—probably a tendon."

"Well, you need to take it easy. You did just go through six weeks of radiation."

"Don't worry. I am," he said, taking a long drink.

51

"Did you know I used to sleep in this same exact bed when I was your age?" Laney asked as she tucked Asher into bed in the little room off the kitchen.

"I know," he said sleepily. "You already told me."

"I did?"

"Mm-hmm."

"Sayin' your prayers?"

Asher reverently closed his eyes and whispered his prayer: "Now I lay me down to sleep. I pray the Lord my soul to keep. Thy love go with me through the night, and wake me up in the morning light. God Bless Mom and Dad and E and Gabe and Ben and Seth and Halle and Mennie and Lucky and me and Uncle Lyle and Aunt Maren and Laurie and Levi and all my loved ones. Amen.

"Night, Mom," he added sleepily.

Laney lightly kissed his forehead. "Night, ole pie," she whispered. "Love you."

"Love you too," he murmured, already half asleep.

Laney sat on the edge of the bed and listened to his soft breathing. She gently brushed his wispy hair back from his forehead and softly whispered her own prayer. "Dear Lord, thank you for giving us such a sweet little boy with such a big heart. Please guide him in everything he does, protect him from the heartaches of this world, and let his life be full of joy and peace and love." She kissed him again, lingering to breathe in his lovely, little boy scent, and whispered, "Amen."

As she stood up, Lyle peered into the room. "Your phone's ringing, Lane," he said.

"Thanks," she said, following him out into the kitchen to answer it. She looked at the screen and smiled. It said: *Home calling.*

She flipped the phone open and cheerfully said hello, wondering which male voice would answer.

Lyle returned to the sink to finish washing the dessert dishes, but when he heard Laney exclaim, "Oh, no!" He looked over his shoulder, turned off the water, and watched the color draining from her face.

"Oh, that's awful," she whispered, her voice barely audible. "Do they know what happened?" She paused, listening and shaking her head, her eyes glistening. "Do you think I should tell him?" she asked finally. "Okay, maybe I'll wait. Call me back when you know more." She nodded. "Love you too."

Laney closed her phone, shaking her head in disbelief, and looked up at her brother's concerned face. "There's a boy on Asher's bus," she began quietly. "He's older and bigger. And he always gives Asher a hard time—always pushing him and calling him names. He comes from a broken family, and he and his brother are famous for being mean and getting into trouble. In fact, at the end of the school year, he was kicked off the bus because he got into an altercation with his brother—who ended up getting expelled." She paused, biting her lip. "Anyway, none of that matters now," she said sadly, "because this morning, his mother found him in his room with a severe head injury. She called nine-one-one right away, but he died on the way to the hospital."

"No way," Lyle said. "Do they know what happened?"

Laney shook her head. "Noah said they took his brother in for questioning."

Lyle gave a low whistle. "What the hell is the matter with kids these days?"

Laney sighed. "I don't know. There've always been bullies even when we were kids. Remember Everett Hanson?"

"Yeah, that kid was mean. But his dad used to whip him with a belt—the buckle end."

Laney looked horrified. "Well, anyway, the problem with kids today just seems to be escalating. They don't even have to be in the same room to bully. They can do it online, which is actually worse because then all the other kids can read it."

"That's exactly why we don't have a computer," Lyle said, shaking his head. "The Internet is evil."

Laney frowned. "It's not entirely evil. It can be educational and amazing if it's used properly. And if Levi and Laurie want to go to college someday, they're going to need a computer."

"Levi's not going to college," Lyle said, shaking his head. "He's already said he wants to take over the farm when he's older. Besides, he doesn't have the grades for college."

"He's only twelve, Lyle. He might change his mind. And what about Laurie?"

"If she needs a computer, she can use one at school."

Laney sighed. "You know, Ly, you've been talking about how hard it is to get by. If you had a computer, you could have an online presence and people would be able to find out about the farm and where it is. It would be a lot better than that old sign down the road. You could even sell products online. There are plenty of farms that do that."

"An *online presence?*" Lyle shook his head dismissively. "I'd rather struggle. The way I see it, Lane, getting a computer is just putting out a welcome mat for trouble."

Laney laughed. "Oh, Lyle, even Mom and Dad have a computer."

Lyle just shrugged. "I'm not interested."

"Maybe you're right," she said with a sigh. "Sometimes, I wish we could all go back to simpler times."

Lyle turned back to the sink, and Laney reached for a dish towel. As she put away a plate, she affectionately elbowed her brother. "This is just like old times, though," she said. "You washing and me drying."

Lyle smiled. "Those were the good, old days. I'd take one of them back in a heartbeat."

"Me too," Laney said wistfully.

"So are you gonna tell Ash about that kid?"

"I am, but I think I'll wait 'til we're on our way home. He's having such a good time. I don't want to spoil it. In fact, I think I'm going to have trouble getting him to *go* home. He'd probably love to stay here so he can help Levi run the farm someday."

"And he'd be more than welcome. After all, he is half Pacey." He looked up and grinned. "Or so you say. . . ."

52

E wrapped his arms around Chloe. "I didn't know you knew the Laughlins."

Chloe nodded. "I knew Jillian. She worked at the Chocolate Sparrow when I first started, but she was constantly calling in because she couldn't get a sitter, and they finally fired her. She worked hard, but they couldn't count on her to show up." She shook her head. "This is so sad. It's like she's losing both sons—one is dead and the other is accused of killing him. I can't even imagine."

E nodded. "Well, Jeff says it was an accident. They were wrestling, and Jared fell and hit his head, but that doesn't explain why he didn't go get help."

"Sometimes life doesn't make any sense. He was only ten years old. Why does God let things like this happen?"

"I don't know, Chlo. I think God has bigger

plans that we can't see or even begin to fathom, and we just have to trust Him. It's like everything that happens is all part of one big story, and we don't get to see how each life is intertwined with other lives; but God sees . . . and He promises to be with us."

Chloe stepped back. "You definitely sound like a preacher's son."

E smiled. "It's how I was raised."

"And you believe all that?"

"I do," he said, nodding. And then he frowned —he was almost afraid to ask her. "Don't you?"

Chloe shook her head. "I don't know, E. I just don't understand why God—who is supposed to be loving and caring—let's bad stuff happen."

"God doesn't *let* stuff happen, Chloe," E said, frowning. "Everyone faces tragedy in life. Life isn't easy for anyone . . . but God has given us faith and He promises to be with us."

"It's great that you have such strong faith, E, but I'm just not as convinced."

E sat on the hood of his car in the beach parking lot and looked up at the long wispy clouds. He didn't know what to say. He loved Chloe with all his heart, but if she didn't believe in God, could they really have a future together?

"Are you going to the service?" she asked.

He nodded.

"When is it?"

"Tuesday morning. In fact, my mom and Asher

are coming home a day early, although I don't think she's told him yet."

"How come? Isn't Jared the one that was giving him such a hard time?"

"He is, but Asher's pretty sensitive, and my mom is worried about how he'll take it. It's funny—even though Jared bullied him, Ash still tried to make excuses for him. He always said Jeff was mean to Jared and that made Jared mean. And he's probably right."

"He's a smart little kid," Chloe said, stepping between his legs and putting her hands on his thighs.

E half smiled and reached for her hands.

"What's the matter?"

"I don't know," he said, searching her eyes.

"Something . . ." she pressed.

He hesitated, trying to think of the right words. "I guess I just need time to think about what you said."

She frowned. "What did I say?"

"About your faith . . . or lack of it."

"Oh," she said, looking surprised. "I was just being honest."

E looked away, his heart aching. "I know."

She started to say something more, but just then, Gabe came up behind her. "Thanks for the pizza today, Chlo," he said, dropping his cooler in the open trunk. "Peanut butter and jelly was getting pretty old."

Chloe smiled. "You're welcome."

E slid off the hood. "I'll call you later."

She nodded sadly and turned to walk to her car, and Gabe frowned, looking from one to the other. "Trouble in paradise?"

E just sighed and shook his head.

53

Laney looked in the backseat and smiled. They weren't even to the highway yet, and Asher had nodded off with his new hat falling over his eyes. She'd been right about leaving. He hadn't been happy—especially since they were leaving a day early. And he'd been especially teary when he'd wrapped his arms around Red, and again when Laurie had hugged him, but when Levi had pulled a new John Deere hat from behind his back and put it on his head, he'd beamed! Then Levi had whispered in his ear, reminding him of the plans they'd hatched for next summer—plans to which Laney had already agreed—and that made leaving a little easier too.

Before they'd left, Lyle had nestled several crates of peaches—not quite ripe—and two cases of peach jam, which Maren had suggested using as wedding favors, in the back of the Pilot. He'd checked her oil and tire pressure and then given her a long hug. "Miss you already," he'd said with a sad smile.

"Miss you too."

"Be safe."

She'd hugged each of them and pulled out, waving. "Thanks for everything!"

"Bye, Aunt Laney! Bye, Ash!" a chorus of voices had sung as Red loped along the driveway, bellowing, and Halle hung her head out the window, barking and thumping her tail.

Forty minutes later, Laney turned onto I-95 just north of Savannah and reached for her travel cup. Maren had made a fresh pot just before they'd left, and it was still hot. Early in their visit, Laney had commented on the unique flavor of Maren's coffee, and she'd told her it was a special blend from New Orleans—her hometown; it had chicory in it. She'd called it her southern comfort in the morning, and Laney had agreed—it was almost as good as Fog Buster.

Traffic was light that Sunday morning, and as Laney took her first sip, her thoughts drifted to the conversation she'd had with Noah the night before. He'd confirmed that Jared's service was Tuesday at ten o'clock and he'd also said they were expecting a large turnout of kids and he wondered if Asher would want to go. Laney had hesitantly revealed that she hadn't told him yet, and Noah hadn't been happy. She'd promised she'd tell him that night, but she was dreading it.

Their hotel reservations were for a Comfort Inn just south of Trenton, but their true destination was Pat's King of Steaks in Philly. They'd stopped at Pat's on the way down, and Asher had loved the famous Philly cheesesteaks so much, he'd begged her to stop on the way home, and Laney had said they'd try. They'd had lunch at a McDonald's in Richmond and then continued north, listening to *Harry Potter and the Sorcerer's Stone*. Laney loved audio books because they made the miles fly by, and she never tired of listening to Harry Potter because the narrator had a wonderful British accent.

Traffic around DC had been stop and go— mostly stop—so it was almost nine o'clock at night when they finally got to Pat's, and they were both starving. They stood at the first window and they ordered "two steaks *wit* onions and provolone" and then stepped to the second window and ordered two root beers and a large fry. When their order came up, they sat at a quiet table on the end with Halle at their feet. As hungry as she was, Laney felt her stomach twisting into knots at the thought of the news she still had to share. She smiled sadly, watching her young son. He was so happy, sitting there, innocently swinging his legs, enjoying his newly discovered favorite sandwich, and sneaking french fries to his best pal under the table . . . and there she was, about to crush his happiness . . . and his innocence.

"I have some sad news," she said quietly when he'd finished eating.

He looked up in surprise, his brow furrowing into a frown under his new hat.

Laney swallowed. "Dad called," she said, biting her lip, "and he said that Jared Laughlin died earlier this week."

Asher's eyes filled with tears. "He did? How?"

"He fell and hit his head."

"Was he riding his bike without a helmet?"

Laney shook her head, picturing Jared on his bike, which, she realized now, he had ridden without a helmet. "No, Ash. Somehow his brother was involved. Jeff said they were fooling around, and Jared fell."

Tears spilled down Asher's smooth cheeks. "That can't be," he said, shaking his head. "Dad's wrong. Jared can't be dead."

"He's not wrong," she said gently, reaching for his hand. "That's why we're heading home early. Jared's service is Tuesday, and Dad thought you might want to go."

Asher shook his head. "I *don't* want to go," he said angrily, his tears falling like rain. "I don't even want to go home anymore."

Laney pulled him into her arms, and he fell apart, sobbing and shaking.

"Oh, hon, I'm so sorry," she whispered.

"It's all my fault," he choked.

Laney pulled him back and searched his eyes.

"It's *not* your fault, Ash. Why would you say such a thing?"

"Because it is," he sobbed.

Laney shook her head. How could her sweet, seven-year-old boy think that he had played any role in this tragedy? "Why do you think that?" she asked, but Asher just buried his head in her chest, and when Halle tried to lick his hand, he pushed her away. "Asher," Laney said sternly, "this is crazy. Jared's death is *not* your fault. I can understand if you're sad, but you can't blame yourself."

"Yes, I can," he said defiantly, clenching his fists. "On the bus, I heard Jeff tell him he was going to kill him. And I—I—" he stammered, struggling with the horrific truth. "I didn't say anything."

Laney raised her eyebrows in surprise, her young son's innocent perception of the tragic events suddenly becoming crystal clear. "Oh, Ash," she said, shaking her head. "*That* does not make it your fault. People say stuff like that all the time . . . and they don't really mean it."

"Jeff meant it. You didn't see his face."

Laney took a deep breath, trying to wrap her mind around this revelation. Suddenly all the training seminars on bullying she'd sat through as a teacher came rushing back to her. *"So many red flags go unnoticed or unreported. Teach your students to report incidents—even if they seem like nothing. We don't want them to become tattletales . . . but then again, we do."* Asher was only seven. Was he supposed to know this already? He obviously did know—he'd heard Jeff threaten his brother, and now he blamed himself for not saying anything. Then again, if she had heard the same threat, would she have taken it seriously? The unfortunate answer was: probably not.

She wrapped her arms around her young son, her heart breaking. "Ash," she said finally, gently brushing away his tears. "I understand, now, why you think you're responsible, but Jared's death is *not* your fault. We don't even know for sure if Jeff purposely hurt him . . . and, sadly, I don't think you saying something would have changed anything. No one would have ever taken Jeff's threat seriously. He would have been scolded . . . or maybe even punished, but in the end, it would not have changed the way he treated Jared. He would have still been mean to him." She held his head in her hands and searched his teary eyes. "So you can't blame yourself, okay?"

Asher nodded slowly, and as Laney held him close, he reached down to pet Halle's soft ears, and she thumped her tail and nosed the edge of the table to see if there were any more french fries.

❦ 54 ❦

"Mom's home!" Ben and Seth shouted, shoving each other as they tried to be the first one outside. In the commotion, Lucky scooted past them and out the door. "Look what you did," Ben accused, pointing as the fluffy orange feline scampered across the yard.

"I didn't do it. You did!" Seth countered.

"Did what?" Noah asked, coming out after them with Mennie at his heels.

"Seth let Lucky out," Ben reported.

"*You* let Lucky out," Seth countered angrily.

Noah groaned, knowing he'd be the one in trouble. "Thanks a lot, guys. Go see if you can find him."

"After I say hi to Mom," Ben said.

"Me too."

Noah frowned, but when he saw Laney climbing out of the car, he couldn't help but smile.

"The house looks great!" she said happily, admiring the fresh paint.

"Thanks!" Ben and Seth said in unison.

"You guys did it?" she asked in surprise.

They nodded.

"And Gabe," Noah added.

"Well, it looks super."

They both smiled, and hugging her, asked,

"How was your trip?" But then spying Asher with a new hat on, added, "Hey, did we get hats?"

"No," Asher answered matter-of-factly. "Just me."

"That's not fair," Seth complained.

"Lord help me, will you two grow up?" Noah asked in an exasperated voice.

Laney smiled, giving her husband a long hug. "They are growing up—too fast!" she reminded.

"Well," he said, shaking his head, "you haven't been putting up with them all week."

"I still know how it is," she replied sympathetically.

Noah turned to the boys. "Okay, you said hello. Now, go find the cat."

"Lucky's lost?" Asher asked worriedly.

"No," Seth said. "He's just outside."

"Outside?" Laney asked, eyeing her husband.

"It *just* happened," Noah explained defensively. "That cat has been plotting his escape all week . . . and he finally pulled it off. Don't worry—he'll be fine. He's not as vulnerable as you think, and I think it's unfair to keep him inside. All he does is sit by the door and cry like he's lost his best friend.

"Speaking of friends . . ." he added, nodding to Mennie who was gazing at his beloved with star-struck eyes, wagging his tail expectantly, and waiting to be noticed.

"Oh!" Laney said, kneeling down to wrap her arms around him. "Hi, there, old pie," she whispered. "Did you miss me?"

"Miss you?" Noah exclaimed. "I have never seen such a sad dog! He moped around all week. What a sad sack!"

"You mean gloomy gills," Asher corrected as both dogs wiggled around them.

"Hi, Mom," Gabe said, coming up behind them as E scooped Asher up and threw him over his shoulder, making his hat fall off.

"My hat!" Asher cried, squirming and stretching out his arms, even though there was no chance of reaching it.

"My hat now," E teased, picking it up and putting it on his head.

"It's too small for you," Asher protested, still trying to reach it.

"Hi!" Laney said in surprise. "What are you two doing home?"

"The beach is closed," Gabe explained, making the sound from *Jaws* for extra effect.

"Yeah," E added, setting Asher down. "We saw one having breakfast this morning, and the water was all red."

"No!" Laney said, raising her eyebrows and mouthing the word *seal* over Asher's head.

E nodded. "Yup . . . and not just one."

"There're sharks at the beach?" Asher asked with wide eyes.

"How about we go inside?" Noah said, eyeing his older sons and changing the subject.

"Okay," Laney agreed. "Do you guys want to help unload?" she asked, opening the hatch.

"Wow—look at those peaches!" Seth said. "Can I have one?"

"They're not ripe yet," Asher explained matter-of-factly.

"Are you the new authority on peaches?" Noah asked, scooping him into a hug.

Asher nodded solemnly, wrapping his arms around Noah's neck.

"Missed you, buddy," he whispered.

"Missed you too, Dad."

Then Noah whispered something in his ear and a smile immediately spread across his face.

Laney eyed them. "What are you two whispering about?" she asked.

"Oh, nothing," Noah answered nonchalantly.

"Yeah, nothing," Asher assured her, using the same carefree tone, but barely able to contain himself.

"Hmmm," she murmured, eyeing them suspiciously.

Carrying duffel bags, suitcases, crates of peaches, cases of jam, and holding their collective breaths, they followed Laney up the walkway, and when she reached the screen door, Noah held it open for her. Giving him a funny look, she stepped from the porch to the kitchen, but then, she stopped in her tracks. "Oh, my," she murmured, looking around at the handsome cherry cabinets and dark granite countertops. "Oh, my goodness! How in the world?" With tears in her eyes, she turned to look at her six men and realized they all looked like cats that had eaten canaries. "You guys," she said, shaking her head. "And you especially," she said, eyeing Noah. "How are we going to pay for this?"

Laughing, Noah looked at his older two boys. "I told you . . ." he said. Then he put his arm around Laney. "It's all paid for."

"Look, Mom," Ben said, flipping a switch, "we even have under cabinet lighting . . . and a new light over the island."

Laney nodded, looking around. "It's beautiful. I can't believe you did this all in a week."

"Hey," Noah said, folding his arms across his chest. "We don't fool around."

"Well, I'm going to have to go away more often."

"They even got you a new sign," Asher said, pointing to a burgundy sign with white lettering, hanging on the freshly painted wall. It read: "NOW FAITH IS THE ASSURANCE OF THINGS HOPED FOR, THE CONVICTION OF THINGS NOT SEEN."

Laney turned to her husband and shook her head. "Thank you," she said softly. Then she looked at each of them. "Thank *all* of you."

"You're welcome," they said, giving her hugs.

"You know what the first thing you have to bake in your new oven is?" Asher asked.

"What?" she asked, hugging him last.

"My birthday cake!"

❧ 55 ❧

By ten o'clock Tuesday morning, the heavy mist had turned into steady rain. It was fitting, Noah thought, as he watched the parade of dark umbrellas making their way through the church parking lot and up the wet slate walk. The sun shouldn't show its face on such a somber day.

The night before, after Laney and Asher's homecoming, Noah had retreated to his study to gather his thoughts, but it had been futile—even though he'd officiated at the funerals of children before, this one felt different. Finally, after staring at a blank Word document for twenty minutes, he remembered a thin volume he'd read in college about writing sermons. It was titled: *Keep It Short, Student*, or as they'd affectionately called it in seminary, *KISS*. He was certain there was a chapter in it focusing on ministering to a congregation after the loss of a child, and he scanned his bookshelves until he found it. When he opened it, he was surprised to also find, tucked between its pages, a faded newspaper clipping and a paper he'd written when he was at Andover Newton. He unfolded the clipping, dated October 14, 1977, and looked at the picture of a boy in a football uniform. The boy's name was John Winslow. Noah distinctly remembered John —even though they'd been on different teams in high school and hadn't been close friends, they'd had several classes together and they'd always said hello. And then, on a crisp Friday night in the fall of their sophomore year, John was injured in a game. Both teams had knelt as John's motionless body was carried off the field on a stretcher to a waiting ambulance, but as the eerie emergency lights lit up the autumn sky and the wailing siren faded in the distance, John fell into a coma. He died three days later. The whole school had been devastated. The school board even brought grief counselors in for anyone who needed to talk. And although Noah hadn't sought counseling, for the rest of that year, he'd looked at John's empty seat and wondered how they'd explained such a senseless loss.

Years later, when he was studying to be a minister, he was given the assignment to write about the loss of a child, and since the only experi-ence he had on the subject was the inexplicable death of his high school classmate, he wrote about John. Noah slowly unfolded the paper, and as he reread the words—now decades old—the grief and sense of loss he'd felt then came rushing back.

When Noah entered the sanctuary, he realized it wasn't as full as he'd expected. Laney and the boys—including Asher—were among the last to file in, and Jillian, who looked much older than her years, was seated in the front row with her sister; but Jeff—who was still being held in juvenile detention—had declined the opportunity to attend his brother's funeral.

"My friends," Noah began solemnly, "we are gathered here this morning to remember the life of Jared Joseph Laughlin—a life that ended much too soon." As he said this, he lit a single white candle and invited them to pray; and then, after singing the hymns and reading the verses that he'd helped Jillian select, he asked if there was anyone who wished to share a memory about Jared. The congregation sat silently, looking around, waiting respectfully, and Noah could feel his own heart beating. There had to be someone who was willing to share a funny anecdote or a fond memory of this young, lost soul . . . but no one raised their hand . . . and no one moved to stand.

Noah nodded solemnly, looking out at the sea of young faces, and silently prayed that the words he'd prepared would somehow touch their hearts. He cleared his throat. "Sometimes, it's not easy to step out of our comfort zones onto a treacherous limb and express how we're feeling.

Kids especially, have a hard time talking about how they feel. The world today is incredibly fast-paced and full of distractions—video games, instant messaging, texting. It can leave your head spinning, and that's precisely why I'm glad to see so many of you here today. Because in our crazy world . . . when things aren't making sense . . . it's always good to take a step back . . . center ourselves in silence . . . and try to understand the things that don't make sense—like how a child . . . a child who is barely ten years old . . . can be called to heaven.

"Many of you are probably wondering how God can *let* something like this happen. How can He let a child—a child who has hardly had a chance to begin living—die? Where is He in such a tragedy? It certainly seems like He's absent or, at the very least, not paying attention. But that is not the case; in fact, it is as far from the truth as can be. God doesn't let bad things happen, but he does promise to be with us and give us the strength we need to get through them. He is never absent; He is with us right now as we remember Jared; He is with Jared's mom in her sorrow; and He is with all of us as we try to understand."

Noah smiled sadly. "This world of ours has been groaning and changing and struggling for longer than any of us can even begin to fathom . . . and in all that infinite time, God has watched over us. He has never slept or been distracted, and although the Bible says we are created in His image, that is where the similarities end . . . because when it comes to comprehending how the fragile threads of our lives are intricately woven together into one luminous and glorious tapestry, we humans fall painfully short. The unfolding story of the world is much greater than our comprehension, but God—from His vantage point—can see how our lives are intertwined and how the decisions we make unwittingly affect other lives—even the lives of people we don't know. In fact, we often never know how . . . or where . . . or when . . . we've touched another's life . . . but God does.

"Jared's life touched many other lives—and although our hearts are filled with sorrow today, we can find solace in knowing and trusting that God has a greater plan . . . and that Jared's life . . . *and* his untimely death . . . will continue to touch us in some way for the rest of our lives.

"Let us pray."

Noah bowed his head, and although, outwardly, he voiced a prayer for Jared and his family, inwardly, he felt his words had fallen short and he thanked God that it was over. He looked up, reached for his hymnal, and said, "Please join in singing our closing hymn, 'Blessed Assurance.' "

"What you said made a lot of sense, pastor," several people said afterward.

"It was a very nice service—touching," others remarked.

"I never thought about God that way," one boy said.

And when Jillian was finished greeting everyone else, she tearfully hugged and thanked him.

"I feel like we're on a roller coaster," Noah mused that evening as he helped Laney wrap Asher's presents. "In the morning, we're attending a funeral, and in the evening, we're getting ready for a birthday."

"That's how life is sometimes," Laney said, tightening a bow.

"None of what I said today came out the way I hoped."

Laney looked up. "It was fine. You shouldn't be so hard on yourself. They were a tough crowd, and I can't help wondering how many of those kids were dragged there by parents who didn't realize what Jared was really like."

"And what was Jared really like?" he asked, looking up.

"He was a bully."

Noah frowned. "He was also a child—a child who was crying out for love, but I couldn't say that in front of his mother. I couldn't say what was really in my heart because it would have broken her heart even more." He shook his head. "God wants us to love those who are the hardest to love, and we failed him."

Laney sat down across from him. "I hate to say this, but the world is a safer place without Jared. Now we have one less angry kid who could potentially show up at school with a shotgun someday."

"That's harsh."

"It's true. How do you rehabilitate a boy like that? In our society, rehabilitation of a child that is innately mean rarely happens. Jared was heartless and cruel and he had no regard for others' feelings or lives. Look what he did to Asher . . . and to Lucky."

"You don't know for certain that he had anything to do with Lucky," Noah refuted.

"I do know it . . . because I've seen the look in his eyes."

"It's wrong to give up on a child. He could've been moved to a loving home and taught responsibility and respect. He might've changed."

Laney looked skeptical. "No court would have taken him from his mother. She wasn't the one abusing him. It was an impossible situation."

"When did you get to be such a pessimist?"

"I'm not a pessimist," she said. "I'm a realist."

She stood up to finish wrapping. "When you asked if anyone wanted to say something, I think Asher wanted to. He sat up and looked around, waiting for someone to get up, and when no one did, he started to stand, but then you started talking again, he sat down."

"He did? I wonder what he would've said."

"I don't know," Laney said with a smile. "He's full of surprises."

"Has he said any more about it being his fault?"

"No, thank goodness. I think it helped to get home to everyone who loves him."

Just then, Mennie moseyed over to the table to remind them that it was past his bedtime. Noah cupped the old Lab's head in his hands and looked into his eyes. "Do you need to go out one more time?" Mennie wagged his tail, and as Noah stood up, he surveyed the pile of gifts on the table as if he was seeing it for the first time. With raised eyebrows, he said, "I don't think you have enough stuff."

Laney looked up at the clock. "Well, it's not too late," she teased. "I can go get more."

Noah shook his head, and when he opened the door to let Mennie out, Lucky scooted in, bolted to his empty food dish, and started meowing. "Well, well, well . . . look who finally decided to come home."

❦ 56 ❦

"Is he coming?" Gabe asked, peering around the doorway into the kitchen, waiting for his cue.

"Yup," E said, looking in and nodding. "Go."

Gabe's long, agile fingers immediately started dancing along the ivory keys of their old piano, playing the familiar melody "Happy Birthday to You" as a chorus of voices joined in. Asher appeared at the bottom of the stairs, wearing his pajamas, his new John Deere hat, and a shy smile on his face. Then his eyes grew wide at the sight of the pile of gifts waiting on the table.

"Wow," he said softly.

With a playful flourish, Gabe finished the song and stood up. "C'mon, bud," he said as he walked by. "You have to open all those before E and I leave for work."

"No more sharks?" Asher asked brightly.

"Nope."

"Are you two ready for your peach hotcakes?" Noah asked, eyeing his two older sons as he slid a spatula under the golden orbs on the griddle.

"We're having peach hotcakes?" Asher asked in surprise.

"Yup," E said, standing behind Gabe with his plate ready.

"How's that new stovetop working, dear?" Laney asked, helping Asher into his chair.

"It's amazing!" Noah teased, as he poured more batter on the griddle. "These are going to be the best pancakes ever."

"Better than Pancake Man?" Asher asked.

"Way better," Gabe said with his mouth full. "And these warm peaches . . . mm-mm," he added, giving Asher a thumbs-up.

Asher grinned. "I told you!"

Noah flipped the next set of pancakes and looked at Ben and Seth. "Ready?"

"Yup," they said, reaching for their plates, standing up, and jostling for position.

Laney cradled her mug in her hands and looked at Asher. "Well? Are you going to start?"

Asher nodded. "What should I start with?"

"Why don't you start with ours?" E suggested, downing his orange juice, "in case we have to leave before you're done."

"Which one is it?"

"The bag," Gabe said, pointing to a green bag with yellow ribbon.

Asher pulled the bag toward him and peered into the top of it. He untied the ribbon, reached his arm all the way down inside, and pulled out a metal toy replica of a 1953 John Deere 40 Orchard tractor. "It's just like Uncle Lyle's!" he exclaimed, examining it carefully. "It even has headlights!"

"Where in the world did you find that?" Noah asked.

"On eBay," Gabe said simply, holding his empty plate out for a refill.

"There's more," E said, motioning to the bag.

Asher reached back into the bag and pulled out two small boxes and studied the pictures on them.

"They're puzzles," E explained.

"John Deere puzzles! Thanks!"

E and Gabe both nodded. "You're welcome."

E looked at the clock. "Well, I'm sorry to say

this, but I think we better go . . . especially if we're going to be home in time for cake and ice cream later."

"Sorry, bud," E added, giving his youngest brother a hug.

"That's okay," Asher said, getting up to give Gabe a hug too. "Thanks for everything. Watch out for sharks!"

They both smiled as they picked up their coolers. "We will."

As they headed out the door, Asher—with Halle and Mennie's help—continued to unwrap, and by the time he was done, the floor was littered with torn paper, and across the table were strewn three new books: *James and the Giant Peach*, *Because of Winn-Dixie*, and *The Fo'c'sle*. "That last one is a true story about a little house that was on Cape Cod. And it's signed by the author," Laney explained. There was also a new pair of running shoes—just like E's but in his size—a Harry Potter Lego set from Ben and Seth, which he loved almost as much as the tractor, a new telescope, and a glow in the dark poster of the night sky that depicted all the constellations and their names.

"Wow!" he said, surveying the pile. "I made out like a pirate!"

"You sure did," Noah said, ruffling his hair and setting a plate of piping hot pancakes in front of him.

"Are all the grandparents coming tonight?" he asked.

"Yup. Gram and Gramp Pacey," Laney said, referring to her parents, "are coming down for the wedding, and they thought they'd come for your birthday too."

Asher nodded as he poured a puddle of maple syrup on his plate and swirled a forkful of pancakes through it. "Are they staying here?"

"No, it's going to be a little hectic here, so they're staying at the Inn at the Oaks again."

"In the Captain's Room?"

"Yes," she said, surprised that he remembered the name of the room they'd stayed in the last time they'd visited.

Noah sat down across from them with his own stack of pancakes and a cup of coffee.

"The cook finally gets to eat," Laney said with a smile.

"Wait 'til you taste 'em, Dad," Asher said with his mouth full of his last bite. As he said this, there was a knock at the front door and Mennie struggled to his feet, barking, while Halle hurried after him to the door, wagging her tail. "I'll get it!" Asher called, pushing his chair back and almost knocking it over.

He pulled open the old oak door and peered outside curiously as the two dogs wiggled outside to inspect the newcomers. The two men who were standing there knelt down to pet the dogs and looked up at Asher. "Hey, sport, we're here to set up the tent."

Asher nodded. "Dad!" he shouted over his shoulder. "They're here to set up for the wedding!"

The rest of Asher's birthday was the best in recent memory. He sat outside all day, with the dogs by his side, watching the workers from Party Tents and More set up the wooden dance floor and the tremendous circus-size tent in the side yard. There was no doubt about it—the excitement was starting to build. In less than six hours, their yard was transformed into party central, and they weren't even done with his birthday yet!

After the men left, he traipsed into the house with the dogs trotting along after him, and seeing his mom up to her elbows in peach peels, asked, "Can we make peach ice cream?"

"Oh, Ash, I'm a little busy."

Looking disappointed, he pressed, "Is my cake done?"

"Yup—it's over there," she said, motioning with her chin.

He walked over to see it. "Wow, that looks great," he said, admiring the frosting image of Harry Potter flying on his quidditch broom. "Mom, you're amazing."

"Flattery will get you nowhere," she said, looking up, "but maybe when I'm done with this, we'll have time to make ice cream."

Later that evening, Asa and Maddie arrived,

bearing gifts and sharing tales of the comical antics of the four fuzzy goslings that they'd left in the care of their fourteen-year-old neighbor.

"Bella's so lucky," Asher said enviously.

"Well, you'll just have to come up and see them," Maddie said, giving him a hug. "They had their first swimming lesson today."

"Mo-om," he called, "can we go see the baby geese?"

Laney looked up from pulling two trays of foil-covered lasagna out of the oven. "Maybe when the dust settles," she called back, sliding two loaves of foil-wrapped garlic bread in.

"Knock, knock," a voice called cheerfully, as Lonnie and Leighton Pacey came into the kitchen through the garage.

"Hi, Gram and Gramp," Asher said happily, running over to give them hugs.

"Hi," Laney said happily, putting down the wooden salad utensils she'd just dug out of the drawer and giving her parents hugs.

Asa and Maddie came over to share hugs too.

"That is some tent out there," Lon said with a smile as he shook Asa's hand.

"I know," Asa chuckled. "I asked Asher if there was a circus coming to town."

Fifteen minutes later, the new kitchen—which the grandparents had been oohing and ahhing over since their arrival—was overflowing with people filling their plates with lasagna and salad and piping hot garlic bread. Glasses were filled with water and wine and iced tea and milk and beer, and when everyone had everything they needed, they gathered around the table and waited for Noah to say grace. They bowed their heads, and he proceeded to solemnly give thanks for bringing them all together, for the delicious dinner, and most of all, for Asher on his eighth birthday.

And when dinner was finished and the coffee was perking, Laney carried Asher's cake out and set it in front of him. Asher paused and looked around at his family, their faces glowing in the warm light of the candles. He looked at their cheerful wrinkles and their smooth, tan skin. He looked at their sparkling eyes and their loving, laughing smiles, and he listened to their lovely voices blending together in song for him . . . and his heart overflowed. Then he closed his eyes, made a wish, and blew. The room fell into darkness and everyone cheered. And then, one by one, the candles sputtered and flickered back to life, and the room filled with laughter again.

57

On Thursday, Gabe and E were dispatched to the store with a list of supplies, and the top item on the list was: "As many tiki torches as you can find."

"What does that mean?" E asked. "Twenty? A hundred?"

"Twenty would be good," Laney said in a distracted voice as she continued to scribble. "And don't forget the fuel. They make a citronella and cedar if you can find it. Do you think you can find strings of little white Christmas lights too? I'm not sure if we have enough."

"Probably," he replied. "After all, it's almost the end of August. Someone must have their Christmas stuff out."

"Well, if all else fails, Snow's probably has some," she said, tapping her pen. Finally, she sighed and handed him the paper. "Okay, I guess that's it, but put your phone on 'loud' so you'll hear me if I think of something else."

E read the list. "What are the ribbons for?"

"The jam jars."

"And what are we using for plates and silver-ware and glasses?"

"The caterer is taking care of all that . . . the bar too. They're dropping off everything Saturday morning."

"Flowers?"

Laney nodded. "Saturday."

E started to realize the magnitude of the planning that had gone into this day, and he shook his head. "If I ever get married, I'm going to elope."

"Oh, no!" Laney said warningly. "There's no

eloping in this house. I'm getting every mother-son dance I have coming to me!"

E laughed. "We'll see . . ."

Just then, Gabe came down the stairs and looked over his brother's shoulder at the list. "What do we need Christmas lights for?"

"They're for under the tent," Laney explained, "to make it look festive."

Gabe rolled his eyes. "I'm sure it'll look festive without Christmas lights." Then he looked at his brother. "You ready? I have to get back so I can organize the music and burn some new CDs."

"I'm ready," he said. Then he looked at his mom again. "How are we paying for all this?"

"Just put it on your card and I'll pay you back."

When they got outside, they found their father and younger brothers watching a tractor trailer trying to back up the driveway.

"What the heck is that?" Gabe asked.

"It's a porta-potty," Asher said excitedly. "The whole trailer is a big fancy bathroom!"

"What those Democrats won't think of," Noah said, shaking his head.

The next morning, Laney felt as if her head had barely hit the pillow when her alarm clock went off. Without opening her eyes, she reached over and clumsily tried to find the snooze button but ended up knocking over a glass of water. "Great," she grumbled, opening her eyes, slamming the clock, and getting up to find a towel.

Hearing the commotion, Noah rolled over. "Are we getting up?"

"Yup," she said sleepily. "It's corn-husking-cobbler-baking day."

By nine a.m. everyone was up, fed, and given their assignments: Gabe and E were setting up tables and hanging Christmas lights; Ben, Seth, and Asher were seated in lawn chairs, husking the corn that Micah and Beryl had brought down from New Hampshire the night before; and Noah was helping Laney assemble six large peach cobblers in new pans lined up on the kitchen counter. "These peaches are amazing," he said, popping a slice into his mouth.

"No more," Laney said as she spread the batter in the bottom of the trays. "Or we won't have enough."

Noah nodded, and when she wasn't looking, he popped another in his mouth.

"I saw that!"

He laughed. "You *do* have eyes in the back of your head."

"Hello! Is this where the wedding is?" a cheerful voice called. The next moment, Micah and Beryl—looking healthy and tan from her tanning visits—followed by E and Gabe came through the door. Their arms were full of vases and votives and Charlotte was carrying a pretty gift bag.

"This is the place!" Laney said with a smile.

"Where should we put these?" Micah asked, glancing around the kitchen.

"Wherever you can find a spot," Laney answered.

They set them down in the only empty spot—on the floor in the corner—and then Micah, E, and Gabe all reached into the bowl of peaches. "I'm not going to have enough," Laney warned, eyeing them.

"The kitchen looks beautiful," Beryl exclaimed, and then spied the jam jars decorated with red-and-white-checked fabric over their lids and tied with white ribbons. "And these look lovely!"

Laney looked up and smiled. "I thought that fabric would go with the sunflowers."

Beryl nodded. "I made labels for the jars, and they have sunflowers on them too."

"Perfect!" Laney said.

As she said this, Micah knelt down next to six-year-old Charlotte and whispered something in her ear. Charlotte looked shyly at Laney and then walked over, holding out the gift bag.

"What's this?" Laney said, leaning down and putting her hands on her knees.

"It's a present," Charlotte said.

"Thank you," Laney replied softly. "Do you want to help me open it?"

Charlotte nodded and reached into the bag. She pulled out a candle, and Laney looked at the label and pulled off the top to smell it. "Mmm . . . summer cotton," she said, holding it out for

Charlotte to smell too. Charlotte smiled and nodded approvingly and then looked up at Micah who motioned that there was more in the bag. Charlotte reached in again, pulled out two envelopes, and handed them to Laney.

Laney opened the bigger envelope first and slid out a gift certificate that had been made on a computer. It was decorated with paw prints and a silhouette of a boy playing tug-of-war with a puppy, and it said: *Good for One Weekend of Boy and Dog Sitting!* "What's this for?" she asked with a puzzled expression.

"Keep going," Micah said, nodding to the other envelope.

Obediently, Laney opened the other envelope. It was a note from Beryl and Micah, thanking her for hosting their wedding, and in a small blue envelope tucked inside, was a gift card for the Century House on Nantucket. "Oh, my goodness," Laney said, looking up in surprise. She frowned. "You didn't have to do that."

"I know we didn't have to," Micah said. "We wanted to."

Laney gave them hugs, and Beryl whispered, "We really can't thank you enough."

"You're very welcome," Laney said. "But you still didn't have to. Thank you though. It's very generous . . . too generous." She eyed Noah. "Did you know about this?" she asked.

Noah just grinned and shrugged innocently.

❦ 58 ❧

A cold front had thundered across the Cape Friday night as they were running through a quick rehearsal of the following day's events, forcing everyone inside, and although Saturday dawned to endless blue skies, the cool, crisp air whispered of September. "I am so not ready for fall," Laney grumbled as she pulled on her old Bowdoin sweatshirt and went out with the dogs. When she came back in, she heard the comforting, cozy drip of the coffeepot, signaling that Noah was up, and smiled.

She surveyed the six golden peach cobblers lined up on the gleaming granite counter and was glad that her preparations for the wedding were behind her. She'd even stayed up late, ironing everyone's shirts and slacks and gave a quick press to her dress, which she hoped would be warm enough. She'd probably have to plan on a shawl or light sweater too.

She heard footsteps on the stairs and looked up to see Noah, buttoning a flannel shirt, his hair still damp from the shower.

"That was quick," she said.

"Mmm," he said. "I hope the boys don't mind if we don't have pancakes this morning."

"I'm sure they'll get over it. We just had pancakes for Asher's birthday."

He filled a mug with coffee. "Okay, well, I think I'm going to run over to the church and make sure they're ready for tomorrow."

"Who's giving the sermon?"

"Karl O'Connor."

Laney smiled, picturing the kind old minister who'd retired several years earlier and moved from Boston to the Cape with his wife, but who still loved the opportunity to "stir the pot"—as he called it—whenever Noah needed a substitute. Mr. O'Connor also led the church's lively, well-attended Bible study, which led Noah to call Karl his godsend.

"I'll be back in a little while."

"Well, don't forget I'm meeting the girls at the salon."

"Oh, yeah . . . what time is that?"

"Ten."

"And what time will you be back?"

"I'm not sure. Hopefully in time for the wedding."

Noah smiled. "What time is the wedding again?"

Laney rolled her eyes. "I guess when the minister decides to show up."

He chuckled as he headed for the door, but then he stopped in his tracks. "Wait a sec . . . who's going to be here for the caterer?"

"Micah, I hope."

"And what time is that?"

"Early."

Noah looked at the clock. It was seven thirty. "You're leaving around nine forty-five," he mused, "so just in case Micah forgets, I need to be back here by. . . ."

Laney watched the wheels spinning in her husband's head.

"Nine thirty," he said, finishing his calculation, "but give E or Gabe a heads-up in case I'm running late and Micah doesn't show."

"E and Gabe won't be here. They're going to Falmouth to pick up the race packets."

Noah shook his head. "You know, we should've never signed up for the race, knowing it was the day after the wedding."

"We didn't know. We signed up in early May, before we—or at least I—knew about the wedding."

Noah sighed. "All right, I'll be back by nine thirty."

Laney nodded, and as he went out the door, she poured a cup of coffee, picked up her Bible, and headed for the porch, and as soon as Mennie and Halle finished their breakfast, they joined her, plopping down at her feet and licking their lips and everything else within reach.

Salon 66—which Beryl's sisters had arranged to be exclusively theirs for the day—was a lot of fun. Rumer and Isak brought champagne, a crudités platter, and tiny cream puffs. The salon had brought in their entire staff, and everyone—from Maddie and Beryl and her sisters to Isak's daughter Meghan and especially Charlotte—enjoyed having their hair, nails, and makeup done. One of the staff members even wove two sprays of baby's breath into wispy halos for Beryl and Charlotte, and although Charlotte adored hers, Beryl wasn't so sure. But when Charlotte pointed to their reflection and whispered that they looked like twins, Beryl realized she had no choice.

A half hour later, Beryl's Mini Cooper, Laney's old Pilot, and Isak's Suburban pulled up to the house and parked next to a large white van with the words "A Moveable Feast" painted on its side. They all climbed out, smiling and chatting like schoolgirls, and stopping to admire the table settings. Beryl went down to the beach to see if the caterer needed anything and found Lucy giving last-minute directions to her staff; when she finished, she gave Beryl a warm hug and grinned. "Nervous?" she asked.

"A little," Beryl said with a smile.

"Don't be," Lucy reassured. "It's going to be wonderful. And it's going to go by very quickly, so enjoy every minute." Then she turned to tend the fire she'd started in the fire pit. "The key to a traditional Cape Cod clambake," she explained, "is to steam everything together on very hot rocks covered with seaweed." She pointed to a nearby bucket of dark greens soaking in seawater. "We've already made up the individual packets of lobster tails, clams, mussels, shrimp, lemon, and potatoes, and we've got the charcoal grill ready for the filets and a big pot of water for the corn. Some people cook the corn in the packets too, but I prefer the corn to taste like sweet, buttery corn, not like seafood."

Beryl nodded. "It sounds wonderful, Lucy."

Just then, Micah snuck up behind them and covered Beryl's eyes, but she smelled his cologne and knew it was him. "Hey, you're not supposed to see me," she admonished.

"I'm not supposed to see in you *in your dress,*" he corrected, looking at his watch, "which you better go put on because it's getting late."

She turned around and saw that he was still wearing shorts and a T-shirt. "And what about you?"

"This *is* what I'm wearing," he teased, wrapping his arms around her. "I thought that's why we were having a beach wedding."

Lucy chuckled and disappeared up the path, leaving them alone next to the warm fire. Micah pulled her into a hug. "I am the luckiest boy in the world," he whispered.

"And I'm the luckiest girl," she murmured, finding his warm, sweet lips.

Just as they started to kiss, they heard a commotion behind them, and Ben and Seth emerged, carrying tiki torches, but when they saw their uncle and future aunt kissing, they snickered and teased, "Get a room, wouldja?" which prompted Micah to pull away from his new bride and chase his giggling nephews down the beach.

Beryl left Micah to help Ben and Seth set up the torches and arrived back at the house just in time to hold the door open for Asa who was carrying a large pot. "Is that your chowder, Dad?" she asked.

"It is . . . and it's nice to hear you call me *Dad*," he said with a smile.

"It's nice to have someone *to* call Dad," she said. "I've never had anyone before."

"Well, I'm honored to be the one," Asa said. "In fact . . ." He paused, trying to find the right words. "I know this may seem like an odd job for the groom's dad, and I don't even know if you already have someone in mind, but since I've never had the opportunity before, I was wondering if . . . what I mean is . . . I'd be honored if you'd let me give you away."

"I didn't plan on having anyone," Beryl said in surprise, "but I'd absolutely love it if you would give me away."

"Okay, well," Asa said, still blushing. "I'm just dropping this off. Now I have to head back, shower, change, and pick up my real date."

Beryl laughed. "Thanks, Dad," she said, kissing his rosy cheek. "I'll tell Laney you were here."

"See you in a bit," he said with a wink.

Beryl turned to hurry up the stairs and found all the women already bustling about, getting ready.

"Hurry up, Gabe," Laney called, knocking on the bathroom door again.

"I have to shave," he called back over the sound of the bathroom fan.

She shook her head. "You were supposed to be done up here by the time we got back."

"I was setting up the sound system," he called back.

Five minutes later, he opened the bathroom door, wearing only a towel, and realized the entire upstairs was full of women. He groaned, and when he walked down the hall, he was followed by the sound of wolf whistles.

"Be nice to him," Beryl called. "He's our DJ."

"Can I make my request now?" Isak teased.

"Wow, Aunt Ber . . . he's cute," Meghan said after Gabe had ducked into his room.

Beryl's eyes lit up at the sudden realization that Meghan and Gabe were the same age. "I'll introduce you!" she said with a smile.

59

"Mo-om," Asher called from the bottom of the stairs. "I'm presentable!"

"Can you come up?" Laney called as she zipped the back of her dress. It had been Noah's job to make sure the younger boys were dressed and presentable by wedding time, but she sometimes worried about Noah's idea of presentable.

Asher appeared shyly in the doorway and looked at everyone all dressed up. "Wow," he said softly when he saw Beryl.

"Thanks," she said, smiling. "You look pretty sharp yourself."

Laney eyed her youngest son. He was wearing stone-colored khakis and a light blue oxford shirt, and he'd had just gotten a haircut so he had a pale line of smooth skin framing his tan face. She straightened the white boutonniere on his shirt and smiled. "You look very handsome."

Asher pushed his glasses up on his nose. "Dad says it's time. Everyone's already down at the beach."

Meghan looked up in surprise. "I think I'm going to head down then," she said, giving her aunt a hug. "Good luck!" she whispered, and as she pulled away, Beryl's heart started to race.

Immediately, Rumer saw the alarm in her sister's eyes and put her arm around her shoulders. "Everything's going to be fine."

"I know," Beryl said softly, her eyes glistening. "It's just I . . . I wish Mom was here."

"She is here, Ber," Rumer said softly. "She's looking down from heaven, and she has a huge smile on her face."

Isak nodded. "I had a feeling you might miss

her more tonight, so I brought something I think she would want you to wear." She held out her hand, revealing a sparkling sapphire ring.

"Oh," Rumer exclaimed. "That's perfect! Not only is it from Mom, but it's old, borrowed . . . and blue!"

Beryl laughed tearfully, slipping the ring that had belonged to their mom on her finger. She held her hand, admiring it, and smiled through her tears—somehow it did make her mom feel near.

"No crying," Isak warned. "Or your eyes'll be red and puffy."

Beryl nodded, showing Laney the ring.

"It's beautiful," Laney said.

"When we have more time, I'll tell you the story."

"I'd love to hear it," Laney said.

After another round of hugs, they went carefully down the stairs and found E and Asa waiting in the kitchen. E knelt down, handed a small box to Asher, and looked him in the eye. "Can you make it down to the beach without losing this?"

Asher nodded solemnly.

Then E held a small basket of flower petals out to Charlotte. "Just sprinkle little handfuls along the path," he reminded, and she nodded too.

The screen door squeaked open, and Rumer's and Isak's husbands, Will and Matt, came in carrying beer bottles. "You guys look maahvelous!"

Matt said jovially, and seeing Beryl, added, "And *you* look gorgeous!"

"Thank you," Beryl said, giving her brothers-in-law each a kiss.

"Umm . . . where are *our* drinks?" Isak teased, eyeing their beers.

"You guys were taking too long," Matt said, offering his bottle to her.

She took a sip and handed it back to him. "Okay, I'm ready. Let's get this party started!"

As they crossed the yard, Beryl noticed Gabe standing near the entrance to the path, and when he smiled at her, she wondered what he was up to. He stood stoically, watching and waiting until Asher, holding the little box as if his life depended on it, and Charlotte, sprinkling golden sunflower petals, passed by with Mennie and Halle—not to be left out—traipsing beside them. Then, as his grandfather offered Beryl his arm, Gabe lifted a brass trumpet to his lips and began to play the beginning notes of Vivaldi's Trumpet Voluntary. Beryl's heart swelled with joy at the unexpected surprise.

Hearing the regal sound, the gathering of friends and family waiting on the breezy beach grew quiet and looked up expectantly. A moment later, Charlotte appeared, wearing her white, cotton sundress and the angelic halo of baby's breath the salon had made for her. But when she saw the crowd of people, she froze, and Asher almost bumped into her. "Char," he whispered loudly. "Whadju stop for?" Still clutching the box, he guided his stage-struck cousin with his free hand toward his father—an act that made everyone chuckle. Next came Laney with her arm tucked into Elijah's, followed by Rumer and Will, and then Isak and Matt, who had to stop to put his beer in the bushes before making their entrance.

Finally, with the majestic sound of the trumpet floating above the thundering surf, Beryl, escorted by her dashing father-in-law and looking absolutely stunning herself, walked across the beach toward the love of her life, and when she reached him, Asa lightly kissed her cheek and placed her hand in Micah's.

Then, under a summer sky streaked with orange and pink clouds, Beryl and Micah stood side by side and promised to love and honor each other forever. And as the stars grew brighter, and they slipped on the golden rings that Asher had been guarding with his life, Noah pronounced them husband and wife. Immediately, the crowd erupted into cheers, and in the flickering light of the torches, Micah gave his bride the long, sweet kiss she so deserved.

"Oh, man, get a room," Seth whispered, elbowing his brother and grinning.

❦ 60 ❧

Just as Lucy had predicted, the evening flew by. Beryl and Micah felt as if they'd been swept up in a glittering dream filled with sparkling lights, clinking glasses, and swishing taffeta, and all with the sounds of Sinatra and Billie Holiday playing in the background. As soon as everyone reconvened under the sparkling lights of the tent, the bar opened and the catering staff began to pass trays of every hors d'oeuvre imaginable, from coconut shrimp to smoked salmon, and mini hot dogs to mozzarella sticks. A long, stationary table was also set up with platters of fresh tomato, mozzarella, and basil drizzled with balsamic vinegar, every variety of shish kebab—beef, chicken, and shrimp—fresh fruit, and an endless array of cheeses. Ben and Seth were overwhelmed by the selection and tried a little of everything, while Asher, intrigued by the fancy porta-potty, visited it at least three times in the first hour. "Did you know there are smelly candles in there?" he reported, tugging on Laney's dress.

"Smelly candles in where?" she asked.

"In the porta-potty," he said in an amazed voice. She laughed. "You mean scented candles."

Finally, Gabe took a sip of the beer E had slipped him, cleared his throat, and turned on his microphone. "Welcome, everyone," he began. "I'm Gabe," he said in the most professional voice he could muster, "and I'll be your DJ for the evening. And just so you know, I *do* take requests." With raised eyebrows, Laney looked across the tent at Noah. He grinned and mouthed, "He's your son." But she just shook her head and pointed back at him.

"I'd like to get this party started," Gabe continued, "but first I'd like to introduce to you —for the first time—Mr. and Mrs. Micah Coleman!" Everyone cheered, and Beryl felt her face blush. But as Micah held out his hand and pulled her toward him, and the sultry sound of Etta James singing "At Last" drifted through the summer night, their surroundings slipped away and she felt as if they were all alone.

As the evening wore on, delicious smells wafted through the tent, but Beryl and Micah barely had time to eat. Instead, they chatted and thanked every friend and family member, only pausing long enough to kiss when the spoons chimed or dance when they were beckoned.

"It's time," Gabe announced later in the evening, eyeing his uncle, "for the special dances." And Micah, taking his cue, reached for Maddie's hand, and as Elvis Presley's haunting song "Memories" started to play, Maddie looked into her son's eyes and tried not to cry.

When the song finished, Gabe suddenly realized

the blunder he'd made and frowned, but Asa quickly came to his rescue and whispered something in his ear. Gabe smiled and nodded as he looked through his CDs. A moment later, Frank Sinatra's smooth, unmistakable voice crooned "I Wish You Love," and Beryl—never expecting a father-daughter dance—followed Asa out onto the dance floor, where he swept her off her feet and showed everyone how it was done.

The clambake was a huge success. Asa's chowder was rich and creamy and loaded with fresh clams, and to everyone's surprise, he willingly shared the Coleman family secret of adding fresh thyme. Even Noah was surprised when he overheard his dad talking about it, but Asa just smiled and said he wasn't going to live forever so he may as well share it.

After the first course, people chatted about the added flavor the seaweed gave the steamed seafood and potatoes; the corn was well-received too, with many guests commenting on how sweet it was; and the filet mignon, cooked whole and served with a warm merlot sauce, was moist, tender, and rare.

The real treat came, however, at the end of the evening when the catering staff brought out Laney's peach cobblers. Even Gabe forgot to put on background music during dessert, so except for the scraping of forks on plates, and the cicadas singing in the trees, the tent was quiet, everyone savoring the sweetness of the peaches and the buttery flavor of the cobbler. Almost everyone came back for seconds, and although Lucy repeatedly explained that she wasn't responsible for the chowder, the corn, or the cobbler, she ended up giving out all the business cards she'd brought with her.

After dessert, Micah and Beryl discreetly disappeared into the house. Ten minutes later, they reappeared, wearing fancy traveling clothes and carrying suitcases. Gabe looked up, realized they were getting ready to leave, and announced, "It's hard to believe that this wonderful night is already drawing to a close. Our bride and groom," he said, motioning to Micah and Beryl, "are ready to leave for their honeymoon, but I know they're hoping everyone will join them for one last dance before they say goodbye." He cued up a CD, and moments later, the haunting voice of Bobby Hatfield singing "Unchained Melody" filled the tent. Gabe looked for Meghan and saw her talking to Chloe and E. He walked over, and eyeing his brother, teased, "You don't get *all* the pretty girls."

E laughed. "I do if you're not paying attention."

Gabe turned to Meghan. "Would you like to dance?"

She smiled and nodded, and he took her hand.

As they walked away, Chloe looked up at E. "I've missed you these last few days."

"I've missed you too," he said, searching her eyes. "I've just been so busy helping . . ."

"I know . . . and it's given me a lot of time to think."

"About what?"

"About what your dad said at Jared's funeral . . . and what you said at the beach that afternoon—about God not letting bad things happen. And about His promise to always be there for us no matter what."

"I truly believe that," E said with a half smile.

Chloe nodded. "Well, it's starting to make sense." She paused, searching his eyes. "I don't want anything to come between us, E. I don't want to lose you."

"I don't either, Chlo, but you can't expect to find faith overnight. It's something that grows stronger with time and, well, when I think of our future . . . I mean, if we were to ever have kids someday, I'm going to want them to believe in God and have a strong faith too. I think it's the most important thing we can teach them, but if you don't feel the same way"—he shook his head—"then I don't know. . . ."

Chloe nodded. "E, I want to have a strong faith too, but like you said, it's going to take time. You have to remember, I just lost my grandfather . . . and then a young boy dies for no reason . . . so I think it's normal to have questions."

E nodded. "Dance with me," he said softly,

pulling her onto the dance floor and wrapping his arms around her waist.

"Still love me?" she asked, searching his eyes.

"Always," he said, pulling her closer.

On the other side of the dance floor, Asa swayed slowly with Maddie in his arms. He looked up at the sparkling Christmas lights, and then he looked around at his family: Noah and Laney; Micah and Beryl; his brother Isaac and his wife, Nina; their daughters—his nieces—two of whom were dancing with Beryl's nephews, Tommy and Rand; his five grandsons; and one sweet granddaughter. Then he looked up at the brightly lit old Cape Cod house in the background—the house where he'd done so much of his growing up—where Noelle had offered him *her* sweet peach cobbler . . . and where Noah had been conceived. He shook his head slowly, trying to wrap his mind around the wonder of it all. Fifty years ago—when he was Gabe's age—he would never have imagined how his life would unfold. And he would never have imagined this glorious night. He was truly blessed.

Moments later, Beryl and Micah climbed into a waiting limo, and as they pulled away, everyone lined up along the driveway, waving, cheering, and wishing them well.

Long after the last guest had said good night, carrying a jar of peach jam, Laney and Noah were still outside, picking up empty glasses and beer bottles. The catering staff had done a great job clearing tables, wrapping up leftovers, and bringing them into the house, but Lucy said there was still more to be done, and she promised they'd be back first thing in the morning to finish. As the catering van pulled away, Noah reached for Laney's hand and smiled. "One more dance?"

She looked at him as if he'd just asked her to climb Mount Washington. "Don't we have a race to run in the morning?"

"Just one," he pressed.

"Okay," she conceded. Wearily, she leaned against one of the tables while he searched the CDs, and as he walked back over to her, she heard the beginning notes and shook her head. "Are you trying to make me cry?"

"No," he said softly, pulling her toward him.

Glen Campbell's unmistakable voice started to sing about the lonely Wichita lineman and tears filled Laney's eyes. "Gramp would've loved tonight," she said, putting her arms around his neck. "He loved it when we all got together."

Noah nodded, tucking her head under his chin.

"Why do the people we love have to go away?" she asked.

"It's part of life," he answered simply.

"I don't like that part," she murmured sadly.

"Me neither."

Hearing music, Gabe looked out from the bathroom window. "Hey, check this out," he said

373

to his brothers who were all getting ready for bed too. They jostled for position, trying to see out the window all at once. They watched quietly, and as the song ended, they saw their dad lean down and kiss their mom.

Seth snickered and Gabe chuckled. "Okay, guys, on three," E, Ben, Seth, and Asher all grinned and nodded. He counted softly, "One . . . two . . ." And on three they all shouted, "GET A ROOM!" Then they fell over, giggling and laughing.

Noah and Laney looked up at the window and shouted, "GO TO BED!"

❧ 61 ❧

Noah tied his running shoes and looked at his watch. "We've got to go," he called up the stairs. He turned to Chloe, who'd arrived early. "Are you sure you don't mind watching from the finish line with Asher?"

"I'm positive," she said. "It'll be fun."

E came down the stairs, wearing his running shorts and a T-shirt. "Hi," he said.

"Hi," she replied with a smile.

He started putting the water bottles Noah had filled into a waiting cooler.

"I think we're going to have to take two cars," Noah said, trying to figure out the logistics of transporting everyone to Falmouth.

"That's fine," E said. "Chloe, Gabe, Asher, and I can ride up together, and then Chloe and Asher can walk to the finish line and Gabe and I can take the shuttle to the starting line."

"I'd like to stay together."

"Okay, well, we'll probably park in the same place we parked last year."

Noah nodded and was about to call up the stairs again when he heard a thundering herd coming down. "Good," he said, seeing Gabe, Ben, Seth, and Asher. "Make sure you have your bib numbers and racing chips and grab a snack if you want one." Immediately, Ben and Seth reached for the Pop-Tart box.

"Ah," Gabe teased, eyeing his younger brothers, "the breakfast of champions."

"Yup! All that extra sugar will give us a nitrogen boost," Seth said.

"And then we'll see who finishes first," Ben added.

"We definitely will," Gabe said. "You two have been slacking all summer."

"No, we haven't," Seth retorted. "We're just well-rested."

"Well, your team won't appreciate you being well-rested when you lose this fall."

"We're not gonna lose," Ben said. "State champs, baby."

Gabe shook his head skeptically. "I'll believe that when I see it."

"All right, girls," Noah said, rolling his eyes. "Go get in the car."

As the boys pushed their way out the door, Asher lingered, retying his new running shoes. "Are you sure I can't run this year, Dad?" he asked.

"You're not signed up, bud," Noah said, tousling his hair, "but maybe next year."

Asher looked disappointed, and Chloe said, "Besides, who would I have to hang out with if you ran too?"

Asher shrugged. "Okay," he said, smiling and reaching for her hand.

As they went out the door, Laney came down wearing running shorts and a bright orange running shirt.

"I guess you don't want us to lose you," he teased with a grin.

She chuckled and reached for the coffeepot.

"I wouldn't do that," he warned, watching her pour coffee into her travel mug.

"I'm not," Laney said. "I'm just having a splash." She scratched Mennie's ears. "Have the dogs been out?"

"Yup, out *and* had their breakfast . . . and we need to go. Do you have your bib and chip?"

"Yup," she said, reaching for her racing packet and holding her mug. "I'm ready. Lead the way."

❧ 62 ❧

Maddie was still sound asleep when Asa slipped from between the sheets. It had been well past their bedtime when they'd gotten home the night before, so he tried not to wake her. A cool ocean breeze drifted through the bedroom windows, rustling the curtains. *What a great day for Falmouth,* he thought enviously, sitting on the edge of the bed. For years, his knee had prevented him from running in the famous race, and he still missed it. *But it doesn't mean I can't go for a run.* He reached for his shorts, and as he did, he heard Harper's tail start thumping against the hardwood floor on the other side of the bed. *That dog doesn't miss a trick.* He peered around the end of the bed and put his finger to his lips, but seeing him just made her tail thump harder, so he motioned for her to follow. She got up quickly, her paws slipping off the braided rug and scratching the floor, and Noah held his breath, waiting for Maddie to wake up, but she only stirred and seemed to reach for him.

"C'mon, you," he whispered, "before you wake her!" Obediently, Harper followed him down the stairs, the tags on her collar jingling like bells. Asa sat down in one of the chairs on the porch to put on his running shoes. "You certainly are noisy in the morning," he said, and she wagged her tail in happy agreement. While he tied his shoes, Harper waited, watching his every move. He looked up. "You don't want to go too, do you?" he asked softly, and she got up and wiggled all around him. "You're silly," he said, rubbing her ears.

As soon as they got to the bottom of the stairs, Harper started sniffing around the yard, but Asa called, "C'mon, this way," and headed down the trail that led past Nauset Lighthouse. Harper—who was still taking care of business—watched him intently and then raced after him, zigzagging every which way, trying to breathe in as many new morning scents as she could while still keeping track of him. When they reached the lighthouse, he jiggled the lock and it clicked open. "You stay here," he said, slipping inside and climbing the winding metal stairs. When he reached the lantern room, he watched the rotating lens for a few moments and then pushed open one of the windows. A fresh breeze cooled his skin, just as it had when he was a boy standing in the very same spot with his arms around Noelle. He looked out at the waves chasing each other toward shore and realized the bittersweet memory could still make his heart ache.

Finally, he headed back down and found Harper waiting patiently, wagging her tail. "Good girl," he said, sliding the rusty lock closed. "Let's go," he called a moment later, and Harper bounded across the deserted parking lot, heading for the steep stairs down to the beach.

Asa looked at his watch and wondered where all the beachcombers were. Seven o'clock wasn't too early to be out scouring the beach, looking for treasure. He trotted down the stairs and walked over to the hard sand along the water's edge. Harper was already gleefully racing through the surf, leaping over the waves, and he wished he'd brought a tennis ball.

"C'mon, girl," he called, turning to jog down the beach. The shiny, wet, black Lab stopped in her tracks, watching him, and then chased after him at full speed. Asa looked out at the orange sun glittering on the water and, as often happened when he jogged, his mind drifted back through the years to when Noah and Micah were younger. Oh, the times they'd had—hiking in the White Mountains, fly-fishing in the cold, clear streams of Maine, reading stories late into the night. He'd never forget the time he'd tried to get through the last agonizing pages of *Where the Red Fern Grows*. Noah had been nestled on one side of him and Micah on the other, and they'd all been misty-eyed as they read about the heartbroken hound Lil' Ann lying on the grave of her beloved Old Dan and refusing to get up. Maddie had even brought them a box of tissues. "I warned you," she said, eyeing him. Finally, Asa just couldn't read any more, and Noah had had to finish the last few pages as tears streamed down his father's cheeks. Sad as it was, Asa thought, it was worth it.

Asa looked down at his damp running shoes. When he was younger, he could run for miles on the beach, barefoot, and not think twice about it, but now he worried that running without shoes would only aggravate his knee . . . and every other ache in his body. He started to feel an odd twinge in his chest and slowed down to rub it. It went away, and he started off again, wondering what people thought about before they died. Did they know, at *the* critical moment, that they were about to die? Some didn't, he decided, like those who were being administered morphine—it was easy for them as they slipped away peacefully without even knowing it, but it wasn't so easy for their loved ones who, with aching hearts, kept watch as they took their last breath. But what about the people who died in tragic accidents? Did they sense, during the day, that the end was near—even before the accident happened? Did they feel any kind of foreboding? Would *he* feel any kind of foreboding before he died?

One time, he'd heard someone refer to the human body as an earth suit and he'd found it fitting. After all, the body's main purpose was to house the soul—it was a suit for the soul while the soul walked around on earth, and when the earth suit failed, well, then there was nowhere for the soul to be housed. He'd always found it difficult to comprehend what happened next though. What happened to the soul when the body died? Was it immediately whisked away to heaven . . . or hell? Or did it linger, hovering around loved ones and witnessing their grief and sorrow? The soul was such a complex entity—it made up a person's laughter, the sparkle in their eyes, their unique memories . . . everything about them . . . but when the body dies, the soul is just *gone*. Where does something so amazing *go?*

He looked out at the waves and thought about how lucky he was to have had such a positive outcome in his bout with cancer when so many others didn't. Some, like Micah's first wife, fought with every fiber of their being and still lost the battle. *Why was it that some folks beat the odds while others didn't? Why were some prayers answered . . . while others seemed to go unheard? How did God choose who would get better and who wouldn't?* Asa shook his head. He knew if he asked Noah that question, his minister son would assure him that God doesn't choose. *Well, if that's the case—if God doesn't play a role in someone's healing—then what's the point of praying?* He could almost hear Noah's answer: "God's job is to be with us as we go through it— no matter what the outcome. We pray to be held in His arms . . . to be in His constant care . . . and for His will to be done."

Asa looked up and watched Harper chasing the

seagulls. He smiled. *Ah, life . . .* he thought. *Why am I dwelling on such gloomy thoughts on such a beautiful morning?* He continued to run, but suddenly, out of the blue, the odd pain in his chest returned, sharper this time. He rubbed it with his palm, feeling lightheaded . . . and as he looked up at the summer sky it started to grow dark. In the back of his mind, he heard the pounding surf and the cry of the seagulls. He felt the wet sand under his knees . . . and then he felt Harper near, licking his cheeks and nudging his hands. "Good girl . . ." he whispered softly.

❧ 63 ❧

Noah tightened his shoelaces one more time and watched as Chloe and Asher, swinging their arms, walked hand in hand toward Grand Avenue. Then he trotted through the shady tree-lined neighborhood to catch up with Laney and the boys, who were already making their way toward the shuttle bus.

The bus was packed with runners, but they all managed to squeeze in for the seven-mile ride to Woods Hole. "Hey, E!" a voice called from the back of the bus.

E turned to look back and saw one of his teammates from college. "Hey, Ty, I didn't know you were running."

"I didn't either until yesterday. One of my friends from high school got us in. Where're you starting?"

"In the fives."

Ty shook his head. "Not me—wait when you get off."

E nodded.

Ten minutes later, the bus pulled up to drop them off and E waited for Tyler. As they chatted, Tyler revealed that he was coming off an ankle injury and was planning to take it easy. E wanted to keep talking, but out of the corner of his eye, he saw his dad checking his watch and said, "Listen, Ty, I gotta go. We'll have to catch up at preseason next week." Tyler nodded and headed off in the opposite direction with his friend.

"You didn't have to wait," E said. "I know my way."

Noah nodded. "I know. I just thought we could warm up together."

"That's fine," E said. "Let's go."

"Wait a minute," Laney called after them, kneeling down. "I have to tighten my laces."

Noah chuckled. "Boys," he said dramatically, "did you know this is how your mother and I met?"

Seth and Ben groaned, and E and Gabe rolled their eyes.

"Dad, we know how you met," Ben said.

"Yeah, you tell us every year," Seth added.

"Mom was innocently tying her shoelaces at the start of the Falmouth Road Race . . ." Seth started.

"In 1983 . . ." Ben added.

"When you rudely . . ." Gabe began.

"And clumsily . . ." E added.

"Knocked her over because you weren't watching where you were going," they all said in unison.

Noah laughed. "Well, that's your mom's version of the story. It was really Uncle Micah's fault."

Laney stood up. "Okay, I'm ready, but let's not go too far. I need to conserve my energy . . . and I need to find a porta-potty."

Noah shook his head. "I told you not to drink that coffee."

"I know—but I only had a little."

Gabe and E both rolled their eyes again, and then E looked over his dad's shoulder and stared. "Um, Dad," he said, pointing.

"What?" Noah said, giving him an odd look. E nodded behind him, and Noah turned just in time to see a short, spry woman wearing a Nike cap jog past them, and like all the other world-class runners in the race, instead of a number on her bib, she had her name printed across it in bold, block letters: JOAN.

Noah's eyes grew wide as he quickly raised his hand in a wave, hoping to get her attention.

"Now look what you did," Gabe groaned.

Noah looked back at Laney. "I just want to say hello," he called. "I've always wanted to tell her . . ." His voice trailed off. Then, somewhere in the back of his mind, it occurred to him that his boys might try to duck away. He turned around. "DON'T YOU GO ANYWHERE!" he commanded in a voice that sounded like it had come from heaven.

The boys watched in dismay and embarrassment as their father flailed his arms, trying to get the attention of the petite female runner before she disappeared into the crowd.

"Seriously, Dad?" Ben murmured.

Laney elbowed him.

"Ouch!" he said, rubbing his side.

"This would really make Dad's day," Laney said sternly, "so I'd appreciate it if you would all . . ."

"Joan!" Noah shouted suddenly, and the tiny, silver-haired lady—along with twenty other people—turned their heads to see who was shouting. Noah waved, and she smiled. Meanwhile, the four Coleman boys and their mother watched as Noah greeted the famous runner and started motioning back at them.

"Oh, great, here we go," Seth groaned, which triggered another elbow to the ribs.

"Ouch," Seth cried.

With a friendly smile, Joan followed Noah over, and as he proudly introduced each of them, she politely shook their hands. "And this," he said, motioning to Laney, "is my wife, Laney." And then, a smile as wide as Texas spread across his face. "I know the race is going to start soon and you probably want to finish warming up, but I've always wanted to have the opportunity to tell you that *you* are responsible for all this," he said, motioning to his family. Joan gave him a puzzled look, and he launched into an abbreviated version of how she'd unwittingly played a role in changing his life.

Joan listened and laughed, and then, with genuine interest, asked the boys how they liked running and where they went to school. She nodded, listening intently to their answers, and then she told them about the 10K race in Maine she had started—it's called Beach to Beacon. The boys all nodded and promised they would look into it for next year. Finally, Joan turned to Laney. "And there's one more?"

Laney nodded. "Asher—he just turned eight last week. In fact, he was born on race day. We were heading to Falmouth that year to cheer on our older boys, but we ended up having to turn around and go to the hospital instead." Joan smiled and shook her head at the coincidence.

"Well, I'm so glad you flagged me down," she said with a smile. "It was a pleasure to meet you and to hear how I helped bring five boys into the world without even knowing it."

Noah smiled. "I wish I had a camera," he said, "but we left all of our phones in the car."

"I didn't," Ben said brightly, pulling his phone

out of an armband. "Mom makes us," he said, motioning to Seth and himself, "carry one whenever we go running."

"Well, it's a good idea," Joan said. "You never know when you'll need it."

Ben nodded and started to hand the phone to Noah, but Joan called a friend over to take the picture of all of them and then Laney took a picture of Joan with just Noah.

"Thank you so much," Noah said.

"It was my pleasure," she replied. And then she looked at the boys. "I hope to see you in Cape Elizabeth next year."

They all nodded, and as she jogged away, the boys started gushing about how nice she was.

"I told you," Noah said with a grin. He glanced at his watch. "Now, are you finally ready to go for a warm-up?"

❦ 64 ❧

Maddie slipped her hand over to Asa's side of the bed but instead of his warm body, she only felt the coolness of his sheets. She opened her eyes and realized he was gone. She peered over the side of the bed and realized Harper was gone too. She gazed out the window at the blue sky and heard the haunting sound of sirens in the distance. In the summer months, a day didn't go by on the Cape when they didn't hear sirens racing up or down Route 6, so it wasn't unusual, but as was her habit, she murmured a prayer for the person or people who needed help.

She got up, pulled on her robe, and as she went downstairs, she realized the eerie sound was getting louder. She went out on the porch to listen, wondering if Asa had taken Harper for a walk . . . or maybe they'd gone for a run. She realized there was more than one siren, and the emergency vehicles had rounded the corner at the Coast Guard Beach and were still coming this way. Maddie's heart pounded. Maybe when Asa got back he would know what happened. The sound suddenly stopped, and she pictured the vehicles with their lights flashing pulling into the Nauset Light Beach parking lot. She wondered if there had been a drowning, or maybe a shark attack—with the growing seal population along this pristine stretch of coastline, there had certainly been more shark sightings, and it seemed like it was just a matter of time.

She whispered a second prayer and then went inside to make coffee, and while it brewed, she went up to take her shower. If Asa had gone for a run, he'd want to take one when he got back, so she may as well get hers out of the way.

❧ 65 ❧

The announcer summoned everyone to the starting line, and although Ben and Seth wanted to start in the first wave with Gabe and E, Noah made them line up in the second wave.

"How are we going to beat them when they have such an unfair advantage?" Seth moaned.

"They're only a couple hundred feet ahead of you, so I'm sure, if you can beat them, you can catch up to them," Noah assured.

"Yeah, a couple hundred feet with a million runners in the way," Ben complained.

"You're quick and agile," Noah said with a smile. "You'll weave through the other runners in no time. Besides, it's based on time, so you could have a better time than they do." And leaving them with that strategy in mind, he walked farther back with Laney.

"You don't have to run with me," she said. "In fact, I'd rather you didn't."

"Why?" he asked, looking wounded.

"Because I'll feel like I'm holding you back."

"You never hold me back," he said, putting his arm around her.

"Well, I've hardly had any time to run this summer, so I'm going all the way back to where the nine-minute milers are starting."

"The nines?"

She nodded. "Maybe the tens—I *am* going to be fifty-three soon, you know."

"You are?" he teased. "When did you get so old?"

"I don't know," she laughed. "I was twenty just yesterday."

"It sure seems like it," he said, stopping. "Okay, so I guess I'll start around here then, on the tail end of the sevens. Good luck!" he added, giving her a kiss.

"You too," she said, smiling. "I hope you don't have to wait all day for me."

"I hope not. Pancake Man closes at two."

"I'll try to be done by then," she said, laughing.

Moments later, after the wheelchair racers took off, the elite runners lined up and the national anthem was sung, followed by the famous trumpet fanfare from Churchill Downs, and then a countdown from ten, and finally, the gun went off. The elites sprinted away, and the first wave started moving. The inspirational theme from *Rocky* along with lots of happy cheering filled the air as E set off at a quick pace with Gabe by his side. Meanwhile, Ben and Seth had to wait several seconds for their wave to start moving, but as soon as it did, they wove through runners with Ben leading the way, trying to catch up to their older brothers.

Farther back in the pack, Noah started trotting along. It was the first year in a long time that

Micah wasn't by his side, and he missed him. He glanced at his watch. It was five after ten, and he knew they'd had an early flight, so if they weren't in Bermuda already, they were at least on their way. He hoped they'd have a good time—they certainly deserved it.

Laney smiled as she ran through the cheering crowd lined up along historic Water Street. She'd always thought the best part of running Falmouth was there was no shortage of cheering spectators. They lined the entire seven miles of the course, inspiring runners to keep chugging along. As she jogged along the narrow, winding, shady roads she thought about the chance encounter they'd had with Joan Benoit Samuelson. Noah had been thrilled, and she was glad the boys had had the chance to meet her. She truly was an inspiration.

When E and Gabe finally reached Falmouth Heights Beach, they were still together. Then they started to hear the crowd cheering, "Go, Joanie!" and they realized the little silver-haired runner they'd met that morning was trotting along—with her unmistakable steady-as-you-go gait—*ahead of them!* They looked at each other and picked up the pace, knowing they would never hear the end of it from their father if they came in after a woman who was nearly sixty years old . . . even if she was a world-class runner! They said hello to her as they passed, and then they raced each other down Grand Avenue, delighting the crowd with their effort, and in the end, it was a photo finish with both claiming victory.

Asher and Chloe ran to meet them as they came out of the shoot. "That was awesome!" Asher said. "We couldn't even tell who won."

"I did," they said in unison, trying to catch their breath.

Two minutes later, Ben came in, and Seth—complaining that Ben went out too fast—came in a minute later.

"Excuses, excuses," Gabe teased.

"Wait 'til next year," Seth said.

Noah was happy to come in at under fifty minutes, but the clock had almost clicked over to an hour before they saw Laney in her bright orange shirt running under the huge American flag that hung over the finish line. "Yay, Mom!" they cheered, and Laney grinned and gave them a thumbs-up.

❧ 66 ❧

Maddie was drying herself with a towel when she finally heard the persistent knocking on the front door. "Be right there," she called, quickly pulling her robe around her. She didn't remember locking the door, so why was Asa knocking? And why was he at the front door? She pushed back her wet hair and pulled the door open.

A young state trooper was standing there with Harper. "Mrs. Coleman?"

"Yes," she answered, feeling her heart start to pound. "Is everything okay?"

The officer bit his lip. "Is this your dog?"

Maddie nodded. Suddenly, she remembered the sirens and blurted, "Where did you find her? Is my husband okay?"

"May I come in?"

"Of course, please," she said, stepping back, and as he came in, he let go of Harper's collar and she immediately sat at Maddie's feet with only the tip of her tail wagging.

The officer took off his hat, and Laney could see tears in his eyes. "Ma'am, I'm very sorry . . . but your husband . . ."

Maddie shook her head. "Noo," she whispered, tears filling her eyes. "Noo!" she cried. "This can't be . . . he just had cancer . . . he was better . . . the doctor said he was going to live a long time."

"I'm so sorry," the officer repeated. "A couple out walking found him," he paused and bit his lip again, trying to fight back his own tears as he stroked Harper's soft ears. "They said your dog was lying next to him with her head on his chest."

Tears spilled down Maddie's face as she looked down at Harper. She tried to speak but no words would come.

"Even after the EMTs got there, your dog

refused to leave his side. They had to pick her up."

Maddie knelt down next to Harper and buried her face in her neck. "You are such a good girl," she whispered, shaking her head. "Oh, God, please tell me this is not happening," she sobbed.

"Is there someone you'd like to call to meet us at the hospital?" he asked softly.

Maddie put her hands on her forehead. "Oh, I can't even think." She paused. "My oldest son . . ." she said finally.

❦ 67 ❦

"Do we still have time to go to Pancake Man?" Asher asked as they walked back to their cars.

Noah looked at his watch. "If we hurry," he said, picking up the pace.

Twenty minutes later, they pulled into the parking lot. It was one thirty. "Just in time!" Asher said excitedly, hopping out. "I'm starving."

E walked across the parking lot with his phone in his hand. "Dad, Grandma called both Gabe and me and left messages to call her back as soon as we could. She sounded upset."

Noah frowned and reached under the seat for his phone. He looked at his screen and realized he'd missed three calls—all from his mom. He listened to the first message: "Noah, please call me as soon as you get this." It sounded like she was crying. Although she'd called two more times, she hadn't left any more messages.

"Lane, check your phone to see if my mom called."

Laney reached into her bag, and as she listened to her voice mail, she nodded, confirming she'd received the same worrisome message. Noah scrolled to his parents' Cape Cod number and pushed it, but the phone just rang and rang. He tried their cell number too, but it went right to voice mail.

Noah shook his head and frowned. "I wonder if we should skip Pancake Man."

"Noo," Asher said, sounding disappointed. "Let's just eat fast."

Noah looked at Laney, who raised her eyebrows. "I don't know, hon. I think we should probably head home and find out what's going on."

"We have two vehicles," Noah said, thinking out loud. "Do you want to stay here with the boys and I'll take the car home?"

Laney shrugged uncertainly. "If that's what you want to do."

Gabe frowned. "Do you want me to go with you, Dad?"

"Don't you want to have pancakes?"

"I can live without them."

"Okay, let's go then."

"Do you want me to go too?" E asked, feeling as if he'd been passed over.

Noah shook his head. "No, you stay and have pancakes with Chloe. It's the least we can do after making her get up early and come all the way down here with us."

"I didn't mind," Chloe said with a smile.

Asher reached for her hand. "Yeah, she didn't mind. C'mon, Chloe, let's go have pancakes."

E laughed. "She doesn't need me. She has Asher."

Noah nodded. "Well, you stay anyway."

He and Gabe got in the car, and Laney signaled for him to call, and he nodded as he pulled back onto Route 28.

On the way home, Gabe continued to try to reach his grandparents. He even tried their New Hampshire number.

"I wish I had Uncle Isaac's number," Noah said offhandedly.

"I can look it up," Gabe offered, going online.

"You can?"

He nodded as he typed. "Providence, right?"

Noah nodded, and Gabe dialed the number and waited hopefully. The phone rang and rang, but when it finally clicked, it was just the answering machine. "Should I leave a message?" he asked.

"Yes, have them call as soon as they can."

Gabe left a message and then looked out the window. "I wonder if she forgot we had the race this morning."

"She probably did. Any other time and one of us would have had our phone with us."

"Are you going right to the house?"

"I guess."

They drove the rest of the way in silence, and when they pulled into the driveway, both of his parents' cars were there. They hurried up the back stairs, and Noah called them but there was no answer. He saw Harper lying on her bed, but when she didn't get up to greet them, he walked over and knelt down next to her. "Hey, Harp," he said softly. The tip of her tail wagged, but her ears were back, and her eyes were full of worry. "What's the matter, girl? Where is everybody? Oh, I wish you could tell me what's going on."

They heard a car door and Noah looked out the window. His heart pounded as he walked outside while the state trooper helped Maddie get out of the passenger side of his car. Gabe stood in the doorway, watching as his grandmother reached up and gently put her hands on his dad's cheeks; he watched his dad's shoulders sag as she spoke and he saw his back shaking as she hugged him. Without seeing his face, Gabe knew his dad was crying . . . and his grandmother was crying too. He didn't need to hear what happened—he already knew. He felt Harper's nose nudging his hand, and he sat down on the stoop and put his arm around her, and as hot tears spilled down his cheeks, Harper leaned against him with the weight of the world.

PART III

Lord, make me to know . . .
the measure of my days . . .

—Psalm 39:4

❦ 68 ❧

Noah leaned against the railing of his parents' beach house and looked up at the stars. He listened to the voices inside, and tears welled up in his eyes again—he couldn't seem to stop them. Laney pushed open the screen door. "I thought I'd find you out here," she said, leaning against the railing next to him and looking up at the sky. "The stars are so bright."

Noah nodded. "I know. Dad loved coming out here to listen to the surf and look at the stars. He knew all the constellations' names. My grandfather told him that Cygnus was his constellation because it was brightest around his birthday." He smiled. "Your birthday too." He shook his head sadly. "I just can't believe he's gone, Lane." Noah's voice was barely audible. "At this time last night, he was spinning Beryl around on the dance floor—and now he's gone. How can that be?"

Laney shook her head sadly. "I don't know. . . ."

Noah watched the light from the lighthouse sweep across the sky. "When I said good night to him last night, he clapped me on the shoulder and said, 'That was the best party I've ever been to.' Those were the last words he said to me. And I hugged him and said, 'Thanks, Dad, I'm glad you had fun.' " Noah shook his head.

Laney smiled sadly. "It's very appropriate. Most people don't remember the last thing they said to someone . . . and other people are filled with regret because the last thing they said wasn't kind, but you two said just the right thing . . . and you'll always have that."

Noah nodded, and Laney looked over, searching his face. "Have you called Micah?"

Noah shook his head, tears welling up in his eyes again. "I don't know what to do. This is the first night of their honeymoon, and if I call them, they're going to turn right around and come home. They've both been looking forward to it for so long. . . ." His voice trailed off.

Laney stood silently next to him.

He looked over at her. "What would you do?"

She sighed. "I honestly don't know what I'd do, but I'm surprised that you, of all people, are struggling with this. You've always been so cut and dry on the subject of being forthcoming . . . no matter what the cost. Your mantra has always been: there's no excuse for holding back—not even to protect someone."

"This isn't the same."

"It's not?"

"No, it's not. This is calling my brother on his honeymoon to give him news that will devastate him."

"And what if the tables were turned? Would you want him to call you?"

"I don't know."

"Well, how would you feel if you were off having a good time and something terrible happened at home, but your family didn't call you because they didn't want to ruin your good time?"

Noah didn't answer, but the tears streaming down his cheeks said it all. "I'd be mad," he said finally. "Oh, Lane," he said, turning to her, his shoulders sagging. "Why did this happen? Why did it have to happen now?"

"I don't know," she whispered, wrapping her arms around him and holding him.

"Dad?" E called softly through the screen.

Noah straightened up and wiped his eyes as E stepped out onto the porch. "I'm taking Chloe back to the house to get her car. . . . She has to be at work early tomorrow."

"Does anyone else want to go home with you?"

"I don't know. Ash's asleep on the couch with Harper, and Seth's half asleep in the chair, and Uncle Isaac and Aunt Nina are going to stay over with Grandma."

"It's late," Laney said, looking at her watch. "I should just take all the boys home."

Noah nodded. "Why don't you guys go in the SUV and leave the car for me? I just want to talk to Mom once more, and then I'll be along."

Laney nodded, and E went inside to round up his brothers.

An hour later, after tucking her three youngest, sleepy, heartbroken boys in, Laney looked in on Gabe and E who were lying on their beds, still talking. "Good night," she said softly.

They smiled and replied, "Good night."

But as she turned to go down the hall, Gabe called her back. "Mom?"

"Mmm?" she said, looking back in.

"Is Dad going to be all right?"

She nodded. "He'll be all right."

"It's just," Gabe faltered. "I-I've never seen him cry like that before."

Laney sat down on the edge of his bed. "I know," she said, lightly brushing his hair back from his forehead. "And when someone who we've always known to be strong and unshakable falls apart, it's scary . . . but don't worry," she said, holding his chin. "It'll take time . . . and I'm sure you haven't seen the last of his tears . . . but he'll be okay."

Gabe nodded, and she gave them both hugs. "Love you."

"Love you too," they said.

Laney collapsed onto their bed and closed her eyes. Moments later, she heard Noah come up the stairs, but instead of going into the bathroom, she heard him stop in the hall and then she heard him talking softly to someone. Finally, she heard the bathroom door close, and when he came into their room, she heard him undress quietly; she knew he was trying to not wake her, but when he slipped into bed, she reached for his hand. "How come you're still awake?" he whispered.

"Waiting for you."

"You didn't have to."

"I know. Who else is awake?"

"E," he said with a sad sigh. "When I came up, I thought I heard something, and I went in to check. Gabe was asleep, but E was lying there with tears streaming down his cheeks. He said he just keeps picturing Grandpa, and he can't believe he's never going to see him again." He looked over at Laney. "It breaks my heart to see him like that. I think he's taking it the hardest of all the boys."

"I don't know. . . . They're all pretty upset. How's your mom?"

"Heartbroken—she can't believe it either."

"Like you."

He nodded.

"Did you talk about a service?"

Noah looked over. "She said he didn't want one."

"What?" Laney said in surprise. "Why?"

"I don't know. She said they'd talked about it a couple of times, and she tried to change his mind, but he was adamant. He said he wanted to be cremated, but he didn't want to be buried in a cemetery. He just wanted his ashes spread near Nauset Light with only family present."

"Wow," Laney said. "Not even a memorial service?"

Noah shook his head. "And, you're not going to believe this, but the headaches he was having last spring were caused by a tumor. He's been having radiation all summer, and he wouldn't let her say anything. He was just cleared last week. They actually went out and celebrated."

"Oh, my goodness! Your poor mom!"

"Now, I don't know whether to be mad or sad . . ."

"Did you ask her about Micah?"

"Yes, she wants me to call him in the morning. She said she's tired of keeping things from people and, honeymoon or not, he should know."

"She's right."

Noah squeezed her hand. "Thank you for being there today," he said softly.

"I didn't do much . . . except cry."

"And listen . . ."

"I learned that from you," she said softly, squeezing his hand.

✖ 69 ✖

As soon as they got the news, Micah and Beryl booked the first flight home. The manager of the resort offered Micah his deepest condolences and said he hoped they'd come back in happier times. He even graciously refunded their entire week's stay. Noah met them at the airport and drove straight to the Cape house so they could see Maddie.

"I'm so sorry we ruined your honeymoon, hon," she said, giving Beryl a long hug and holding Micah's tearstained face in her hands.

Micah just shook his head, and in a voice choked with emotion, asked, "Do they know what happened?"

"Without an autopsy, they can't be sure," Maddie said, "but after I said he'd recently complained about pain in his leg, they think he may have had a blood clot that traveled to his heart."

Micah shook his head. "I just can't believe it. He seemed fine at the wedding. He seemed so happy."

"He *was* happy," Maddie said softly. "He was so very happy . . . and he was so proud of you boys and the lives you've made for yourselves."

Micah turned to search his mom's eyes. "And how are you?"

She smiled sadly. "As good as can be expected, I guess . . . I miss him. And poor Harper is such a lost soul. Did Noah tell you how they found her?"

Micah nodded, and the image of Harper lying on the sand with her head on his dad's chest triggered a new wave of tears. "She's such a great dog."

Maddie nodded. "She adored your father, and I

think she's just as heartbroken as the rest of us."

"Noah said he didn't want a service. . . ."

"No, he was definite about that. I tried to change his mind, but you know him, once he gets an idea in his head, that's it. So he's being cremated, and we're going to spread his ashes on Friday morning." As she said this, she looked up at Noah for confirmation and he nodded.

Micah wiped his eyes. "Where is Harper?" he asked, looking around.

Maddie motioned toward the kitchen. "On her bed. She doesn't have much of an appetite, and she hardly gets up. She won't even play with her ball."

"That's not good." He looked at Beryl. "Want to see if she'll go for a walk?"

Beryl nodded, and as Noah carried their suitcases upstairs, Micah went into the kitchen. When the little black Lab saw him standing there, the tip of her tail started to wag, but she didn't lift her head until he came over and sat next to her, and even then, she had the same sad, worried expression on her face that she'd had for days. Micah stroked her soft ears and told her everything was going to be okay, and she licked his hand and rested her head on his thigh. Finally, he asked her if she wanted to go for a walk, and she wagged her tail and got up. Micah clicked her leash to her collar, and he and Beryl walked with Noah out to his car and then continued up the road—away from the beach. When they got back a little while later, Harper nosed around her food dish and finished most of what was there.

"Well, that's a little better," Maddie said with a sad smile. "I guess it's just going to take some time."

❧ 70 ❧

Friday morning dawned cloudy and cool, and by the time they'd walked to a spot from where they could see the lighthouse, it had started to drizzle. Everyone pulled up their hoods or stood under umbrellas. "Well, I guess this is appropriate," Noah said with a sad smile. "Dad . . . Grandpa . . . never minded a day like this, no matter how gloomy. He always said it was the perfect opportunity to settle into his favorite chair and read a good book. And if he wasn't reading, he was standing on the porch, watching the waves roll in.

"Even though he didn't want a traditional memorial service, I think we would be remiss in our duties if we didn't say a few words; so with that in mind, I'd like to read a verse that I've always found to be a source of comfort for those who are left behind." He slipped a small, dog-eared copy of the New Testament from his pocket, opened it to John 14 and read, " 'Let not your hearts be troubled; believe in God, believe also in me. In my Father's house are many rooms; if it were not so, would I have told you that I go to prepare a place for you? And if I go and prepare a place for you, I will come again and take you to myself, that where I am you may be also.' "

Noah looked up. "Let us pray.

"Dear Lord, bless the soul of our beloved husband, brother, father, and grandfather. He was a good and faithful servant who loved You and showed his love by sharing his time and talent with anyone who asked. We are thankful for the time we've shared with him on earth, and we know in our hearts that he is now in Your heavenly care . . . in a room that you've prepared just for him. Amen."

Noah nodded to Gabe, and Gabe stepped forward and unfolded a tearstained piece of paper. Clearing his throat and wiping his eyes, he looked up and whispered solemnly, "This last poem is for you, Grandpa. It's from Tennyson. . . .

'Sunset and evening star,
And one clear call for me!
And may there be no moaning of the bar,
When I put out to sea.

But such a tide as moving seems asleep,
Too full for sound and foam,
When that which drew from out the
    boundless deep
Turns again home!

Twilight and evening bell,
And after that the dark!
And may there be no sadness of farewell,
When I embark;

For though from out our bourn of Time and
   Place
The flood may bear me far,
I hope to see my Pilot face to face
When I have crost the bar.' "

Noah put his hand on Gabe's shoulder and smiled. Then he reached for the box in E's hands, opened it, took a few steps away, lifted it high, and turned it on its side. Just as he did, a gust of wind swept past as if it had been beckoned and carried the dull gray ash out across the waves. And at that moment, as they watched in amazement, a bright ray of sunlight broke through the dark clouds and streamed across the ocean, causing the ash to shimmer and sparkle as it drifted away.

When they finally got home late that afternoon, E and Gabe grimly set to work packing and trying to get organized. Noah and Laney were taking them back to their respective colleges the next morning for their weeklong cross-country preseason—E to Amherst, and Gabe to Amherst's rival, Williams.

Laney stood at the bottom of the stairs with a

pad and pencil in her hands and called, "I'm going to the store. Do you need anything?"

"Deodorant," E called.

"Me too," added Gabe, "and toothpaste."

"I'll take toothpaste too," E called.

"Is that it?" Laney asked, jotting down their requests. "Does anybody need laundry detergent . . . dryer sheets . . . shampoo . . . soap?"

"I do," they both called.

"Which?"

"All of it," they both called.

"Snacks and Gatorade too," E added.

"Are you making cookies?" Gabe asked hopefully.

"If I have time . . . after buying out the store."

"What's for supper?" E called.

"Spaghetti."

"With sausage?"

"Maybe."

"And garlic bread?"

"Possibly."

"Can Chloe come?"

"Yes," Laney called. "Anything else?"

"Can you also get those little cups of microwavable macaroni and cheese?" Gabe called.

"You're pushing it!" she said, and she heard them laugh.

She stopped to peer into Noah's study and found him staring at a blank document on his laptop screen. "Need anything?"

"A sermon," he said, turning around and smiling.

"I don't think they have those at the store. Besides, hon, I honestly think the congregation would understand if you took Sunday off."

"I know they would, but I took last Sunday off," he said, closing his laptop. "I think I'm just going to go for a walk, and hopefully, I'll think of something."

Later that night, with boxes piled everywhere, and bags of running shoes piled on top, they gathered around the candlelit table, said grace, ate spaghetti with sausage *and* meatballs, garlic bread, salad, and apple pie until they thought their sides would burst. They snuck tidbits to the dogs, teased one another, made faces, told jokes . . . and laughed. Noah looked around the table at their smiling faces, glowing in the candlelight, listened to their laughter, and he was amazed by the buoyancy of the human spirit—in spite of their shared sorrow and broken hearts, they had each found a way to laugh.

He looked across the table at his favorite old soul and knew, by the look in her glistening eyes, that she was missing her boys already. It would be Thanksgiving before they were together again, and he knew she was holding them close . . . never wanting to let them go.

❧ 71 ❧

After they'd sung the middle hymn, Noah looked up and gazed out at his congregation with tired eyes. He felt as if he'd aged ten years, and when he'd looked in the mirror that morning, he'd decided he looked it too. The day before, they'd loaded up Laney's SUV and E's old Civic and driven all the way across the state to drop the boys off at school. And the trip hadn't started off well because it was Saturday and all the homebound vacationers were trying to get off the Cape too—Route 6 had been backed up for miles.

E's car had been busting at the hinges, and although he was keeping his car at school, they didn't want to just send him off on his own. They wanted to help him move in and make sure he had everything he needed, so they stopped at Amherst first and then, after they'd tearfully hugged him and Laney had thoroughly embarrassed him by going through their ritual good-bye in front of his friends, they headed north to Williams—where Gabe made sure no one was around when he and Laney kissed each other's palms and murmured, "I love you . . . keep the faith . . . fight the good fight . . . I can do all things through Christ which strengthens me . . . inch by inch, it's a cinch!"

"*Your* mother," Noah teased.

"Hey," she said defensively, smiling at her tall, handsome son. "It's tradition, right?"

Laughing, Gabe gave his mom another hug. "Yup, Mom, it wouldn't be the same if we didn't do it."

After leaving him, they'd stopped at a diner for a bite to eat, and when they finally got home, Noah still had his sermon to write. He'd had plenty of time to think about it, but it was still a matter of organizing his thoughts into something that made sense . . . and, hopefully, had a meaningful message.

He looked down at his notes before speaking, praying that he'd get through the first sentence. "As most of you know," he began, "my dad passed away last Sunday." As he said this, a quiet wave of surprise and sympathy rippled through the sanctuary, and he had to fight back his tears.

He wiped his eyes and smiled sadly. "Through the years, most of you have gotten to know my mom and dad—they've been coming to church here in the summer for a very long time. The rest of the year, they've lived in New Hampshire—in the house where my brother and I grew up, and in a town where they both spent their lives teaching. My mom taught kids with special needs, and my dad taught English." He paused, looked up, and smiled. "My dad loved teaching. . . . He loved books and poetry and plays, and although he

415

never published a book, he filled countless notebooks with poems. And although he never wrote a play, he had a favorite—in fact, many of you have probably heard me talk about my dad's love for Thornton Wilder's timeless American play *Our Town*.

"At least once every four years—for the last forty years—my high school has put on a production of *Our Town*, and my dad has been at the helm, directing it. Before he retired, he directed it for the tenth—and last—time." Noah smiled. "But years earlier—my senior year—I landed the coveted part of stage manager—which is where I discovered my gift for oration."

At this, the congregation chuckled warmly.

"Anyway, my dad made sure that play was put on once every four years because he wanted every class to have the chance to either see it or be involved in it. The play's poignant message was that important to him.

"For those of you who aren't familiar with it, *Our Town* takes place in the early 1900s, and it portrays American life as it was at the turn of the twentieth century—a time of innocence before the Great War. *Our Town* is set in the fictitious town of Grover's Corners, New Hampshire—a town very much like the one in which I grew up.

"As *Our Town* opens, the narrator, or stage manager—as he's called in the script—stands to one side and briefly introduces the play and gives the demographics of Grover's Corners; he then directs the attention of the audience to the lives of the Gibbs and Webb families and explains how George Gibbs and Emily Webb—once neighborhood playmates—have become romantically involved. In fact, it's over an ice-cream soda at Morgan's corner drugstore, that George and Emily realize they are in love, and soon after this realization, George decides to forego college and work on his uncle's farm so that he and Emily can marry."

Noah looked up and smiled. "They are married in the Grover's Corners Congregational Church—with all of their friends and family in attendance."

Then he paused and looked around. "*Our Town* has three parts, and the last part opens in the Grover's Corners cemetery up on the hill; nine years have passed. As we all know, in real life, joy and sorrow often walk hand in hand, and it's the same in this play. The enduring happiness George and Emily always hoped for comes to an abrupt end when Emily dies in childbirth.

"But the most moving scene in part three is when Emily ignores the warnings of the nine other dead souls in the cemetery and returns in spirit to the home in which she grew up. She wants to relive a happy day—her twelfth birthday. She stands to the side in the kitchen and watches her mother bustling about with early morning chores; she hears her mother call her down to breakfast, and she watches the interaction they share. Emily realizes how wonderful life is—even the mundane and everyday moments. Suddenly, she is overcome with grief and begs to be returned to the dead, her heart aching for the loveliness of the life that has rushed by . . . and she ponders out loud man's inability to savor the preciousness of every minute."

Noah paused and looked up at Maddie, who was dabbing her eyes with a tissue. She was surrounded by family—Laney and the three younger boys, Micah, Beryl, and Charlotte, and Isaac and Nina, and their girls, and then he looked around at all of the friendly, familiar faces of his congregation. There wasn't a single person who hadn't faced sorrow. "If you're wondering if there will be a service for my dad, there won't be. He didn't want one, and so last Friday, we honored his request with a simple ceremony on the beach . . . and sent him off with a blessing and a poem.

"Life isn't easy. In fact, when I think back over the last few months, life has been one long roller coaster ride of emotions . . . and I know I'm not alone in that sentiment. There isn't a soul in this sanctuary who isn't familiar with that ride. In fact, there isn't a soul on earth who hasn't been on it." He looked up. "In real life, you can be on top of the world—you wake up in the morning and take a quick inventory: the sun is shining, the bills are paid, everyone's healthy, the kids are doing well in school, that funny sound the car was making stopped on its own. But on that very same day, your world can crash down around you—the school calls to tell you your child fell in the playground and is being rushed to the hospital, a pipe breaks at home and floods the basement, a credit card bill shows up in the mail that knocks the socks off your budget, someone dear to you is diagnosed with cancer . . . or maybe it's you who, with a sinking heart, feel an odd lump. Now, the clouds roll in . . . and they are big and dark and ominous . . . and we look heavenward and ask, 'What happened to that sunny day? Don't you know I was enjoying it?' "

He paused and looked up. "I recently found out that my dad had his own bout with cancer . . . and won. My mom said they celebrated. . . . She said they felt as if they'd been given a new lease on life, and they were going to make the most of it. One week later, he had a heart attack.

"Life is messy—there's no doubt about it. It's hard . . . and it often sets us back on our heels . . . but that still doesn't mean it isn't glorious. God gave us this glorious life to see what we would do with it . . . and He gave us resilient spirits and a promise to always be with us . . . through every struggle. My dad understood this about life . . . about God . . . and he made the most of it. His favorite psalm was Psalm 8—the one we read this morning." Without looking down, Noah recited several verses from memory. " 'When I look at the heavens, the work of thy fingers, the moon and the stars which thou hast established; what is man that thou art mindful of him, and the son of man that thou dost care for him? Yet thou hast made him little less than God, and dost crown him with glory and honor.' "

Noah looked up. "My dad was a great man . . . he was a good and faithful servant . . . he shared his time and talent with anyone who asked . . . and he embraced the come-what-may life God gave him. He was a loving son, brother, husband, father, grandfather, and friend . . . *and* he was a great teacher. He shared the play *Our Town* over and over because he believed its simple message was profound and timelessly poignant . . . and I think he felt that if he taught us kids nothing else, he could teach us the importance of embracing and savoring *every* moment. That was how he lived his life—he wrapped his arms around it, and come what may, he lived it to the fullest."

Noah looked up and smiled. "None of us will live forever." He paused and looked around at every face. "What will you do with the measure of your days?" he asked solemnly. "How will you spend your precious and glorious life?"

He opened his hymnal. "Please join me in singing one of my dad's favorite hymns, 'All Creatures of Our God and King.' "

❧ Epilogue ❧

The last week of August turned out to be the hottest of the summer, and even though Noah had promised they'd make a point of going to the beach, it was just too hot. On several occasions, they went down in the evening for a swim, but during the day it was miserable. Ben and Seth were constantly caught standing in front of the new refrigerator with the door open; Laney took to turning on the weather in the morning to find out if there was any end in sight to the heat; and on Saturday morning, as Asher—who'd come down late—ate warmed-up pancakes, he listened to the weatherman's colorful descriptions and asked, "Why do they say, 'It's as hot as blue blazes'?"

Laney looked up from putting breakfast dishes in the dishwasher. "I'm not sure, but I think it's because the hottest part of a flame is blue."

Asher nodded and took another bite of his pancake. "And why do they call it 'dog days'?"

Laney started to answer, but Noah—who'd just come in to refill his coffee cup—said, "I know! I know! When I was little, Grandpa told me it originated a long time ago when the Romans associated hot weather with the star Sirius. Sirius is the brightest star in the constellation, Canis

Major, aka Great Dog. Sirius is also called the Dog Star, and it's the brightest star in the sky."

Asher's eyes grew wide. "Sirius is also Harry Potter's godfather . . . and his animagus is a black dog!"

"Well, there you go," Noah said with a smile as he headed back down to his study.

Asher brought his plate over and handed it to Laney. "I'm not hungry," he said glumly.

"How come?" she asked in surprise, looking down at the syrup-smothered pancakes.

He shrugged.

She frowned and put her hand on his forehead. "Do you want me to save them?"

"You can give them to Mennie and Halle," he said, plodding gloomily out to the porch.

Laney scraped the soggy pancakes into the dogs' bowls, and before she'd had time to put the plate in the dishwasher, they'd both hurried over and gulped down their portions. Laney poured the last of the coffee into her mug, dumped the grinds, washed the pot and filter, and wiped down the counters. When she finally finished, she looked out on the porch and saw Asher curled up on the floor with his arm around each dog and Lucky curled up in her favorite wicker chair next to them.

She went out and peered down at him. "What's going on?" she asked softly.

"I don't know," he said.

She scooped him up and pulled him onto her lap. The dogs looked up in dismay and then got up to move closer. "You guys are silly," Laney said.

"They just want to be near us."

"They were near us."

"They like to lean on us."

Laney smiled, and they sat quietly, watching the birds flutter back and forth to the feeder. "Did you know there's a bird's nest under the shed?"

Asher nodded. "Dad showed me. I saw the babies too, but now they've all flown away."

Laney rested her chin on his head, and Asher fiddled with the string on his shorts. "I miss everybody," he said, his voice full of sadness.

"Oh, hon," Laney whispered, "I miss everybody too."

"I think I'm having a heart attack."

"You do?" Laney asked in surprise. "Why?"

"Because my heart hurts," he said.

"Sweetie, you're not having a heart attack. . . . Your heart is aching because you're sad, but it won't always be like this. You won't always feel sad."

They were both quiet for a time, and Laney pulled him closer and began softly, "Once upon a time, there was a handsome prince who fell into a deep sadness, and no matter what he did, he couldn't seem to overcome it. All of the sages and advisors in the court tried to discern the reason for the young prince's somber mood, but no one could. Finally, on a crisp autumn morning, the gardener invited him to visit. The prince accepted, but when he arrived, he noticed that all the blossoms had gone by and most of the branches were bare. Seeing his dismay, the gardener quickly pointed out that the garden was still beautiful in its gold and rusty hues. The prince nodded, watching the chickadees, cardinals, titmice, and nuthatches fluttering busily among the vines and berries, and the gardener explained that it wasn't his mind or body that suffered—it was his soul. She went on to say that all mankind endures the ebb and flow of life's joys and sorrows—'the rhythm of the tides' she called it—much like the earthly change of seasons—and she assured him that his heart would once again know joy.

"The handsome, young prince considered her words and asked her how she'd come by such wisdom, and the gardener showed him an ancient sundial hidden among the roses. On it were engraved the words, 'This too shall pass.' "

Asher sat up and looked at her. "Did someone tell you that story?"

Laney smiled and nodded. "My grandpa."

He leaned back against her. "Did Grandma go back to New Hampshire?"

"Mm-hmm."

"I can't believe school starts next week," he said gloomily.

"I can't either. It seems like summer just started."

"Can we go see the baby geese before we go back?" he asked brightly.

"Well, we can't go today. Dad has to finish his sermon."

"Can we go tomorrow?"

"Maybe. It would have to be after church."

"Wait," Asher said, turning to her. "Tomorrow's your birthday."

Laney's eyes grew wide as she pretended to have forgotten. "You're right—it is!"

"Well, we should definitely go then."

"Why?"

"Because it's Grandpa's birthday too."

She nodded thoughtfully. "That's right . . . which means tomorrow would be the perfect day."

Beaming, Asher hopped down and happily announced, "I'll go tell Dad," and with Halle at his heels, he raced down the hall.

Laney and Mennie watched them go, and then Mennie sat up and leaned against Laney's legs. He rested his noble head on her lap, and she stroked his silky ears. "Do you want to go too, old pie?" she asked softly, and Mennie thumped his tail and gazed at her lovingly . . . and his solemn, brown eyes said it all.

Want to bring some of that Cape Cod flavor into your home? Try one of these beloved Coleman family recipes!

LANEY'S GEORGIA PEACH COBBLER

7–8 fresh peaches, peeled, pitted, and sliced
¼ cup brown sugar
¼ cup white sugar
¼ teaspoon cinnamon
Sprinkle of nutmeg
2 teaspoons lemon juice
½ tablespoon cornstarch
1 cup all-purpose flour
¼ cup brown sugar
¼ cup white sugar
1 teaspoon baking powder
½ teaspoon salt
6 tablespoons chilled, unsalted butter cut into small pieces
¼ cup boiling water
2 tablespoons white sugar
½ teaspoon cinnamon

Directions:

Preheat oven to 425 degrees. Lightly butter 9-by-9-inch glass baking pan.

In a large bowl, combine peaches, ¼ cup brown sugar, ¼ cup white sugar, cinnamon, nutmeg, lemon juice, and cornstarch. Spread peach mixture in bottom of pan. Bake for ten minutes.

While baking, sift together 1 cup flour, ¼ cup brown sugar, ¼ cup white sugar, 1 teaspoon baking powder, and ½ teaspoon salt. With pastry blender or fork, cut in butter until evenly crumbly. Stir in boiling water until blended.

Remove peaches from oven and drop the dough in spoonfuls onto the hot peaches. Spread a bit and sprinkle with sugar and cinnamon. Bake for 30 minutes or until topping is golden brown.

Serve with vanilla ice cream. Yum!

Recipe can be doubled for a 9-by-13-inch pan.

BERYL'S MANTRAP GRAVY

1 lb. pork sausage links
2–3 tablespoons olive oil, divided
1 lb. ground beef
1 large onion, finely chopped
2 cloves garlic, minced
3 tablespoons fresh basil, torn
½ teaspoon dried oregano
¼ teaspoon dried rosemary
¼ teaspoon dried thyme
2 cups red wine, divided
2 29 oz. cans tomato sauce
1 6 oz. can tomato paste
8 Roma tomatoes, seeded and diced, or
    2 14.5 oz. cans of petite diced tomatoes
Freshly grated parmesan cheese

Directions:

Preheat oven to 400 degrees. Place sausage links in foil-lined baking pan and bake for 30 minutes. Turn links over and bake for additional 30 minutes until brown. Slice into bite-size pieces.

In a large skillet, heat 1½ tablespoons olive oil and brown ground beef until no longer pink. Set aside.

In a large pot, heat 1½ tablespoons olive oil and sauté onion. When onion is tender and lightly browned, add minced garlic. (It browns quickly.) Mix in all spices until fragrant. Add ½ cup of red wine and mix well.

Add browned beef, sausage, tomato sauce, tomato paste, and Roma or diced tomatoes. Simmer for one hour and add 1½ cups red wine or more depending on preferred consistency.

Simmer on low for 2 to 3 hours, stirring occasionally, adding more wine if necessary.

Serve over your favorite pasta and sprinkle with freshly grated parmesan cheese.

For printable copies of the recipes found here, please visit www.nanrossiter.com and email Nan.

Discussion Questions

1. Faith is a predominant theme in this book. Do you think people shy away from openly talking about their faith? Why?

2. Many people are turned off by religion and don't even like to see it included in books. It seems Christianity is increasingly a target for oppression—especially at Christmastime. Why is this happening? Do you think it plays a role in the decline of our society?

3. One night at dinner, Asa, Maddie, Micah, and Beryl discuss the behavioral problems of today's children. Asa blames the lack of discipline in the home and the breakdown of the family structure; Maddie, on the other hand, believes the inherent personality of the child must also be considered. With whom do you agree? Why?

4. Asher witnesses Jeff telling Jared he is going to kill him. Do you think if Asher had told someone it would have made a difference? In today's society, threats are often taken lightly. How should this issue be addressed?

5. After Jared's funeral, Noah and Laney have a similar discussion. Laney believes the world is a safer place without Jared. Noah counters that if Jared had been placed in a loving home and taught responsibility, he could have been rehabilitated. Who do you think is right? Do you think a boy like Jared—who seems inherently cruel—can be rehabilitated?

6. Laney worries that Asher will be a victim of cyber bullying someday. At the same time, she's dismayed when he reveals he might not want a Facebook page. How has cyber bullying become a problem in our society and is there a way to prevent it?

7. One theme that threads through the book is the struggle to be forthcoming. Laney, Asa, and Asher all withhold critical information. Discuss their reasons and the impact their decisions have on others. Do you agree with their decisions?

8. From the beginning, it is clear that Noah feels very strongly about being honest and forth-coming . . . no matter what the consequences. In the end, his conviction is shaken. What is his dilemma and how is it resolved?

9. The Coleman household is often filled with chaos, or as Noah likes to call it, "blessed

pandemonium." Our lives, too, are filled with appointments, meetings, deadlines, and demands; and the overwhelming expansion of technology only seems to exacerbate the situation. Do you ever wish for simpler times? What are some ways we can slow down and get back to the basics?

10. In real life, joy and sorrow often walk hand in hand. How is this reflected in the story? Has it ever happened in your life?